Rimworld

-Militia Up-

D1521737

JL Curtis

Books by JL Curtis

The Grey Man- Vignettes

The Grey Man- Payback

The Grey Man- Changes

The Grey Man- Partners

The Grey Man- Twilight

Rimworld- Into the Green

Short Stories by JL Curtis

Rimworld- Stranded

The Morning the Earth Shook

The Grey Man- Generations

(Kindle only)

Anthology Collected by JL Curtis

Calexit- The Anthology

Author's Note: This is a work of fiction. Names, characters, places, and incidents are a product of the author's imagination. Locales and public names are sometimes used for atmospheric purposes. Any resemblance to actual people, living or dead, or to businesses, companies, events, institutions, or locales is completely coincidental.

Published by JLC&A. Available from Amazon.com in Kindle format or paperback book, printed by CreateSpace.

Rimworld- Militia Up/ JL Curtis. -- 1st ed.
ISBN-13: 9781790774036

DEDICATION

To my loyal readers who've stuck by me. This is for you. You give me a reason to get up and write, and I thank you!

Who knows what else may be accomplished or seen in our lifetimes? Our children's? Our grandchildren's? We can only guess.

ACKNOWLEDGMENTS

Thanks to the usual suspects.

Special thanks to my editor Stephanie Martin

Cover art by Tina Garceau.

Table of Contents

Prologue

"So, based on the problems everyone is having, I'm going to approach the GalPat Det about providing some additional security to all of your feeder locations. I also want each of you to deploy sonic fences at all feeder and subfeeder sites. I'll download the mods to you for the programming to add the human range. Any questions," Mikhail asked.

Ethan Fargo, lean and compactly built, leaned back against the wall thinking, *This whole deal is sounding screwier and screwier. Why would anybody want to knock down the Tight Bridge Tech? Our worlds depend on it for power, e-tainment, and communications, unless… Nah, I'm just being paranoid. But, this isn't Hunter. Mikhail Radovich what have you gotten us into?* Unconsciously, he straightened up off the wall into a more balanced stance. He slid his elbow down, confirming the pistol was still secure in its holster on his belt. His change in posture caught Mikhail's eye, and Fargo shook his head minutely.

Mikhail, tall and dark, his Slavic features giving him a grim appearance, was wrapping up the meeting with the TBT techs on the planet Endine in Ivan's office in Capital City. Ivan March, small, red headed, and feisty, was the lead tech on Endine, working from Capital. Mike Hartwell, bald, sunburned, and middle aged, worked out of Archer City. Jean Gauntt was the only female, compact, dark haired, tired-looking, and very quiet. She worked out of Canyon City and William Beamon, lanky and gray haired, worked out of Paradise on the southern coast. Beamon was the only one openly wearing a pistol in a well worn holster.

Ivan replied, "Gonna be hard for me to do that. The TBT feeder is right up against one of the slums that is expanding out of the city center. And my subfeeders are on those roofs."

Mikhail grimaced. "Well, do the best you can. If nothing else, secure the equipment huts with the switching gear. Anybody else have a problem I need to know about?"

Pulling out his data comp, he quickly called up the modification for the sonic fence system, pushed it to the local server, and heard all four data comps ping in response. "Don't load that until you have the fence up and running. You'll have ten secs to get out of the perimeter before it takes effect. To get in, you'll have to remote in and kill the update. Understood?"

Fargo moved to the door as Mikhail stood. "Alright, we'll reconvene for dinner at, say eighteen? Then I can update you on the outcome of the meeting with the GalPat Det. Can you give us a minute and then we'll be ready to leave."

Ivan hopped up. "I'll drive you over, it's a pain in the ass to maneuver around over there with all the blocked streets and checkpoints."

Fargo stopped abruptly. "Blocked streets and checkpoints?"

"Yah, they've restricted access due to the protesters getting a bit out of hand a couple of times."

"Didn't they put them down?"

Ivan snorted. "Not really, more like let them run out of steam and gently *pushed* them back out four or five blocks."

The hair on the back of Fargo's neck started standing up and he shook his head. "So are we even safe to go down there in a marked vehicle?"

Ivan laughed. "Even the proles like having their power. Never had a problem anywhere on the planet. I'll get the van ready when you are."

Mikhail turned to Fargo. "What's wrong Ethan?"

"I'm not sure, but as your security, I'm getting worried about not only your, but our safety. This isn't Hunter, and I'm not sure what the real situation is here on Endine. I wish we had a better read on GalPat and some intel feed from them or somebody."

"It's Planet Security here. They provide a feed to our folks for things that might affect them."

"So they aren't getting anything from GalPat? That's strange."

Mikhail shrugged. "Different planet, different set of reactions. That's one of the things we have to deal with in TBT. You're just being paranoid."

"Former Terran Marine and GalScout. I was paid to be paranoid, that's why I'm still here."

***

A half div later, Ivan blew his breath out noisily. "Well looks like this is as close as I can get. Something must have happened." He pointed to a gate a block away and continued, "That's the gate you need to go through. It leads directly to the admin building, which is just on the other side of the wall. I'll find a place to park and wait here for ya."

Fargo extended his empathic sense as far as he could, but didn't sense anything other than some low level discontent. Getting out quickly, he settled his pistol then said. "Okay, let's make this as quick as we can, Mikhail. I don't like this at all."

Mikhail looked at him. "Are you okay, Ethan? You know you can call me Misha. We *are* family."

"Come on, let's move. Something's going on here that I don't like. Call it a hunch, or a gut feeling, but…"

Mikhail shrugged. "Okay, quick like a nearbunny, we will be." He took off at a fast walking pace, Fargo following closely on his right, watching both sides, and ahead of them. As they cleared the buildings, Fargo's paranoia increased, seeing the broad empty avenue they had to cross, and the small crowd gathered fifty yards from the gate.

Glancing both ways, Mikhail started across as Fargo shifted to the left side, putting himself between the crowd and Mikhail. They made it across the street with no issues, and Mikhail went to the man door in the gate, twisted the handle and was surprised when the gate didn't open. Instead a voice came from a speaker overhead, "State your business."

Mikhail looked up and saw the speaker and a camera off to the side of the gate. "Mikhail Radovich. Tight beam technology manager for this sector. I have a meeting with a Colonel Zhu."

The speaker spat out, "Wait."

Fargo glanced up. "Not too friendly are they?"

"Apparently not. One would think this gate would be mann—"

Fargo shoved him violently to the ground as he saw a figure detach itself from the crowd at a dead run toward them. Mikhail asked indignantly, "What the hell was that for," as he started to rise.

Fargo hissed, "Stay down. Shit's going down, *now*." He committed the cardinal sin of taking his eye off the threat, as he glanced down to make sure Mikhail was still on the ground. He sensed hate now mingling with joy, and snapped back to honor the threat, drawing his pistol as he turned, shielding Mikhail.

The small figure had a weapon in hand, pointing it directly at him, close enough that Fargo saw the finger tighten on the trigger button as the whine of a needle gun firing was crossed by the flat snap of his bead pistol. The small figure started crumpling to the ground as Fargo felt the incredible pain of the flechettes tearing into his shoulder outside the vest, *Oh fuck that hurts. Gotta get Mikhail somewhere safe.* His left arm dropped limply and he almost passed out from the pain before the pharmacope kicked in.

Leaning over, he said, "Mikhail, are you alright?"

Mikhail replied shakily, "I'm… I'm not hit, if that's what you mean."

"Good, stay there." Fargo leaned against the gate, pistol at low ready as he scanned the crowd both visually, empathically, and with his psi senses after a quick glance over his shoulder and down the street they'd just left. It was so quiet he could hear his blood plopping on the stones in front of the gate, as the speaker squawked, "Stand clear. Opening gate now."

Fargo pushed himself off the wall with his elbow, keeping the pistol trained on the crowd, who were backing away in fear. He took a step to the side and felt the world go gray as the pharmacope dumped more painkillers. "Mikhail, get yourself in the…"

***

Mikhail got an arm under Fargo, half drug him through the gate and screamed at the sergeant. "Medical, he needs medical! What the fuck are you people doing? How did you let—?"

Two medics with a gravsled ran to where Fargo lay slumped on the ground, and they quickly loaded him onto the sled, asking. "Who is he? Blood type? What the fuck did he get shot with?" The lead tech quickly scanned Fargo, getting a lot of beeps and sirens that didn't sound good to Mikhail, as he put the sled in motion.

Mikhail answered, "Fargo, Ethan, NMN he's in the GalPat, no GalScout database. I think he's O positive." For reasons Mikhail didn't understand, he reached over and took Fargo's pistol, dropping it in his pocket, as he followed the medics toward the main building at a run.

They had gone through a set of doors, telling Mikhail he couldn't enter, sterile zone, and to wait. Fifteen minutes later, a dour, ethnic Asian in dress blacks walked slowly down the hall toward him, obviously listening to his earbud. He stopped in front of Mikhail. "I am Colonel Zhu, you are Mikhail Radovich, correct?"

Impatiently, Mikhail replied, "Yes, what is being done for Fargo? And why were we not allowed in the gate? We had an appointment scheduled!"

Zhu replied enigmatically, "Security. There are *issues* right now with a very small segment of the population, here. We are working through those."

"Issues my ass, when they are trying to take down the TBT system, and we get shot by people in a mob, that's a little more than issues."

"Why did you initiate contact with the protesters?"

Mikhail goggled. "Initiate? We didn't initiate anything! Whoever that was came charging out of the mob, firing some kind of needler, and next thing I know, I'm on the ground with Fargo bleeding all over me, just before he passed out."

"Why didn't you retreat? You had ample option to do that."

Mikhail started to reply when an older lady, granny glasses perched on her nose, curly hair adrift came stalking by and went into the medical area. He noticed Zhu at rigid attention, and asked, "Who was that?"

"Director Vaughn. Your man must be badly hurt, if she deigned to come down here." Zhu turned around and marched away, leaving Mikhail standing in the corridor by himself.

Two divs later, Evie landed the shuttle in the forecourt of the building, the two med techs pulled Fargo out on a gravsled, and he was loaded into the Med Comp installed in the shuttle. Another two divs, and they were back aboard *Hyderabad*, when Mikhail realized he never got a substantive conversation with Zhu on the problems on Endine.

***

Fargo came to slowly. Reaching out with his senses, he didn't feel anything, which scared him. His arm and shoulder throbbed in time with his heartbeat. He looked out the port to his left and saw a bulkhead, looking out the port to the right, he saw a small sickbay with a compartment number he recognized. *I'm on Hyderabad. Where is Mikhail, is he...*

Captain Jace came quickly through the door, closely followed by Mikhail. "Ah, I see our lazy guest has finally deigned to join us in consciousness."

Fargo lifted his right hand, extending the middle finger. "Why am I hurting?" He looked at Mikhail's drawn face, "You alright? Not hit?"

Mikhail said softly, "No I'm okay Ethan. Much better than you. You saved my life. I don't…"

"You don't owe me anything. If I'd let you get killed, Luann would have killed me. Still haven't answered why I'm hurting."

Jace answered, "Simple. Your shoulder is blown up. It exceeds the capability of the med comp, manual intervention is required, and you can't go into Cryo, so we're hauling you back to Hunter."

"What, err, why not treat me on Endine?"

"They wanted you off planet immediately. Apparently the woman you killed was the daughter of one of the powers that be on Endine. Well, that and the fact that the Director, who's a surgeon herself, took one look at your injuries, along with your medical history and scans, and said you needed a galaxy class surgeon to even attempt a rebuild."

"Oh. That bad, huh?"

Captain Jace added. "Yes, that bad. OneSvel will meet us in orbit, perform the needed surgery, and do your follow-up care."

"But…"

"We know who he is, Mikhail has been briefed and agreed to say nothing. As far as anyone is concerned, the surgery will have already been done. OneSvel will *just* be the med tech taking care of you in zero-G, until your shoulder is stabilized."

"How long?"

"One to two weeks. It'll take the nanos that long to rebuild the bone structure, plus there are something like thirty pieces of bone still floating around in there. Evie will fly Mikhail down to Rushing River as soon as we hit orbit and pick up OneSvel for the trip back."

"What about the techs? Are they…"

Mikhail winced. "So far, they're still alive. Director Vaughn has given authority to the GalPat Det to up security as required to protect the assets. I never got to have my meeting, so I'm getting this from comms after the fact and two FTLs we've had enroute back here."

Fargo turned to the captain, "Scans?"

Jace nodded. "We didn't have your history or medical scans in the med comp, so OneSvel sent them. The system is now holding you stable, but it can't start the rebuilding process until all the bone chips have been removed. We're at point six G, trying to keep them from moving around anymore than they already have."

Fargo mumbled, "Oh, lovely," as darkness overtook him again. His last thought was, *This getting shot crap is getting old. I just hope this time it's not weeks…*

Recovery

Fargo swam slowly back to consciousness, opened his eyes, and saw OneSvel leaning over the open medcomp. "Mphfff… wa—"

One of OneSvel's pseudopods pushed a straw between his lips as another pseudopod gently squeezed the bulb of water. Fargo sighed blissfully as he felt the water in his mouth, then swallowed.

OneSvel extruded another pseudopod and gently touched his temple, "*How do you feel?*"

Fargo projected, "*Lousy. My shoulder feels like it is on fire, and my nose itches. How long have I been out?*"

"*Long enough. We will speak now.*"

"How do you feel?"

Fargo took another swallow of water and scratched his nose with his right hand. "I feel like hell. How long have I been out?"

"Nineteen days and a few divs this time. The repairs on your shoulder have been completed, and the nanobots are finishing knitting the muscles back together now."

Another head poked over the edge of the medcomp and he looked up to see Captain Jace, "Where are we?"

The captain said, "Holding orbit over Hunter. They let us park here, in case we needed to get you on the ground quickly. We can burn down in about four divs if we need to."

"Mikhail?"

"Evie dropped him off two weeks ago. We have a number of messages in the queue from various people for you. Whenever you feel up to it, you can at least listen to them, if you desire."

Fargo reached out and grabbed the bulb of water as it started to float off, and squeezed another drink out of it. "Later." Glancing at OneSvel he asked, "How did the surgery go?"

"Thirty-seven pieces of your shoulder blade and collarbone were removed, ground down and fed to the nanobots. The rounds missed your pharmacope by about an inch. And the medcomp made almost three pints of blood for you. Other than that, fine. The basic structure has been rebuilt and the bots filled in the holes while we have been in zero G."

Fargo shrugged then winced. "Ouch!"

OneSvel's GalTrans gave the equivalent of a laugh. "Movement is not advised. Do I need to put you back under?"

Fargo held up his good hand. "No! I won't do that again anytime soon. But I really need to go to the fresher."

OneSvel cocked an eyestalk. "Can you manage?"

The captain interrupted, "We can get him there and back. And it has straps." The captain opened the side hatch, as OneSvel extruded a pseudopod, gently helping Fargo to sit up and dangle his feet off the side of the medcomp.

"Do not be stupid Fargo. I am tired of putting you back together. And there is no rush. Those that need to know your situation do, including Command."

"Did you get a report off?"

"Yes, including the situation on Endine from Mikhail, and your mumblings."

"Mumblings?"

"Something about ice mining and an insurrection. No real specifics, but I included it anyway, along with the world's location."

"Gently now, Fargo. Let the Captain tow you to the fresher. You don't need to be bouncing off bulkheads in your condition."

Fargo put his right hand on the captain's shoulder, and glanced back at OneSvel, who were holding themselves in position by numerous pseudopods, attached to the bulkheads. *So that's how he's doing that. That's... cheating,* he thought muzzily. He let Jace tow him to the fresher, then entered and cycled the hatch closed, saying, "I can do this part myself. Can I at least have a wrap?"

Jace chuckled. "Why? You are the only *human* aboard, remember? *Hyderabad* is a RIG ship, and I am Jace, Joint Autonomous Controller Element, I and all the crew are simulacrums. You and OneSvel are the only two living organisms aboard. And I don't think OneSvel cares."

Fargo rolled his eyes at the door. "Because I don't want to catch any dangly bits on anything, okay? Just humor me."

"Your wish is my command, Captain," Jace said with a laugh.

"Oh, stuff it—" Fargo grumbled as he eased himself around and used the fresher, then set the fresher for clean, started the suction, and then the spray. *Not going to screw that up again… Ever!* He got wet, cycled the spray off and soaped up as the suction pulled all the water bubbles out of the fresher. He rinsed off, and ten segs later, after the last of the water had suctioned out, he swam out of the fresher. He found a wrap floating in front of the door, and barely managed to get the wrap fastened, when Jace opened the hatch.

"Feel better now?"

"Much! But I've been out nineteen days. I don't care how sterile that damn med comp is, I needed out for a little bit. Has OneSvel been here the whole time?"

Jace shook his head. "No, he's been coming up when we come back into orbit to check on you."

"Come back into orbit?"

"Well, just because you're tying up the med comp doesn't mean we're not working and making credits. We've been running miners and supplies out to the belt, and as a bonus, getting them four days of acclimatization to zero G," he said with a smile.

Jace towed him back to the sick bay, and maneuvered him back into the med comp, "There you go, nice and clean."

Fargo sighed and looked over at OneSvel, "Why zero G? I mean, all my other med comp stays have been in G."

OneSvel chittered and his GalTrans spit out, "Because you heal faster if the reconstruction nanites don't have to fight gravity. Granted you are losing muscle mass by not having G on you, but since you're *missing* most of your shoulder muscles, and the bones had to be rebuilt too, this probably reduced your time in the box by fifty percent."

"Oh…"

"And we don't mind getting a little time in zero G, since there are no hydrotherapy pools on Hunter. When you have as much bulk as we do, reducing the stress on the pseudopods is always a plus. We don't have any bones in them."

Fargo looked startled, "What? I… didn't know that. I always thought…"

OneSvel's GalTrans gave the equivalent of a snort, "Thought and never learned. Typical human. Making assumptions, rather than getting facts."

"I'm… sorry. I…"

OneSvel waved a pseudopod. "That is why we are the doctor, and not you. Now, for the next eight days, you will work on your rehabilitation for three divs per day. The captain was good enough to set up a portable AI rehab unit in the training compartment. I have programmed it to bring you back to at least fifty percent of strength and mobility in that time. When you are not in the unit, you will be here, in the med comp. Is that understood?"

Fargo looked up mutely, and OneSvel extended a pseudopod. "*It is important to get you back to health as soon as possible. There are things occurring that you need to involve yourself in.*"

"Uh, yes. I will do the rehab." Fargo projected, "*I wasn't expecting that forceful a statement. You know I always do my rehab.*"

"*That was for the captain. I sense that he is shielding.*"

Fargo smiled, *If you only knew.* "Ah, understood."

OneSvel retracted the pseudopod. "Captain, can Evie take us back down? We think Fargo will be good for the next few days. When you come back this time, we'll get him to his cabin and you can go back to having your ship be something other than a sick bay for him."

"Certainly. Anytime you are ready."

***

Jace took the data comp that Fargo had pushed his way, "Are you ready to go back under?"

Fargo nodded. "This rehab is kicking my ass. I hurt."

"What is the old Earth saying? That which does not kill…"

"You makes you stronger," Fargo finished the quote. "But dammit, that automated program is tearing me up. I know you lose muscle, but my legs are cramping, my thighs feel like they are on fire, and my shoulder feels like there is a knife stuck in it! *And* OneSvel turned off my damn pharmacope!"

Jace winced. "I think that is probably because it would counteract the med comp's treatment."

"Where are we?"

"About six divs out of the belt. We'll drop the four modules in five divs, and the miners' shuttle will be alongside in six divs."

Fargo nodded. "Wake me in four. I'd like to at least say I've seen the belt."

"Will do."

Five divs later, Fargo sat strapped into the captain's chair on the bridge as Evie smoothly maneuvered the *Hyderabad* into the edge of the belt, keying on the flashing beacon bobbing in front of them. Peering through the pilot's windscreens, he could see a mishmash of rocks of various sizes, seemingly spinning out of control in a variety of directions that made no sense. Looking up at the plot, it was even more nightmarish, with vectors seemingly going in random directions, and a few red ones pointing at the ship.

His attention was drawn to another vidscreen showing the bottom of the ship, as what he could only think of as tugs moved underneath them. A speaker crackled, "Okay, we're in position, drop the load."

Captain Jace toggled a switch and the four containers and block of ice floated slowly away. The tugs each took one, and the last tug grabbed the ice block, wheeling away and following the others toward the mass of rocks. The speaker crackled again, "Shuttle inbound. ETA two segs."

Evie replied, "Shuttle, you are cleared Bay Four starboard. Wipe your feet before you come in."

A chuckle was heard over the speaker, "Got it. And we wiped our feet. Locked onto the approach beacon."

A seg and a half later, Evie said, "Shuttle, standby for tractor in three, two, one. Locked." The ship trembled gently as the shuttle was tractored into Bay

Four. "Passengers will be disembarking through Bay Four. Please queue up with the crewman at the bay door, please ensure you have all of your belongings. It will take approximately fifteen segs to pump down."

The passengers were loaded onto the shuttle, it was pushed out of the bay, and the ship turned for Hunter. "Nothing going back with us?"

The captain shook his head. "Nope. Maybe one trip in four we get something or somebody that wants to go in."

"But there were, what, thirty bodies on here? Where…"

"Don't know, and not going to ask. If we don't ask, we get more business."

Fargo leaned back in the chair, "Bullshit. This is a collection platform. You have your ways…"

The captain put his hand to his brow, "How could you possibly believe that poor little us…"

Fargo rolled his eyes, and the captain became serious. "They are building a refinery on one of the bigger asteroids. And they've lost at least three runabouts in the last month. So that's at least nine dead. They need people. And only two of those containers were supplies. The other two were Hab modules."

"Why leave the ice block? I thought those were only used for micrometeorite shields on external cargo."

"Water. They don't have any, and regardless of what the scientist's papers say, you can't recycle enough to live more than about thirty days in these conditions. That tonnage will last a couple of months.

They go out and laser off chunks at a time, plop it in their hydro system, purify it, and live on it. Sometimes they extract enough material out of them to pay for a new block."

"Pay for it?"

"Yep, a thousand credits per ton."

Fargo whistled as he unstrapped, "That's... expensive."

"Not if it keeps you alive. You going down?"

"Yes. I think I've got eight divs before the next session of folding, spindling, and mutilating."

"Just think, only four more days of this."

Fargo shook his head. "I'd rather not."

***

Fargo groaned as he released the straps on the rehab unit, "Fuck you, you piece of shit. Never again. If I could, I'd blow you into bits and pieces."

Jace chuckled. "Such language for an inanimate object. I'm shocked, shocked I say."

"Inanimate my ass. That damn thing is *way* too animated to suit me. I'm gonna talk to OneSvel as soon as I land about that rehab schedule he set up."

"Speaking of which, he's going to ride down to your cabin. We're going directly there."

Fargo replied, "Um, not going to work. If I don't land in Rushing River, Luann is going to kill me."

"Mikhail, Luann, and the children are down at White Beach. Mikhail messaged you a couple of divs ago."

Fargo just looked at Jace, who cocked his head. "I see everything. You keep forgetting that. We will pick up OneSvel at the space station, then drop to your cabin. You might want to let Luann know you'll see them when they get back."

Sarcastically, Fargo replied, "When will they be back?"

"Three days. Mikhail is meeting with the planetary governor over expansions to the TBT network. He decided to take Luann and the kids to give them a break and see something different."

"Okay. Can I at least run through the fresher first?"

Two divs later, OneSvel came aboard, and immediately marched Fargo to the med comp, "Let me get a scan and see where we are."

Grumbling, Fargo climbed into the med comp, "Did you ever learn about bedside manners?" OneSvel ignored him as he extruded various pseudopods and activated the med comp, noting various readouts, and finally opening the med comp.

He reached out with a pseudopod, gently touching Fargo's temple. "*You appear to be in one piece again. How do you feel?*"

Fargo projected, "*I guess about eighty percent. But I really want to talk with you about the damn automatic rehab torture machine.*"

"*It did not break you. And I estimate you are at ninety percent. Better than expected. Zero G and rigorous rehab seems to speed up the healing process.*"

"*Why is my pharmacope off line? I've hurt after every session on that damn machine.*"

"*It was necessary for you to heal more quickly in the med comp. The pharmacope would have attempted to mitigate the pain, which was counter to the med comp's feedback requirements."*

Captain Jace walked in, "Are we ready to go to the shuttle?"

Fargo looked at OneSvel, who answered, "I believe so. There is nothing to be gained by leaving him here any longer. Can you transfer the auto rehab unit to the shuttle?"

Fargo interrupted, "Oh hell no. I'm done with that sumbitch. I have exercise…"

"Please put it on the shuttle. We will take it to the clinic. We believe we can use it to help other people during rehab with what we have learned with Fargo. And if Fargo doesn't progress as expected, we can put him back on it."

"Arghhh… alright, I'll keep up the exercise."

Four divs later, the shuttle landed softly a hundred yards from the cabin. As the hatch opened, Fargo saw a liteflyer parked outside what he thought of as his garage, but didn't see anyone around. He shuffled down the ramp, a little unsure of his balance after almost a month in weightlessness, and was puffing slightly as he finally got to the steps. The door opened and Cattus and Canis came charging out, knocking him on his butt, as they happily licked his face. Urso came bounding up the landing strip, moaning in happiness, and he scrambled to his feet.

Looking up, he saw Nicole standing in the door, her hand over her mouth, "You can go ahead and laugh. I know you want to." Then he saw tears running down her face.

Visitors

Fargo sat morosely in the living room of his cabin, staring at the e-tainment console as he scrolled listlessly through the myriad of emails waiting for his attention. Nicole had gone back to Rushing River that morning, and Fargo missed her already. *I never thought I'd find anybody again. And now… I really don't want to live in town. I like my solitude. Except now...*

OneSvel had told him recovery was going to be slow, but dammit, this was getting ridiculous. It had been almost a month, and he was still getting twinges in the shoulder when he did the littlest things. Like picking up the damn coffee pot.

Taking a sip of coffee, with his right hand, he selected the next email in the company queue. He started poring through the monthly equipment listings, number of rounds expended in training, and suit maintenance issues. *This is why we had company clerks. Thankfully Horse is getting it done, well, he and the women.*

Cattus and Canis suddenly came bolting into the living room, snarling and growling. Fargo looked at them, "What the hell?"

Canis stood between him and the door, ruff fully erect, as Cattus stalked to the window and peeked out, tail lashing. "What has got into you two now?" Both of them ignored him, and he heard a thump and muted growl outside the door. Getting up he grabbed his pistol as he said, "External cameras."

Nothing showed in the pictures, but Urso was prowling back and forth on the porch, rumbling, growling, and staring down the length of the landing strip. Grabbing up the binoculars off the side table, he moved toward the door, only to be blocked by both animals. "Alright you two. Enough!" Extending his empathic sense, he sensed worry/fear from all three of the animals. He tried sending a command to them to stand down, but he wasn't sure they were even paying attention.

Slipping the pistol in his pocket, he hip checked Canis out of the way, and slowly opened the door. A moment later, he slipped onto the porch, closely followed by Cattus and Canis, as Urso bawled and turned toward them. Ignoring them, he focused the binoculars on the end of the landing strip and saw two squat figures, standing in plain sight. He picked out the uniforms, realizing they were GalPat camo, and remembered, *There were two Scouts with the company Nan dropped here. Two, what did they call themselves? Darkies.* Zooming on the faces, he nodded, *Heavy world build, Amerind heritage, definitely from Anadarko.*

He felt a gentle pressure, *"We come in peace. May we approach the house?"*

He projected, *"Please do. The animals will not harm you."* Then threw up his 'wall' as he thought of it, protecting his mind.

The two figures began walking toward the house, and he concentrated on the animals, projecting friendship, and no harm. Urso grumped, and sprawled in front of the chairs letting the sun hit her on the back. Cattus jumped off the porch and circled the cabin as Canis parked herself on his boots, but her hackles slowly went down.

Fargo debated going back into the cabin to get refreshments, such as they were, but thought better of it. He pulled a chair out from behind Urso and seated himself, setting the binoculars on the table, and waited.

A few segs later, the two scouts stood just off the porch, and he could see that they were a mated pair, one male, and one female. The male said, "Captain, we are MobyDineah. We are…"

"You are the scouts attached to the GalPat Company temporarily detached here. I saw you at the ceremonies."

He felt a push for lack of a better term, and lowered his wall. He felt what was almost like a double or echo, "*They did not tell us you are a level five psi!*" Cattus prowled behind them, causing the female, who he thought of as Dineah to turn and watch him.

"Cattus! Dammit cat, come here!" He projected calm, and patted the deck next to his chair. Cattus swished her tail, but hopped onto the porch, and flopped bonelessly down, her eyes never leaving the two scouts. "*Sorry about that. They're a bit protective.*"

Dineah looked at Moby, then said, "Captain, did you know there are animals that communicate with each other? Once we began climbing the foothills, there were at least three species that watched us all the way here." She looked meaningfully at the three lying on the porch deck.

Fargo sighed, "Yes, at least three that I know of. And they are matriarchal, from what I've seen. Please come up and let me introduce you to them.

They both smiled and slowly stepped forward. He got up and walked off the porch, meeting them at the bottom of the steps. "Canis, come." Canis came down and sat beside him, "This is Canis, she's a… I guess the term would be wolf. Canis, friends." He shook hands with Moby, then Dineah, and both offered their hands for Canis to sniff.

"Cattus, come." Cattus yawned, showing a mouthful of teeth, but came down the steps and the exercise was repeated, followed by Urso. He escorted them into the cabin, and asked, "Would you like something to drink? I can offer whatever we can get out of the autochef, or I have fresh water."

He felt that push again, and Dineah smiled as Moby said, "Fresh water, please. I get so tired of processed water."

Dineah asked, "Coffee?"

Fargo smiled. "Would you like real coffee? Handmade, real coffee?"

Dineah squealed, "Oh! You have… Oh yes, *please*! I haven't had real coffee in *so* long!"

Fargo noticed they were both wearing backpacks, "You can drop them by the door. The animals will not bother them." They both eased out of the packs, and he noted they were very solidly built, and very flexible, as they set the packs by the door. He set about making a pot of coffee, after delivering a large glass of water to Moby, and motioned them to the couch, "Have a seat, this will take a couple of minutes."

"*Captain?*"

"Yes?"

He felt them probing the animals, "*You realize the animals are bonded and linked to you?*"

"*Yes, I know. But I can only perceive basic emotions. I am closest to Canis, because I felt her in her mother's womb.*"

Moby and Dineah exchanged looks, and he felt Dineah's mind for the first time, it was slightly *softer* if that could describe it. "*In her mother's womb? How?*"

"*When her mother was hurt by a Silverback, I put my hand on her to calm her with my empathic sense, and... I felt, that's the best word I can come up with, Canis. Maybe she was closest to my hand. I don't know.*"

Moby and Dineah talked softly in a sibilant language that left Fargo wondering what they were saying, and he dropped out of the psi link, reaching down to stroke Canis.

Moby said, "My apologies. Some things we need to talk out."

"Not an issue, but I have to ask, what were you speaking?"

Dineah laughed softly, "Apache. It's a version of Athabaskan, which is a group of Native American languages. Similar to Navajo."

"Are you both Apache? But your names? And that brings up another question, Darkies?"

"Yes, Mescalero Apache. We are known as Darkies because the first troops we interacted with had problems with Anadarko on the radio. Too many syllables, and too close to one of their brevity codes." Dineah laughed, then glanced at Moby, then continued, "Our true names are secret, known only to our tribe. When we bonded, we became MobyDineah. That is what we are known as. But we were actually talking about totems."

"Totems?"

Moby said, "Totems are the spirit animals we adopt after our vision quests. My totem is a dolphin, and hers is a whale."

The coffee pot burped its last, and Fargo took two cups down, "Anything in your coffee?"

"Just coffee, please."

He poured two cups, took one to Dineah, and sat slowly in his chair. "Dolphin and whale? I thought Indians had things like wolves, eagles, and such."

Moby laughed. "Oh we do. But many others too. We only have one apiece, but you seem to have three."

Fargo shrugged. "For what good it does me."

Dineah projected, "*Have you tried working with them like this?*"

"*No, I didn't think it was possible. I tried, but I never did get any responses.*"

"*We sensed them, but at a much lower… Frequency, if you will. And they communicate over long distances.*"

"*Like you did from the bottom of the landing strip?*"

Dineah smiled. "*It does have its advantages.*" She reached for Moby's hand and grasped it, "*We can communicate about a mile.*"

"*Lower, you said.*"

Moby projected, "*Down here.*" Canis and Cattus both sat up, as Urso growled softly.

Fargo had *heard* Moby, but it was fuzzy, so he consciously tried to send a thought to Canis much lower than before, "*Canis, come.*"

Canis cocked her head, and padded over to him, then lay her head on his leg. He felt a response from her, but it didn't make any sense. It was mélange of sensations and 'smells', more than anything else.

Fargo said, "I got something, but it was like senses, sensations, smells, something… It's hard to describe."

Moby replied, "They don't think like we do. At least our animals on Anadarko don't. Sensations are about all we get. And only the ones we bond with. I've never encountered what you have here, with cross species communication."

"That's because this planet was planned as a hunting preserve by SierraSafari. I think they genied some of the species on purpose. I haven't felt any others, well, other than Silverbacks."

Cattus interrupted their conversation when she padded over to Dineah, then flopped down in front of her, paws in the air. Dineah laughed and projected, "*Belly rub?*"

Cattus reached up with both paws, tugging Dineah's hand gently down, and Dineah projected, "*Belly rub.*" She started stroking Cattus softly, and Cattus started a rumbling purr, closing her eyes in ecstasy.

Urso moaned from the door, and Fargo got up with a smile, "*I know what she wants.*" He went into the kitchen and pulled down a sealed canister, spooning out some of the honey from the bee tree. He tried to project "*Sweet, good, like,*" to Urso, and she sat up on her hind legs. He sensed desire from her, but he wasn't sure if that was because she already smelled the honey, or his projection.

He held the dish out and Urso took it delicately, then rolled on her back, slurping nosily, as everyone laughed.

Canis whined and went out the door, jumping over Urso and Moby projected, "*Did you catch that? I think something called her.*"

Fargo shook his head. "*No, I didn't really…*" He stepped out onto the porch, along with MobyDineah, and Cattus followed. "*Well damn. She did get called. That's her mother,*" pointing a hundred yards out, to Canis and an even bigger wolf standing nose to nose.

Fargo turned to them, "That makes me wonder, how did you project a thought all the way up here to me? That's… almost a thousand yards from the bottom of the landing strip."

Moby projected, "*We just pushed the thought a little harder. At least that's what we call it. Depending on your strength and level of talent, some can project further than others. Just like some have to physically*" *touch someone, like most level ones. As the level increases, the ability to communicate over distance increases in most cases.*"

Fargo held up a hand, "This may be interesting." Pointing to the wolves, who were trotting side by side toward the house, "I don't know what is going to happen. I've never seen her do that before when anyone else is here."

Dineah projected, "*She's curious about us. And I think her… cub shared our scent. I think we should sit.*"

Fargo glanced at her, shrugged and pulled three chairs over. "Okay, sit it is." They all sat down as the two wolves came up on the porch. The matriarch came to him first, licked his hand, he felt a 'tickle' in his mind, as if she was trying to communicate with him. She cocked her head as if to say, "Well, are you going to answer me?"

Fargo tried to go as far down in what he thought of as frequency as he could and projected welcome and peace. The matriarch wagged her tail a couple of times, then stalked over to Dineah, sniffed her hand, then put her paws on her leg and sniffed her face and neck. Dineah smiled without showing any teeth, and didn't move as the wolf licked the side of her face, then giggled, "*That tickles.*"

Fargo picked up Dineah sending something like friendship and honor. The wolf licked her again, then repeated the process with Moby, who also projected the same thing. The matriarch then stalked over to Cattus, who rolled over and showed her belly in subservience. After sniffing her, the matriarch went to Urso, who did the same thing.

She finally came back to Fargo, licked his hand again and he sensed approval from her. She bounded off the porch and trotted into the woods as the three humans looked at each other. Dineah projected, "*Well, that was interesting. It was almost like she was verifying what Canis had told her, for lack of a better term. And she was definitely checking to see if we could communicate with her.*"

Moby nodded. "*I think so. And her checking Cattus and Urso was… different. Then she projected approval at you.*"

"*Based on what I've seen over the last couple of years, I think she was checking up on Cattus and Urso, and is going to tell their mothers they are doing okay. I know the three species communicate at some level, and I wouldn't be surprised if your scents aren't also passed along.*"

Dineah shivered a little, "*This is truly strange. In all the years we've been scouting, I've never seen or heard of anything like this. I can't help but wonder if they are actually sentient, within the GalPat rules.*"

Fargo winced. "Ah deity. That would be a can of worms I don't even want to think about. But I don't think so, at least not under the sentience rules we had with GalScouts. I haven't seen any tool use, or any of them building anything. Which is a requirement."

Moby added, "You're right. Communication, in and of itself, is not enough."

"Speaking of communication, would you be willing to help me?"

MobyDineah nodded in concert, "If we can."

Learning Curve

After a quick lunch from the autochef, and another coffee for Dineah and himself, Fargo leaned forward, "Um, I have a confession to make, and I could use some help."

Moby and Dineah glanced at each other, and he could sense they were *talking*, but he couldn't pick anything up. Moby looked at him and asked, "Is this about your psi talent?"

Fargo projected, "*It is… But*"

Moby interrupted, "Talk please."

"Uh, yes. I've never had any training… and I don't want anyone to know I have it."

Dineah sat bolt upright, "What?" Canis and Cattus bolted up, and they heard Urso moaning from outside the cabin, "Oh, sorry…" Fargo felt her projecting calm and the animals calmed down, with Cattus climbing on the couch and rolling over for a belly scratch. She continued, "You were never trained? But you're a strong psi, maybe as strong as we are."

"Let me explain. I was originally a level five empath. We, my team and I were on a scout mission, I was a GalScout team lead and we were attacked. It came down to two of us left, myself and my comms/intel guy, who was also a level five psi. We were linked when he died… and something broke in my head. I don't know any other way to describe it."

He saw both of them wince at that, and Canis laid her head in his lap, trying to comfort him. "I woke up in the med comp, and thought I was crazy. I was hearing things in my mind…"

Moby asked, "Hearing things?"

"Like they were discussing my treatment. But I was hearing their thoughts, I guess is the best way to put it."

"Did the doctor note it?"

"No, I never told him until later. And it was never documented. I was medically retired from the GalScouts due to the fact that I can no longer go into cryo or stasis." Fargo decided not to tell them about the current tasking, no need for them to know that, or about OneSvel and what he really is, either.

Moby and Dineah looked at each other again, and once more he sensed them *talking*. Finally Dineah asked, "So you have never had any training? No one ever tried to help you and you never asked for help?"

Fargo shook his head. "No. What I know I got off the net and from practical experiences, mostly bad."

"Do you have to be close to someone or do you have to have physical contact?"

He blushed, thinking about Nicole, "Uh, physical contact makes it stronger, but I can sense people from a distance. I don't know how far, as… Well, on Endine, I felt the anger and her thoughts about killing Mikhail from that woman at probably thirty feet, maybe more."

"What about in a crowded environment?"

"It's like the Tower of Babel. Some beings are strong, some are weak, but a lot…I kinda build a wall when that happens so I don't hear them. But I have to work at keeping that up. But when I do that, I lose my empath sense too."

Dineah asked shyly, "Could I maybe have another cup of coffee, please?

Fargo moved Canis off his lap, "Damn, dog. How did you weasel your way into my lap? Down!" Canis grumbled as she slid off his lap and sat cocking her head at him. He got up and picked up his cup, grabbed Dineah's and walked slowly into the kitchen. As he fussed with fixing another pot of coffee, he sensed them talking again, and he shook his head in frustration. *They can block me easily… so frustrating. Why wasn't I taught anything? Maybe the colonel didn't want anybody to know… or did he even know? I need to talk to OneSvel!*

He carried the two coffees and a water back into the living room, handing the coffee to Dineah and the water to Moby. He sat down and Moby said, "We will do what we can to help you. We cannot hope to give you the benefit of our lifetimes of training, but we can try to give you the basics to keep you safe and sane."

"Safe and sane would be good."

Dineah projected, *"First is how to keep others out of your head. Block me if you ca…"*

Fargo threw up his wall, and Dineah smiled. "Very good. But did you hear Moby? Or did you notice the animal's reactions?"

Fargo projected, *"You told me to block you."*

"I meant for you to only block me."

"How? I mean… I only know how to block everything. How can you block just one?"

Moby asked, "How do you visualize your wall?"

"Uh, a wall."

"No, what kind of wall? Light? Plasteel? What? Project it please."

Fargo thought for a minute, then projected, *"Like this? A block wall. Stone."*

"Something you've seen before?"

"A castle wall in Euro."

"Euro?"

"Earth. Euro, ancient Germany."

"Ah. So nothing in or out, right?"

"No, when I put up the block, even my empathic senses go away. I didn't see what Canis and Cattus did, either."

Moby sighed, "Put up your block again and watch them."

He put his wall up again, watching both animals. They both reacted, snapping around to look at him, and Canis put a paw on his leg, almost like she was looking for a physical connection. Cattus snarled silently, tail twitching. When he dropped his wall, they both relaxed.

Dineah thought, *"You cut their link too, and it worried them. Remember, they are bonded to you, which means they expect to keep that link alive. Maybe this will help. Here is how I think of my wall, if you will."* She projected something that Fargo could only describe as a lace curtain.

He imagined he could see through it, and didn't see how that could possibly work. *"How can that possibly work? It's full of holes!"*

"Try to penetrate it then."

He could sense her thoughts for a second, then it was like the holes closed. But he could still sense her talking with Moby, and catch parts of the thoughts. He pressed harder, and got nowhere. Slumping back in the chair, he asked, "How did you do that? I caught a second of your mind, and I could sense you and Moby still talking, but that's all I got."

Dineah smiled ruefully, "*You are very strong. You should not have caught anything. I just closed the holes in your direction, shielding me from you. But I could still sense you, and yes, Moby and I were talking, as you think of it.*"

Moby projected, "*Try this. This is the block I use.*"

Fargo got an image of a wall of plasglass with holes in it. "*So I need to be able to 'see' through it? Like a window rather than a wall?*" He felt pressure and tried to fill the holes enough to stop the penetration, while watching Cattus and Canis. He seemed to be succeeding, until Moby increased the pressure, and Fargo reverted to his wall, knocking Moby's probe away, but also losing the connection with the animals. Urso moaned and stuck her head in the door, as if she was going to come in the house, which she hadn't done since she was a little cub.

Fargo shook his head in frustration, "Dammit! I can't hold… Argghhh, now I've got a damn headache!"

Moby smiled. "It takes practice. We've been working with you what, two divs?" It took me seven GalYears to be able to control my communications! You're doing better than I did for a couple of years, and you've never had *any* training."

Dineah smiled ruefully, "Maybe we better stop for now. When I got headaches and tried to push through them, I hurt for two days."

"Where are my manners, would you like to eat? I didn't realize how long we've been working. Can I offer you the spare bedroom? It's clean and has its own fresher."

Fargo sensed them talking, and Dineah smiled. "We would gladly accept. Both offers. *I* would like a fresher after the hike up here, and a chance to wash my hair."

Moby rolled his eyes, "There goes all the hot water!" He dodged Dineah's elbow strike and picked up his glass, "May I have another glass? This water is… unusual."

Fargo took the glass and smiled. "Let Dineah have the fresher, and I'll show you." Moby and Dineah both got up, and Dineah stuck her tongue out at Moby as they headed for the door. Cattus and Canis beat them out the door, and they promptly jumped on the sleeping Urso as Fargo lead him around the back of the cabin, pointing to the waterfall that fell 500 feet from the cliff a half mile behind the house. "The water comes from there. I have a collector up there, piping down to here," he pointed to the top of a mostly buried plascrete tank. "And this system cleans the water, holds two thousand gallons, and provides pressure to the freshers in the house."

Moby whistled, "Do you know what… Does the waterfall ever stop?"

"Not that I know of. It's snowmelt from higher in the mountains. It's pretty pure as is, and the filtering, if you will, is limestone. The only thing I add to it is some fluoride."

"Anadarko is an arid planet. I don't think I've ever seen a waterfall that massive, nor one that never stops."

"Water is always precious. That's probably one of the biggest issues we had doing planet surveys with the GalScouts. A lot of other things can be overcome, but we can't exist without water."

Moby smiled. "Like the ice blocks the colony ships carry, and the freighters. You have a large number of blocks in the parking orbit, too."

"Yeah, that was kind of a surprise. I didn't expect to see that many of them on the rim. Apparently a lot of them are pretty worn down, which is why they got dropped out here. Some of the rim freighters use them as micrometeorite shields for cargo, just like the interstellar freighters do."

***

Fargo lay in bed, flipping and flopping as he thought over what MobyDineah had showed him, *Yeah, they truly are one entity. Two bodies, two minds, but one entity… And now I know just how little I actually know about my psi talent, and how to use it. I wonder…*

Two divs later, he woke up and groaned as he sat up on the side of the bed. Reaching out with his mind, he felt them in the guest room, and could sense they were carrying their mental blocks even while asleep. He also sensed Cattus and Canis, sleeping in the living room, and Urso out on the porch. He started trying different ways of imagining a block, imagining raising and lowering various *things*. At one point he slipped and brought up a full stone wall block, but quickly dropped it.

Even as he did so, Canis and Cattus shouldered through the door, both of them sitting in front of him and putting paws on his leg. He also felt a sleepy thought from Moby, "*We will work more with you in the morning. Please go to sleep.*"

He mumbled, "Okay, okay. I give." Pushing their paws off, he said, "You two, out. I'll be good." The two animals continued to stare at him, and he flopped back on the bed with a sigh. The next thing he knew, the sun was shining through his window, and he heard rustling in the kitchen.

Yawning, he ran quickly through the fresher, put on a well-worn shipsuit, and walked into the living room, scratching his chest. Dineah looked up at him over a cup of coffee, "Why do all men scratch their chests in the morning?"

Fargo stopped, "Uh, it itches?"

Dineah laughed. "My father, Moby, my brothers, you… all of you scratch *something* in the morning."

Moby came in with a glass of water, "Morning, Captain."

"Morning, sorry about waking you up last night."

"No problem. It's just that we're attuned to any psi talent, and your actions kept bouncing our shields."

"Even while you were asleep? How…"

Dineah gave a rueful grin, "Uh, practice. Did you come up with an image that works for you?"

Fargo threw up his hands, "I don't know. Maybe. Moby's comment about water yesterday got me to thinking, what about rain? Or fog. Make it thicker, let the other things slide off… And with fog, I *think* I might be able to close that around me in a crowded environment."

Moby said, "We'll stay the rest of the day, and work with you again. As strong as you are, you definitely need to learn to control your talent. A lot of that is going to be getting out and mingling with people and practicing."

"How do you *practice*, as you call it?

Dineah grinned, "We listen in on the captains, and the CSM. And the Intel officers and chiefs. That way we have time to plan, and always looked smarter than we really are when asked questions about scouting."

Fargo laughed. "Oh deity… that is *so* perfect. I wonder…" *I wonder if that is how Diez always knew what was coming down.* "Let's eat and I'd appreciate it if you would run me through the simple things I need to know to not screw up."

Moby and Dineah both nodded, and Dineah asked quietly, "Coffee? Please?"

Searching

The e-tainment system sounded a siren, then flashed a red screen, pulling Nicole's attention from the shop books, and she yelled for Holly, "Come here, we've got an emergency!"

As Holly came through the curtain, the screen changed, showing a picture of a young girl, then flashed the information underneath.

NAME: BAER, MELISSA
AGE: THREE STANDARD YEARS
STATUS: MISSING SINCE 1300. LAST LOCATION .5 MILES E OF RUSHING RIVER

SEARCH TEAMS MUSTER AT ROCK POINT LOCATION FOR ASSIGNMENTS, ALL AVAILABLE PERSONNEL REQUESTED.

They looked at each other, and Holly asked, "Shelly's daughter?"

"Has to be. But what… Dammit, I'll bet Shelly took her out while she was collecting berries."

"We're going, right?"

"Yes, lock up and we'll swing by the house on the way." Glancing at the clock, it showed 1400, and Nicole winced. "Not much time. If she's not found by dark… I don't want to think about it."

Holly nodded as she slipped off her apron, headed for the kitchen to shut off the cookers and ovens.

Twenty minutes later, they were gathered with thirty others at Rock Point, as Sergeant Omar squirted assignments to the individual team's wrist comps. Nicole glanced at hers when it pinged, and said, "We're going to be in for a rough one. Glad we brought gear." Holly had her med kit over her shoulder, and Nicole had emergency blankets, water, and nutrition bars in her backpack. They both had pistols on their belts, and jackets rolled on top of their packs.

Holly checked her wrist comp and winced. "We're gonna be wet and tired. At least we're not in the wood line. That place scares me."

Nicole asked the sergeant, "Any chance of a flyover?"

Sergeant Omar twittered and the GalTrans spit out, "Requested I have, but time we do not have. Two divs it would take. Lightflyers we will task. Altitude, they cannot use, beams too low."

Sobbing, Shelly Baer stepped forward. "Mel was tethered, and I was in a bunch of nearberries. When I backed out, I turned around and she was gone. It couldn't have been more than five minutes…"

Sergeant Omar interrupted, "Exact location, please for this?"

"Oh, yes." Shelly scrolled back through her wrist comp, then keyed the location, "Here it is. I looked and looked, and called her." She broke down in sobs again, "And Jonathan is at White Beach, and I had nobody to watch her."

Luann put her arm around Shelly, and led her quickly away, as Doc Grant stepped up. "You find her,

ping me, if she's hurt, give me an emergency ping.
OneSvel and I will be in the middle of the search area,
so we can respond in any direction as quickly as
possible.

Nicole thought of Fargo, *Dammit, I wish Ethan
was here. He might be able to find her quicker than
any of us, but he's still recovering. Or is he climbing
out of bed and heading this way? That crazy…*

A half div later, as they crossed yet another stream,
Nicole looked up and saw Fargo's lightflyer go over,
almost hovering at times. It moved across to the wood
line, and she yelled over to Holly, "He must be using
IR goggles. Maybe he'll get lucky."

Holly waved back, "The sooner the better. The
damn bugs are about to eat me for lunch. I *knew* I
forgot something."

Nicole slanted her way, knowing the next creek
had only one ford, as she pulled her pack around. She
got there first, and pulled out the bug spray, handing it
to Holly as she puffed up. "Do your arms and clothes,
and I'll do your back. Then you can do mine."

Holly quickly sprayed herself down, then stepped
behind Nicole and sprayed her back. Nicole took the
spray and sprayed Holly's back, then shoved the spray
into her pack. "Looks like another div of light. We'll
cover at least ninety percent of our search area. I'm
thinking we should modify our track, and work from
distant to close, rather than the way they laid it out."

"Sounds good. I still don't understand why they
did what they did."

"Probabilities. That is what always drives stuff like
this."

Holly snorted. "Which is why it's a good thing I didn't go into the GalPat."

Nicole took another drink of the electrolyte, capped the bottle and shrugged. "Probably right. Let's get this one. We'll finish this leg then rotate the tracks ninety to the left. Okay?"

Holly hoisted her pack without a word, and resumed the spacing, as they trudged toward the wood line.

***

Nicole and Holly walked dispiritedly through the dusk back to the winery, "Where could she have gotten to? She's only three. We should have found her!"

Nicole replied, "I don't know. Six divs is a long time. And if she went into the wood line…"

"Is Fargo coming over?"

"No, that stupid ass shouldn't even have come down, much less flown two divs of search patterns. He didn't bring his meds, and he was hurting, which serves him right, damn him!"

"He's a male, he's stubborn, or stupid depending. But I do like him." Holly sighed, then switched subjects, "If we didn't find Melissa, I'm afraid she's gone."

"I know."

They dropped their packs on the step, and headed for the winery, each lost in their own thoughts.

Holly said, "I'm going to close down the processor."

"Okay, I want to see how much sand we have left."

As they approached the processor they heard a soft "Wuff", and a full grown wolf stepped boldly into the light from the door. "Mom!"

Holly started to reach for her pistol, and Nicole said, "Wait. Stop, don't move."

Holly had already stopped and started to protest, but Nicole held up her hand in silence. The wolf padded over, sniffed Nicole's hand, and gently took her wrist in its mouth, tugging slightly.

"Mom? What is…?"

"I don't know. It's like it wants me to go somewhere."

The wolf tugged again, and Nicole involuntarily took a step, then another. Nicole looked over her shoulder at Holly, "I'm going with it. Stay here."

"No! I'm coming with you. If you get bit, I think I can kill it before it kills me. At least I'll try, but I'm not staying here," Holly hissed, as she followed Nicole. She pulled out her taclight, putting it on the lowest setting, and made sure her pistol was loose in the holster.

The wolf led them through the vineyard, across the intervening field, and toward the wood line. As Nicole's eyes adjusted, she realized the wolf leading her was a female, and she wondered, *Is this Canis? I don't think so, she looks too big. But what in the hell is she doing? And why did she come to me? Dammit Ethan, why couldn't you be here? And she's got my damn pistol hand in her mouth. Shit…*

A quarter div later, deep in the woods, the wolf stopped at a magnificent old oak, then whined. What Nicole could only describe as a meow sounded and what she'd thought was a pile of brown moss uncoiled, and she involuntarily stepped back as Holly shrieked softly behind her. A full grown mountain lion yawned, showing a mouthful of teeth, then bent and licked something lying on the ground. Holly shined her light, and Melissa Baer asked, "Mommy?"

Nicole reached down gently, "No, honey. But we're going to take you to her, okay?"

The little girl reached up and replied, "Okay."

The mountain lion reached up and licked the girl's hand, she giggled and said, "Tank you, kitty."

Nicole turned, "Now I've got to figure out where we are. Holly, can you use your comp to get us home? I'm going to have to carry her."

Holly rolled her sleeve back, swiped a couple of times, and replied, "Okay, I think so. I didn't think to track us in, and I don't remember all the direction changes, but I can get us back to the winery. Or do you want to call for help from here?"

"No! Who would believe us? Let's go, while I try to figure out how to explain this."

Holly headed off, with Nicole carrying Melissa. Escorted by a wolf on one side, and a mountain lion on the other side. *How do I...* Nicole shook her head, *I can't explain this. I need to talk to Fargo. Somehow this has to tie into his animals. That sumbitch did this to me, somehow. But we found Melissa... Gotta call him before we talk to anybody.*

A quarter of a div later, they were back in the vineyard, and Nicole stopped suddenly. "Holly, can you take Melissa for a few minutes?"

Holly glanced down at the wolf and mountain lion, then edged closer. When they didn't respond, she gathered the girl onto her shoulder, "Still asleep?"

"She's been asleep the whole time." Nicole turned to face the two animals, crouched down, and projected empathy as hard as she could, saying, "I don't think you understand, but thank you for saving her life."

First the wolf, then the mountain lion licked her hand, and then moved to sniff Holly, before turning and disappearing into the night, side by side.

"Mom, what did you just do? Were you trying to talk to them? What?"

"Later." She got up slowly, and they continued toward the winery as she pinged Fargo on her wrist comp.

A groggy Fargo answered, "Nicole? Whazza you want?"

"We found the girl."

"That's great! Where?"

"Deep in the woods. A damn wolf led me to her. And she was being kept warm by a… mountain lion. Kinda like your two or three."

"Shit." A now fully awake Fargo continued, "Lie. Don't tell them about that. Say you found her in the tree line. We can't…"

"Fargo! She remembers! And she thanked the kitty for keeping her warm."

"Make up something. We can't let anybody know about the animals."

Grumbling, Nicole finally said, "I'll try. We're back at the winery. I've got to go report this. You and I are going to have a talk about this, you understand?"

"Fine. We can do that. Does Holly know?"

"Yes, she was with me the whole time."

"Okay, bring her with you the next time, if she'll come?"

"She'll come. We both want answers." Nicole disconnected and called Sergeant Omar, telling him she and Holly had found the girl and were at the winery. Holly quickly checked her for any problems, let her go to the bathroom, and cleaned her up as well as she could as people descended on the winery.

***

Two days later, Fargo sat gingerly at the table with Nicole in the Copper Pot, twisting his coffee cup in his hands, "So, nobody asked any questions?"

"No. They were so happy to get Melissa back, they bought the fact that we found her in the wood line behind the vineyard. Apparently, Melissa thinks it was all a dream, even the *kitty*. What I want to know is why they saved her, and why they picked me! Ethan, that is just *not* normal behavior!"

Fargo held up both hands, "I'm not sure. I know, well, you know too, they can and do communicate both within and across at least three species. Why they saved the girl? I have no idea, other than they thought she was a cub. I do remember all of the animals at the waterfall coming and smelling me when they left. And Cattus, Canis, and Urso all have smelled you and know you won't harm them. I just…"

Doc Grant and OneSvel came through the door, and Doc said, "Ah, two birds with one stone! Just the people I wanted to see today."

Nicole nodded at them, "Anything to drink Doc? OneSvel?"

OneSvel's GalTrans said, "Fargo, you are coming for evaluation today, correct?"

Fargo nodded. "At fifteen. What did you need to see us about, Doc?"

Doc said, "I'd love a real coffee."

OneSvel extruded a couple of pseudopods, and his GalTrans said excitedly, "Disaccharides, we sense you have unprocessed disaccharides here. May we… indulge?"

Nicole looked up at him, "Uh, what?"

"Maltose, turanose, kojibiose. They are in a concentration that includes…" One of the pseudopods looked like it was sniffing, "They are mixed with monosaccharides, fructose, and a flower."

"Oh, you mean honey? Yes, I do have some that I've collected up at Fargo's place. I haven't processed it yet, to make sure it is safe."

"May I have some? Maybe an ounce or two?"

"Now?"

"If we may, yes, please." OneSvel almost seemed to be trembling, and Nicole shook her head, got up and went into the kitchen. *That's strange. I've never seen that kind of reaction, and I guess it's true, Taurasians really can sift through the atmosphere and pick out minute particles. That honey is in sealed containers to prevent contamination. I wonder why they want it.*

She brought Doc's coffee, and two ounces of honey in a small bowl with a spoon, back to the table and set it in front of OneSvel. She handed Doc his coffee cup as she watched curiously. Yet another pseudopod extruded and delicately touched the honey.

OneSvel quivered, a reddish color running over his skin, as the GalTrans moaned, "Oh. So pure. Must resist…" Suddenly the pseudopod slurped up the remaining honey in one swoop, and OneSvel's skin turned bright red, as thousands of little hair like pseudopods popped out then disappeared. The eye stalks closed, the Galtrans spit out gibberish, as they slowly collapsed on the floor, shaking the entire building.

Nicole looked at Doc. "What the hell?"

Doc laughed. "If I remember my physiognomy correctly, what we now have on our hands is a drunk Taurasian."

"What?"

"Apparently, raw disaccharides are, to a Taurasian, the equivalent of hundred proof alcohol to us. What you just did was give them enough put them out like a light."

"So, how do I deal with them?"

Doc shrugged. "Leave them lay? I don't think we can move OneSvel. It should wear off in an div or three. OneSvel told me that's why he's never gone beyond medtech. He's the Taurasian equivalent of a drunk."

Fargo and Nicole looked at each other, as Doc continued, "The reason I wanted to talk to you Nicole, is that when we examined Melissa, I found hairs on her clothes. Those hairs came from animals. Specifically, a mountain lion, and a few hairs from a wolf, according to research I had OneSvel do. Now we know both those species have a history of savaging humans on Hunter."

He glanced between Fargo and Nicole, "Fargo, now he's a GalScout, retired. He's comfortable in the wild, lives up in a remote area. But he's never been bothered, other than that one incident at the waterfall, right?"

Fargo nodded. "I see them occasionally, but that's all."

Doc faced him directly. "Bullshit. The last time I cleaned the exam room after you left, I noticed there were hairs everywhere. I compared them under the scope, and they're the same."

Fargo was a bit startled when OneSvel projected, "*Careful with your answer.*"

"I."

Nicole threw up her hands. "Fuck it. I'm tired of lying. You want the truth? *This* is the truth. A wolf came up to me, took my arm in her mouth, and led Holly and me to the girl. A full grown mountain lion was keeping her warm. They let me pick her up, and escorted us back to the vineyard."

Doc rocked back in his chair. "Wh…eh…that's not…"

Nicole was in full chief sergeant mode now. "Not possible? Of course it's not possible, except it happened. And," pointing to Fargo, "*He* has one each: wolf, lion, and bear that are *bonded* to him. And he communicates with them. How's that for impossible, Doc?"

Doc asked softly, "How?"

OneSvel, still prostrate on the floor, projected, *"Well, that cat is now out of the bag, as you speak."* It was all Fargo could do not to flinch, thinking OneSvel was unconscious.

Fargo thought, *"As you say. Since the truth is now out, I guess I'll lay it out for him.*

"If necessary, Doc can have an accident. And I am not drunk, my host is drunk."

Fargo shook his head. "Okay the truth is that I used empathic projection to get close to a female wolf who was hurt at the waterfall. I treated her and felt the litter of pups she had. And, oh by the way, those three species were fighting the Silverback in concert. They can talk, I guess is the word, mentally within their species and across species. They all came up and smelled me when they left. Four months later, I got three females dropped in my lap, literally. One wolf pup, a bear cub and a lion cub. They bonded with me, and although I can't talk to them, they do sort of respond to commands. They also alert me when things happen and I can sense their mental states. Nicole knows about it, she's been up at the cabin and interacted with them."

Doc said wonderingly, "Wolves noses are over a hundred thousand times better than ours. That would explain them coming to Nicole. But why?"

"Payback for my killing the Silverback? Payback for saving the she-wolf? I don't know. What are you going to do about it?"

Doc looked at Nicole. "Uh, could I have a drink please? Something strong?"

Nicole stomped over to the bar. Pulling a bottle out from under the bar, she sloshed a glass half full and set it in front of Doc. "What are you going to do?"

Taking a sip, he said, "I… I don't know. The scientific…" He tossed off the drink with a shudder. "No, that won't work. We would be invaded with eco-nuts and the xenos. How about we keep this between us? I won't even tell OneSvel. I'll… figure out something to tell him."

Nicole raised an eyebrow. "Why? This could make you famous."

OneSvel projected, "*Doc has his secrets too, and he has no desire to interact with the larger GalPat. He will never tell anyone. I can sense his resolve in this.*"

"*So we should agree and let him drop it?*"

"*Yes.*"

Fargo said, "Okay, I'll buy that. We're done here. Never to be mentioned again, agreed?"

Nicole looked sharply at him, as Doc nodded his head. "So, what do we do with them?" Pointing to OneSvel."

"Let them sleep it off. It's only fourteen, so you've got what, three divs before it gets busy?"

Nicole rolled her eyes, "I guess I'll just lock the door."

Twenty minutes later, Holly stepped out of the kitchen. "Mom, I heard everything, but I can keep a secret."

"Good. Because a lot depends on it."

OPFOR

Fargo walked into the GalPat admin building adjacent to the space port, looking around in interest. He'd seen the buildings being unfolded and set up, but this was the first time he'd actually been in one. An androgynous chief master sergeant sat at a workstation in the entry way, and looked up politely, "Can I help you?"

Fargo nodded. "Fargo, Hunter Militia, I'm here to meet with a Major Culverhouse?" *Winged foot emblem, dammit... Oh yeah, Hermes. Hermaphroditus or Hermaphroditos, child of Hermes and Aphrodite. Mated with a... Nymph? Hence hermaphrodite.* He consciously didn't probe the Chief, working on the shielding he'd discussed with MobyDineah.

The chief stood, "I'm Chief Aphrodite. You are expected. Major Culverhouse, Captain Culverhouse, and Captain Garibaldi are in the captain's office. This way, please." Major Jackie Culverhouse sat behind the desk, with her hubby Captain Mack Culverhouse, sitting to her left. Captain Bob Garibaldi sat on the couch, a bulb of something in his hand.

Fargo had a momentary start, as he tried to figure out whether he was supposed to report, or... Major Culverhouse got up, "Mr. Fargo? Or is it Captain? Come in, we don't stand on ceremony here."

She extended her hand, as Fargo stepped in front of the desk, "Um, well, since this is an *official* meeting, I guess Captain Ethan Fargo. Or just Fargo." He extended his psi sense and felt curiosity from all three of them, and humor from Captain Garibaldi. None of them seemed to have any psi talent, nor did the chief.

Captain Culverhouse stepped up, "Mack. Pleasure to finally meet you. We've heard from our scouts about you and your hideaway up in the mountains." Taking his hand, Fargo sensed a wistfulness, and honesty.

"Mack, I usually just go by Fargo. It's a long story."

Captain Garibaldi stood languidly, "Bob. I'm the old fart here, and junior to boot. I'll defer everything to my 'seniors' here," he said with a laugh.

Fargo saw that Garibaldi was a fireplug of an officer, short and wide. And from his handshake, *very* fit. "Fargo." He sensed that Garibaldi was the prankster of the group, but also the smartest one in the room.

"Bulb?" Matt asked, pointing to the small autochef sitting on the sideboard.

"Coffee, please?"

"How do you like it?"

"Program sixty-two please. No adds."

A seg later, bouncing the bulb in his hand, he sat around the conference table with the others, as the chief went back to its desk. Major Culverhouse opened the discussion, "Colonel Keads told me I needed to get in touch with you about providing some OPFOR for the company we've got here on a det."

Fargo sensed humor from Bob, and worry from Mack as he nodded. "We could probably do that. Depends on how much and what type of OPFOR you want."

Jackie plowed on, "Colonel Keads told me a little bit about your company. Well, more than a little bit. Like it's *all* Ghorkas, and retired chiefs, CSMs, and warrants. And you have armor."

Sensing her nervousness, he smiled. "Yeah, you might say the company is a *bit* different."

Bob laughed. "Really? A whole fucking COMPANY of Ghorka? Oh my God, what I wouldn't give…"

Mack looked over at him, "Shaddap Bob. Just shut up. We are *not*…"

Fargo glanced between the two of them, then at the Major. "Lemme guess. The troops are getting a bit *uppity*?"

Jackie rolled her eyes, "A bit. Well, maybe more than a bit. They're getting barracks fever. And they are pissed they didn't get called to participate in the search for the missing little girl."

Surprised, Fargo said, "I didn't know that. I was in my liteflyer, not working the ground end. Our militia company wasn't called up either. We have SAR protocols for each community, based on time delay, search area, and other factors. The rule, if you will, is that we do not extend searches past sunset. Too many things outside the settlements will eat you for dinner without a second thought. The only allowable darkness search mode is airborne, preferably from a shuttle. Liteflyers are only allowed if they can glide to a safe area. And she was found just before sunset."

Mack and Bob exchanged glances and Fargo sensed that they knew that was a lie. Shaking his head, he continued, "So, what kind of OPFOR do you want?"

Jackie rolled her hand at Mack, who said, "Preferably multiple. Some flat, some wooded, some mountainous. We had thought about some night, but maybe we need to rethink that."

"Armor or no?"

Bob chimed in, "Maybe a mix of both? Some, shall we say, local resistance, moving up the complexity chain to armored attack and defense of positions?"

"How badly do you want them beaten?"

Jackie bristled, then thought for a second, "Do you really think?"

Fargo smiled. "Major, do you really want me to unleash a hundred CSMs and warrants on your troops? Most of our company has a minimum of forty years of service. Our average age as of last month was eighty-nine."

Bob laughed. "Oh hell yes! This is gonna be epic!"

Mack just shook his head as Jackie's eyes got big, "I didn't think…"

Fargo grinned, "How about subduing a local resistance hotbed in an outlying village. No armor. Lasers simulating firing. Pain threshold say… Two? And kills are paralyzed for the remainder of the exercise?"

"Um, I guess."

Fargo glanced at his datacomp, making a couple of swipes, "How about this weekend? We're drilling this weekend."

Mack looked at him, "I'm afraid to ask, but where?"

Fargo's grin got wider. "Oh, how about the Enclave?" He tapped the holo and entered the coordinates, then sat back.

The other three looked at the holo, then Mack expanded it, "Damn. That's…"

Bob finished the statement, "A friggin fortress! Who the hell would voluntarily…"

Jackie said softly, "The Ghorka, right?"

Fargo nodded. "And it's almost eight thousand feet up. And chilly. And no way to approach covertly."

Jackie looked at the holo, then rotated it, "That. Is. A. Killing. Field. I wouldn't even put armor in there. I'd nuke it from orbit and be done with it." Sitting back, she looked at the two captains, "You want to try this?"

Fargo said, "I'll sweeten the pot. I'll give you a three to one advantage. Fifty against your entire company. And only half of those with rifles."

Mack and Bob's eyes met across the holo, and they both nodded. "We're in. We'll need lift."

Fargo replied, "There is a ship in orbit called *Hyderabad*. She's on contract. She can lift the entire company."

Jackie shook her head. "Captain Fargo, may I observe from the… Enclave, as you call it?"

"Certainly."

***

Fargo leaned against the building, looking at Lal, Jiri, Horse, and Nirvik. Nicole had disappeared with a few of the women, and he worried about what they might be planning, but that was out of his hands. "So, we're going to use second platoon and part of third as the rebels. Everyone is kitted out with the laser modules for their rifles and pistols, right?"

Jiri nodded. "Everybody including Yash and Kamadev. They'll play snipers."

Lal glanced at Nirvik, "Are you sure you want to play the leader?"

Nirvik grinned through his gray whiskers, "I'm old. I'm bent and broken. They will not suspect me. They will look at me as a cast off."

Fargo got up the nerve to ask, "Nirvik, how old are you?"

Nirvik laughed. "Something between one thirty and one forty. I lost count. Maybe Lal knows, he keeps all the records. I just make *kukris* now."

Lal shook his head. "Dammit Nirvik, you know you're a hundred and thirty eight. You are eighteen years older than your wife, and she had a birthday on Tuesday." Turning to Fargo he continued, "Ekavir, you and the major will be in the eagle's nest to observe. She will have to be blindfolded to be led there for security purposes."

"Eagle's nest?"

"It is one of our lookout posts. You are of this tribe. You may know the way. She is not, and may not." Glancing at his wrist comp, he said, "And you need to be going that way."

A shuttle popped over the cliff, spiraled down for a landing, and they watched with interest as Colonel Keads stepped off, along with Major Culverhouse. Kulbir came trotting up, "Want me to escort the colonel?"

Fargo nodded. "I don't know where he will want to go, but feel free. Lal, who is going to escort us to the… nest?"

Lal grinned, "I am."

The colonel and major walked up, "Captain, Warrant, and Kulbir. Are we ready?"

Fargo nodded. "Anytime you are, Sir. Where would you like to observe from?"

"Kulbir, what would you suggest?"

"Colonel, I can show you a number of places with the rebels," Kulbir said with a grin.

Keads smiled. "That will work. I've never seen this side of an exercise."

Fargo turned to the major, "Major, if you're ready? We have an overlook to observe from."

She nodded. "That's fine. Colonel, I'll meet you back here at the end of the exercise."

Keads nodded distractedly, "Fine. Lead on, Kulbir!"

***

Fargo and Major Culverhouse sat in the Eagle's Nest, looking out over the Enclave and the approaches, "Amazing view. And I can see why they don't want us to know how to get here. They really are security conscious aren't they?"

Fargo nodded. "And paranoid to boot." Cocking his head, he said, "Sounds like a ship. Here we go!"

The *Hyderabad* swooped in, grounding for less than one seg, as a platoon boiled off a mile away. It hopped east, grounded again, another platoon off, and grounded to the southeast, remaining on the ground as the last platoon debarked, all three platoons in soft armor.

Fargo laughed. "Interesting... A mile out? Maybe a little overconfident?"

Jackie winced. "I... I don't know what they are thinking. I'm not sure they've been out of battle armor in over two years. And I know they haven't done any VRs like this." Turning to Fargo she said, "This isn't going to end well, is it?"

Fargo shrugged. "Honestly, I don't know. I wasn't involved in the planning. But probably not. A mile, across open ground? Even in soft armor they are going to be ripe for the picking. Did they...ah well, too late, so never mind."

Lal said softly, "Here they come."

Major Culverhouse and Fargo both brought binoculars to their eyes and watched as the platoons closed on the Enclave. Fargo asked, "No ferrets?"

Her shoulder slumped, "I haven't seen any launched. Bad..."

"Who planned this?"

"Mack and Bob are all about getting the troops involved. I'm guessing they gave it to the sergeants to plan, and the chiefs to review."

"If they were in full armor, yeah, but this..." He chuckled as he watched Bob go down, "They just took out Bob. Hope he's comfortable. At least he's lying on grass."

Jackie swung her binocs and sighed. "Mack is down too."

"They're going to take care of the flankers, then handle the middle platoon."

Ten segs later, intermittent sniping fire from the village, then concentrated fire on the flanking platoons had caused both of them to be effectively annihilated. The villagers had done their best to drop them in comfortable locations, but a couple ended up sprawled across rocks in what had to be uncomfortable positions. *I hope they call it before those Herms end up badly bruised and cramping up, but they do sort of deserve it, all things considered.* The snipers turned their attention to the center platoon who had hung back, waiting for the flankers to get into position. Only a few random troops in the center platoon were down, along with both lieutenants, but Master Chief Aphrodite was still upright and leading that platoon. They were less than fifty yards from the village when they realized both sets of flankers were down, and started to move faster. They were singing something that Fargo didn't recognize as concentrated fire took out the master chief, and two other chief sergeants, leaving what looked like one senior sergeant in charge. And charge she did. But only about fifteen troops were left who followed her into the center of the village.

Fargo leaned forward, wondering what Jiri had up his sleeve, when the troops started kicking in doors, "Oh not good. That's going to piss off…"

Suddenly Nirvik stood in the center of the street and yelled something, but Fargo didn't hear it clearly. The senior sergeant did, as she charged toward Nirvik, discarding her rifle and pulling a combat knife. Fargo got up, "No! Lal, she's going after Nirvik! FINEX this damn thing before he gets hurt."

Lal replied calmly, "We can't get down there before whatever is going to happen, happens."

The major was on her radio yelling, "FINEX, FINEX, FINEX, all troops stand down, this exercise is terminated! FINEX, NOW!" She yelled, even as the senior sergeant closed with Nirvik, blade flashing in the afternoon sun.

Fargo watched as Nirvik somehow eluded her blade, and seemed to slide to one side as she charged by. Turning she came back at him and Fargo realized he had his *kukri* out. "Shit. Nirvik is going to try to defend himself. Lal, get…" The two closed again, and once again, Nirvik seemed to slip aside, but this time there was a scream, and the senior sergeant went to her knees. Nirvik kicked something to the side, and yelled something in the Ghorka dialect. As he did, all of the other troops collapsed on the ground.

***

Two divs later, debrief completed, the colonel, major, captains, Lal, Jiri, and Fargo joined the picnic being held in the center of the village. Nicole smiled at him as she handed him a plate, "Very lightly seasoned, just for you."

"So this is what you were up to?"

Nicole replied, "Well, we didn't want to send them away mad. Besides they needed to cycle some foodstuff that was getting close to expiring. And it's mostly made friends with them."

Fargo glanced around, noting Ghorka and Herms intermingling around the center of the village, and nodded. "Damn good idea. What did they do with that senior sergeant? Is she still alive?"

"Hera? Yes, Nirvik only took her hand. He didn't kill her, and our medics jumped in. She was onboard *Hyderabad*, and in the med comp before you ever got down here. Oh, and the colonel busted her to private on the spot."

"Considering the alternative, she should be glad of that."

Lal said, "But she will never be allowed back here. And will be shunned by all Ghorka for her actions. To continue the attack after the exercise was ended, much less for the fact that she attacked a clan elder, much less a *kukri* maker… she's lucky she's leaving here alive."

Fargo grimaced. "Including the Fleet, right?"

Lal nodded grimly, "Everywhere there are Ghorka."

"Then her, its, career is done."

Nicole tugged his sleeve, "Fargo, look!" She pointed to Nirvik sitting in a chair in front of one of the houses with a broken door, and Master Chief Aphrodite on her knees in front of him, her hands clasped together. As they watched, Nirvik reached out gently and touched Aphrodite on the head, almost as if blessing her. They saw her nod, then rise and walk blindly out of the Enclave, toward the *Hyderabad*.

Nirvik saw them looking, and waved. He got up slowly and limped over, "Ekavir, you saw what happened?"

Fargo nodded. "I did. I tried…" He reached out to Nirvik with his psi sense.

Nirvik waved him off, "We left her *alive* since she was a hothead. We counted on the fact that she would go off and try something stupid. We just didn't realize how stupid." Fargo grimaced as he touched Nirvik and felt his absolute certainty that he could have and would have killed the Herm, as Nirvik continued, "I heard the FINEX call, and that is the only thing that saved her. If not for that, I would have killed her."

"I'm amazed she didn't get you. She's younger, fitter, and…"

"Doesn't have over a hundred years of knife fighting experience. She was so predictable, everything by the book. And I literally *wrote* the book," Nirvik laughed, then said, "But who is going to fix my door? It was open, and they were supposed to be simulating that!"

"Maybe a working party from the losers?"

"Ah, that would be appropriate!"

"Captain Culverhouse," Fargo yelled. When he turned, "Join us please?"

Mack and Bob came over, and Fargo said, "Gents we've got busted doors, and they need to be replaced. Would you mind putting a working party together to make that happen? Especially since the doors were open?"

Mack nodded. and Bob said, "I'll get right on it. *Hyderabad* has a shop on board, right?"

"That it does. Coordinate with Captain Jace, if you would."

"Consider it done."

***

A week later, Fargo was back in the major's office for the out brief. "Did you ever figure out why that sergeant went nuts on Nirvik?"

The major rolled her eyes as Mack said, "According to the Chief Sergeant, she was the catcher in her latest relationship and apparently a little *too* submissive. She'd apparently been dumped the night before the exercise, and had been ranting and raving about how she wasn't submissive and dared anyone to tell her so."

"So she tripped off line, and attacked a hundred and thirty-eight year old icon in the village?"

Bob sighed, "Well, she was also one of the planners for the company's approach, and we all saw how well *that* worked out, didn't we. Or should I say those of you that didn't get killed *immediately*, saw how it worked out!"

"What's going to happen to her?"

Jackie replied, "She let her guard down, and was vulnerable in the relationship. Not a good place for her to be. She's not exactly under guard, but we're watching her. She's finally realized what she did, and knows it's the end of her career. She'll be admin'ed out at the end of the deployment, and sent back to her planet of origin, but not with a negative discharge. At least that way she can find some other kind of employment." She turned to Mack and Bob and continued briskly, "Now, about the debrief…"

Three divs later, two very abashed captains walked out of her office, and Fargo asked, "Weren't you a little hard on them?"

"No, they frikkin well knew better. They knew from the start your folks were going to hammer them into the ground. They should have stopped the planning and redirected it to a more workable solution, but no…" she said with a sigh.

Fargo nodded. "Okay, for the next one, you want to do armor? It might be safer for all concerned."

"Oh hell yes. Because *I* will control the armament. There will not be another screw up like this one."

Job Offer

Fargo sat on top of the Hab van, scanning for any sign of the Silverbacks he could sense. *Dammit, the sooner we finish this feeder, the better I'll feel. This one has been jinxed from the get-go.* Jiri, Kamala, and Daman filled out the rest of the security team for the feeder installation, keeping watch twenty-four/seven for predators and other things until the site was in; the sonics up and working.

Kamala's sultry voice came through the earbud, "Movement northeast and just below the lip of the ridge. Mammal of some type, maybe a cat."

Reaching out with his empathic sense, he touched two minds, but they weren't like Cattus or the Silverbacks. These were pure predators. He tried to project a sense of danger to them, but that didn't work, and he sensed them slinking closer. He flipped his mic to on, "Everybody under cover?"

Kamala came back, "All inside. You're the sole outside person."

"Okay, two predators. I'm going to try to take them out. See if you can see where the second one goes after I hit the first one."

"Wilco."

Reaching down, he picked up his 16mm bead rifle and flipped the holo sight on. He brought it slowly to his shoulder, let a breath out slowly, and locked on where he thought the cat would appear. He sensed it creeping closer, and took another breath, just as the first cat came over the ridge. Just as he pressed the firing stud, the second cat popped up, and he didn't even think, just put a second round into it.

Both cats went down, and Kamala asked, "Did you get them both?"

"Yes. Ask Daman to come relieve me and I'll go look at them. They are *different*."

Daman came on the net, "On the way." Less than a seg later, he was settling into the chair and said, "Those are... Nearcats?"

Fargo shook his head. "I think nearleopards. I'll go see."

"I don't think I've ever seen one. The spots are pretty."

"And damn good camouflage. They're normally only seen in warm veldt type climates."

Daman laughed. "Like where we are? You know the women will want those for collars for their coats."

"We'll see. Kamala yes, but the other one? That might bring some money off planet." Fargo climbed down, looked around then headed toward the two nearleopards.

Jiri stuck his head out of the Hab, "Need any help?"

"Nah, I'll skin them out real quick. Go back to sleep."

Jiri disappeared back into the Hab, as Fargo leaned his rifle against a boulder that hadn't been moved because it was too heavy. Dragging the first of the cats over, he pulled out his knife, clicked it on, and quickly skinned the first nearleopard. Pulling the second one over, he skinned it out, noting it was female, and was pondering the pair's method of hunting, when Kamala screamed, "Fargo!"

He looked up to see a Silverback in mid-leap, and threw the carcass of the nearleopard up as he frantically rolled toward the boulder. He felt a sharp pain in his left arm as he grabbed his rifle, dimly hearing another rifle firing. He spun, saw the Silverback biting the carcass, and triggered four shots into its rear end, praying he was hitting the hearts. It screamed and collapsed, as he fired one final aimed shot at where he knew each heart was. He opened his empathic sense in panic, knowing the other one was somewhere close. He felt the second one scrambling up the slope in a killing rage, saw it out of the corner of his eye, and scrambled frantically behind the boulder, resting the rifle on it with one hand as he took a sight on the lip of the ridge. He started to feel lightheaded, felt the pharmacope kick in, and started to feel his senses fading. *Dammit, don't tell me I'm going to get killed by my own damn stupidity... Gotta hang... on...*

The second Silverback charged over the lip of the ridge, and Fargo pumped rounds into it until the rifle was empty and the Silverback was piled up against the opposite side of the boulder. Sliding down, he leaned back against the boulder as the rifle slid from his hand. Looking down at his left arm, he saw that he was bleeding heavily and most of his bicep was hanging loose. *This isn't good. Not good at all...*

He heard Jiri and Daman yelling and wondered why they were so far away as he blacked out. What he didn't know was Jiri was holding his brachial artery closed to keep him from bleeding out, as Daman frantically got a tourniquet on. As soon as they did that, they pulled the bicep back up and wrapped it in a sterile bandage, while Kamala called for Mikhail to bring the shuttle back.

Three days later, he felt a touch in his mind, *"Fargo are you there?"*

"Where is here? OneSvel?"

"You're in the med comp at Rushing River. What did we tell you about being tired of fixing you back up?"

"Uh, you weren't happy?"

"You are correct. You are lucky to be alive. If it had not been for your pharmacope, and Jiri and Daman, you would be dead now."

"I know. I was stupid, I lost concentration. I missed…"

"Only the fact that Mikhail was within twenty segs of the site saved you. And our having four units of blood expander in the onboard emergency kit. Otherwise, you would have bled out."

"My arm itches…"

"Good, that means the nerves are regenerating. Now go back under."

***

Fargo looked at Luann, "I'm sorry. I *do not* have a death wish. I *am not* trying to kill myself!"

She banged a skillet down on the heating unit with a loud clang, "Ethan, twice in three months is too close for comfort. I'm thinking you need to move down here, and start working with us. I think you've got some issues," she tapped her head, "that you're not willing to admit to."

It was all Fargo could do not to use his psi sense to see what she was really meaning, since he'd never told her or Mikhail about that new ability. But she was radiating concern and anger in equal proportions that his empath sense readily picked up. He sighed as he tried once more to calm her as he projected calm, "Luann Jean, I have a life. I'm not going to kill myself. And I've been checked out by both Doc Grant and OneSvel. There is nothing wrong with me. I made a mistake…"

"A mistake? *A mistake*? Ethan James Fargo you are the *only* family I have left. I will not see you dead because of your own stupid masculine ego!"

He projected calm and tried a different line of answers, "So, you want me to not protect Mikhail? You want me to not protect our community? Is that what you really want?"

Luann threw up her hands, "Oh hell, I don't know… I just don't want you dead," she cried.

Tears rolled down her face, and Fargo gently gathered her in his arms, "I don't want to be dead either."

She pushed him away, "Now get out of here. I'm trying to get dinner ready."

He nodded gently, "Okay."

He eased out of the kitchen, and met Mikhail in the hallway. Mikhail was projecting worry, and Fargo sighed mentally, *What the hell is going on around here*

*today? First Luann melting down on me, and now
Mikhail is worried as hell about something.*

Mikhail cleared his throat, "Uh, Ethan, I've got
something I need to talk to you about." He waved a
printout vaguely, "Can we talk in the office?"

"Sure."

Mikhail sat down heavily, still holding the
printout. "What would you think about a security
contract to protect TBT equipment?"

Fargo cocked his head. now very alert. "What and
where?"

"Endine." Shoving the printout at Ethan, he sat
back and steepled his hands. "I've been waiting till
you got well. It's for a minimum of ninety days."

Fargo quickly scanned the printout. "This is for...a
full blown Grey Lady security contract. I don't..."

"Aren't your guys and girls working for Grey
Lady?"

"The militia? Yes, but..."

"The Earth office wants the system protected, and
GalPat doesn't have the personnel to loan out, even if
we paid for them. Grey Lady does this, and your
folks..."

"All four feeder sites? That's... probably fifty
people. Plus some support." He glanced at the printout
again, "How much?" He whistled when the numbers
sorted themselves out in his head, "Damn, that's full
combat pay!"

Mikhail held up his hands. "I doubt that combat
will be required. It's just to keep the sites safe until the
company gets a grip on their security issues. All I
know is what you see there. I had put the request up

channels after what happened to us a few months ago, because of the potential damage to our systems on Endine."

Fargo leaned back. "I can't speak for the company. All I can do is bring it before them, and I'll have to let the GalPat Det at White Beach know. But since there is a GalPat company parked here right now, it might be doable."

***

Fargo walked into the clinic, looking for OneSvel. He needed to get this out to the GalScout command, and see what they thought. "Hallo?"

OneSvel came thumping down the hallway. "Fargo? Anything wrong?"

Fargo projected, "*Is anyone else here?*"

OneSvel answered, "No, Doc Grant is down in White Beach for the quarterly medical updates. Why?"

Fargo held out the printout. "This is why…"

OneSvel took it with a pseudopod, then his GalTrans spit out tones Fargo had learned were the equivalent of laughter. "I was going to message you to come in. This solves that problem. Command is aware of this, I believe they engineered it. There are concerns over the possibility that the Traders or Dragoons have a foothold in that system, possibly on Endine. If the Dragoons are there, they are obviously covert. There are also questions about ice mining, and there is an ice moon in that system. There is an adjacent system where Command thinks there is ongoing extraction of hydrocarbons, based on things that are being seen. Their solution was to have the Grey Lady be contracted, knowing you and your militia are the only Grey Lady component within this sector of the Rim."

Fargo shook his head. "A little presumptive aren't they? Assuming me or any of the militia are willing to go haring off for probably four months? Even at full combat pay, I'm not sure how many…"

"One million credits a month. At least. Two million credits a month if you take the entire company. You will have to turn people away. These are proud people. We have researched them. This would allow them to expand their enclave, and bring more Ghorka here."

Fargo sighed, "Maybe. So this is all being orchestrated from Earth?"

OneSvel 'laughed' again, "Who knows? We do not. You have only yourself to blame. Had you not gone and been hurt, it may well have never come to Command's attention."

"Well, I guess I better to beard the lions in their den."

"Beard the lions?"

"An old Earth saying. My father said that when it was something he didn't want to do, like arguing with my mother." Fargo turned and headed for the door, "I'll head out there now. I'll let you know as soon as I get an answer."

Four divs later, Fargo landed at the Enclave. As he walked up toward the village, Kamala rushed out to meet him, "Ekavir, I am so sorry, I…"

Fargo held up a hand, "Nothing to be sorry for. I was stupid, not you. Your warning saved my life. That and getting Mikhail there as soon as you did."

"But…"

Fargo stopped, "Kamala, I'm here, alive, and fully recovered. I bear you no ill will. None. Shit happens."

She shrugged. "But I still feel bad."

Fargo started walking again, "Do you know what happened to the nearleopard pelts?"

"Jiri has them, along with the Silverback pelts. Nirvik cured them. They are beautiful!"

"Where is Jiri?"

"He, Horse, and Lal are in the weapons building. They are doing maintenance on the equipment, along with others."

Fargo angled toward the building, "Thank you."

He went through the front, didn't see anyone, and opened the door to the bay with the armor. Hearing a string of what he guessed were curses in Nepalese, he followed the sound until he stood in back of one of the armored Phantom IIs. Lal and Jiri were up on a work stand, holding a pair of legs, as a voice continued cursing from deep in the suit.

Lal saw him, said something and he and Jiri hauled a still cussing Horse out of the armor, "Dare I ask?" he said with a laugh.

Jiri smiled. "Horse is complaining the left haptic actuator for his leg is not calibrated properly. He has been *adjusting* it without success, since it passes BIT every time."

A red faced Horse dropped a tool with a clang. "F'ing thing is off, it throws me off balance when I accelerate. I don't care what BIT says."

Fargo asked, "Did you adjust it with your AI? And that didn't work?"

"Adjust it with the AI? That's not…"

They cracked up at the expression on Horse's face. "You mean…"

Lal shook his head. "Didn't bother to read the manual on the *new* armor, did you?"

Horse opened his mouth, shut it, turned red, and jumped down from the maintenance stand, mumbling under his breath as he stalked out.

Lal and Jiri hopped down, and Jiri asked, "You here for your pelts? I hope? Sushma keeps trying to get me to give one to her. She says…"

"Let me guess, it will make a warm collar."

"How did you…"

"Kamala already told me that. I have no problem giving the women *one* of them. Just make sure Kamala gets a good piece of it," he said with a smile.

Jiri laughed in relief, "Good!"

As they walked out of the weapons building, Fargo pulled the printout from his shipsuit, and said, "But I'm actually here for something fairly serious. We've… the company has been offered a contract through Grey Lady to go provide security for some TBT systems on Endine." He handed the printout to Jiri. "I figured we need to have all of the company in on the discussion."

As Jiri read it, Lal asked, "Did you bring Nicole with you?"

Fargo's stunned expression caused Lal to burst out laughing, "Forgot her, didn't you."

"Oh shit. She's going to…"

Lal looked at the field, "You brought your liteflyer? You wouldn't have had room for her and the pelts both."

"I guess I better call her, are we going to meet in the community hall?"

"Yes, I'll start gathering folks up. You go try to mollify her before we get there."

Four divs later, it came down to drawing straws to determine who would, and would not go to Endine. Nicole had been icily polite, said she was going, brooking no argument, and hung up over a div ago. Fargo sat off to the side, eating a Rasbari milk ball, and sipping the tea Sushma had brought him. *OneSvel was right. The whole damn company wants to go, along with half the women. I know this would mean a lot more credits, but dammit, there isn't any way to justify that many bodies. Crap… OneSvel can't go. We're going to need a medic. And a maintenance person… I wonder if we can borrow them from GalPat…*

Fargo got up and wandered out to the head, verbalizing a note to check on those people tomorrow with Colonel Keads. He debated trying to call Nicole, but decided that would be worse than talking to her face to face. She was pissed, to put it mildly, and he knew it was his fault. That was *not* going to be a fun conversation.

Loggie Time

Fargo and Jiri sat on one side of the table, with Colonel Keads, Major Culverhouse, and WO Boykin on the other. Multiple empty bulbs sat at each place, along with numerous notes on paper, in addition to the notes on the data comps. A holo of Endine rotated slowly in the center of the table with the sites of the feeder locations marked.

Keads leaned back. "Is that it? Have we got everything sorted?"

Fargo looked at Jiri, raising his eyebrow, "Jiri?"

Jiri rubbed his face, "I don't like going short on the armor, but this isn't a combat situation. I think four at each site will work. And loaning us a maintainer is a great help. That's the one thing we don't have in the company."

Fargo nodded. "And the Hab modules, and maintenance module. They're used, but they will work."

Culverhouse shrugged. "Well, they're just sitting there since the company at Rushing River got the barracks up and the admin building operational. You'll be back before they need them again."

Boykin leaned forward, "Colonel, I need to go, too."

The all looked at her in surprise, and Fargo felt determination radiating from her. Keads asked, "Why?"

Boykin held up a hand, fingers extended, "One. No shuttle pilot. Endine has a three decimal human requirement. Evie cannot meet that." She dropped one finger. "Two. I'm tired of ass and trash. I talked to Lieutenant Edwards out at Rushing River. He thinks my job is the greatest thing since molycircs. Four months of flying Stuttering Sally might cure him of that notion." Another finger dropped. "Three. We don't have good Intel on Endine. Remember the questions about the last Det that was fired? Boots on the ground. I can collect data in case we need to respond there again."

Keads pinched his nose, "Stuttering Sally? Ass and trash? Really?"

A small smile crossed Boykin's face, "She's a tad touchy. She's old. She has to be babied. I want to fly a new one! And you know damn well what I'm talking about with ass and trash, present company excluded."

Keads let that one pass, "Where are you going to get... Ah, one from Rushing River?"

Nodding toward the major, she replied, "Since Meacham is going to be here, they'll have a spare. I've already talked to the major, and she's willing to let me take Wizard. It has a collection suite incorporated. Did you forget that I was an Intel weenie in my previous life?"

Culverhouse nodded. "Current data is always an improvement over suspect data, Colonel."

Keads sighed, "Guilty. And the more I think about it, it makes sense. Plus you would provide a senior GalPat rep to ride herd on the maintainer. He might not listen to a mere militia captain."

Fargo laughed. "It's not *me* he needs to worry about, it's a butt load of WOs and CSMs that will rip him a new one that he *really* needs to worry about. WO Boykin, I believe I can speak for everyone when I say we would be delighted to have your accompany us."

A smile flashed across Boykin's face, and she nodded toward him, "Thank you, Captain."

Keads slapped the table, "We're done. I'm sure… And I just thought of one other item. Major, your folks can backfill for Fargo's troops if anything comes up, right?"

"Yes, sir. I've already been talking to Lalband… um."

Fargo laughed. "Just call him Lal. He's fine with that."

"Oh, okay. And yes, we'll back them up, and they will back us up. Plus the Herms want some more OPFOR," she said with a rueful grin.

Fargo just rolled his eyes.

***

Mikhail brought the shuttle in for a landing well away from the *Hyderabad*, once again parked over the river, with both front and rear hatches open. Fargo and Nicole were in their grays, *kukris* prominently displayed, as they unstrapped their trunks and toggled the leashes on. Mikhail hugged Fargo, "Ivan will be your local contact, I've already messaged him that you're on the way. Stay safe. If you don't, Luann will never forgive me." Turning to Nicole, he continued, "Thank you for coming to dinner last night. I think she's much more comfortable with you looking out for him. And if Holly has any problems, she can call me."

Fargo replied, "We'll do our best. Should see you in about six months. Ivan March, right?"

Mikhail squirted the data to his data comp, "Yes. Here are all the contacts. Things are *stable* right now, for versions of stable. Everyone has the sonic fences operable. You may need to expand those perimeters."

"No issue. We'll work that as necessary."

Fargo and Nicole walked down the ramp, each lost in their own thoughts. As they crossed the field, Nicole said, "I don't see the shuttle."

"Boykin is going to pick up the maintainer and his maintenance van when she takes the old shuttle to Rushing River. She's going to meet us on orbit."

"Oh, okay." She squinted then started laughing, "Oh my deity…"

"What?"

"Liz is here."

"Liz?"

"Liz Hand. Chief Hand." Waving she yelled, "Liz. Liz!"

A small gray haired lady turned, grinned and started trotting toward them, "Cole! By all that's Holy! Girl, I haven't seen you in ages!" Hugging Nicole, they both laughed, and she looked at him, "Fargo, right?"

"Yes, ma'am. Are you coming with us?"

"Yep, Wallace and I both. You're gonna be in Indian Country, so I'm going to ride along and run the Mod Thirty and comms for y'all."

"Sweet! Let me dump the trunk and we can talk."

As they cleared the end of the forward ramp, Fargo heard Master Chief Hand laying into somebody, "You don't dump shit at the hatch. You carry it all the way back to the storage area marked for that material. And stack in properly. If you don't, you'll be restacking the entire hold!"

Fargo chuckled. "Afternoon, COS."

Wallace turned, coming almost to attention, "Afternoon Cap'n. Are you the HMFIC of this cluster?"

"Fraid so. I take it you hired on again? And although I hate to ask, what's wrong?"

"Yep, me and Liz. Cap'n Jace figured he needed somebody to ride herd on this bunch. We're behind. All this shit should be loaded and we should be starting to load armor."

Fargo said, "Let me dump my trunk and I'll see what…"

Wallace replied, "Don't worry, Cap'n, I'll handle it."

Fargo sensed the Chief of Ship's iron determination as he headed up the ladder to his stateroom, *Whew, the COS is on a roll. Why do I think this is going to be a classic irresistible force versus immovable object paradox… We're supposed to lift off in five divs. I'm betting we'll make it with room to spare…*

***

Four divs later, the IC pinged, "All pax please finish storing your gear and report to your respective lounges or messes in fifteen segs for safety briefing.

Captain Jace strode into the crew's mess ten segs later, a smile on his face. "We're loaded. Only had to kick one stray off. Hatches are closed, and we're shifting power now. Since all of you have had the safety brief, this will be quick and dirty." Five segs later, he was done, and turned to Fargo, "I've had Wallace and Liz put on this deck. There is one stateroom with a bed big enough for a Taurasian, so I've given it to them. They will be down the passageway from you. We'll lift at nineteen, and rendezvous with Boykin and the shuttle at twenty three, then pick up the Habs and an ice block and should be on our way by zero six tomorrow. Ship time is the same as local here, which is within one div of local on Endine."

Nicole asked shyly, "Captain, could I watch the takeoff? I've never actually seen one from the bridge."

Jace smiled broadly, "Of course! I know you'll be much better company than Captain Fargo!"

She stuck her tongue out at him, as everyone laughed. Fargo shook his head, and walked out without a word, but he was smiling.

Fargo, Nicole, and Jiri were in the crew's lounge going over deployment plans, watch schedules, and personnel allocations when the IC pinged, "Shuttle inbound. Set maneuvering watch. Stand by to receive shuttle Bay Three, port forward." They stopped as the wall screen came alive, showing an external shot with the blinking lights of the shuttle in the center, and a split screen showing the Bay Three doors sliding open. They saw Wallace shuffling slowly toward the middle of the bay, with what looked like a pair of sticks under his arm. Jiri asked, "What is he doing?"

Fargo shrugged. "Guess he's going to bring her in manually. We used to do that in the Corps. It was an emergency procedure, but we practiced it quite a bit."

Nicole shook her head. "He's f'ing crazy! There is *no* way I'd want to be in a zero G, open to vacuum bay, with something that big coming at me."

Liz walked in laughing, "I heard that 'Cole. And yes, he's crazy, but he's *my* kind of crazy. He actually has had to do that a time or three. Got an MSM out of one of them."

"Still crazy…" Nicole muttered.

They heard a pop over the speaker and Boykin saying, "Dropping van in three, two, one."

It gently floated away from the shuttle as Wallace said, "Nose or tail first?"

Boykin answered, "Nose, then spin."

They saw Wallace look up and confirm the lights were flashing red and yellow, "Confirm zero G, no atmo."

"Roger zero/no. Have the ball, closure thirty fps." They watched as the shuttle closed the side of the *Hyderabad*.

Wallace held up one stick, now lit green. "Bring it."

Jiri watched in amazement, "She's going to run into the back of the bay!"

Wallace said, "Drop ten."

"Twenty fps."

"Keep it coming. Two hundred, centered."

"Roger."

"One hundred, centered, drop ten."

"Ten fps."

Wallace started waving the wands, moving slowly backward as the shuttle nosed into the hangar. Moments later, he crossed them over his head, "Spin it."

"Going left."

"Stop. Down. Three, two, one. And you're down. Standby for locks."

"Standing by."

Wallace was shuffling back to the interior bulkhead, and they saw him pull a switch down, then look back at the shuttle, "You are locked."

"Roger locked, starting shutdown." The bay doors started closing and the van started drifting toward the ship.

Jiri looked up, "What the hell?"

Liz replied, "Moving over the van, going to tractor it into position. Then we'll go get the others."

Jiri shook his head. "Give me the ground any day."

A half div later, WO Boykin, Senior Sergeant Ian McDougal, and Senior Sergeant Kelly Grayson walked into the crew's mess.

Fargo smiled, remembering McDougal from the formation earlier. He was surprised to see the medic, Grayson and asked, "Why are you here, Grayson?"

"Colonel Keads told me to get on the shuttle. Said for me to collect what medical data and enviro I can. That, and he wanted to get me away from Palette and Cameron for a while."

Boykin grinned, then coughed to cover it. "The Captain has already given them the safety brief, and assigned them billeting. I wasn't sure where you wanted to site them."

Jiri and Fargo looked at each other, and Jiri wearily pulled his data comp out, as Fargo said, "McDougal will be at Feeder Three. That's where the maintenance van will be." Looking at him, he continued, "You're assigned a billet in the Hab van at that location. How much equipment did you bring?"

McDougal shrugged. "Standard detachment kit. Comms, sonics, spare Ferrets, some armor spares, a small fabber, and a standard load of feed material for it. Standard tool kit, and a few spares for the oddball things that tend to show up."

Fargo nodded and turned to Grayson. "You bring any medical supplies?"

Grayson nodded. "Two pallets. Standard detachment load out. But I hear they have real hospitals there, so I'm looking at load and go if we have issues. I'll distribute the medical kits to the sites, as soon as I find out what, where, and how many personnel will be at each site. I've got *my* kit, but nobody touches that but me."

Jiri said, "Well, Senior Grayson, I think the best place for you is going to be in the Palace. All the Habs are full, and you weren't a planned inclusion. Since the warrant is also going to be based there, if there is an issue, she can get you there and any injured back quickly."

Grayson's face lit up, "The Palace? Like a real Palace?"

Fargo laughed. "Not really. It's a compound where the director and the GalPat Det are headquartered."

Grayson's face fell, as he mumbled, "Oh frikkin great. More brass. Dammit…"

McDougal yawned, and Fargo said, "Why don't you go ahead and hit your billet. Ship time is the same as Hunter local, and it's midnight."

The two senior sergeants left, and Fargo turned to Boykin, "I saw that smile. What did Grayson do?"

Boykin laughed. "Oh nothing much. Just gave Palette two injections, one in each butt cheek that had him so sore he couldn't sit down for two days. And it was apparently a placebo! Palette is notorious for thinking he's catching something."

Fargo and Jiri both laughed at that, and Jiri said, "Noted, never piss off the medic. But he's pretty damn good too! I saw what he did on the raid."

"Hit the rack Boykin. We're done. You're up here with us, and this is our mess."

Boykin nodded and said, "I *am* a bit tired."

Jiri headed for his stateroom, and Fargo sat watching the arrangement and tractoring of the remaining Hab modules, more than a few times laughing at the invective COS Hand used with the tug drivers, as he maneuvered in a hard suit. *Got your pilots license out of a tub of Martian Sea Crackers… Oh that was a good one! Those are some nasty damn crackers. They are worse than e-rats.*

Once they picked up the ice block, he saw the stars pitch, and headed for his stateroom. He made a quick pass through the fresher, got in the rack, and pulled the acceleration netting over himself.

Intelligence

Fargo and Jiri were announced and led into the director's utilitarian office. Director Vaughn said, "Welcome gentlemen. Captain, I am most pleased to see you looking much better than the last time I saw you."

Fargo extended his empath sense as he nodded. "Thank you ma'am. Apparently I owe much of that to you. This is Warrant Officer Mankajiri Rai, my XO."

Jiri smiled. "Just call me Jiri, please."

The director nodded then said, "I…we couldn't do much for you other than expedite your departure. Sit, please. You know Colonel Zhu?"

"Yes, ma'am." Fargo and Jiri sat at the end of the conference table, taking out their respective data comps. "Ma'am, we brought enough people to set up security on the TBT feeders that supply power here on Endine, but I really need to know what we may be facing."

He caught a glance between the director and colonel, then she slowly replied, "Well, there have been a couple of instances of some of the rabble trying to shut down the power grid…"

Colonel Zhu interrupted smoothly, "Captain, *we* felt it would be better to bring in your militia rather than more GalPat troops, since there are so few in this star system. The Grey Lady security contract is fairly specific on what you're allowed to do."

"I know that. I've reviewed it in depth with my troops, but I need boots on the ground Intel as to what *threats* we are really facing."

Director Vaughn asked, "When are you going to begin protecting the feeders?"

Fargo pulled up the schedule on his data comp and pinged it to both her and Colonel Zhu, "We are getting our ROE confirmation and we will depart this afternoon for the ship. We'll conduct a final briefing tomorrow morning at zero seven, and will start dropping the first Habs and personnel by zero nine. We should be complete by eighteen, and on line at each site no later than twenty-two."

The director looked quickly through the schedule and nodded. "I see you're saving feeder three until last?"

"Yes we are. That site is the largest and that is where we will place the maintenance module, which requires a separate trip, since the shuttle can only carry two modules at a time."

"Why there and not here?"

"It's a large enough area to place the additional module, and also large enough to land the shuttle. At the other locations, the shuttle can only tractor items up or down."

The director turned to the colonel, "Will this be a problem? This won't restrict any traffic?"

Colonel Zhu shook his head. "No, ma'am. It's on the outskirts of Kwamaine, and the area does not include any roads, tracks or paths. We don't have room here for an additional module and an additional shuttle, unless we move a shuttle outside the containment. And we'd prefer not to do that."

She turned back to Fargo, "Where will *you* be operating from?"

"Colonel Zhu has been kind enough to give us office space in the GalPat area. I and Jiri will work from there, along with the medic, and our shuttle pilot will also be in that office when she is not doing lifts. She will also assist the GalPat detachment as necessary."

"Very good. Now, what can I help you with?"

"Intel, ma'am. All we really know is from the TBT techs, that someone is attempting to sabotage the feeders."

Director Vaughn glanced at them in turn before saying, "That's hard. The patrollers have not been successful in tracking down who is actually making the attacks. And GalPat is so limited with their other responsibilities…"

The colonel interrupted, "We've provided forensic support to the director, but have not been able to determine anything unusual about the attacks. None of the feeders have video circuits tied to them, so no video of any attacks. Or at least none since the sonic fences and videos have gone in."

"If there haven't been any more attacks, why are we here?"

Director Vaughn replied, "We are hearing rumors about more attempts to strike a blow for freedom as they are saying. The patrollers are picking up some low level chatter in the lower quarter housing, but nothing that can be tied to any one group. The corporation would prefer not to have wide scale destruction take place, if at all possible."

"Why not have GalPat step in, if you're taking it that seriously?"

"The corporation would prefer it be handled at the lowest level of force possible. That is why Grey Lady was contacted, and why you are here. We believe your force will be the deterrent that will stop this mess."

A functionary stepped in, "Ma'am, Landholder Perez is here."

The director said, "I'm sorry, I must meet with him. Colonel Zhu can give you any additional details you may desire. I look forward to working with your company."

Fargo and Jiri rose, as did the colonel, "Thank you for your time, ma'am. We will do our best." They followed the colonel out of the office, past the functionary and a scowling potbellied Latino man, who glared at them as they walked by.

Colonel Zhu turned toward his office as Fargo and Jiri continued toward the canteen, "Coffee?" Fargo asked and Jiri nodded. After getting their bulbs of coffee, they sat at one of the small tables off to the side of the canteen, "Well, what did you think?

Jiri glanced around, "Lot of hiding going on. This is some of the worst BS I've ever seen. The colonel is in the dark, but I don't understand why. And that director… she's probably been told what to say by the corporation, which is effectively don't say anything."

Fargo grimaced. "I think you're right. Let's finish the coffee and go see if the good colonel is any more forthcoming without her in the room. We'll talk more once we get back aboard."

***

Colonel Zhu glanced up as Fargo knocked on his door, "Yes?"

"Colonel, I think there is more happening than the director is telling me. Do you have anything from Intel that might give us a clue?"

Zhu leaned back, steepling his hands, then rubbing his moustache. "Come in. Sit." Fargo and Jiri took the straight backed chairs facing Zhu's desk as he continued, "What little we've picked up seems to be some low level, possibly long term, ongoing conflict between what they call Firsties, those that were in the first wave colonization, and the latecomers from the second and third wave."

Fargo tapped his data comp, then looked up. "So ninety years, there can't be many of those left alive." Glancing down, he continued, "Sixty and thirty years for second and third. So most of them are alive."

Zhu nodded. "Second gen on the first wave. The young ones think their shit doesn't stink. Mainly large landholders. They raise the majority of the edibles on planet. Lot of them use autoag machinery or tenants."

"Tenants?"

"Second and third wavers that work for them."

Fargo tapped on his desk comp for a minute. "So, second wave was primarily service types, third was tech?"

Zhu shrugged. "Best guess. I've only been here a little over six months. Walked into this one cold. The previous GalPat group didn't leave us a lot of notes or

Intel, nor was there a lot in either the GalPat or corporate databases. A lot of these planets on the Rim are strange. We came over from Titan Three, when they elected an autonomous planetary council and petitioned for GalPat to be removed."

"You never got a handover?"

"No. There was a half company here as caretakers for the facility, but nobody above the rank of lieutenant. He had the keys, but not much else. They were hunkered down here, no patrols, and no shuttles, not much of anything."

"You didn't find that strange?"

"Oh, exceedingly. When I FTL'ed the General, I was told to liaise with the Director, and build our own database. Something about the previous one being *corrupted*."

"Where did the previous detachment go?"

Zhu threw up his hands, "Not a clue. The only thing in the log was that they were being recalled."

"Some, but not all. That is odd."

"Those left were the last replacements, we rolled them in to our detachment, since we lost about that many to orders, pensioning out, and we also had two deaths."

Fargo got up, "Thanks Colonel, so not a lot to go on, or something buried real deep that the Director and others don't want us to know."

Zhu grimaced. "Probably. You have the ROE briefing, correct?"

Fargo nodded. "Given already. Weapons tight unless we are attacked, minimal response if we are, no escalations."

"Did you bring any armor?"

"Four suits for each feeder site. Locked down to self-protect mode only."

"Oh deity… Keep those out of sight. I did one training evolution two weeks after we got here, and the director threw a shit fit. She doesn't want them seen in public at all. We now do our training in remote locations in the outback."

"Ours are stored. Two in the Hab modules, and two in the surveillance modules."

"Good, keep it that way. Don't bring them out, ever!"

Fargo glanced at Jiri, "Well, if there isn't anything else, Colonel?"

"I don't have anything else."

"Then we'll depart and head back up to the ship. We'll start drops tomorrow at zero nine, in the order I pinged to you."

"Very well."

***

Back onboard the *Hyderabad*, Fargo sat in the crew's mess with Captain Jace, Nicole, Jiri, and Boykin running through what they had, and more importantly, hadn't learned from the director and colonel. "I'm convinced the director is hiding something, I sensed she was nervous, not about us, but something else she was hiding. The colonel is worried, but I sensed that was more of a military capability worry than hiding something. I think he was curious as to what she was going to say, too." Finally, he turned to Nicole, "Were you able to pull anything else out of the systems?"

She shrugged. "Not much. I did find that the previous detachment was recalled and broken up. Most of them were sent back to line units, and the colonel was *allowed* to retire."

"Lovely. Just… lovely."

Nicole cocked her head, "I do have an idea." The others all stared at her, and she continued. "I could go in under cover," looking at Captain Jace, "you could send me over to the space station in the shuttle, right?"

Jace nodded. "Yes, but why?"

"I could go down to Endine and get a job in a restaurant. That would allow me…"

Jiri interrupted, "A restaurant? What good…"

"If you'll let me finish, yes, a restaurant. Preferably an upscale one, of which there seem to be three. People ignore servers, hostesses, and any staff. I'm a trained hostess and certified sommelier. That would almost guarantee that one of the three would hire me. And there is a *lot* of cross talk among restaurant employees."

Fargo asked, "But what would you… sommelier, isn't that something to do with wines?"

Nicole held up her hand, "Be right back." She jumped up and left the crew's mess.

Fargo looked at Jiri and the captain, "What can this buy us?"

Jace answered, "More than you know. If she can deploy some mini-mics, we would be able to monitor conversations, and who knows what we might hear."

Nicole came back and lay a small silver and red pin on the table, "Scan it," she said peremptorily.

Curious, Fargo waved his data comp over the pin, and it dinged as it uploaded the embedded data. LEVESQUE, NICOLE- CERT MASTER SOMMELIER- 27700312 PARIS, EU EU/NA/AS/GAL ALL SPIRITS. MBR- CURRENT. Fargo cocked his head. "All spirits?"

"Wine, beer, hard liquor, any liquid intoxicants. Any continent, any planet, anywhere in the galaxy. It took me *seven* damn years to get that qualification."

Jiri asked, "But how could you justify coming here?"

Fargo cut a glance to Jace, "What if you were, say a Star Lines shipboard or maybe star cluster sommelier? Maybe you could be…"

"On vacation or a sabbatical. Taking a couple of months or more off. Travelling looking for more, different, local wines."

Jiri cautioned, "But you would be, ah, on your own."

Captain Jace interrupted, "We could put a set of LOs out, give you a discreet for your wrist comp or something else, that only hits them, and have that as an emergency call."

Fargo added, "Yeah, we're going to need those low observable sats up. I don't think they have much for coverage out here, much like Hunter. Corporations tend not to spend that kind of money if they don't have to."

Jiri nodded. "Makes sense." Glancing at his data comp, he said, "I need to get ready for the brief. Meet you in the passenger lounge in a half div?"

"Sure. We won't say anything about Nicole going undercover."

"Agreed!"

Jiri slipped out of the mess, and Nicole picked up the pin, "I'm going to hit the fresher while I can."

After she left, Fargo looked at Jace, "Can you help protect her?"

Jace's smile was definitely feral, "More than you know. There was a Star Liner in this cluster two weeks ago. I can print her a data chip that says she's been employed by them for, say, forty years, based out of…" Fargo knew Jace was accessing his network and waited, "Orion cluster. I just inserted her into their system, if anybody wants to actually do a background check."

Fargo shook his head. "Really?"

"I have access to any system in the galaxy. Something like this is easy."

Nicole came back into the mess, "Dammit, I'm going to need clothes."

"Clothes?"

She glared at Fargo, "Yes, *clothes* I can't go down to Endine in my grays. I didn't bring any dresses, or…"

Jace interrupted, "We can fix that. You tell me what you need and we can fab it."

She smiled nicely at the captain, "Thank you! Now I will go finish my briefing, what little there is."

Fargo shook his head again, "Women…"

Three divs later, the briefings were complete, people were doing final checks on their equipment, repacking their trunks, and the site leads were meeting with Boykin to coordinate their drops.

Fargo had just finished his repacking, shoved his trunk into the space between the two bunks, and laid down, when there was a soft knock on the hatch. Curious, he got up and dilated the hatch, and was startled to find Nicole in his arms. "What are you—"

Nicole kissed him passionately, and he groaned as she said, "Now. I want you now."

Fargo started to shake his head, then realized he'd already felt her mind, and he wanted her as much as she wanted him. He closed the hatch, locked it, and carried her back to the bunk. A div later, Nicole lay across his chest, both of them sweating from their exertions, and she said, "I know I said we'd wait, but I may not see you until the detachment ends. I love you, Fargo. Damn your hide!"

He chuckled. "Is that damning with faint praise? Or a statement of anger, or…Ouch!"

Nicole had grabbed him and twisted. "You want to rephrase that?"

He enfolded her in this arms, whispering, "I love you too. And I don't like this any better than you do. If anything, and I mean *anything* starts looking skosh, send up a call and we'll extract you in armor. ROE be damned."

"I will. And now I need to go hit the fresher and get some sleep. The captain is ferrying me over at ten divs in the morning." Kissing him softly, she quickly slipped back into her greys and stood at the hatch, "Um, you've got to unlock it."

She went quickly back to her stateroom, and Fargo was thankful no one saw her coming out of his stateroom.

On the bridge, Jace smiled as he scanned the video, and added a notation to his database that paired Fargo and Nicole. He also upped her security classification within his system, and prioritized data collection to support her. He added an extra sensor on orbit, Geostationary over Center, with tracking of her data chip.

Insertion

At 0600, the first two modules and Barun's troops dropped at Feeder One, three divs early, just in case somebody leaked the times. No one noticed, other than a wolf like creature that whined and took off into the brush. It hadn't liked the noises, and there wasn't anything to eat up there anyway. Boykin goosed the shuttle back into orbit, loaded the next team on board, eased out of the shuttle bay, and tractored the next two modules. Horse leaned into the cockpit, "Any problems on the first drop?"

"Nope. Clean as a whistle. But number one is out in the sticks. The next three are nearer population centers, so I'm sure there will at least be notice, if not reaction. I'm weaps white, but I can go red in a half a heartbeat if needed."

"Modules first?"

Boykin nodded as she spooled the shuttle up, dipping toward Endine, "Drop them first, then y'all, just outside the containment. You've got the code to shut it down, right?"

"Yes, if there is no action, I will deactivate the containment as soon as the modules are placed."

Boykin nodded. "Good. Now go away and let me drive."

Horse smiled. "Of course. Good driving is appreciated."

Boykin brought the shuttle to a hover over Feeder Two, tractored the Hab and surveillance modules into the spaces designated, as Horse leaned out the back hatch, shutting the sonics down. A few people watched curiously, but not a soul moved toward the shuttle as it touched down lightly outside the containment. Horse and his team were off in ten segs, and inside the containment in another five. "Okay, WO, we're snug. Thanks for the lift."

Boykin smiled in her helmet, "You're welcome, WO. Stay snug."

***

Nicole stepped up to the check station, handed her ID across, and the rotund mousy woman behind the desk asked in a bored tone, "What is the nature of your visit?"

"Sabbatical. I'm touring the Rimworlds, looking at different vineyards."

"Vineyards?"

"Wineries, people that make wine or sell grapes."

"Oh, arm please." Nicole stuck out her arm, and the woman pressed the device against her.

She felt a momentary stab, "What's that?"

"Verifying you're human. We don't allow others here." She glanced at the readout, "Luggage?"

Nicole placed the trunk on the table and cycled the locks open. "Anything to declare? Plants, animals, weapons?"

She reached in the trunk, pulled out the small bead pistol and cycled the case open, "Only a Ladies Aide."

"Frangible ammunition?"

"Right here," Nicole said, handing over the small package of beads. The woman opened the package, extracted one bead and passed it over something behind the desk. Then put it in an envelope.

Nicole asked, "What are you doing with that?"

"Evidence if you shoot somebody and run." She riffled through the trunk, grunted, looked curiously at the data pod, and nodded to Nicole, "You can go now. Enjoy your stay."

Nicole repacked everything, then headed for the shuttle line down to Capital, mumbling, "Yeah, right. Enjoy myself. Fat chance."

Getting in the queue, she slid her chip across and received a data chip for the shuttle, no choice of seat assignment. And it wasn't for the shuttle leaving in a half div. It was for the next shuttle in 3 divs. She went over and parked her trunk, sat down next to it, and reconfirmed her reservation at the Women's Lodge in Center, updating her arrival time from the land time of the shuttle.

***

Boykin shut down in the bay long enough to grab a bite to eat, as the fourth team loaded up. Fargo checked with her for any issues. Boykin indicated she didn't have any, so he went back to herding the cats that were left. Shanni and his team were loaded by the time she got back from the fresher, and they did a quick consult on the aft ramp, making sure they both understood the sequence. Boykin slipped back into the cockpit, picked up the two modules, and drove toward Endine and Feeder Four a little faster than she had the others. Feeder Four was outside Coventry and there were a few people with protest banners but they were well away from the feeder and where the shuttle would be setting down. Boykin warned Shanni and made sure when she landed, it was as close to the containment/sonic as she could stick the tail and not have it impact the troops coming off. Shanni and his team were already doing comms checks before she hit orbit for the last modules, and she laughed to herself, *Funny how having people watching tends to speed up the whole security process. At least the modules are secure against anything below a seventy-six.*

***

Four divs later, tired, hungry, and grumpy, Nicole collected her trunk at the baggage claim. Keying her code to it, she walked out of the terminal, the trunk obediently following behind. She looked around, and saw nothing resembling a ground transport. A person walked around the corner of the terminal, and she politely asked, "Ground transport?"

"You gotta reserve it. Only got three working now. All have done gone to Center. Gonna be a while, if they come back at all." The person turned around and scuttled back around the corner of the building.

Nicole walked back inside, and finally found an e-board with notices posted. She paged through and found one labeled Taxi. Only one number was listed, and no address went with it. With a sigh, she activated her wrist comp and told it to call the number.

Another half div later, she finally got to the Women's Lodge. After signing in, and confirming that she would obey the rules of the Lodge, she was finally squirted a code for the room. When she asked about food, she was told by the AI at the check-in counter that the autochef was being serviced and would not be available until morning between six and eight divs. The AI did offer that the room water was potable.

***

Boykin and Fargo stood on the shuttle deck, watching the last team for Feeder Three load, "You doing okay, WO?"

"I'm hanging, Captain. I don't do a lot, just fly the bus and monitor the instruments."

Fargo reached out cautiously with his psi sense, and realized she was telling what she thought to be the absolute truth, but her shoulder and hip were hurting, and were being ignored.

Daman walked forward, "We're loaded. Got the maintainer, and the medic is passing out med packs."

Boykin cocked an eyebrow at Fargo, who held up a hand, "Anybody seen Jiri?"

Jiri came jogging through the hatch, "Just got a download from the Captain, latest updates from the LEOs he's deployed. Looks like there are people massing at Feeder Three."

Fargo hunched his shoulders, "Shit. I was hoping we'd get everybody down before we got a reaction." Turning to Daman, "Put somebody in armor. Make that two somebodies. Full stealth. I want them off first."

Daman nodded. "Nil, Karun, mount up! Take two Phantoms from the storage. Weapons tight. Full stealth, now!"

Fargo said, "You know those suits don't have any weapons loaded, right?"

"Yes, but if we have to, they can get to the Hab and get one out that does."

Fargo nodded, as Boykin said, "So much for being on the TOT. I can make up some time, but probably not all the segs that we're going to be behind."

"We'll deal with it. I'd rather get folks down in one piece, than be on exact time on top."

Boykin grinned, "Your circus, your monkey. I just drive the bus. I'm going to go squirt the data I've collected to the Captain. I'll be back in ten."

Fargo rode in the copilot's seat, noting the torches, *Torches? Really? Are they that backward? Or is this a show of force to try to scare us off?* He turned to Boykin, "A little hotter reception this time."

Boykin nodded as she dropped the first two modules, keeping her nose pointed at the crowd just outside the range of the sonic containment. "Yep, apparently the word got out. Or got passed. Each drop has had more action."

"Let's hope this is as far as they go."

Boykin nodded as she backed the shuttle down and tractored the maintenance module down. Sidestepping the shuttle, she eased forward with the nose almost against the sonics, "Just in case."

Fargo nodded as she keyed the IC, "All ashore that's going ashore. Aft ramp going down now. Rear approaches clear."

Nil and Karun stepped off the ramp as it touched the ground, placing themselves side by side in front of the Hab module's door. Daman yelled, "Alright, everybody off! Single file. First man blocks the door open."

Hari went down the ramp at a run, trunk bobbing in his wake, his rifle up at high ready, as he sprinted to the Hab. Quickly popping the door, he dropped his trunk, and bladed up, rifle at his shoulder. The rest of the team moved quickly, with McDougal bringing up the rear.

Boykin smiled. "Listen to this."

She hit a button and voices came through the cockpit, "Something is out there. I can't tell…"

A female voice said fearfully, "They wouldn't have armor, would they?"

Another voice answered, "Nah, not after the stink we raised before. These are some cheap security types they hired from some backwater planet. I doubt they could even run a suit."

The first voice said quizzically, "Maybe a heat mirage, that door's right behind the engine on that side."

The female said, "Well, that one at the door with the rifle isn't a mirage. I wonder if it's loaded."

The second male snickered, "Probably not. Their rules are so strict I don't think they could shoot if we were over running them. We made sure of that."

Fargo turned, "Can you get video?"

"Got it, good video of the first male and female. Second male is behind them. No good video of him yet."

"Keep trying."

Boykin just looked at him.

"Sorry. Sorry… Not trying…"

Daman came over the radio, "We're in and clear. What do you want us to do with the spare armor?"

"Keep it. And load it. If you have room, put it in the maintenance module. If you have to, park it between the modules in full stealth."

"Roger, thanks for the ride, WO. We should be up in a couple of divs, Captain."

Boykin looked at Fargo and he nodded. She replied, "No worries. We'll be around if you need us." Lifting off, she overflew the protest, maybe a little lower than she should have, and she cussed, "That son of a bitch turned away. No video of him, but we've got good voice ID. And I've got pics of most of them now."

"Good. Let's get to the Palace and call it a night. I know you have to be tired. Jiri and I will pick up the comms checks and check-ins."

Boykin nodded and swooped toward Center. A div later, she gently grounded in the spot she'd been allocated, "Do we let GalPat know we have an enhanced shuttle?"

"You mean the data collection issue?"

"Yes."

"Up to you."

"I'd rather not. I'm still not sure what's going on here, and some Intel doesn't need to be shared."

Fargo glanced at her, "Your call."

Boykin stretched, "Then no."

A half div later, Fargo and Jiri finished setting up the comms consoles, and were starting their checks, as Grayson stuck his head in, "Need me for anything, Captain?"

Fargo shook his head. "No. Quarters okay?"

Grayson smiled. "Oh yeah. I got officer billeting!" With that, he disappeared down the hall, whistling.

Fargo went back to running the checklists, confirming the surveillance modules were feeding into the molycirc storage they'd set up, getting comms checks with each site, and confirming the watch schedules were on track. Shanni called in with an issue, they had two storage lockers filled with winter gear. Fargo and Jiri looked at each other and sighed, neither said a word, but they smiled at each other. Finally at 0200, he turned to Jiri. "I think that's it. We're up and online. The one thing we didn't think about was manning this site."

Jiri shook his head. "Damn, you're right. That… was stupid on our part. And nobody caught it."

"Screw it, I'm going to set it up to ping our comps. That's about the only thing I think we can do. Maybe talk to Boykin and Grayson and see if they'd mind helping us out." Getting up, he stretched and groaned, "I'm too old for this shit. Let's call it done until zero eight."

Jiri nodded. "Sounds good. I'll get a cot to put in here tomorrow, if I can find one."

Fargo followed Jiri down to their rooms at the end of the hall, their trunks bobbing along behind.

Fargo shoved his trunk in the corner, made a quick lap through the fresher, and collapsed on top of the covers. He was asleep before he could even roll over.

Settling In

Fargo dialed up a bulb of coffee, and a high protein breakfast from the autochef as he tried to stretch his aching muscles, *Damn, I'd forgotten how bad Fleet beds could be. I swear I've slept on softer rocks.* Jiri came in smiling as usual and Fargo grumped, "Guess you slept well?"

Jiri laughed. "Of course, my captain. Nobody was shooting at me!"

The autochef spit out Fargo's breakfast and bulb, and he carried them to a table off to the side, as Jiri selected his breakfast. Slumping down, Fargo winced as his back complained about the hard chair. He sighed, and juggled the bulb, waiting for it to cool. Reaching out cautiously, he sensed Colonel Zhu coming down the hall, and cocked his head toward the hall as Jiri started to say something.

The colonel came into the mess, saw them, and crossed to their table, "Morning gentlemen. What is your status?"

"All four sites are up and on line, Colonel. Insertion was done without any problems. There was a fairly large crowd at Feeder Three, but they took no action. We have initiated video surveillance and I'll be getting those downloads every twelve divs. To who do you want us to pass them?"

The colonel thought for a second, "Let me think on that. I'm not sure we necessarily need to let the administration know we're doing that. It was also brought to my attention that your shuttle pilot didn't use standard approaches when the modules were emplaced."

Jiri interrupted, "Colonel, we weren't told we had to use any particular approaches, and she used the most secure approaches to the sites. Not overflying populations, and minimizing any potential interactions with any flights."

Zhu nodded curtly, "Makes sense. If there are any reactions or protests, notify me immediately, any time."

They chorused, "Yes, sir." And Zhu headed for the door.

Jiri mumbled, "Damn martinet …"

Fargo coughed to cover a smile, "Garrison folks are a little different."

Jiri smiled wryly, "Give me the field and a real enemy anytime. Them I can deal with. Backstabbing and politics, not so much. It's not in our genetic makeup to deal gently with those."

Fargo coughed for real as he snorted coffee out his nose, "Damn Jiri… You said that with a straight face… Don't do that to me."

Jiri's smile broadened, "We are what we are. Granted our reputation precedes us, but that is who we are. Deity knows, we deserve it."

WO Boykin and Senior Grayson walked in together, and Fargo marveled at the size difference.

Grayson almost made two of Boykin, and their personalities couldn't be much more different. But, in the situation they were in, he was happy to have them both, and he knew they were both professionals. That was all that mattered.

Fargo waved them over, and they sat as soon as they'd gotten their breakfast. He turned to Boykin, "Well, you got caught out on the surveys. How did they colonel put it? It was brought to his attention that you didn't use standard approaches when the modules were emplaced."

Boykin shrugged. "So?"

"Jiri covered you nicely. Today is probably a good day to go make nice with the pilots here, and see what else you can find out." Turning to Grayson, he said, "You getting settled in?"

Grayson nodded around a mouthful of food, holding up a finger. "Yes, sir. I'll check out the facilities today. Got the spare stuff stashed in the shuttle for a quick react." Plucking at his sleeve, he said, "These grays are pretty nice. You sure I won't get in trouble?"

Jiri replied, "In accordance with GalPat Rule thirty-one, three-eighteen, blah, blah, you're authorized indigenous uniform when temporarily additional duty to indigenous forces. Which we qualify as. Voila, grays. And yes, they are probably better than your issue ones."

Fargo got up, "Time for morning reports. I'll go collect those. Jiri will you follow-up with the colonel? WO, Senior, y'all are on your own."

They all nodded, and Jiri got up, "Since the colonel is already here, I might as well go beard him now. You know where our office is, right?"

The warrant and senior both nodded. As Jiri walked away, Grayson asked, "So if I'm in grays, why aren't you, WO?"

Boykin laughed. "Well, if militias had combat shuttles, I would be, but since I'm flying the latest and greatest combat shuttle, it's kinda hard to say I'm not GalPat."

Grayson leaned over, "Have you seen their damn armor?"

Boykin nodded, looking quickly around. "Yeah."

"It's a helluva lot better than ours. And ours is supposedly the best in the universe. How the…"

Boykin interrupted him, "Grey Lady. They do testing for De Perez."

"De Perez? But why in the back of beyond on a dirt ball like Hunter?"

Boykin shook her head. "You really don't pay attention, do you Grayson?"

"Huh?"

"Have you looked, I mean really *looked* at who is in this particular militia company?"

Grayson shrugged. "Little, old guys. And they all carry those funky antique knives."

"You don't get out much, do you?"

"What?"

"You ever hear of Ghorkas?"

"Yeah, the CSM in boot was one. Why?"

"You ever see any other ones?"

"Not really. Treated a few when I was with the Fleet."

"Never did a ground pounder tour, did you?"

Grayson sighed, "Where are we going with this, WO?"

Boykin put her hands on the table and looked directly at him, saying softly, "Those little old men with the funky knives as you call them, have an average, *average* of over forty years of service, and an *average* rank of E-nine. You never see them anywhere but in combat outfits for the simple reason that they *love* to fight. And they smile when they do it." She leaned back. "And *that* is why they're here, and we're here. And why *they* are doing testing for new armor. They have more combat..."

Grayson held up his hand, "So, what you're telling me is I fucked up, right?"

Boykin smiled, holding her fingers about an eighth of an inch apart, "Just a *little* bit. There may be hope for you yet. Go on the net and look them up. You might learn something."

Grayson nodded. "Will do, WO. As soon as I finish breakfast."

"Good man. Now I have to go see a pilot about a schedule."

***

Fargo sat down in front of the communications suite, made sure the data logger was on, and started calling the four sites.

Shanni at Feeder Four noted they had seen evidence of at least one disturbance higher up on the mountain behind Coventry, but it didn't appear to have fresh tracks in or near it. They had hooked the location, and would continue to monitor video. They had also dropped a Ferret near the location and their two man patrol was out for another two divs.

Feeder Three reported in, with Daman identifying what appeared to be an observation post, watching the feeder and their operations. He squirted a vidcap, and Fargo pulled it up. The hairs on the back of his neck stood up, and he said, "That looks almost like a sniper's hide. Are you getting any transmissions from there?"

"Nothing in the RF band, we've got a patrol out, talking to mostly shopkeepers in the area.
When they get close, they're going to launch a Ferret, and we'll fly it up to the window, and see what we get."

"Copy all, update at sixteen unless something happens between now and then. Good catch, guys."

Horse reported in for Feeder Two with no unusual activity, and very little movement around the site. Barun reported in for Feeder One, and due to their more remote location, their patrol had already been out and back. The closest village was over a mile away, and nobody had reacted to them at all.

Fargo wondered again about the feeder placement, *Should have asked Mikhail about that. Their layout is entirely different than Hunter's. Which reminds me, I need to get with Ivan and get the maps for the cross feeds, sub-feeder links, and links to the remote farms. Don't want to have the warrant inadvertently flying into those. Maybe task her for some overflights of the outlying areas around the locations. Totally different feel than Hunter.*

Jiri came in with a worried expression. "Are we running armed patrols?"

"Why?"

"The colonel is apparently already getting complaints from the 'natives'."

Fargo picked up the mic. "Feeder Three, Base."

"Go Base."

"Daman available?"

"Standby one."

"Feeders One, Two, and Four, listen up." He heard double clicks from the other sites, and fidgeted as he waited for Daman. "Colonel pissed?"

"He wants to know what *kind* of patrols we're running."

Fargo scrubbed his hands over his face, "Well, apparently the locals have some kind of organization that is intent on making our job interesting."

The radio squawked, "Daman for Fargo."

Fargo keyed up, "Daman, give me a description of the patrols you're running."

"Standard two man patrols. In grays, sidearms and slung rifles."

"So GalPat standard, right? Rifles slung down the back?"

"Correct, no overt show of force. Just introducing themselves to the shopkeepers. Vidcams on the lapels. Handing out the holocards of what we are here for."

"Anybody doing anything different?"

Barun reported from Feeder One, "Well, we're not giving cards out. Only thing out here is animals and I don't think they are sentient, much less able to read."

That prompted a round of chuckles, and Fargo keyed up, "Thanks, Daman. We'll handle it from this end." Fargo got up, "Well, let's go see how unhappy that makes the good colonel."

Ten segs later, they were finally admitted to the colonel's office, and he waved them in peremptorily, "Well?"

Fargo replied, "GalPat standard two man patrols. In grays, sidearms and rifles slung down the back. Strictly non-threatening. The patrols are introducing themselves to shopkeepers, and giving out these," he handed the colonel one of the holocards.

The colonel tapped the card to activate it, watched it in silence, and then looked up, "Non-threatening?"

Fargo reached out very tentatively, sensing worry on Colonel Zhu's part, and the fact that he had already been called by the landholder he'd seen once before, Perez. "Non-threatening. No riot gear, no protective gear at all. Standard comms devices, lapel vidcams. So we have recordings of every interaction."

"That's not what is being reported."

Fargo was getting frustrated, "Colonel Zhu, I need details to be able to see if we have an issue anywhere."

Zhu reacted, "Well, I don't have details. You people haven't even been here a day, and already causing problems."

Fargo sensed Zhu's frustrations overlying his worries about who was doing what on the planet. It was obvious that Zhu wanted to have control, but he didn't know who to try to control, much less what the underlying issues were. "Sir, if you get specifics, I'll be more than happy to investigate them. But in the meantime, I plan on continuing random patrols, non-threatening, boots on the ground, which is well within the ROE we've agreed to."

The colonel glared at him, "Dismissed. When I have more information, I'll call you."

Fargo and Jiri came to attention, executed precise about faces, and left the office. Fargo stalked back to their office waved Jiri in, and closed the door. "Well, *that* didn't go well."

Jiri slumped in a chair, "Not like we had a lot of options there. We are in compliance with the ROE, but something tells me we're upsetting what is it they say, somebody's cart?"

Distracted, Fargo said, "Apple cart. Don't know why, but it's an ancient English saying. My mother used that one a lot. Especially when people were unhappy."

"What do we do?"

Fargo pulled up the manning list, "Double up on patrols, at least every other, or every third day. Randomize the schedule twenty-four/seven. Still should give the folks enough rest. Need to go find Boykin. I want her to do some more flying."

Jiri nodded. "I'll man the radios."

Fargo got up and stalked out, getting the feeling that they might be in trouble. There was a lot more going on than was being admitted to. He reached out with his psi sense, deciding all was fair in love and war, and this sure as hell didn't look like love.

Boredom

Fargo sat in front of the comm suite, toying with a bulb of coffee as he waited for 0800, to start the morning reports. It had been a quiet week, none of the sites had reported any problems, and none of the observation posts they'd observed had been occupied. Fargo had continued the daily patrols, and only Feeder Three had reported any issues. Daman had said that their patrols were being followed, and had launched Ferrets to follow the patrols, getting video and some audio of two younger techies.

Fargo had pushed the video over to the colonel, but nothing had been heard back from him, nor had anything been heard from Nicole, which was beginning to worry Fargo. At exactly 0800, Barun called, "Morning Base, Feeder One, nothing to report, unless strange sand snakes count."

"Sand snakes?"

Barun chuckled. "Pics inbound. Karun managed to step on one. It bit his rifle instead of him, but he had to come back in and change shorts." The system 'dinged', Fargo pulled up the pictures, and whistled. The sand snake was at least 12 feet long, and had a head the size of a dinner plate, which was still attached to the fore grip on the rifle. It had apparently bitten through the heat shield and either trapped its fangs, or Karun had been awfully quick with the *kukri*. Fargo marveled at the picture, even with the snake laid out on the sand, it was almost impossible to see.

"Where was it when it attacked Karun?"

"Right across the path where we go in and out of the sonics."

"Did Karun take it out with the *kukri*?"

Barun laughed. "Oh yes, one cut. According to Balraj, he didn't even get turned around before Karun had the head off, the rifle off, and was standing six feet away, panting."

Fargo shook his head. "Amazing what a little adrenalin can do. I suppose Karun wants to keep the skin?"

"He does. He also wants to clean the fangs out, and leave them embedded in the rifle as a reminder."

Fargo shrugged. "That's your call. Tell him if he poisons himself, it's all on him."

The other sites reported in with no issues, and he trooped down the passageway to the colonel's office, knocking on the door, he said, "Colonel, nothing to report. All four sites normal."

Colonel Zhu glanced up. "Good. I like quiet," then went back to his data comp.

***

Nicole dressed with care, with no perfume or powders, choosing an outfit that was nice but not dressy. She concealed her pistol on her thigh, made sure the vidcorder was fully charged, and headed out. She'd only found two stores that sold wine, and the one called Makers was having a tasting at noon. She'd thought that was a little odd, but she was discovering Endine was a little strange anyway.

Makers was what she would call a decent place, with a more varied collection of wines than she would have expected, this far out on the rim. When she walked in the door, she saw the young clerk that she had talked to earlier in the week, and walked over to speak to him, "Morning, Renard. I would like to attend the tasting. How much is it?"

"It is two hundred credits, Madame." He proffered the chip reader, and she scanned her ID chip into it, approving the withdrawal. "We will start exactly at twelve, and everyone will enter together. Feel free to browse until twelve."

"Thank you. Do you know how many will be here?"

Renard shrugged. "Not sure Madame, I know the buyers for the three restaurants, and maybe a couple of the Firsties. I know Senor Perez will be here, since two of his vintages are being revealed, and the supply ship brought a good variety this time."

"Thank you." She turned and walked around the store, noting the Perez varietals, and some interesting bottles that resembled the classic Italian bottles known as Chianti. She quickly made a vid of those bottles, then went back and made a vid of the Perez bottles. *Huh, looks like two vineyards on the planet. That could be good or bad.* She took a closer look at one of the Italian bottles, and noted the name Abruzzi, and the name Abboccato. *Italian name, white wine, Abboccato means mouth filling. I wonder…*

At noon, there were ten people milling around when the door to the tasting room was opened. Since she was across the store, she was the last one through the door, and immediately noted a strong odor of aftershave, *Why, why must there always be one? Do they not understand that we need to smell the wines? Whoever it is, I'm staying as far away as possible.*

She glanced around and saw that she was the only woman, and that this would not be a seated tasting. There was a table with what looked like crackers and cheeses for cleansing the palate, and she was relieved to see large plastic cups, obviously meant to be spit cups. Although she'd taken the precaution of taking a pill ahead of the tasting, just in case, if she had to drink too much so that she we feel logy by the end of the tasting. The layout of the bottles was interesting too, it seemed the Perez offering was the premier, since they sat on their own table, while all the other bottles were crowded onto one table.

Since everyone else crowded around that table, Nicole eased around to the second table, munching a cracker, and picking up a spit cup. The young girl doing the pouring looked at her nervously, "May I pour for you, Madame?"

She pointed to one of the Abruzzi bottles, "The Barbera, please."

The young girl found the bottle and poured a generous half a glass, and Nicole whispered, "Not more than two sips. About half of what you gave me. Tastings don't get much wine in the glass, just enough to get the aroma, and a taste."

The girl nodded gratefully, "Thank you. I have never had to do this before."

Nicole moved away, swirled the wine gently in the glass and sniffed, *Oh, that is… nice!* Taking a sip, she slurped a little air with it quietly, and swished it around in her mouth, holding it for about ten seconds, *This is as good as I've tasted at home! Berries, nice and full, somebody out here is good!* She spit the mouthful in the spit cup, and set the glass down, quickly noting her impressions into the vidcorder.

She went back and asked for the Sangiovese, and this time the young girl poured just the right amount. Nicole smiled, and whispered, "Perfect." The young girl looked relieved and turned as one of the men came up. Nicole stepped away, repeated the tasting, and marveled at it, *Damn, another good one, Cherry, nice tannins, now I want spaghetti or lasagna. This would go great with anything Italian.*

Nicole continued to circulate, trying the different wines, and watching the others. The older Latin was the one with all the aftershave, and he stood off to the side of the Perez table, with a proprietary look in his eyes. She'd picked out the buyers for the restaurants, and a couple of others that might be buyers from other towns. One older man had come in late, but he didn't seem to be tasting anything, just watching. And when he did, one of the buyers suddenly became very serious. *Wonder if he's the restaurant owner? Or I should say which restaurant owner…*

She tried one more wine from the crowded table, but it was barely fit as plonk. She quickly spit it out, and grabbed a couple of crackers to try to clear her palate. Since the others had finally moved away from the Perez table, she eased over and asked for the Chardonnay. As she swirled the glass, she smelled the aftershave overlaying everything as the little Latin man stepped over to her, and into her personal space. "Who are you, and what are you doing here? I don't know you."

His attitude immediately pissed her off, and she deliberately took a sip of the wine, then spit it in the cup before answering. "I'm not from here. I'm on sabbatical from Star Lines. I'm a sommelier, looking for new and different wines that might please the palates of our customers," Nicole said in her best hostess voice.

"I'm Perez. My wines are the best on the Rim, but they do not come cheap." He turned and stomped off, obviously irritated by Nicole's failure to respond immediately or cower before him.

They are cheap wines, at least they're not sleazy like you, you little... She tried the Cabernet Sauvignon, and it too was middling at best, *Gran Cru my ass. And I'm beginning to wonder where those grapes came from.*

Her thoughts were interrupted by the older man, who stopped a respectful distance away and merely waited until she had spit the wine out. "Madame? May I inquire?"

Nicole smiled at him, "I'm a sommelier on sabbatical from Star Lines looking for some new, different wines and liquors. We have found some interesting wines are being bottled out here, and our customers are adventurous enough to be willing to try them, especially paired with local cuisines from their planets of origin."

"My name is Vincent DuMaurier, I own the Endine Inn and Restaurant, among other things. I couldn't help but notice that you don't seem impressed by the offerings of the Perez winery. What would you recommend from this group?"

She laughed. "Nicole Levesque, I'm a poor sommelier, I'm not allowed to buy, only recommend. And I'm not sure I would want to recommend without knowing what kinds of meals one serves."

DuMaurier smiled and nodded. "Spoken like a true sommelier! My father told stories of working with his sommelier back on Earth, before we came out here."

"You have a vineyard?"

"No, we... we have cattlelows and vegetables, and a couple of restaurants. We took the food trade as a secondary skill. Would you be interested in some consulting? For a fee, of course?"

Nicole cocked her head, *Ah, the in I was looking for. Now to not appear to jump too quickly.* "That might be possible."

"It would be appreciated, and we will comp you all meals, of course. Would you be willing to come to the restaurant this afternoon and discuss our menu with the maître and the chef? Around sixteen?"

She nodded. "I believe that would be possible. The address?"

DuMaurier touched his wrist comp, and she saw the address pop in on hers, "Until this afternoon. Pleasure to meet you, Ms. Levesque."

"And you, sir."

***

Horse called in for Fargo, and Grayson finally tracked him down, in the mess, "Horse is calling, something about liberty for the troops, Captain."

Fargo sighed, "Figures it would be Horse. I swear... Is Boykin around?"

"No, sir. She went flying with one of the other warrants. Something about planetary approaches."

"Okay." He finished the bulb of coffee, flipped it at the disposal, and missed. With a groan, he picked it up and carefully placed it in the bin, "That's why I don't play Tri-D ball."

Grayson grinned, but didn't answer, as they walked back down the hall to the detachment's little office. Fargo flopped down in the chair in front of the comms unit, calling up Feeder Two's location on the holo. "Feeder Two, Base. Fargo for Horse."

"Standby by, Base." A seg later, Horse came on, "Oh great leader, we need some relief. The men would like to get some time away from the site on their down time."

Fargo laughed. "Feeder Two, Base, they need time, or *you* need time?"

"Um, Base, of course I would have to verify..."

"Feeders One, Three, and Four, are you listening?"

"One's up."

"Three."

"Four's here."

Fargo looked at the site, distance from it to Archer City, and then quickly pulled up the other sites. Feeder One was outside Capital City, Three was at the Kwamaine village, but the city was Canyon, and Four was outside Paradise. "Let me work on something. Plan on four pairs men a week, for each site, which would give them... Liberty every third week, let's say." He pulled up the schedules and winced. "Looks like some people are going to have to double up, since if we give liberty, I want it in daylight. I'll need to work this out with the WO, and with the GalPat colonel."

All four sites rogered up, and Fargo pushed back from the comm unit, scrubbing his hands over his face, "Liberty? Really, Horse, *liberty*? And over an open damn channel, so all the other sites would hear it?" He laughed. "You are one sly sumbitch, sir. Yes you are."

Grayson burst out laughing, "Sly? That damn warrant is *twisted*. It's no wonder everybody gave him a wide berth on the ship."

"So, Senior. What kind of issues are we facing if they go to town?"

"Uh, nothing they haven't already had vaxes for. Endine is surprisingly clean. No real plant, water, or bugs we haven't already mapped and checked."

"What about foods?"

"Well, I haven't seen any warnings, other than the usual off limits locations on the planet for *other* issues. But I gotta admit that damned Vindaloo they have here should be classified as a bioweap. That shi… crap burned from end to end!"

Fargo covered a laugh by coughing, "Okay, good to know. Would you mind getting a list of the off limits locations planet wide, please?"

Grayson reached for his data comp and squirted a file to Fargo's, which pinged with an incoming message, "There you are, sir. I keep that on mine for purely professional reasons if I need to assist the local troopers."

Fargo did laugh, "I can't believe you actually said that with a straight face, Senior. But okay. If you see the WO in your wanderings, could you let her know I need to talk to her?"

"Yes, sir."

                              ***

Fargo, Jiri, and Boykin had spent most of the previous evening running through various plans for setting up liberty runs to the four main cities nearest each site. Fargo had decided not to allow liberty in Kwamaine, due to the potential for hostile action, but he did want to keep the regular patrols working.

Since Boykin already did twice weekly runs to the sites, it was more a matter of revising the days and times than anything else. They had checked and found they could draw supplies for the sites on any day, and chose to move to first and fourth days. Since sixth and seventh day were considered weekends/religious, he didn't want troops in town during those days, even though seventh day had provided a quiet time for Boykin to get in and out of sites.

She had come up with at least two locations where she could land for each site, except Feeder Three, that was inside the perimeter, which made her happier. And it would give her more *excuses* to shoot a variety of approaches.

What Horse had not planned on, and Jiri laughed about, was Fargo's decision to add surveillance modes to each liberty. All of the troopers would wear their grays, but would add the lapel cameras and do data collections on all of the towns. He also laid on a tasker for each of the team leads to meet with the TBT techs in the major cities at least once per month.

"Fargo, you know Horse is going to have a Slashlizard when you put this out. He's not going to like the surveil requirement, that means the guys can't *play*."

"I know. That's part of why I did it. We're only here three months on the initial contract, and they *should* be able to do that standing on their heads in a corner. Horse started it, all I'm doing is finishing it."

"And adding the off limits places?"

Fargo grinned, "Cherry on top."

Ramping up

"Base, Feeder Three. Base, Feeder Three, come in!" Fargo scrambled into the chair as he glanced at the clock, 0730. *What the hell? Daman doesn't sound happy...*

"Go Feeder Three."

"We've got protesters. They're throwing rocks and bottles. They started moving in right at sunrise."

"What's your status?"

"Everybody is under cover. I've got Rana and Rai in armor between the Hab and maintenance vans, just in case. Squirting video now."

"Good. Break. All sites, perimeter check."

"Feeder One, two- maybe three people. Nothing being thrown. But I don't see a lot of people moving around either, which is not normal. We're in soft armor."

"Feeder Two, Horse here, we have a few rowdies, maybe thirty total. Mostly young. Everybody in soft armor.

There was a pregnant pause as he waited for Feeder Four. After almost a seg, he said, "Feeder Four? Shanni, come in Feeder Four!"

After a half seg, an out of breath Shanni came on, "Base, Feeder Four. Sorry. Had to go get Mr. Beeman through the sonics. He was attacked this morning at the Paradise main link. We've got probably forty or more. Working on a good count now. Right now nothing is being thrown, and they're staying well back. Something took down the primary antenna, we're on a backup right now."

"Drone or something else? Squirt the video over the last twelve divs. Matter of fact, everybody squirt their video. If you had anybody on liberty, squirt their video too. I'm going to go see the colonel as soon as he gets in to see if they are getting any intel."

Shanni chucked, "Unless drones out here bleed yellow and have real feathers, it wasn't a drone. And the damn black flies *loved* whatever blood that was."

"Copied all."

He pinged Jiri, Grayson, and Boykin's comps with the message- LOW LEVEL ALERT. SITES HAVE ACTION. While he waited, he started scanning the video from Feeder Four, and finally saw something hit the antenna around 0500. It was too dark to actually make it out, but when he replayed it in the enhanced mode, it looked like two birds. The bigger one chasing another smaller one, with the first one cutting around the antenna, and the second hitting it squarely, and biting through the antenna in one bite. He winced, *Don't know what that was, but I don't want to meet one. Anything that can bite through a half inch of composite isn't something to fool with. Better find out just what that was.*

Grayson was the first one through the door, still getting into his grays, "What have we got, Captain?"

"Nothing serious, yet. No injuries reported, wait. Check with Feeder Four. Beeman the TBT tech was attacked this morning, check with them on his condition. I need to hit the head."

"You got it boss." Grayson flopped down and grabbed the mic as Fargo headed toward the head.

He met Jiri coming down the hall, "Nothing major. Gotta hit the head. Can you grab coffee for everyone?"

Jiri nodded and headed for the mess as he opened the door to the head. When he got back to the office, Jiri had coffee bulbs sitting on a tray, with everyone waiting for his return. He looked at Grayson, who shrugged. "Minor bruises. Little cut on his head. Apparently more pissed than hurt."

Boykin looked up from her comp, pointing at the screen, "That thing looks like what they call a Condor here. But it's more like a cross between a Condor and a feathered Velociraptor. Wingspan is about twelve feet, it's got a lot of teeth, and it's carnivorous. I've seen a couple since I've been flying around."

Jiri shook his head. "Oh *hell* no. A KEW from orbit works for me."

Fargo chuckled. "Bad experience I take it."

Jiri nodded. "Yep, and I don't even want to talk about it. Took a twelve mil laser to kill the damn thing!"

"Okay, y'all go eat. WO, after you eat could you prep the shuttle, just in case?"

"Yes, sir."

"Senior…"

"Already got a full go pack aboard, and that's where my armor is parked. Right next to yours and the WO's, Captain. I'll move my go bag aboard as soon as I eat."

"Jiri?"

"I'll go. It's my turn to get out of the office. Besides, you can use your *other* talents on the Colonel."

Fargo rolled his eyes, "Okay. This *has* to be coordinated at some level. I'll work with the colonel on that. I'll go hit the mess right quick and come back." *I wonder what, if anything, Nicole has heard. I worry... Stop that. She knows what she's doing, and Jace would keep me informed.*

Jiri smiled. "Food is good. Go ahead, I don't think anything is going to happen in the next fifteen segs."

At 0800, Fargo stood bouncing on the balls of his feet as he waited for Colonel Zhu to put in an appearance. He'd snapshotted the apparent leaders of each of the protesters, and already sent them to both the colonel and his intel officer. Finally the colonel came down the hallway, a bulb of coffee in his hand. He nodded curtly to Fargo then motioned to his office as he opened the door. "Problems, Captain?"

Fargo nodded. "All sites are being, I guess, *protested*; there are anywhere from three to forty people depending on the location. At Feeder Three, they are actively throwing things at the personnel, mostly rocks and bottles. No one has been seriously hurt, yet. I wanted to see if you've gotten anything from your Intel section?"

Zhu sat slowly, then brought up his holo. Quickly scanning the incoming, he said, "Nothing. It looks like the only thing I've gotten is from you."

"That's pulls from our surveillance vans. This has to be a coordinated effort. Can we..."

Zhu cut him off, "I'll go talk to Director Vaughn and see if her officials have seen or heard anything. I don't want your people out stirring shit up among the natives."

Fargo bristled, and reached out with his psi sense, *He's worried, no… he's afraid. Why? What else is going on around here?* He risked a little deeper probe and wasn't happy with what Zhu's emotions and thoughts revealed. *Crap, he's sure there is a bunch of rebels and he doesn't know who they are, or where they're getting their information and support. And the director's people aren't letting him have any intel. That's… not good.*

"Keep me in the loop, Fargo. And keep your troops under control." Zhu got up and motioned Fargo out of the office, as he headed for the door, an angry expression on his normally stoic Asiatic features.

***

Jiri and Fargo spent the next four divs monitoring the feeds and radio traffic between the four sites, but there weren't any additional actions by the protesters. Suddenly at thirteen, all of the protesters turned and walked away, as if they'd been programmed to only protest for a specific length of time. Daman called in, "Base, Feeder Three, got something interesting. Squirting data now."

Fargo jerked out of his trance, realizing he'd been watching the vid feeds without even seeing them, per se. "What have you got?"

"Base, finally got a face in that window we picked up as being an overlook. And he's on a comm unit just about the time the protest stops. Managed to hack the local's security system, followed him out to the local shuttle port. He got on a shuttle to Capital at fifteen thirty."

"Daman, did you get a name on him?"

"Negative, didn't try to hack the database that far. Figured you might be able to do a *legal* search from your location."

Fargo nodded to himself, "Makes sense. I'll see what I can find. Maybe I can get eyes on when the shuttle lands here. Thanks Daman." He quickly pulled up the vid and looked at the capture Daman had sent, then sent it to the GalPat Intel section with a request for an immediate ID. Pulling up the shuttle schedules, he saw that the shuttle from Canyon would arrive at seventeen. Scanning back through the vid, he saw what Daman was talking about, and smiled grimly, *This guy is definitely a player. But I'm guessing he's reporting to somebody, or taking direction from somebody or bodies.*

Jiri came back in, "Want a break?"

Fargo stretched, "Yes. I need to go beard the lion again. He dismissed me this morning, and went stomping off. Hopefully, he's found something we can use. What do you think about dropping the alert with the warrant and Senior?"

"I think so. Looks like they've stopped the protesting, and I never did like keeping folks on alert for nothing. It's not like we can't call them if we need them."

"Do it." Fargo got up, ceding the chair to Jiri and stretched again, "I'm going to hit the head, then the colonel. Want a bulb when I come back?"

Jiri laughed. "No! Any more bulbs of coffee, and I'll be wired for three days."

"I think we might need to be." Fargo hit the head, then went back to the colonel's office, knocking on the door he asked, "Permission, Colonel?"

"Come in. Why did you send a picture to my Intel section asking for an ID?"

Fargo stopped in front of his desk and reached out, *Whoever that was, he's not happy about the ID. Wonder if he'll give me the name?* "That was a person we observed at Kwamaine, apparently coordinating the protesters. Who was he? He never got off the shuttle here."

Zhu looked up sharply, "Didn't get off the shuttle?"

"Our people tracked him to the Capital shuttle at fifteen thirty. When it landed here at seventeen thirty, he never got off. The next stop is Archer City."

"He's… from a prominent family, *very* prominent. How confident are you…"

Fargo said earnestly as he gave the colonel a little *push* with his psi sense, "We think he's one of the coordinators of the protests. We'd really like to put a marker on him and track him."

Grudgingly, Zhu said, "Smallwell. Eric Smallwell. His family is one of the original families. They own…a farm or something called the Oasis. It's west of Archer City. He's the third generation, they…use a combination of indentured and mechs to farm over ten thousand acres. I don't know…" Fargo pushed again, "Well, maybe if we don't advise the director, I guess we could put a marker on him."

"Thanks, Colonel. Any more information?"

Zhu shrugged. "Not much more than what you heard originally. The company doesn't want us nosing around, saying *they* are investigating some *rebellious* young people. No names, supposedly no idea what they want, yada, yada."

Fargo mumbled, "Bullshit." He looked up at the colonel, "So, all the data we provided has gone nowhere?"

"Not that I can tell, Captain. I would suggest you might want to bring your people to a higher level of alert."

Fargo looked at him, *Does he not understand we've been there since day one? The only way…* "We'll look at what we can do, Colonel. If there is nothing else?"

"Not at this time. If… if anything else comes in, we will advise you. And in the future, please route all data through my office, don't send anything directly to my Intel shop."

Fargo stood, came to attention, and left the office, *So, who is covering for who, with what? By us going directly to Intel did we upset his or somebody else's apple wagon? Dammit, I wish Nicole were here, she'd know the answer and probably how to work around it!*

***

Lev stepped into the Hab module and glanced at Shanni, "You ready? I'm hungry. I want to try that Star of India place that Thak found."

Shanni finished pinning his lapel cam on, making sure it was as discreet as possible, "Sure, we can do that. Although I'm not sure Thak is a good reference. He'll eat damn near anything."

Chuckling, Lev answered, "Well, it is Thak. But he said they actually do the food with the right seasonings. And I checked, it's not off limits, yet."

"Yet, only because I haven't talked to Ekavir about it. It should be. It's *not* in a part of Paradise that we should be entering at night. Remember what Mr. Beeman told us? Only go for lunch. And he's a native, and well known."

Lev shrugged. "Well, we're the last ones to get liberty, so after we go, maybe you should call him. Everybody else has had their chance at it."

"Probably. Let's go before it gets completely dark. At least we'll only have to walk one way in the dark."

A couple of divs later, Shanni pushed back from the table, "Wow. That… that was fantastic. Almost like we were back in the enclave. Now I need a gravsled to move my ass back to the Hab!"

Lev laughed. "Oh yes. Very good. Maybe we shouldn't put this off limits. This would actually be a pretty nice place to have a party before we leave. But we don't have a gravsled, and I'm not carrying your fat ass."

Shanni got up with a groan, and they walked slowly to the door, saying "Salam" to the hostess and her husband as the left. They immediately started moving, unconsciously falling into the standard two-man tactical spread, even though they had no weapons beyond their *kukris*. They hadn't moved more than a couple of blocks when a gang of men came out of an alley, knives and batons or pipes in their hands. Shanni quickly shifted into the roadway, "Hey guys, we're not after you. We're just going back to our Hab."

Lev quickly hit the emergency call on his wrist comp saying softly, "Need some help, guys. We're about to get stuck in. Two blocks from Star of India, main drag." Drawing his *kukri*, he slid to the left as Shanni ducked an awkward blow from a pipe.

Shanni knocked the pipe away, stepped in close, and hammered a fist the man's brachial plexus, knocking him out of the fight as he went to his knees. He got an arm up, deflected a baton as he drew his *kukri*, and then sliced the baton wielder's tendons just above the wrist, putting him out of the fight. In the roiling fight that followed, Lev managed to get his back to a wall, ducking blows and weaving away from multiple strikes, smiling as the attackers kept getting in their own way. He took out two more of the attackers before one snuck a knife into his ribs as he ducked a baton from his other side. The attacker paid with his life, but Lev knew he was in trouble. "Shanni, I took one. Not good."

Shanni fought his way to Lev's side, dropping his third attacker. He flipped his knife to the other hand, and hooked his arm under Lev's armpit, "Gotcha. There are only two left, let's get across to the next building and…"

As they passed the mouth of the alley, a hooded man stepped silently out and fired needle gun rounds into the backs of both men, before disappearing back into the darkness. The two surviving attackers that could still move ran back toward the rough part of town as four of the Ghorka came charging down the street, rifles up.

***

The dual suns were peeking over Endine's horizon when Fargo finally was granted permission to remove Shanni and Lev's bodies. Jiri was doing his best to keep the rest of the company from going on a rampage, while Horse paced back and forth across the mouth of the alley, as he had been doing for most of the night, since Boykin had picked him up from Feeder Two. Thak and the others gently rolled Shanni and Lev into body bags, reverently replacing their bloody *kukris* in their sheaths without cleaning them.

That had been a totally separate battle with the local law enforcement, who wanted to confiscate the weapons as evidence. It finally took Colonel Zhu stepping in with the director and her personal orders to the locals to allow them to be released back to Fargo. Horse stomped over, "Ekavir, this I have found, there was one camera that shows what we may be able to get processed into a usable vid for facial recognition. These others were nothing but... *Trash*. I pulled Shanni and Lev's lapel cameras, and scanned them, they were attacked without warning or talk. But I do not want those to disappear into this mud ball's *law enforcement*. Our people need to know they went out fighting."

Fargo nodded choppily, "Agreed. According to the colonel, all six of these", motioning to the bodies now lined up on the street, "are indentured employees who've *escaped* from their servitude and *disappeared* into the nether world that apparently exists here. Yet *another* thing we weren't briefed on."

Thak approached them, "Captain, we are ready."

Fargo nodded and keyed his comm unit, "WO, we're coming. Drop the ramp when you see us please." Turning to Thak and the others as they hoisted the bodies onto their shoulders, he said, "If you will." He and Horse stepped out into the street and began the slow march toward the shuttle a block away in the middle of a major intersection. The GalPat troopers snapped to attention and saluted as the small procession passed them on the way to the shuttle.

Once they were lowered gently to the deck of the shuttle, he climbed into the cockpit, "Straight back to the Palace please."

Boykin nodded silently as a tear rolled down her face, then she faced forward and gently lifted the shuttle into the air on the anti-grav.

Aftermath

Nicole came in to hear Ophelia breathlessly saying, "Apparently they killed two of those off world security guys last night. My uncle says the two of them killed six of the people that attacked them." She stuffed her bag in her assigned cubby, walked toward the vidscreen, picking up the scheduled menu offerings on the way. She stood looking at the reservations for the night as she heard Ophelia continue, "Apparently they landed a shuttle right in the middle of the main intersection blocking traffic for *divs*!" *I need to talk to Ethan. If those were our folks that got hit… I'm not sure how much good I'm actually doing here. Lots of loose talk, but nothing really odd, or that I could actually point at as… rebellious. Maybe it's time for me to come in out of the cold and help.*

Nicole notice there were two private parties scheduled, one labeled Perez and one labeled 3G. As she was puzzling that out, Raymondo swished into the work area, clapped his hands, and said effeminately, "Girls, girls! We're going to be *so* busy tonight! We have two privates and three quarters of the other tables are full. Mr. DuMaurier wants to make sure *everybody* is on their best behavior tonight, *capiche*?"

A mumbled round of "Okay, yes," and groans followed Raymondo's announcement, as he swished over to Nicole. She glanced down at the menu, noting a number of Italianish dishes, and smiled.

Raymondo stepped up and whispered, "You're not to work the Perez party, only his estate wines will be served, so there is no reason, according to him, for a sommelier. Apparently Mr. Perez doesn't like you for some reason, but I need you to work the third generation party and the main room."

Nicole smiled up at him, "Oh, I know why. And the further I can stay from him, the better I like it. Do you want me to at least to make sure the room is prepped correctly?"

"Please. Go do what you do so well!" He said with a smile.

Nicole laughed softly, "I will." *Oh, will I ever.* She strolled back to her cubby, dug in her bag and pulled out her sommelier pin from her clutch, while palming two more Ferrets. The previous ones had been placed in various locations in the main dining room, and she wasn't sure if they'd actually done any good, but at least they were passing data, she hoped. She'd already programmed these for passive record and burst transmit after the restaurant closed, and only needed to do the final activation step, which consisted of pressing the gray side of the cube. She snagged a clean towel off the stack and held it casually as she said, "Going to check the private rooms and swing through the main."

Raymondo nodded distractedly as he was deep in conversation with Otto, the head chef. Nicole remembered her earlier conversation with Raymondo, or Ray, his actual name. *Ray's sharp as a tack. He plays the high queen role well, and it makes people underestimate him. He's a big part of the success of this place, and Mr. DuMaurier knows it. Ray reads people like a book, which kinda scared me that he would see through my act but I guess I've carried it off so far.*

Nicole checked the first private room, reserved for Perez, and noted it was set for twelve. Five on a side, and one at each end centered in the room. Looking around, she decided to place the Ferret on the ornate frame of the photo mosaic screen that served as a vidscreen if desired. Pulling a chair over, she quickly depressed the gray side, and the Ferret unfolded into its tactical bug like shape as she stepped up in the chair. She found a particularly busy section of the frame and gently pressed the Ferret to it. It automatically attached, changed colors to match the background, and she looked closely as the very small lens swiveled up. *Bet that is going to scare the hell out of whoever looks at the initial images*!

She replaced the chair, wiping it down to make sure no footprint was visible and repeated the steps in the second private room. It was set up with four tables, so she placed the Ferret on the top of the curtains at the end of the room. *Probably lose any low voiced conversations at the far tables, but what the hell. Something is better than nothing.* A pass back through the main dining room, and she headed back to the kitchen. She found Otto giving low voiced instructions to the sous and pastry chefs, once he was finished, she asked, "How many of the Italian dishes are light and how many are heavy?"

Otto waggled his hand, "Even split. The red sauce ones are all heavy, the white or no sauce ones are light. And I have the local version of cheese for a variation on Caprese for the salad."

"So I better go check on the Abruzzis we have in the cellar and make sure we have enough bottles left. I *hope* somebody puts an order in for more of their wines."

Otto raised his hands, "Not my job! I only do food, you have to deal with Raymondo for those sins," he said with a laugh.

***

Fargo flopped down in the chair angrily, as Jiri looked at him, "Didn't go well?"

"No, not at all. Apparently the GalPat Intel folks have a *higher* priority than seeing if they can do anything with the video to enhance it so they could actually catch that son of a bitch. The colonel *assured* me it will get worked on soonest, whenever the hell that is."

Jiri cocked his head. "Odd thought, what about pushing the video and other stuff up to the ship? Maybe Liz could do something with it? I know she's EW, but a lot of those folks are…"

Fargo slapped the desk, "Dammit, why didn't I think of that? Deity… how stupid can I be?"

"Well, you haven't had any sleep in over twenty-four divs, and you haven't taken any stims."

"Still should have thought of it," Fargo muttered as he quickly typed a message to Captain Jace and attached all the surveillance data and videos to it. He hit send and leaned back, "And more hurry up and wait."

Grayson walked into the office juggling a bulb of coffee, "Hot, hot, hot! Dammit... I'll relieve somebody." He looked at Fargo and continued, "And that somebody is you, Captain. You look like hammered lizard shit." He dropped the bulb on the edge of the desk and rummaged through his pack, came up with a little red pill and said, "Take this with a *full* bulb of enhanced water. It'll give you six divs down."

Fargo started to protest, and Grayson looked at him. "This, or I give you an injection for twelve divs. Your choice."

Fargo grumbled, but he took the pill and got up slowly. "If anything, and I do mean *anything* comes in, get my ass up. Understood?"

"Yes, sir. Warrant, you need some down time too."

Jiri nodded. "I caught a couple of divs. A few more wouldn't hurt. As soon as the eighteen reports come in, I'll go down."

Onboard the *Hyderabad*, Jace processed the message traffic and was glad that both Wallace and Liz were down, and he didn't have to put on an act, even as he wished he *could* strike something. Less than ten segs later, he'd enhanced the video to the point that when he started the worm searching the world's database, it should give at least a 50% correlation. That would be good enough to at least start a physical search for the individual. Jace snarled to himself at the cluster of separate databases, lack of continuity, and just plain sloppiness he saw, including in the GalPat Det's on-planet database.

In the process of scanning through the databases, he was surprised to learn that none of the first families were actually tracked in any way, only the second and third wave of migrants were tracked daily. Jace figuratively cocked his head, wrote and loosed more worms, and set up tracks on all of the citizens. *Something else going on here. This isn't just about some rebellious young people. What else is going on? Twenty-eight days until I can pick up the surveillance drone we dropped on the way out last trip. That will take eight divs, unless…*

Jace processed the track of the drone, calculated its path around the dual suns, and looked at known ship tracks coming into the system. He figured if he powered the drone on low power and change the trajectory, he could shorten the delay to 23.3 days, and it would take the *Hyderabad* 10.4 divs to retrieve it on the way out. He sent a request for a move order to Orbit Control for 24 divs out to conduct maneuvering in local space for pilot training, citing upgrade training for the second pilot. Jace laughed as he did it, deciding to see if Wallace wanted to try to fly the ship a little bit on training orbits while *Hyderabad* did its own searching.

***

Nicole sat down next to Raymondo and grimaced as she kicked off one shoe, rubbing her foot. "What happened," Raymondo asked.

Nicole wiggled her foot and sighed, "One of those oafs in the three G party stepped on my foot. I think on purpose. He made a grab for my boob and I *might* have accidently hit his arm with a wine bottle as I fell against the table."

Raymondo dropped his effeminate act. "Which one? Describe him?" He hissed quietly.

"Blondish hair, rather long, swept back. Faux glasses or at least don't look like there is any correction in the lenses. Blue eyes, about my height, probably weighs one ninety. Seemed pretty fit. And was acting like he was drunk when he stepped on me, then laughed about it when I was limping away."

Raymondo shook his head. "Hayden Archer. He's a shit. He likes to hurt people. Normally he only picks on the younger girls, don't know why he went after you. His family are the founders of Archer City, and according to his *daddy,* he can do no wrong."

Nicole snickered, "Well, he won't be doing any wrong with his right hand for a while. And I'll guarantee he's going to have a bruise. There was an interesting dynamic going on in that room too. Archer and five or six others seemed to be in charge, and everyone else there was… it was almost like they were trying to suck up. When I left, the six guys and one girl were at one table, and their dates or husbands or wives or whatever were at the furthest table away from them."

"I'm not surprised. At least they hopefully don't do too much damage tonight. Mr. DuMaurier made them pay up and banned them for three months after the last fight. They really don't have jobs, or they are just jobs in name only. The only one of that generation that I can think of that actually does anything… well, two of them, are the Abruzzis, Dominick and Elena. They actually work, really work, in the winery. Dominick is learning the grapes, and Elena is managing the sale and distribution."

"So two out of how many?"

"About a hundred. There've been a lot of consolidations since the Firsties hit the planet. Some died, some went broke, and some got broken…"

"And on that note, I'm going to take my sore foot back to the Women's Lodge and see if I can trick the fresher into letting me soak tonight," Nicole said as she slipped her shoe back on and stood.

Otto came into the break room carrying a small hot pack and a cold pack. He saw Nicole and handed them to her, "Some salad and my version of Arribbiata, you never stopped long enough to eat."

She took them and nodded. "Thank you, Otto. Tonight was a little busy. Oh," she turned to Raymondo, "We need to order more Abruzzi wines. We went through most of the stock tonight. Even some of the more expensive ones."

Raymondo grimaced. "I'll talk to Mr. DuMaurier. Mr. Perez is trying to get him to only carry the Perez wines."

Nicole shook her head. "Big mistake. Perez stuff is average at best and way overpriced. Abruzzi's is good and reasonably priced. He'll lose customers if they don't have an option."

Otto looked at her, "Really? I mean I know sommeliers pair wines, but would they really leave if the right wines weren't available?"

Nicole laughed. "There was a case a couple of years ago where a multi-planet corporation threatened the Star Lines with a boycott over wines from an inner world they dropped. They said if the Lines didn't pick the line back up, the company would take their millions of credits worth of travel elsewhere. Star Lines reordered that wine the next day, with apologies."

Otto shook his head. "Glad I only cook."

***

Fargo and Jiri sat in the little office looking at personnel files, putting people in different columns until Jiri finally said, "Ekavir, it just makes sense for me to go out there. I'll take Dhiri from Feeder Three with me. You can put the GalPat tech, Mac in the watch section. That is the least impact."

Fargo scrubbed his face, "I know. I *think* it might be better to go ahead and pull Nicole back in. Maybe she could sort this intel crap out and help us find out who killed Shanni and Lev. And with you leaving, it's going to be me and Grayson standing watch. Can't put Boykin on the schedule, since she's got to be available to fly. It's going to mean some long days, but we're down to only a few weeks left." His data comp pinged, and he glanced at it curiously, then smiled viciously as he projected the picture on his screen, "Looks like this is the perp. Just got this from Captain Jace. If his folks can't do it, this should at least get the locals started."

"You going to see the colonel with that?"

"As soon as I get the morning status. I'll tell him you're going out to replace Shanni. I… think I'll send the warrant up to Hyderabad with Shanni and Lev. Get the bodies taken care of, since we're not leaving them here." He quickly pinged the picture to the colonel with a cover note.

Jiri nodded. "They deserve to go home and be buried there."

"I'm not leaving anyone behind."

Five segs later, Barun called in, and reported all normal. He was closely followed by Horse, Daman and Thak, who was standing in for Shanni. Only Feeder Four had any protesters, and it was less than a handful if you had the Terran normal of five fingers. Fargo put out the plan of Jiri and Dhiri moving to Feeder Four, and then told everyone he was going to see the colonel and would be back up in a div with any further information.

As he headed for the colonel's office, he passed the mess and saw Grayson and Boykin sitting at one of the tables. Swinging in, he said, "Senior, can you cover the radio till I get back, please? Jiri is going out to Feeder Four." Grayson nodded, and he turned to Boykin, "WO, can you do a lift out to Three, pick up Dhiri and drop the two of them at Feeder Four, then go up to Hyderabad and leave Shanni and Lev's bodies with the ship?"

Boykin smiled sadly, "Taking them home, Captain?"

"Yes. I'm damn sure not leaving them here. I don't…" He shrugged. "Sorry, every once in a while the Marine kicks in. We were taught not to leave any of ours behind."

"That's the right way to do it, too bad GalPat has never learned that. I'll be ready to lift in thirty." She finished her bulb, dropped it in the recycle, and headed for the door. Grayson had already gone, so he continued to the colonel's office.

He knocked on the colonel's door and Zhu motioned him in, "Morning, Captain. I got the picture. How are your people holding up?"

That caught Fargo by surprise, and it took him a moment to think, "Uh, not well. They want to go after the perp or perps, they want to find them, question them, and go after whoever paid for this. It was a targeted attack, no question. And Shanni and Lev weren't doing *anything*. They only wanted to get something to eat. They hadn't harassed anybody, none of our people have. Colonel, have you ever been around the Ghorka for any length of time?"

Zhu leaned back in his chair, "Other than basic, not much. When I had a company, I had one as a CSM. We didn't interact that much, I pretty much let him do what he needed to do."

"Colonel, what they *need* to do is find the killer and take care of him. Right now they're waiting to see what the local law enforcement and GalPat are going to do. But if they don't see progress, they're liable to start looking on their own. That's why Jiri is going out to Feeder Four. He can sit on them for a while."

The colonel snapped forward, "What are you saying?"

"Colonel, to put it bluntly, I'm sitting on a powder keg. I have almost fifty *senior* combat veterans, mostly E-eights, and E-nines. They *know* how things should be done. If they don't *see* things getting done, they might start helping things get done. Remember, two small men, only armed with personal knives, took on at least eight men who attacked them. They killed six, and disabled at least one more. If they hadn't been shot in the back, they would have survived."

"I'll get this out to the director and her head of security immediately. And I'll make sure to *impress* her with the fact that this one shouldn't be dropped."

"Thank you, now if you'll excuse me, I need to get folks moving. By your leave, Colonel."

Zhu looked up at him curiously, "Will there be a service or memorial?"

Fargo shook his head. "No, sir. We will take them back home. The service and interment will be on Hunter."

"Very well, dismissed.

Abandoned

Two hyper jumps away from Endine, a star liner is in trouble...

Lherson groaned as he tried to roll over, *What the hell? Feels like my damn ribs are broke...* Consciousness came flooding back, and with it a red haze. He finally realized it was blood inside of his helmet, he frantically gasped for air, and was thankful to find there was air, even as his ribs spasmed from the pain. *I'm outside, I'm alive. I'm in zero-G. I was working on the forward particle shield power connector. What happened? Did something hit me? Am I a Dutchman?*

He tongued the mic, "M-twelve, maintenance forward?" He didn't hear a reply and tried again, "M-twelve, calling maintenance. How copy?" He tweaked the squelch and heard static in the speakers, so he knew he was getting out, or so he thought. Extracting one arm from the arm controls, he reached behind him and pulled out a Sani-wipe, scrubbing it over the inside of the helmet. He almost wished he hadn't, when his mind registered what he was seeing.

He was pin wheeling slowly in space, and looked down to see he was still boot locked onto Star Liner number 133, *Destiny*. His tool bag tugged gently at his waist, as it floated at the end of its tether. He looked forward to where Duggan should have been tethered, and only saw a flopping tether, with nothing attached. Shuffling painfully forward, he tongued to all-call, and steeled his voice to calmness, "M-twelve, on all call. Anybody there?" He heard pops again, but no answer. Not even static.

Reaching the tether, he coiled it in, and found the end of it burned, almost like a laser cut. He'd seen those before, in his *other* life, as he called it. "Is there anybody out there? Hellooo?" Turning around he gasped as he looked aft, the stern third of the ship was… gone. *Well shit. That kind 'splains things. Fourteen years in GalPat and two major battles, we got one minor hole. I get out for something safer, and I get my ship blown out from under me on my second underway. A diplomatic underway at that. Some fucking spacer I am.*

A flashing alert caused him to glance up at the HUD, and he saw an amber LOW O2, ONE DIV REMAINING, roll across the top of the HUD. *One div? These tanks are 24 div tanks. I must have a leak, or was I out for, shit. How long were we working on the shield? Half div, one div? It was programmed for a two div EVA, total. So maybe twenty divs?*

Shambling back to the airlock, he popped it open, unclipped and stepped through. Cycling it closed, he noted the emergency lights on, and saw the no pressure indicator on the interior hatch. He hit the emergency override, and cracked the hatch, peering carefully out into a deserted, eerily lit passageway.

Carrying his tool bag, he moved aft toward the maintenance shop, amid the clutter and detritus of what had obviously been an explosive decompression. He saw a couple of reddish smears in his helmet light, but knew better than to look too closely at them.

He had to cross Main Street, as it was called, to get to the space, and as he put a glove on the wall, he felt a tremor. He stopped, then felt again. Was that something he had done? Or? He stood there for a minute or two, then felt a tremor again. Leaning his plasteel helmet against the bulkhead, he could vaguely hear three fast taps, three slow taps, and three fast taps, repeated over and over. *Where the fuck do I know that from? Ah shit. Code! Somebody's alive somewhere.*

Dropping his bag, he took out a spanner, and frantically thought back to his training, then laboriously tapped out W H E R E R U. He was getting ready to try it again, when a series of taps came back, F W D M E D. Forward Med? Where the hell is, oh yeah, that's the pressure space up on deck six. Tapping back, he sent R U O K H O W M N Y. moments later, he heard 4 N D O 2 H 2 O. *Four alive. Need O2H2O, what the… Oh, need O2 and water. Forward Med is configured for overpressure, up to two atmospheres. Now where the hell was that connection? Shit.* He tapped back, S T B Y, then moved as quickly as he could to maintenance forward.

The space was predictably trashed, but he found two O2 bottles still in their racks. He quickly set up a hose and pressure filled his reservoir, then pulled the second bottle out of the rack and gathered up a hose connector. Pulling up a schematic in his HUD, he started slogging forward and down to deck six, he felt like it was taking too long, but he couldn't risk screwing up the valve on the O2 tank. He finally got to the forward bulkhead, and found the access panel.

Tapping out, S T B Y O 2, he plugged the hose into the coupling and gently cracked the valve, slowly bleeding air into the space. He could feel taps, but couldn't separate them out from the vibration of the O2, and continued for another ten minutes. Then he tapped B T T R. He got a tap back of O K, followed by N D H 2 O.

Flipping quickly through his cookbook on his HUD, he shook his head, *Crap. No way, unless I can put a portable lock on the door. There's one in the forward damage control spaces, I think.* He tapped out, W R K O N I T S T B Y.

Wrapping the O2 bottle in some dangling cabling, he started forward toward the damage control locker, and saw another alert pop up on his HUD- LOW BATTERY CHARGE REQUIRED IN ONE DIV. "Well isn't that just fucking great? There aren't any working chargers. Dean old boy, you're about fucked, unless you can figure something out." Pulling up his cookbook again, he found the battery was in his right thigh area, and he just might be able to change it, if he could find a spare.

The damage control locker was closed, and he gingerly opened the hatch, not knowing what to expect. Surprising him, most of the equipment was still in the respective racks. There was one portable air lock, latched to the bulkhead, just forward of the hatch. He also found spare batteries, and managed to get his battery pack changed out. By the time he was finished, he was sweating and hurting, so he popped an analgesic tab and electrolyte replacement to choke it down with. *Water, where the hell… None in here. Did any of the escape modules go? They've got E-rats and water. Now where the hell is the closest one?*

Twenty segs later, he floated through the tunnel and into escape module 7, which would have been the one the bridge crew would have used. *Damn, this means nobody on the bridge got out. Well, let's see…* He popped open the hatch marked emergency supplies, and was greeted with a blizzard of pacs floating out. He grabbed one, flipped it over and confirmed it had both E-rats and water. A body bag floated out of the hatch and he snagged it, then loaded it with all the pacs he could corral quickly. Tethering it behind him, he started back down to medical.

Tying the body bag off with the O2 tanks, he went back for the portable airlock. As he was pulling it off the bulkhead, he knocked over a rack of radios, and picked two of them out of the vacuum, sticking them in an outside pocket of his soft suit. Another thirty segs, and he finally had it in front of the hatch into medical. He tapped out, P O R T A I R L O C K, a pause then E R A T S, another pause and R D O I N B A G. He got back a tap O K. Taking the radios out, he shoved them in the body bag. He wrestled the airlock over the hatch, braced it with his suit, and hit the sealing charge. There was a flash of light, and he felt a clang as the airlock mated to the bulkhead. He shoved the bag into the lock, then sealed it.

Moving over to the O2 tanks, he plugged the hose into the airlock, cracked the valve, and waited until the light on the lock showed green. Shutting the valve, he tapped on the bulkhead, P R E S S E Q, a pause, H 2 O B A G. He got back O K, then felt a grinding as the hatch was cracked open. He moved over to the small view port, and saw a slim female he recognized as the assistant astrogator, *Solly? Yeah, Solly... Bridget? Or was that just what they called her.* Tapping on the view port, he saw her look up, then nod as she pulled the body bag through the hatch.

A seg later, he heard a click in his speakers, and a tentative voice, "This is Solly. Thanks for the O2, water and food. Who's in the suit?"

He tongued the mic, "Spacer Second Lherson, ma'am."

A click, "What happened?"

"Dunno, ma'am. The back third of the ship is gone. As far as I know, you and whomever else is in there and myself are the only ones left alive."

"Damn."

He thought for a second, "How many of you?"

"Four now. Doc committed suicide."

Lherson sensed there was something she wasn't telling him, but he didn't have time to worry about that. He tongued the mic, "I'm going to see if there is anyone else alive. Be back in a div or so. Will you be okay until then?"

Click, "I think so. Now that there is some water and food. Nobody answers on any channel?"

"No. Not a soul. And we're tumbling. I didn't see any other ships either."

***

Two divs later, he was back at the hatch, he tongued the mic, "Ma'am, looks like we are it. The

escape modules are still in place, as far as I can tell.
There is a shuttle in the forward bay…"

Solly interrupted hopefully, "A shuttle? Which
one?"

Lherson stopped, "Uh, the fancy one. Not the one
the crew uses. But what good does that…"

"We have soft suits in here. If we could get to the
shuttle, and it has fuel…"

"Ma'am, I didn't check. Why the shuttle and not
an escape module?"

She sounded more hopeful as she keyed up, "More
room and more range. And I could navigate it, as
opposed to the EMs, which go to the nearest habitable
planet."

"Oh. Want me to go check?"

"Please. Do you know what to look for?"

"Yes, ma'am. I'm a former GalPat spacer."

"Good!"

"I'll raid the modules too. Back in a div or so."

Lherson made his way back to the forward bay,
floated in the back hatch of the shuttle, and made his
way forward, realizing there was no atmosphere. *Shit,
gotta figure out a way to get atmosphere in this thing.
Didn't we have cylinders that had normal atmosph…?
Crap that was on the combatants. Not sure they've got
that capability here.* Easing into the cockpit, he
steadied himself and found the master bus switch.
Flipping it, he was startled when alarms started blaring
in his headset, and the board lit up red. He found the
reaction mass gauge, and saw the tanks were full.
Quickly shutting the switch off, he backed carefully

out, checking the various lockers and hatches. *Plenty of room to store E-rats. Now I just need to get some.*

Two divs later, he tongued his mic, "Ma'am, I've got the shuttle full of E-rats. I've located a cylinder of compressed air, and I can put atmosphere in the shuttle once I get you and the others on board. I'm about at the end of my rope, though. I haven't slept in over two days, and I'm running on stims and meds."

He heard a click, "Understood. I will get the matriarch out of the med comp, its battery is down to two divs anyway. I think I can get her in the soft suit, and I'll get the young ones in another two. I'm going to need help to get them to the shuttle though."

"Matriarch? Young ones?"

"I'll explain later," came across the speakers forcefully.

"Yes, ma'am. I'll be there in twenty segs."

"Once I get them in the suits, I'll need you to bleed off the pressure. I don't know where the manual controls are in here."

"I can do that. Heading your way now."

Thirty segs later he heard, "Okay, bleed the atmosphere off. We are all in soft suits."

Lherson had rigged a hose with a valve to the feed valve on the medical spaces and slowly cracked the valve, feeling it trying to move him down the passageway. Clamping in, he quickly bled off the rest of the atmosphere, watching the lights on the airlock. When it showed green again, he dropped the hose and spun the locking bar on the airlock.

He was not expecting to have a fully grown Dragoon shoved in his face, and recoiled across the passageway, reaching for a weapon, before he realized it was a she, and she was unconscious. She seemed to be missing body parts, but he couldn't tell for sure, as it was quickly followed by a second soft suit, containing one very alive and agitated young Dragoon. That was followed by a third soft suit, containing a very young human female. His speakers clicked, "I've strapped them together, if you take the matriarch, I'll bring up the rear."

"Yes, ma'am. Be aware, lots of stuff floating and panels down. We'll have to go careful."

"Fine. Lead on."

A div later, he had them in the shuttle, not without a few scares, and it was pretty clear that Solly was one determined young officer. They decided to crank the hatch closed, rather than power up the shuttle, until it had atmosphere, so he was back outside, running more hoses and connecting to a port on the servicing panel of the shuttle. He tongued the mic, "Starting flow. I have no idea how much is in the bottle, but there is an O2 bottle here if we don't get adequate pressure."

Click, "I won't hit the master bus until the soft suit deflates. That will at least give us an idea of pressure."

"Yes, ma'am. Standing by for your call."

Thirty segs later, he heard a click, "Okay, they're deflated. Powering up the master bus now," a pause, then, "About thirteen and a half."

Tonguing his mic, he said, "Okay, switching to the O2 tank." While it was emptying, he floated across to the hangar door, looking at the emergency releases. *What the hell, I gotta do this sooner or later...* He clamped his boots onto the hangar deck, and with some trepidation, fired the left emergency releases. He *felt* two 'tings' through his boots, and the left side of the hangar door started moving outward. He unclamped and floated over to the right side of the door, clamped in, and fired the emergency releases on that side. Two more 'tings' and the door disappeared as the door's rotation no longer matched that of the ship.

Crap, I didn't think about that. How the hell are we going to get the shuttle out? As soon as we…

He was interrupted by a click and "Spacer, we've got fourteen point five. What did you do?"

"I got rid of the hangar door, ma'am."

Click, "Good thinking. Are you coming aboard?"

"Let me disconnect the O2, and I'll come in through the back airlock. Where are the pax?"

Click, "I have them strapped in seats, for now, and still on their bottles."

Lherson climbed wearily up to the shuttle lock, cycled in, and clamped his boots to the floor. Cracking the seals for the first time in almost two days, he sniffed the air, and realized he could breathe. Easing himself out of the suit, he strapped it into the bulkhead, then floated forward and into the cockpit, steering clear of the two Dragoons. Solly was out of her soft suit, strapped into the copilot/nav chair, and she turned, "My God, you *stink*!"

"Sorry, ma'am, I been in that suit for almost two days. Why aren't you in the pilot chair?"

"I'm an astronav, not a pilot. I looked you up in the system, you're a qualified cox'n, right?"

"I was in the GalPat, but that was on much smaller things than this!"

Impatiently she said, "Well, you're a better choice than I am, Spacer Lherson. Do you think you can get us out of here?"

He looked at her, "Either that, or kill us. Not like we have much choice, is there?" Solly just looked at him, and he shrugged. "Binary solution set, ma'am." Lherson strapped himself into the pilot's chair, scanning the instrument panel and mumbling to himself. Touching the joystick, he looked at the thruster controls, "Huh, like a scooter, maybe I *can* do this."

Pulling up the emergency checklist, he powered up the APU, and heard Solly gasp, "What are you…"

"Gotta have power. APU points up, and the hangar should be high enough that I'm not setting it on fire. Scratch that, no atmo, no fire." As systems came on line, he ran through the checklist, with more mumbling, then finally said, "Okay, we can't cycle the Nav and Stab systems, since there is no power and no stability. Gonna have to try to fly us out, assuming the guillotines work to disconnect us from the hangar deck. Would you go check and make sure the others are strapped in tight? This is probably gonna be a rough ride."

She looked a bit miffed, but did as he asked, then came back, "Passengers are secured as tightly as I can make them. What do you want me to do?"

"Right now, nothing. If we get clear, then you're going to have to try to cycle and sync the Nav system."

"Okay." She pulled her straps tight, turned to him and said, "Okay Spacer, let's do this."

Escape

Lherson brought up the power to 5%, and felt the shuttle react against the pitching. He gingerly moved the joystick, and felt the resistance of the shuttle reacting against the clamps holding it. He closed his eyes, and taking his hands off the controls, mimicked the movements his mind said he would have to do to get them out the hangar door and clear of the ship.

He started combat breathing, deep breaths and measured exhales, slowly placed his hands back on the controls, and said quietly, "Here we go."

He slammed the guillotine switch, brought up the power, twisted the joystick as he twitched it to the right and spun the shuttle on its axis. Pushing the stick forward, he started rolling the shuttle left to try to match the tumble of the ship, and *almost* made it out the hangar door clean. He scraped the right side, almost trapping the shuttle as the tumble of the ship slowed the momentum and starting to bind the shuttle in the hangar door.

He frantically slammed the joystick all the way over, ran the power all the way up, and muttered, "Come on you bitch, get the fuck out!"

Suddenly the shuttle came clear, and blasted out into space, rolling wildly. He vaguely heard a scream, as he muttered, "Nose, wings, power. Nose up, wings level, minimum power, nose…" after a few segs, he had the shuttle more or less stable in space, drifting freely and clear of the debris from the ship.

He cranked up the plates to 1G relative, and signed as his butt settled into the chair. He turned, "Can you get the Nav up, Ma'am? I need to go hit the fresher, if you don't mind."

"No fine, err, yes, go I think I can get the Nav up."

He staggered as he got up, then walked slowly out of the pilot station, holding his ribs. *Gotta find a pain pill. Can't believe I didn't kill us, but I gotta go now!*

He found the fresher just forward of the passenger compartment, and quickly used it, then stepped into the wash section, still in his undersuit, and stood there while he punched the refresh setting.

Solly found him there, almost a div later, collapsed on the floor and sound asleep. She shook her head, and went to check on the others. She eased the matriarch out of her soft suit, but she still did not regain consciousness. The younger dragoon had thrown up in his soft suit, so she left it on him for now, after freeing his head. He snapped at her, and she batted him saying. "No! Stop that." She moved back two rows and knelt in front of the young girl, "Cedar, are you okay?"

"Want mommy and daddy. Scared, and my arm hurts."

Solly got Cedar out of her soft suit, and said, "Okay, honey. Let's see about that arm." Taking her arm gently, she felt it and saw what was going to be a bad bruise, but thankfully nothing was broken. "Let me get you an analgesic. I think you just bumped your arm. You need to go to the 'fresher?"

She nodded solemnly, and Solly led her to the aft fresher. After she'd finished, she got a couple of E-rats out of the bag, and handed one to Cedar, then carried the other up to the young Dragoon. Peeling it open, she dropped it in his lap, and moved over to check on the Matriarch. She was still breathing, but the bag attached to her pic line was empty.

Cussing, Solly went back to the bag, rummaged around and found four more bags. She carried them back and, after a minute, puzzled out how the bag attached. She disconnected the empty bag, replacing it, and giving it a squeeze to start the flow.

She walked back to the forward fresher, looked down at Lherson, and then nudged him with her foot. "Wake up, Spacer."

He jumped and scrambled halfway up, then collapsed back with a groan. "Oh, my fu… my ribs. What the hell?"

"You've been passed out in here for over a div. I figured out where we are. What's the matter with your ribs?"

Gingerly getting up, he cupped his ribs, and replied softly, "I think I broke some ribs when the ship was attacked. I guess I just pushed through. Can you find a med kit? I really need something for the pain."

She looked at him, "Oh, let me go find one. Just… I'll be right back."

He eased himself back down on the toilet, and sighed, *Scatterbrained? Or just a youngster, fresh out of academy? Well, for better or worse, I'm stuck with her…*

Solly handed him a packet, "This should help. I need you to get us on course as soon as you feel up to it."

He got up with a groan, after choking the tabs down. "Now sounds like a good time." He looked back into the passenger compartment as he turned toward the pilot's station, asking quietly, "How are the others doing?"

She shrugged. "I don't think the matriarch is going to make it. She lost a leg and didn't handle the surgery the doc did very well. The med comp was keeping her stable, but all I can do now is give her the stuff through her pic line. And we're down to four bags of that left. Her... Son? Grandson? Threw up on himself, so he's still in the suit. The little girl, Cedar wants her mommy and daddy, but..." I tear ran down her face. "Her mom went back to their cabin to get a form..."

Lherson eased into the pilot's chair. "Okay, where are we, and where do we need to go?"

Solly sighed, "We're two jumps from GalPat space. We're in a dead system. There was apparently one habitable planet here, but it was destroyed sometime in the past. Two jump points are the only reason to drop in here."

"Well, that and the forward particle shield failing. That was why we dropped here. Can't go into hyper without it."

She glanced at him, "We're a little over a light second from the jump point. We need to head one three five, up eighty-eight. We don't have enough mass to get there, so I'd recommend full power until we're at fifty-four percent of mass, then cut power and drift at whatever speed we get. I figure we've got thirty-four days of food, water, and unlimited air, as long as the scrubbers hold out."

He threw up his hands, then groaned. "Shit. Really? So all we can hope is somebody comes through here in the next thirty-four days is the best you've got?"

"The jump points here are unmanned. If we get close enough, maybe we can hit a beacon that will be picked up and relayed. Our other choice is point this thing at the sun and ride it in. *I* would prefer not to do that."

Strapping in, Lherson said, "One three five, up eighty-eight, max power. Aye, aye, ma'am." He gradually fed the power in as he fiddled with the joystick until he had the shuttle on the required course. Mumbling to himself, he scanned the displays until he found the mass totalizer. Looking at the flow rates, he did a quick set of calculations and said, "Looks like twelve, maybe thirteen divs unless we start getting vibrations."

Solly nodded. "Okay. Do you mind if I get some rest?"

"Go for it, ma'am."

"Call me Bridget, please. What's your name?"

Surprised, he turned and looked at her, "Uh, Dean Lherson, ma... Bridget."

She stuck out her hand, "Pleased to meet you Dean, and thank you for saving our lives. I'll come back in four divs and give you a break."

"Thank you."

She eased out of the pilot's station, and disappeared aft. He thought, *Well, that's fucking strange. Never had any officer in the line ask my name, much less give me their first name and want to be called that.* Settling back in the chair, he stared morosely at the panels as he tried multiple frequencies to see if there was anyone in the system. *Do I really want to hit the beacon now? What if whoever shot at us is still here? Nah, I'll wait until… Bridget comes back and we can discuss it.*

***

Twelve divs later, Lherson watched the mass totalizer run down to sixty-five percent and shut the power down. Solly still hadn't come back to the cockpit, so he confirmed the heading was still good, put the sensors in AutoDetect, and got up, stretching slowly because of the ribs. He moved quietly back to the passenger compartment, noting Solly passed out and curled up in one of the seats, with Cedar sleeping in the next seat, a hand touching Solley's hip.

He checked the matriarch, and she was still breathing, the IV running a slow drip. The young dragoon appeared to be asleep as well, and he moved cautiously by it. He found the e-rats and pulled out four energy bars. None of them looked that appetizing, but he needed to eat, so he peeled one and started chewing away. Taking the other three, he started walking back forward as the young dragoon yowled. He dropped one in its lap, and smacked the dragoon on the nose when it snapped at him, "*Not food,*" pointing at himself. Pointing to the e-rat, he said, "food. Eat it."

That woke Solly up, and her moving woke Cedar, who sobbed quietly. Lherson handed the energy bars to both of them, "L… Bridget, I shut power down early. I forgot we need to conserve mass for the APU. We've got a little over two hundred eleven thousand meters per second of speed now. I figure we'll get within maybe a half light second before we run out of fuel and food."

Solly groaned and scrubbed her face and head, "At least we'll have a chance if somebody drops into this system."

Nodding toward the dragoons, he asked, "What are we going to do with them?"

She smacked her head. "Dammit, I forgot." Scrambling up, she went forward to a compartment behind the cockpit, and he heard, "Ha! They're here!" She came back dangling something on a lanyard and he realized it was a GalTrans.

"What are you going to do with that?"

"Give it to the little Dragoon. He doesn't have one yet. The matriarch told me they were on their way to Star Center for his implant." She followed her words with actions, and walked back to where the Dragoon was still strapped in his seat. Punching a couple of buttons on the GalTrans, she looped it over the Dragoon's head and let it settle against his chest. The lanyard automatically retracted until the device was nestled in the area of his throat, as he looked curiously at them, growling.

Solly waited a couple of minutes, then said, "Do you understand me?"

The GalTrans emitted a series of sounds and the young Dragoon looked down at himself, then yammered something. The GalTrans spit out, "What is this? How can I understand you? I thought…" He looked at the matriarch, and growled. "My Mother? She lives?"

Solly reached over and checked the IV and life signs, "She lives. She was badly hurt saving you. We are doing what we can."

The dragoon gave his equivalent of a nod, "She lives. She must live!"

Lherson asked, "Do you know how to use the fresher? Can we trust you to do that?"

More growls and a whine, "Filth off! Clean, yes." Straightening, he looked squarely at Lherson, then gave a long answer in his language, "I, Ton'Skel, heir to Ton'Mose do give my parole."

Solly and Lherson looked at each other, then Lherson released the straps, helping the young Dragoon up and back to the aft fresher. He walked back forward to Solly, "Uh… Bridget, what they hell was that all about?"

She shrugged. "I'm not sure. But we'll see what happens. While he's back there, I'm going to take Cedar up front and let her clean up."

"Okay. I'll wait here."

***

Six days later, the matriarch's IVs ran out, and she passed quietly, never regaining consciousness. Ton'Skel curled up next to her body and cried for over four divs, before finally passing out. They let him sleep and grieve, moving Cedar into the cockpit and letting her play with the controls after Lherson safed them. Cedar finally fell asleep in Solly's arms, crying for both her and Ton'Skel's losses.

The next clock day, Ton'Skel finally came awake and turned to Lherson and Solly, his GalTrans spit out, "My mother's body must be preserved until she can be properly buried according to custom."

"Dave, what can we do? If she stays in here, she's going to decompose, she's already started..."

Lherson nodded. "Let me check something. I'll be right back." He disappeared through the aft hatch, mumbling to himself. A half div later, he returned to the cockpit. "I think we can put her in the aft airlock and bleed it down. That should mummify her body to the point that it keeps him happy, and doesn't contaminate the rest of the shuttle. If we seal her in the soft suit, maybe... I don't know..."

"I think that would work. The question is, will he accept that?"

"If he doesn't, I'll space his ass too!"

"Quiet! Let me go talk to him, okay?"

"Go ahead."

Solly came back a few segs later, "He agreed. He made me promise you, we, will not space her body. I think he's in shock right now. Cedar is sitting with him, holding his hand."

Rolling his eyes, Lherson reached up, "The sooner the better."

"What are you doing?"

"I'm going to drop the grav down so we can move her. I'm not up to trying to maneuver that much weight under one G."

"Let me warn them first, okay?"

"You've got a seg to do it."

Solly left, mumbling under her breath. As the clock ticked down, he dropped the G to .3G and swam out of the cockpit. Ton'Skel was crooning something in their language, as Cedar cried quietly in her seat. They waited until he finished whatever he was doing, and gently closed her back into the soft suit, sealing the tabs and gently picking her body up. Ton'Skel cradled her head, tears rolling down his face, as he continued crooning softly. They moved the body back to the aft airlock, and gently placed it on the floor, curled up and facing away from the inner lock.

They had to pull Ton'Skel back into the shuttle, and Lherson slowly closed the inner hatch. Once it was closed and locked, Ton'Skel pasted his nose to the viewport, and watched as Lherson slowly lowered the pressure to a couple of pounds, explaining to Ton'Skel that he would leave pressure on the airlock to prevent either door being opened.

Lherson went back to the cockpit and cranked the inertial compensation back up to 1G, then turned to Solly, "I'm going to run one air cycle for the emergency scrubbers to get any particulate that may be in the shuttle. It'll take about a half div, if you want to warn them. Then I'm going to climb in the fresher and try to get myself clean."

She nodded and left without saying a word.

Missed Me

Back on Endine, things are happening…

McDougal bitched to himself, *Bad enough I get left behind on a colony world, but insult to injury has me on a Det with the local militia. I'm getting behind on the booze making, can't do it out here, light years away. And these guys don't break shit, so I'm bored… And now we're locked down because two of them got murdered.*

As he stepped out of the Hab, he habitually jumped down the three steps, and survived the needle gun shot that was supposed to take him in the chest. He was on the ground, crouching behind the barrier before his brain caught up with what had just happened, *What the fuck? These turds just tried to kill my ass! Sonics may stop them from physically getting in, but that don't stop anything else from getting in…*

McDougal scrambled around the corner of the Hab, jumped through the door of the maintenance module, and leaned against the wall, absently brushing the dirt from the front of his shipsuit.

"Hey, anybody see who shot at me?" He asked over his wrist comp.

"What?"

"Somebody just tried to kill me, Rai! Didn't you get that on surveillance?"

"You didn't jump and fall?"

"Nooo, I think it was a needle gun."

"Standby… Okay, yeah we missed that one. We were watching a disturbance down by the feeder. Might have been a decoy."

Oh good, now they're using decoys… I'm gonna fix that shit… Damn "So?"

"Yeah, we got video, Senior. We're putting it out, he'll be on the arrest list in a few minutes."

"So, what good does that do us?"

"Gonna put a warning out. You're supposed to check surroundings before you open the Hab or any other external door, you know that."

"Yeah, yeah. I hear you."

McDougal powered up his maintenance system, pulled up the latest armored system diagrams and started drilling down, *I know these fuckers have a repulsor module. Where is it? And how big? Ah, there you are you… Damn, that thing isn't little! Hmmm, specs…*

He pulled up the sonic fence specs on another screen, started comparing ranges and dug deeper into the repulsor module, *If I back that range requirement down to… Match the sonics placement. Overbuilt to hell and gone. If I reduce that by a factor of… Three? Four, no, five.*

That reminded him that he was going to work on an embedded code for the wrist comp that would allow the militia and GalPat to pass through the sonic fence by setting the mid-point to zero dB at six feet on approach and run it back up when the wrist comp was six feet past. *Lemme see, 3 miles an div, that's… 4.4 fps, I want 12 feet, so... three second off pulse, mid-point between any two legs. That'll also take care of the requirement to go exactly between the two designated legs, controlled by security, which should reduce the threat to us. And even better, I won't have to walk all the way around the damn module when I need to get to the RCA.*

Pulling himself away from that, he got back on designing a repulsor module that was only twenty pounds and a little over a foot in diameter. In order to solve the angularity issues, he decided to mold in two feet that aligned to the flat plate angle, and orthogonal to the gravity plane, which meant it *should* effectively brace itself against the planet itself. In addition to the feet, he decided to color the mold a dark gray on the external face, and white on the internal face, *Even a GalPat troop can't screw this one up! Maybe I should have directions, maybe something like front toward enemy... Didn't they do something like that back in ancient history?*

He occupied himself with revising the programming for the sonics while he waited for the fabber to spit out the module he'd designed. *Now, where can I test this? Sure as hell ain't going out there to do it. Wait a minute, I've got a sim here...*

McDougal set up the simulator to duplicate a section of sonic fence to specification in quarter scale. Inserting the programming into his wrist comp, he walked up to the beam, watched it cut off, and restart four seconds later. When he moved off center, to either side, he felt the tingle of the fence, which meant he'd gotten it right.

"Hey, Senior."

The call interrupted McDougal and he growled as he came up from the maintenance documents, "What?"

"Senior, Master Chief Magar over at Feeder One. Did you file an incident report on that attempt on you this morning?"

"Uh, no? Didn't know I was supposed to."

"Ah, that explains why I have this uncorrelated report from Chief Rai on my datacomp. I'm pushing the report form to you. Please get it back in thirty. I have to brief the Captain at sixteen on status."

"Uh, I'm in the middle of…"

"In thirty, Senior."

"Yes, Master Chief." McDougal glanced at his desk comp to see a flashing red icon in the middle of the screen, sighed, and reached for it, punching the icon as he did so.

Mumbling to himself, he wrote up what he remembered, tagged the security video camera and timeframe, re-read it twice, and submitted it. *Thought security was supposed to take care of that shit…*

***

"So, that's all I've got, Captain Fargo, one probe at Feeder Four around zero five, and the attempt on Senior Sergeant McDougal at Feeder Three at zero eight. Perp was identified, arrest warrant issued, and he was taken into custody at eleven." A picture flashed up in the holo, "Fedorice, Maurice. Age is thirty-six. Identified as anti-tech member. Works as a baker in an organic bakery in Center City. He's not talking."

Fargo growled, "What is it with these fuckers and needle guns?" Shaking his head, he asked more civilly, "Any idea why he was all the way out in Kwamaine? Also, any change in the frequency of attempts, Master Chief?"

Master Chief Magar shrugged. "They're about the same, across the board. This is only the second attempt on one of the troops, and both of those have occurred at Feeder Three. I think that's because that site is the most spread out. Remember, we couldn't nestle the Hab and maintenance modules right at the Feeder because of the terrain. That's why we put McDougal and the big module out there. It's also the only one where the shuttle can actually land inside the perimeter."

"Recommendations?"

"Double up security. Put an additional three-sixty view system up there, put two more people on watch. I know that is gonna impact their quality, but we were planning on rotating teams around anyway, just to keep them fresh and alert."

"Do we move the big module and McDougal?"

Master Chief grinned, "I wouldn't. He's out of everybody's hair out there. And frankly, he's pretty clueless when he went to town. His situational awareness sucks. Besides, if we move him, it'd have to be someplace else big enough to take the shuttle."

Fargo leaned back and groaned, "You do have a point. Tip of the spear, he's not. Okay, tomorrow we'll do a few bounces with response teams. I want to make sure we do one at Feeder Three, fangs showing. Maybe that will slow them down a bit."

The holo dinged three times, indicating an override, and a harried GalPat Lieutenant popped up, "Captain Fargo?"

"Go ahead."

"Sir, that man arrested for the attempted murder at Feeder Three just suicided. Some kind of pill. We've notified the locals."

Fargo slumped, "Suicided? Really? How did he manage…? Oh, never mind. Duly noted, thank you."

Fargo and the master chief exchanged looks over the vid, "This isn't good. They're escalating."

Fargo nodded. "That's what I was thinking. Put an alert out to everybody."

***

McDougal popped the first module out of the fabber, checked the metals levels and added another fifty pounds of plasteel pellets, making a note to order spare materials. He idly wondered if he could snag some run time on the big fabber GalPat had in Center City, but decided to wait until he had two units to see if his idea actually worked.

He glanced up and was surprised to see it was seventeen already, and he got up slowly, stretched and set the prototype repulsor on the bench. Deciding he was done for the day, he quickly calculated the capacity of the fabber, added two more bars of metal, and programmed for two more modules, figuring it would take most of the night for them to run. He hit start, then checked the perimeter that he could see before opening the door, quickly closing it, and scampering into the Hab module.

He headed to the autochef, fed in his order and turned to the little dining table, "Hey, Rai. Anything on that guy from this morning?"

Rai grimaced. "Dammit Mac, don't you *ever* check your datacomp? They caught him, questioned him, and he suicided. It was on the alert broadcast an div ago."

"Oh. Uh, I… I was busy."

"Well, thanks to you, we're going to be doubling up. The captain is bringing another three-sixty head and monitoring station up here tomorrow. That means we're going to have four on watch at a time. Which means we're basically on port and report. You're not qualified to stand watch are you?"

McDougal replied, "No, I'm only certified for maintenance. But I am duty maintenance for the entire Det, not just you guys. And I'm the *only* maintainer out here."

Rai grumbled but subsided, when McDougal pointed that out, "Okay, okay. We're going to be rotated in a week anyway, so maybe we'll rotate home before we have to come back up here."

McDougal gave him a hands up gesture, "Sorry. It's not like I did it on purpose."

The autochef dinged, then spit out McDougal's dinner. He grabbed it, flopped down at the other table, and ate as quickly as he could. He dumped the plate into the autochef's return slot, and made for his coffin. Sliding in, he racked the desk comp, checked the system alerts were all clear, and racked out.

***

McDougal made it to the maintenance module without getting shot at, which was, in his mind, a good

JL Curtis / Rimworld- Militia Up / 191

thing. Two more units sat on the out tray of the fabber, and he sat them on the bench beside the original one. Running a check on the fabber, he grimaced, *Dammit, out of metal. And I'm down to three barrels of plasteel. Maybe I can get some on the shuttle today, if I talk nice to supply...* Flipping through the forms on his desk comp, he found the supply request and plugged in enough metal bars and plasteel barrels to do at least six more units.

Once that was done, he rooted around in the parts bin, finally found the right cable and connected the mini-repulsor to the maintenance system. He gingerly applied power, and sighed with relief when the unit powered up without arcing or sparking.

Flipping back to the systems diagrams, he cobbled together a BIT test for the module, made sure it was facing away from him, and hit start. Thirty seconds later, it completed, and from all appearances met spec as he had modified it.

He duplicated the testing on the other two units, and only had to replace one molycirc that had a temp fluctuation issue that worried him. That one passed on retest, and he dug around for more cable. Finding one two hundred foot length, he called Chief Rai on his wrist comp.

"Rai, Senior here. I need to run a quick test on a piece of hardware outside the module. Is the area clear where I can set up two units two hundred feet apart?"

"Standby."

Mac drummed his fingers nervously, until finally Rai came back, "Yeah, quiet as a mouse out there today. Not even the usual protesters by the gate."

"Okay, thanks. I'll be out for about fifteen." He picked up one unit, connected it to the cable, and carried it out toward the end of the compound until he ran out of cable. Hustling back, he connected the second unit to the other end, made sure the cable was taut, and plugged a second cable into that unit. Running it back in the module, he plugged it into the maintenance station. He started to power up the minis, but stopped, went to the door and looked out, confirming the white side faced him. Satisfied, he powered the units up, ran the BIT again, then hit activate for thirty seconds. There was a little instability for about ten seconds, but everything looked like it smoothed out.

He stuck his head back out the door, and was surprised to find the unit closest to the door buried about three inches in the ground. *Huh, wonder what… Oh wait, if it braces, it might try to balance the forces across all the modules.* Trotting out to the other module, it was sitting on rock, but there was a little indentation, so maybe his idea was right.

He powered the modules back up, stepped out of the door, and picked up a handful of the gravel that was everywhere. Flipping it at the imaginary line between the two units, he was gratified to see it cross that line and fall to the ground. Stepping back inside, he fiddled with the programming, truncating the outside halves of the modules, and only running full power between the two. He walked back out, picked up some more gravel and flipped it, with the same result. Walking well around where he thought the edge of the field was, he got on the gray side, picked up more gravel and flipped it at the line. It seemed to stop in mid-air and bounce to the ground. Picking up a bigger rock, he threw it at the line, it did the same thing, only bouncing back a bit further.

His wrist comp beeped, and he glanced down at it, SHUTTLE INBOUND. ETA 6 MIN. "Shit, gotta shut this down," McDougal grumbled to himself. He ran quickly back to the module, checked that the power feeds were still good, and powered the system down to standby.

***

Fargo looked over the Feeder Three site, mentally cataloging the issues, as he walked toward the perimeter. He saw a cable running to a strange gray and white object partially buried with another cable running from it to what looked like another one some distance away. Turning, he followed the cable with his eyes, surprised to see it terminating at the maintenance module. *What the hell? What is this…?* He walked over to the module, opened the door and found McDougal deep in a maintenance screen, "Mac?"

McDougal looked up, then popped to attention, "Sorry, sir. Didn't hear you come in."

"What's the gray and white ball that's half buried out there?"

"Um, err… Something I'm trying out, sir."

Fargo made a come on motion with his hand, "And?"

"Well, we had an attack out here, and… Well, I, uh… I kinda built a little repulsor module test bed."

"A what?"

McDougal got, "Lemme show you, sir." He stuck his head out the door, confirmed there wasn't anyone near the two units, and powered them back up to full power. He walked out, Fargo following, picked up some gravel, and said, "See, from this side, it's non-functional, err… It doesn't stop anything." He flipped the gravel over the line, and it fell to the ground on the other side. Walking around the module, he picked up more gravel and threw it at the line, where it bounced and hit the ground, "This side, it stops things from coming in."

Looking around, he found a bigger rock, maybe ten to fifteen pounds, and heaved it at the line. It bounced too, landing about three feet from the line. Fargo cocked his head. "You did this, Mac?"

"Yes, sir. I, um… I downsized a repulsor module from the armor, and…"

McDougal went down the nearrat hole into schematics, leaving Fargo shaking his head, until he interrupted, "Mac, I think this has some potential…"

"You do, sir?"

"At least for here, Mac. How many of these things would you need to cover the perimeter for each site?"

"Uh, standby one…" Turning to his datacomp, he quickly ran a set of calculations, "Um… Twenty-one. I can piggy back sonics modules…"

Fargo held up his hand, "No, we've already got those in place. I'll hit GalPat for, what nineteen more modules? Can you send the data to their fabber?"

McDougal nodded quickly, "Yes, sir. Got it right here." He typed something into the datacomp and continued, "It's on queue for their fabber now. Just waiting for command approval."

Hunting

Fargo had gotten a rush order for the fabber at the Palace after Planet Security caught a protester with needle gun at Feeder One, who admitted under questioning, he was supposed to shoot the sonics and see if they failed. Four days later, Boykin picked up McDougal along with his gear, and the newly manufactured repulsor modules. They went to each site with Mac modifying the sonics to allow them to enter and exit between two units, and emplacing the repulsors. They checked them with rocks, and he tuned each one to ensure they were high enough to prevent anyone shooting down into the sites from the nearest rooftops. All of the troops wanted to know what was happening with the search for the killer, but Fargo couldn't give them any more details than what he'd passed earlier. *Every* Ghorka was less than happy, and there was a lot of under the breath grumbling, but nothing he could hear well enough to call anyone out on. He reiterated that both the GalPat Det and Planet Security were poring through databases to try to get a match, but without success.

Jiri called him to the side at Feeder Four, "Ekavir, I'm not sure how much longer I can keep the guys from going hunting on their own. They're pretty sure they can *shake* some answers out of the people out here."

He sighed, "Do the best you can. If somebody goes out, at least give me a heads up, that way if the shit hits the impeller, I can try to save their dumb asses."

"Will do. But you know as well as I do the geeks have already hacked the local systems and are digging through them on their own."

"I'm hoping to hear back from Captain Jace. I sent it up to him too. Maybe Liz can pull something out. She's an intel type.

"Let's hope so. Where are you headed next?"

"Back to the Palace. I've got a meeting with the senior TBT rep. He's offered to give us back door access to their systems. Problem is, I don't have anyone that can actually execute on that."

"What about GalPat?"

Fargo looked at him, "Would *you* give them access?"

Jiri wouldn't meet his eyes for a second, "No, I guess not. I…"

"I'm going to see if I can get Liz hooked in. Maybe…" He glanced over to see Boykin signaling him, "Looks like we're ready. Check in at seventeen like normal. As soon as I have something, I'll get it out."

Jiri nodded as he turned away and headed for the shuttle's ramp.

***

Fargo stared at the emails on his datacomp and snarled, "This isn't going to end well." Jace had sent them encrypted to his personal account rather that his official account and Fargo knew if these had gotten in the system, there would have been hell to pay.

The first said that when he searched the world's database, it finally popped out a 96% correlation with one Smallwell, Eric a div ago. All of the other correlations were less than 40%, and most were even lower. Jace had started a worm running in Endine's TBT system, looking for any mail, vid, audio, or stills from any system on the planet. He also ran a check on all of the Ferret uploads from Nicole, and found three audio correlations over 65 days of data, and also found vid correlations from the Canyon feeder site's data. That was enough for Jace to decide to act.

His email said he had carefully crafted an innocuous seeming message that apparently issued from the GalPat detachment's own system, advising the Endine director and chief of security that a 'watch' should be placed for Smallwell, Eric, with a detain if found. He said he had inserted the proper documentation and enhanced photo into the GalPat Det's system, and tagged it to send right at the end of the shift in three divs with a detain and question warrant.

Basically, the second said there were at least two plots ongoing, based on the recordings from the Ferrets Nicole had emplaced. In one that Jace had attached, the person identified as Eric Smallwell had bragged to the other five young people at the table how he'd killed Shanni and Lev from behind, and maybe this would motivate the rebels to get more aggressive. He had also laughed that they would never catch him, and if they did, he'd get off.

The other plot Jace had identified was much more nebulous, and involved a much older group of men, most of whom were first families, according to Jace. Perez, Archer, Smallwell, Hartsorn, and Eggleston were apparently all large landholders and raised the majority of food stuffs and protein animals for the world. Their conversation was elliptic, even in the supposedly private room, and hinted at what could be a takeover of the world, if Jace's analysis was right. Apparently only the Smallwell and Archer families were involved in both plots, which was rather interesting. He'd also said not to pass anything to the GalPat Det, it was being addressed via a *different* avenue, so he must be sending it as a RIG dataset to HQ GalPat. That was scary, if the local GalPat Det wasn't to be trusted.

Fargo shook his head, *I already don't trust them, why am I even thinking that. Are these two plots connected? If so how… if not… Are they at cross purposes? Third generation wanting what? To go back to the pre power days? Do all these landholders have their own power generation? They must, considering the size of their holdings. Nuclear? Probably, since they only date back ninety something years…*

Grayson walked in yawning, "You ready for chow, boss?"

"Is it that time already?"

"Eighteen, straight up. It's some kind of noodle dish. Spicy noodles and mystery meat. The warrant took one sniff and went to the salad." Grayson belched, "Ohhh, gonna pay for that later tonight."

Fargo shook his head. "Okay, here's the latest. All sites quiet at sixteen, three had a few rock throwers earlier, but they bounced. Four had a delegation from

Archer come up and want to apologize for Shanni and Lev's deaths. According to Jiri, they were the business leaders and owners of the restaurant. He was polite, and turned them away without allowing them inside the perimeter. Nothing from one and two."

"So you're saying tonight is either going to be boring as shit or it's going to blow up in my face, right?"

"Not going to jinx you. What will be, will be. Remember, put the forward to my comp on at all balls, when you secure the watch."

"Yowza, boss. Have a good night."

***

Nicole clocked out, chatting with Raymondo and the other staff as they walked to the corner. When they turned away from the others, he finally said, "You were prowling like a damn cat tonight. What's going on?"

Nicole shrugged. "Not sure. I just feel antsy. I've been here almost three months, I think it's about time for me to move on. I do have a real job to go back to and this sabbatical has been almost six months long. The only decent wine on the planet is from Abruzzi, and I'm not sure they could produce enough to make it worth Star Lines time to order it."

Raymondo nodded in the pale light coming off the street lamps, "You've been pushing it pretty hard, and I'm hearing their sales have gone up about twenty percent. Perez isn't happy with that or with you. He talked again tonight to Mr. DuMaurier about firing you. Otto overheard it. But Otto is liking the chance to play with more Italian cooking too. I swear his

heritage must be more Italian than German. I think…
Lombardian?"

Nicole laughed. "One more reason for me to look
at leaving, sooner rather than later. With Otto just like
anyone from Old Earth, each is a polyglot by now,
simply due to travel over the last what, five hundred
years? Much less when you throw in the genie mods."

"Point. But still, the name and physical
characteristics…"

"But who knows what genied DNA went into his
family when? Granted his coloring and build are
Central Euro, not Mediterranean Euro if Italian was
the primary. Maybe there's an Italian grandmother
somewhere in the family tree. That would explain the
Tuscan dishes."

At the next corner, they parted ways and Nicole
hitched her backpack up to a more comfortable
position as she walked slowly toward the Women's
Hotel. A half block later, as she crossed the mouth of
the last alley, she heard movement and started to run,
until she was struck by a charge from a stun pistol. She
slumped to the ground, unconscious, scraping the side
of her face and one arm on the rough surface of the
sidewalk.

A grav car slid to a halt as two men lifted her limp
body into the back of the car, with one retrieving the
backpack and throwing it in on top of her, and
slamming the hatch just before the car sped away.

Two hundred miles above them, the satellite
Captain Jace had placed in Geosync'ed orbit picked up
the voltage change across Nicole's wrist comp and
pinged an alert to the *Hyderabad*. Jace took one look

at the feed, did a pingback for vitals, and waited impatiently for almost a seg before it came back, indicating probable unconsciousness and movement.

Fargo was regretting the noodle choice as he rolled over in the bunk, trying to decide if a trip to the fresher was worth it. Suddenly his wrist comp and data comp both blared an emergency alert tone, yanking him out of his misery. He jerked upright, slapping at the wrist comp even as he reached for the data comp. He read the alert and pinged both Grayson and Boykin with emergency pings, CH SGT LEVESQUE TAKEN RESP TO SHUTTLE FOR IMMED TRACK/RECOVER.

Pulling on his shipsuit, he debated notifying the GalPat Det, but the earlier warning stopped him, *We take care of our own. We'll get her back, one way or another.* Five segs later, he waited impatiently as Boykin ran a fast external preflight and Grayson trotted through the aft hatch, "What the fuck, Captain?"

"Somebody grabbed the chief sergeant. Apparently stunned into unconsciousness. In some type of vehicle, almost to the port."

"Where's the GalPat response team?"

"Haven't notified them, not going to."

Grayson started to say something, then looked at Fargo. He shook his head, then said, "We take care of our own, right?"

He nodded as Boykin pounded up the ramp, "Close the ramp and strap in, auto start sequence is almost complete. As soon as I strap in, we're lifting. Captain, feed me tracking data as soon as you get it."

Grayson scrambled for the ramp controls as Fargo squirted the track data to her comps. They both flopped into seats and had just finished strapping in, when the G load hit as she took them vertical. She unloaded the G at 30,000 feet, causing their stomachs to try to come out of their throats, and Fargo glanced down at his comp, "Shit. Apparently dumped both her comps. Getting an intermittent track on her chip now." He yelled up to the cockpit, "WO, can you follow that track?"

She clicked the PA, "Not directly, but I'm trying to match it to radtrack, IFF, or IR on any skimmers, liteflyers, or shuttles heading in that direction. Three possibles. Stable for now. How do you want to proceed?"

Fargo realized he hadn't thought that far ahead, and slumped, *Shit. We never actually discussed this. What the…* He glanced at Grayson and saw that he had the issue sidearm, and he was startled to realize that somewhere along the way, he'd also put his on. *Pistols against what? What other…* looking at the forward end of the bay, he saw three sets of armor racked. "One of those yours, Grayson?" He pointed at them.

"Yes, sir. The one on the right. Warrant Jiri's is on the left, yours is in the middle."

"I don't know what we're walking into, but pistols aren't going to be my method of choice."

"Didn't the colonel say something about not using armor?"

"He did, but I don't give a shit. I know you've done an airdrop before, feel up to another one?"

Grayson grinned, "A HALO, hell yes!"

"Let me go talk to the warrant. But I'd best start suiting up."

He got up and climbed into the cockpit, noting that Boykin had reconfigured one display to show three different views of sensors. Before he could ask, she glanced at him, "This is probably the vehicle. It's approximating the chip track in both course and speed. The other two diverged a while back. According to the trackline, the only thing out this way is the Perez compound." She pointed to her nav screen, and a blinking object, "Big enough field for a shuttle. At these speeds, be there in fifteen segs. How do you want to play this?"

"I'm thinking airdrop us in armor. From altitude. You could overwatch and take care of anything we don't see."

"Good enough. You'll have to go off the ramp on my call. I'm darkship, emcon anyway, so at forty k, nobody will hear or see me. That would give you... a... call it four seg drop. If they are landing there, I can kick you out while they are on approach, and you'll land about the same time they do."

"Sounds like a plan. I'll go suit up."

"You've got nine segs then I open the hatch."

"Yes, ma'am."

Fargo bolted down the ladder and started stripping off his grays as he hit the deck. He saw Grayson already had his suit kneeled, and was in the process of climbing in, smiling from ear to ear. He finished stripping, threw his clothes, boots, and pistol belt into a storage compartment above the seats. Scrambling across the decking, he knelt his armor, hoping to hell there was an undersuit in it. If not, it was going to be a bit uncomfortable, to put it mildly.

Thankfully, there was an undersuit sitting on the pads. He quickly wiggled into it, then mounted the armor. Sliding in, he hit the hatch closure and felt the momentary disorientation as his mind and the AI connected. "Good evening, Captain."

"Cindy, emergency BIT, combat drop in… four segs."

"Captain that is not recommended."

"Troop in danger, emergency drop required. Connect to ship's AI, please."

"Emergency BIT in progress, connecting."

"You up, Grayson?"

"Yes, sir. Up and BIT good."

"WO?"

"Five by. Skimmer is descending and slowing. IR shows a hot shuttle on the ground at the location. Estimated track for skimmer puts it landing adjacent to the shuttle."

"Shit. What kind of shuttle?"

"Unknown. Depressurizing now, releasing clamps. Ramp in one seg."

"Copy." He slewed his view to see the clamps retract on Grayson's armor. "You're free, Grayson."

"You too, sir. Lead on."

He thought for a second, "Grayson, I want you to go full stealth. I'm going to land no stealth directly in front of them. I'm going to free fall to minimum altitude then full braking."

"Aye, aye, sir. I'll land offset to your right as you face them."

Fargo started slowly shuffling aft as the ramp cracked open and slowly went to full down. He got in position, called up the ship's feed in his HUD, and felt Grayson come up next to him. "In position, WO."

"Go in five, four, three, two, one, now!"

Fargo fell off the ramp, automatically swinging slightly left to make sure he separated from Grayson, visually verified the separation, and concentrated on the landing pad below him, saying a quick prayer, "Deity, keep Nicole safe, and let us rescue her without harm, if it be your will."

Cindy said, "BIT complete. All systems nominal. Stealth?"

"Negative, Cindy. Deploy laser as soon as we land."

"Will do. Full power?"

"Yes."

Two minutes later, Cindy said, "Switching to onboard cameras. Eighteen thousand feet to go. ETA one seg, thirty three."

"WO, you got us?"

"Roger, high cover in place. Medium prob shuttle is Trader. And it's hot. Skimmer ETA one seg."

"Copy. Grayson?"

"Copy."

The seg felt like a div, until the armor finally kicked on the anti-grav, punishing Fargo with six Gs as it rapidly slowed the suit from about 170 miles per div to ten feet per second. He saw Nicole being dragged out of the skimmer by two men, with a small older man following them. He felt the laser deploy, and saw the carat pop on in his HUD as he

concentrated on landing and staying upright. He saw
the men looking up, and he assumed they heard the
armor.

The old man grabbed Nicole around the throat,
pulling something from his pocket, as the other two
pulled weapons from under their jackets. The armor
crashed down, splattering the rock that made up the
landing pad, as he put the laser cursor on the man's
head. He keyed the external speaker. "Release the
woman."

The old man cackled, "You're gonna be in so
much trouble. Armor isn't allowed. Besides, by the
time you can get out of that, I can do anything I want
with her. You move, I kill the puta.

Fargo projected, lightly touching Nicole's mind. It
seemed fuzzy for lack of a better term. *"Nicole, can
you hear me?"*

"I... Ethan? Wha..."

*"You've been stunned, I need you to drop, be a
dead weight."*

"Now? M'kay."

He saw her sag, but the carat never moved from
the man's head as he triggered the laser. The head
exploded and the body and Nicole slumped to the
ground together.

*"Nicole! Nic, answer me, oh Deity, please answer
me."*

"M'cold. And wet. My... head..."

Grayson and Boykin both said, "Shuttle is lifting."

Fargo glanced over, then back at the two men, now
frozen with their hands halfway up, "Drop your
weapons and prone out, *now!*"

They did so, and he said, "Grayson, clear the skimmer."

Grayson walked over, rapped gently, well as gently as one could in armor, on the cockpit, and he heard Grayson order someone out. Another man came out trembling and with a wet spot in his crotch, as he went prone as soon as he was on the ground.

"Cover me, getting out."

Just as he started to pop the hatch, he heard Boykin say calmly, "Shuttle is confirmed Trader. And it's firing on me."

Fargo smiled ferally, "Weapons are free, splash it."

"Rog."

He quickly dismounted, moved the weapons well away from the two men, and rushed to Nicole, gathering her in his arms.

She looked up at him muzzily, "Wha happened? Where?"

"You got stunned and kidnapped. We rescued you."

"M'kay. Don't feel so good. Tired. Thank you later."

Fargo smiled softly, "You're alive, that's what counts. I didn't lose you."

"Not gonna happen."

A boom interrupted him and he looked up to see an explosion and a trail of fire heading toward the horizon. He heard Grayson's PA, "The warrant got the kill. She'll ground in five. Give me a thumbs up if the chief is okay."

Fargo gave him a thumbs up, and sat down, cradling Nicole until Boykin landed.

Inquest

Boykin grounded and came down the ramp in a rush, her bright red hair matted to her head, sweat rolling down her face, and sweat stains showing on her flight suit where the straps had held her in the pilot's seat. "Is she okay?"

Fargo looked up, "Thanks to you, yes."

"The blood?"

"Not hers," he motioned with his head, "His. I took his head with the twelve mil laser."

A Cheshire cat smile crossed her face, "Oh, most excellent!"

"You took out whatever that ship was?"

"Yeah, confirmed Trader shuttle, and it was armed. When I lit it up, it fired on me. ORBCON might be a bit miffed at me right now."

Fargo cocked his head. "Why?"

She grinned, "Well, I *might* have been a tad late IDing myself. I was a little busy for a couple of minutes. Oh, and the cavalry is on the way."

"The cavalry?"

"ORBCON broadcast a grounding order and put out a kidnap in progress alert. GalPat was, shall we say, less than pleased to be the last ones to find out."

They were interrupted by the whine of a grav sled, and a shouted command, "Hey, what the hell are you people doing? You, freeze. Nobody move." A large

Hispanic looking male, running to fat came into the lights of the landing pad, a pulse rifle at his shoulder and finger on the firing stud.

Before Fargo could say anything, Grayson's external speaker said, "You might want to drop that weapon and hit the ground, Sport. Mine's bigger than yours."

The man swung the rifle toward the sound, then gaped as Grayson dropped the stealth on the armor. "On the ground, *now!*"

The rifle clattered to the ground, and the man proned out, mumbling under his breath.

***

Two divs later, the landing pad resembled a circus more than anything else. Both Fargo's and Grayson's armor knelt where they had been left, as GalPat security, planetary security, and assorted cats and dogs milled aimlessly about. Nicole had been lifted out by skimmer to the Palace and was under the care of Dr. Vaughn, in the infirmary. She'd partially recovered, enough to bitch at Fargo for getting blood on her good dress, and that had prompted a laugh and a hug from Boykin. *Women. Never understand them in a million years,* Fargo thought at the time.

The four men that had been subdued had been put in flex restraints, and flown somewhere by planetary security for further questioning, after multiple vids had been taken by the GalPat investigator and security investigator. Finally, Grayson was allowed to put the armor back in the shuttle, and Boykin clamped it in. Fargo was curious, but refrained from asking, figuring it wasn't the time or the place.

Boykin had been questioned, and he saw a data cube come off the shuttle. He guessed that would also include his suit data, since he'd never dropped the link to the ship. She was still smiling a little bit, and he remembered that feeling. *I fought, and I won! I'm alive and my enemy is dead. I know I should mourn them, and maybe later I will, but right now, I'm alive!*

An argument caught his ear, and he turned to see Colonel Zhu in an argument with a heavyset local in a planetary security uniform, "I want his ass. He killed one of the leading members of a founding family. He's not getting away…"

Zhu interrupted, "He prevented a kidnapping. The man, Perez," Zhu said, jabbing a finger at the body still lying on the pad, "Had a gun to her head and you've heard and seen the recording."

"But that could have been faked!"

"Oh bullshit. Those systems are locked down. They *cannot* possibly be faked."

"He killed…"

"Enough! He killed somebody that needed killing. Period. He's GalPat's, not PLANSEC. If I were you, I'd take a hard look at how many *other* bodies might be out here that you don't know about. If, big if, you come up with anything, bring it to the inquest."

A burly sergeant came up, "Sir, we found two boys, tentative ID is Perez sons. They were in the house, and both of them are high as hell on Synth. What do you want us to…"

The Planet Security man said, "Load 'em up. We'll question them in Capital. Make sure they are in separate cells. No law givers, no medical treatment, no one visits. *Totally sequestered.*"

"Yes, sir."

Fargo walked over to where Boykin was looking up at the side of the cockpit, seeing a gouge in the airframe, he whistled, "That was close!"

Boykin bounced on her toes, "Yep! I made the mistake of letting the bastard get a head to head on me. That was one of his first rounds."

"Would that?"

"Would that have killed me, you bet your ass. I saw the flash and jerked right. If I hadn't, I wouldn't be standing here, and Wizard would have been the flamer not him."

"Nice reactions!"

"That's why I'm a shuttle pilot. Did I hear them saying something about other bodies?"

Fargo sighed, "Yeah, the colonel intimated there might be other bodies buried out here."

"Interesting. I was doing a multispectral scan when I was coming in, and there are some awfully regular rectangles in that vineyard over there," she said, pointing to the vineyard behind the pad.

"Did you tell anybody?"

"Not yet. Think I should?"

"I'd tell the colonel, privately, or maybe show him. You can replay, right?"

Boykin waved a hand airily, "Any time. If you're curious, I can show you the shoot down."

He nodded. "That would be interesting, I've never seen an actual one. Is there much to see?"

She laughed. "Hell, I'm not sure. I was a *little* busy about then."

Grayson ambled over, "What a cluster. Idiot wanted to know why I didn't try to save, Perret, Perez, or whatever. Told him it was kinda hard without a functional brain attached. Wanted to know why *I* didn't notify planet security. He didn't get the fact that I work for you and GalPat, not him. Egotistical little…"

Colonel Zhu came striding over, obviously angry. "Mount up, Grayson. I need to talk to these two." Grayson looked at them, and Fargo nodded. When Grayson was on the ramp, he turned on Fargo, "What the fuck were you thinking? Do you know how this is going to be taken?"

Fargo bristled, "Colonel, one of my people was taken. I got her back. Sorry I had to kill him to do it, but she is much more valuable than he was. *We* don't leave people…"

Zhu cut him off, "Fucking *armor*? We'll never hear the end of this. You've irreparably harmed our relationship with the Director."

"I got my troop back. *That* means more than anything else."

Zhu turned to Boykin, "And you… you shot down a shuttle, for Deity sake! What were you thinking? And how did you supposedly *track* an individual with an assault shuttle? That's…"

Boykin smiled at him and said quietly, "Star thirteen alpha, Colonel."

Zhu's expression paled, his jaw dropped, and he literally backed up a step, "Ah, I… Load up. Return to the Palace. You are all restricted to the compound. Boykin, consider yourself grounded until further notice. A team from ORBCON is on the way down to debrief you."

She saluted, "Yes, sir. Oh by the way, Colonel, there are a number of suspicious depressions in the second and third rows of that vineyard over there," pointing to the vineyard behind the pad. "You might want to have a forensic team take a look, you might find something interesting. I'll squirt the picture to you momentarily." Turning to Fargo she said, "Shall we, Captain?"

Fargo nodded and they walked up the ramp together. Fargo stopped and hit the ramp controls, shaking his head in amazement. Grayson was already belted in and appeared to be asleep, head pillowed on his uniform in his lap. He climbed into the cockpit, "What did you mean with that code, WO?"

She met his eyes, "I know what *Hyderabad* really is. And I figured you didn't want to try to explain away how we did that. Plus he doesn't need to know what this baby will actually do. And you never heard that code, understand?"

He took one look at her icy green eyes, and said, "What code? I didn't hear anything."

"Good. Strap in, I need to go pee."

***

A wan Nicole sat in the office, arguing, "Dammit, I need to go back to work. I've got to retrieve…"

"No, you're not going anywhere by yourself. And we're damn sure not walking into that place to retrieve any Ferrets. Send a remote kill to them, and have them self-destruct. Sergeant Mahan will escort you to the Women's Hotel to retrieve your stuff there, and you *will* come straight back here."

"Arghhh. Men! You're all overprotective assholes! I'm not defenseless…"

Fargo tried to take her hand, "Nicole, I don't want to lose you. I need you here to look at the data we're getting. I…"

Fargo projected, "*I love you, dammit. I almost lost you. I don't want to lose you. How much plainer can I make it?*"

She blew out a frustrated breath, shook her head, and finally smiled. "Since you put it that way, I guess…" She got up, walked around the desk and hugged him, finally kissing him gently on the cheek, then whispering, "I love you, too."

Boykin laughed from the door, and they quickly separated, both blushing. "Bout damn time," she said. "Everybody knows you two love each other, so stop trying to hide it."

Fargo leaned back with a sigh, "How did the inquisition with ORBCON go, WO?"

The Cheshire cat grin was back, "Once they understood the impact of what happened, and reviewed the tapes and vid, they were *very* apologetic. They didn't even know that shuttle was in atmosphere, and have no idea where it came from."

"Isn't that special."

She shrugged. "Not my problem. I got good data on it. Now ORBCON is looking all over hell and half of space for its mothership. Oh yeah, Ryerson is gonna be pissed. I blooded Wizard, and he didn't. And she'll go home wearing a zap for the kill."

Nicole asked, "A zap? That's… not something I've heard before."

"It's an outline of the type ship killed, or tank, or whatever. Wizard was brand new when she was dropped at Hunter. This was her first combat. So I'll always be in her logbook with the first kill."

Fargo winced. "And that's important to y'all, isn't it?"

"Well, that and this kill makes me an ace."

"Ace?"

Nicole chimed in, "Five kills, right?"

"Five *airborne* kills. And I just heard in the mess that they'd found sixteen bodies in the vineyard at Perez."

"Damn," Fargo and Nicole said in unison.

"And the asshole that showed up with the rifle? He was the overseer for the entire Perez operation. He's singing like a nearcanary in a mineshaft. The two guards that surrendered to you both had slave chips embedded, and they found kill boxes in the main house and in the overseer's house. Apparently that was how Perez kept control. Oh, and one other thing, GalPat found a drug lab hidden in the winery. Guess what they were making? Give up? Synth."

Fargo whistled, "That's… confiscation, which means they, well, the family, lose all those lands. That's gonna leave a mark."

***

Two days later, Fargo, Boykin, Grayson, and Levesque, all in grays, sat in front of the long green table in straight backed chairs as the members of the inquest filed in. Fargo was surprised to see the Director, Doctor Vaughn, sitting in the witness box. Colonel Zhu, followed by Major Johns, from ORBCON, filed in, followed by a lean old man in a black robe with a fuzz of white hair, and glasses perched on his nose. *Ferman, no Freeman. He's the chief justicer for Endine.* A fat man in the browns of Planet Security followed him, *Meechum. He's head of PLANSEC. Rumor has it he's a toady to the first families.* He projected to Nicole, "*You doing okay?*"

He felt her grumpiness, "*I've got stuff to do. Don't understand why I'm here. I was the victim. I don't remember shit.*"

"*I think they're going to try to get into what you were doing here. Remember, that's…*"

"*I know, I know. I'm Intel.*"

"*Love you.*"

"*Shut up. Time for that later.*" She shook her head minutely, and he withdrew, the ghost of a smile on his face.

Two more people, one man and one woman followed Meechum to the table, neither of whom was known to Fargo. Three more people filed into the witness box, including a youngish svelte girl/woman in ORBCON blacks with senior sergeant insignia gleaming on her collar. The fat PLANSEC man from the landing pad was the last one in, and a recorder took a position at the end of the table.

A woman walked slowly to the table to their left, depositing a number of data cubes on the table as she nodded to the panel. Freeman return her nod, and cleared his throat. "I, Chief Justicer Freeman, call this court of inquest to order. All proceedings will be recorded, and Mr. Oh will provide a separate transcript of all testimonies. This will be a closed, restricted inquest due to a number of… security issues." He cleared his throat again and said, "This inquest is into the death of one Hector Perez, which occurred on thirty-two Septober, twenty-eight twenty-five. Mrs. Park will you please present the facts collected thus far."

He projected a probe and felt Zhu's mind, sensing his quandary about the use of force, frustrations about the hearing, and wondering what he didn't know about what they were doing. His face might be inscrutable, but his mind wasn't. Mrs. Park stood and started with a bare recounting of the facts from the time Nicole left the restaurant, enhanced by vid captures, including one of Nicole being stunned and carried to the vehicle. She pointed out that the vehicle was owned by Perez LTD, and the fact that not only Nicole's DNA, but her wrist and data comps were found in the vehicle at the port. This was followed by a second vid from the port, showing a limp Nicole being loaded into the skimmer by the two men, closely followed by Hector Perez. Fargo glanced at Nicole, who was staring rigidly at the screen, apparently not paying any attention to Mrs. Park.

She skipped forward to the vid from Grayson's armor, showing the relative positions of all parties, and Nicole slumping as Fargo had fired the shoulder mounted laser over her to explode Perez's head. Fargo was amazed he hadn't singed Nicole, seeing the shot from a different angle.

Next, she showed the vid from Fargo's armor, without commentary. Nicole glanced at Fargo and then back at the screen, and he saw her hands tighten in her lap. *I guess she just realized how close I came to killing her too. Hindsight, I shouldn't have taken that shot. But thankfully it worked. There's really nothing weapons wise on the armor that is… suitable for something like that. Should we have…No! Shoulda, woulda, coulda doesn't apply. We did what we could, with what we had.*

Mrs. Park jerked him out of his reverie, "Ms. Levesque, remembering that you are under oath, were you aware of any, or did you have any disagreements with Mr. Perez?"

Nicole answered, "I know he did not like the fact that I did not recommend his wines for many meals at the restaurant. But that was a quality issue, rather than a personal one. I do know, from Raymondo, the maître, that he did not want me serving any table of his or his parties at any time."

"Do you remember at any time being aware you were being followed?"

"No, I do not."

"Did you hit your emergency alert on your comp?"

"I do not remember doing so."

"What is the first thing you remember?"

"Being cold, and wet. And lying on the ground, smelling long pig. And that's hazy."

"So you have no memories of your abduction, or your rescue?"

"No, ma'am."

"Thank you."

Mrs. Park stepped behind the table again, "I call Senior Sergeant Ramirez from Orbital Control. Senior Sergeant, would you take the witness chair, please?"

The sergeant took her place in the witness chair, hands crossed demurely in her lap, "Senior, would you please tell us what ORBCON has determined from their investigation?"

"Yes, ma'am. My cube is number twelve."

She inserted it, and the senior sergeant ran down the results, including the facts that the skimmer was owned by Perez, had never activated their beacon as required after takeoff, no flight plan filed, and contained shackles under the aft seats. When the next visuals came up, Fargo sucked in his breath. It was from Boykin's shuttle, and he was amazed to watch the maneuvering Boykin was doing, hearing the grunting, panting, and cursing as she fought the Trader shuttle. Ramirez' cold recitation of the facts made it even more stunning, and when the Trader's back track came up, he watched Colonel Zhu closely. Zhu was frowning as the senior sergeant admitted they had no idea where the actual mothership was or had been. *He's not liking that. But he's not about to stick his nose in.* They had no incoming track, and only bits and pieces of planetary tracking, including a possible stop at Hartshorn's ranch. What caught his attention was the fact that DNA had been recovered from the crash site and been matched to both Derrick Hartshorn and Aldridge Archer, two Firsties who were compatriots of Hector Perez. *Zhu didn't visibly react, but damn, that*

sent his mind into a tailspin, wondering what other
data he didn't have. He's really pissed at the previous
Det commander now.

Mrs. Park finally asked, "Do you have any issues
with the fact that Warrant Boykin did not properly
notify you of the situation in a timely fashion, nor did
she activate her beacon until after she engaged in
combat with the alleged Trader shuttle?"

"No, ma'am. GalPat protocols allow covert
maneuvering by their assets depending on the
situation. She obviously followed the tenants of all
pilots, in that she aviated, navigated, *then* when she
could, she communicated. We, ORBCON, do not find
her in non-compliance."

"Thank you, you may step down."

Mrs. Park looked at her list, "Mr. Reynold, senior
investigator for PLANSEC, would you take the
witness chair, please?"

The heavyset man stepped up and sat, saying,
"Cubes six and seven."

She nodded and inserted them, and he walked
through the investigation from the time Nicole had left
the restaurant, including being followed in the vehicle
by Hector Perez. He jumped forward to the killing of
Perez, stating, "While we believe there were less lethal
options available, a question of timeliness in acting
makes those moot. While we believe we should have
been notified to effect the rescue, PLANSEC does find
this to be a line of duty shoot, complying with all
applicable Endine directives."

She nodded and asked, "What was the result of the
search of the vineyard directed by GalPat?"

He hung his head, saying quietly, "Cube six please. There were sixteen bodies, or parts of bodies recovered from the vineyard. Fifteen of those were missing females going back thirty years. Additionally, we discovered another one hundred sixty-four bodies dumped in pits near the river. These all appeared to be indentured. Some… were shot. All had slave chips, and many of them were apparently killed by the chips. There were male, female, and children found."

"And what is the disposition of the four men who were arrested on site?"

He looked up at her with a pleading expression, "Is it necessary to get into that here? Now?"

"Yes, it is relevant."

"One, the pilot, was killed in lockup. The two guards and supervisor were found dead, apparently by injection of Synth. Possibly murder/suicide."

"Thank you, you are dismissed. Director? If you would, please?"

Director Vaughn took the chair, "I don't have any cubes. All data is entered in the autopsy record, and Ms. Levesque's medical file.

"Two questions, Director. Was Ms. Levesque physically harmed?"

"Other than being stunned, no. She was not molested in any way. Other than bruising, apparently from hitting the ground, scratches from where her wrist comp was torn off, and some burned hair, she needed no treatment."

"What was the cause of death for Hector Perez?"

"Stupidity?" Which elicited an unexpected laugh from everyone. "Hector Perez died of excessive trauma to the head, to the point that it was effectively vaporized courtesy of a twelve millimeter laser from a range of less than thirty feet. His BAC was point zero nine, and had traces of stims in his bloodstream. Since there was no head left, I could not do any review of brain tissue for lesions or anything else. The remainder of the body was non-remarkable for a ninety-eight year old longevity recipient."

"Thank you. You are dismissed." She turned to Chief Justicer Freeman, "Sir, this completes the presentation. We find that Hector Perez was legally taken under fire in commission of a criminal act, within the continuum of force for law enforcement, and no charges or penalties accrue to Captain Fargo, Senior Sergeant Grayson, or Chief Sergeant Levesque. For Warrant Officer Five Boykin, we find she acted within all applicable GalPat regulations and MOA with Endine in her use of force to protect GalPat assets."

Freeman hit a button and a privacy shield rose, blocking both the view and sound, and incidentally, kicking Fargo out of Zhu's mind. *Huh, didn't know that was possible. Strange that a privacy shield would block thoughts, but I don't know enough... Oh well, I know which way he's going to vote.*

Chief Justicer Freeman dropped the privacy screen a couple of segs later, looked up and down the table, "Do I hear any objections? Hearing none, I concur with the results, and close and seal this case. Let no one go forth and speak of this under penalty of law, pursuant to Endine Charter and Law Giving section thirteen, paragraph six, sub paragraph nine alpha. Case closed. You are dismissed."

Colonel Zhu motioned Fargo and Boykin over to the end of the table, "You two are cleared, but I don't want to see a repeat of this behavior, period. You're off restriction, Boykin, you can go back on flight duties. One more action like this out of either of you, and you'll regret it. Do I make myself clear?"

They answered in unison, "Yes, sir."

"Get out of my sight." Zhu turned and stalked out of the room.

Attack

Fargo's comps pinged simultaneously, and he rolled over with a groan. Peering blearily at his wrist comp, he saw it was zero four. He opened the alert and bolted upright, "Dammit, dammit, dammit, now what?" The alert simply said- FEEDER THREE UNUSUAL ACTIONS OCCURRING. NEED BASE CONTACT.

Fargo quickly pulled on his grays and trotted down the hallway to the office, carrying his boots in his hand. Opening the door, he flopped down, scrubbing his face, "Feeder Three, Base."

Daman answered immediately, "Base, Three. Got something strange going on. Got a crowd, estimated at one hundred and growing forming in the village, but not coming out. We're watching that window that we ID'ed as an overwatch and are seeing multiple people and movement."

Fargo shook his head as he slipped on his boots, *What the hell? We've seen nothing to indicate… Wait, what did the Ferret from the restaurant…* "Uh, rog, standby Three. One, Two, Four, are you seeing anything?" Fargo booted the data comp scrolling back through the downloads, looking for the message from Jace about the recordings, and finally found it. POSSIBLE SECONDARY OR TERTIARY ATTACK PROFILE IS TO HIT FEEDER SITES,

THE TWO PLOTS MAY NOT BE CONNECTED
OR AWARE OF THE OTHER PLOT. YOUNGER
SMALLWELL, ET AL POSSIBLE LEADERS OF,
OR COORDINATORS OF ACTIONS ALL THIRD
GENERATION ATTACKS BASED ON IDS.
OPTIONS INCLUDE ATTACKS AND ATTEMPTS
TO OVERRUN SITES, GETTING MULTIPLE
RIOTERS SHOT TO PROVIDE PRESSURE
AGAINST LEADERSHIP TO REMOVE
SECURITY. APPARENT GOAL TO REMOVE
POWER TO CITIES, FACILITIES NOT
OWNED/RUN BY FIRST FAMILIES. POSS GOAL
OVERTHROW OF COMPANY/REVERSION TO
FIRST FAMILY CONTROL OF PLANET. GOALS
BASED ON RESEARCH OF PREVIOUS
PLANETARY TAKEOVER ATTEMPTS YEARS
2250-CURRENT.

"Feeder One has about ten, maybe fifteen
protesters, Base. Base, Feeder Two, maybe a few.
They may be in that little canyon. Feeder Four, zip
nada Base." Jiri came on, "Base, Four. None here. You
want us to mount a QRF?"

"Negative. I think I'll alert GalPat, they have a
QRF platoon that's supposedly on call."

"Captain, you… We're here if you need us. Just
saying."

"Copied all, WO. I am going to put Boykin on
standby."

Fargo sent a ping to both Boykin and Grayson,
asking them to report ASAP, to the office, then ran
down the hall to the mess, quickly punching up a
coffee and a quick breakfast. Juggling them he made it

back to the office before either of them showed up. He keyed the radio, "Feeder Three, can you push your video feed, please?"

Daman came on, "Pushing. I have twenty segs to sunrise. What do you want us to do?"

Fargo leaned back in the chair as Boykin and Grayson came into the office. They both looked at him curiously, as he pointed to the wall vid. He heard Boykin say softly, "Damn. That's… interesting." Grayson just whistled.

He keyed the mic, "Uh, Feeder Three, nothing for now. Sonics and the maintenance guy, Mac's repulsors are running, right?"

"They are. I'm seeing a few at a time joining the crowd, but they're not approaching, yet."

"Copy, as soon as GalPat comes in, I'll advise them and get the QRF on standby. All sites keep an eye on your perimeters, please." He spun the chair around, "What say you, WO?"

Looks like somebody is ramping up the…"

Nicole came in, running her fingers through her hair, "What's going on?"

Fargo shrugged. "Not real sure. Feeders One, Two, and Three have protesters congregating. Feeder Three has the most, estimated one hundred plus." He pointed up to the wall vid, "That window in the top center display is apparently where they have an overwatch on us. They've seen movement up there already."

He saw both Nicole and Boykin looking at the window speculatively, and wasn't sure he liked either expression. Boykin broke the silence, "I can slip a round through that window no problem."

Grayson grinned and nodded until Nicole said meditatively, "Any audio? Or is it too far away?"

"Too far away. Crap… Should have had them fly a Ferret over there."

Nicole smiled sweetly at him, "Now you think about that. That's why you have intel support, to think about those *little* things like that."

Grayson laughed. "She got you on that one, boss!"

Fargo glared at him, "You can get something to eat. I think we have time before anything blows up in our faces."

Grayson rubbed his belly, "Food good. Ladies?"

Boykin just shook her head. "Men." Nicole nodded and they walked out of the office, whispering to each other.

***

Colonel Zhu wasn't happy to see Fargo, "Now what?"

"Colonel, I've forwarded you the vids from this morning. There is a large crowd at Kwamaine, and smaller crowds at Capital and Archer City. We think this might be a precursor to a large scale demonstration and attempt to overrun the feeder site at Kwamaine."

"Oh, come on, Fargo. Really? A bunch of protesters are going to overrun your site? You've got sonics. They can't get through that, and we both know it."

"Nothing has happened yet, but I wanted to advise you, and make sure the QRF was available if…"

"QRF is drilling in desert rescue today. They won't be available until after fifteen. These idiots haven't done anything up to now, why do you think they will do something today?"

"We've never seen this level…"

Zhu cut him off, "Come talk to me if they actually move on your sites, otherwise don't bother me."

Fargo stood stiffly, "Yes, sir." He did a precise about face and left the office, detouring by the mess to get a bulb and calm down before he got back to their small office.

A couple of segs later, he walked back into their small office and Nicole looked up. "Didn't go well, did it?"

He took a sip from the bulb, "What gave you that idea?"

"Other than the fact that you look like you have a ramrod up your butt, nothing… Sir."

"The good colonel thinks we're *overreacting*, and oh by the way, the QRF isn't available until fifteen."

Boykin glanced up from her data comp, "You want to go hang out, Captain? If I put a full bag on, I can loiter for about seven divs."

Grayson got up, "I'll go get chow. Box lunches okay?"

Nicole looked up at him, "You're going, aren't you? Which means *I* get stuck here, right?"

Fargo almost reached for her shoulder, but instead projected, "*I need to be out there, able to protect the troops. You can do more here, spotting things I'd never see.*" He glanced at Boykin and Grayson, "We need…"

Nicole hung her head, "I know, I know. Intel weenies get stuck behind the scenes," she said bitterly.

"I didn't mean it that…"

"I know you didn't, but dammit, I'm not a damn breakable doll. I've done field work, hell I've been in combat before! I…"

"Calm down, dammit! If this goes sideways, you don't have any armor here, and I'm not going to risk you on this damn dirtball!"

Boykin interrupted his thoughts, "Um, do we need to leave? I'm gonna go preflight the Wizard. I'll be ready to lift in thirty. Come on, Senior." Grayson got up and followed her out without a word.

Fargo shook his head in frustration as Nicole turned away and picked up the mic, "All sites, this is Chief Sergeant Levesque, I have the radios here. The *captain* will be launching in thirty segs to provide top cover and a reaction force. Please forward all intel feeds to me here, starting now. I will select what will be forwarded to GalPat." She looked up at Fargo, made a shooing motion, and said, "You might want to hit the fresher before you mount up."

Fargo threw up his hands, and stalked out, muttering to himself.

***

Two divs later, Boykin once more circled over Feeder Two scanning with the multispectral systems and looked over a Fargo, "Nothing changed. Still about sixty protesters, but they're staying back. Can you grab me a box lunch when you go down to the hold?"

Fargo nodded. "Yes, ma'am. I can take the hint." He got up, stretched, and clambered out of the cockpit. Glancing over, he saw that Grayson was sprawled bonelessly across three seats, apparently sound asleep. *Don't know how the hell he does it. I tried that, I'd be hurting for a week.* He hit the rudimentary fresher on the shuttle, replugged his catheter and readjusted his undersuit, *PITA, I hate those damn things, but if the crap starts, the last thing I need is to forget that. I don't feel like...*

The ship suddenly swung hard, bouncing him off the bulkhead and spilling Grayson onto the deck, "Captain, you might want to get back up here," Boykin called over the IC.

He grabbed the box lunch, scrambled up into the cockpit, handed it to her, and asked, "What happened?"

"Apparently, they're crowding the sonics at Feeder Three, pushed a bunch of what look like children to the front. We're thirty segs out unless I go ballistic, that will cut ten segs off that time." She reconfigured the copilot's screen, "This is what the chief is pushing right now. She's advised GalPat, but they can't get there in under two divs."

"Shit… It's going down." Fargo looked at the screen and winced. "I hope they're not pushing those kids into the sonics. If that happens, it could really go rodeo." He looked over at Boykin, "Push it up, WO, push it up. I'm going to go gear up."

Boykin nodded as she started talking to ORBCON and pointing the nose of the shuttle at the sky. Fargo slid down the ladder to the bay, and glanced around. He didn't see Grayson, then saw the fresher light was on. *Smart, always take a piss when you can, especially before gearing up.* He climbed up on his armor and reached in, hitting the power button. He felt the frisson of the AI connecting and said, "Cindy, BIT check. Twenty segs to launch."

He 'heard' her snippy response in his mind, "At least this time I actually have the segs needed to do a real BIT check. Commencing."

"I'll be back." He hopped down as Grayson stepped out of the fresher, now wearing his grays. "What are you doing?"

Grayson cocked his head. "Well, Captain, if you're gonna need a medic, it'll be kinda hard for me to do medic things in a suit."

"But this could be a hot landing."

"That's why I get the big bucks. I'll take my chances. Saving lives is what I do, Captain. Can't do that… Besides, you've got other suits out there, right?"

Fargo thought for a second or two, "I guess that makes sense. At least put on soft armor. And a helmet."

"I'm getting there. Had to piss first. I'll be ready. And I'm not going charging out when we hit the dirt. I'll evaluate before I stick my pretty little pink butt out the hatch, trust me." Grayson turned away and started pulling his soft armor out, along with his pistol.

Technically, he's not supposed to carry a pistol, but I'm not going to argue with him. And he does have a point, Fargo thought. Mounting up, he wiggled into his armor, hooked up his tubes, and closed it up, "Connect to ship please, Cindy."

"Connecting."

He brought up the feed from Nicole and watched it as he thought through options. The vid feed seemed to be static, and he noted the troops appeared to be under cover, with one suit standing between the maintenance van and the Hab, in full stealth. Blinking on the suit ID, it came up as Paras, and he nodded to himself as he tongued the comms over and said, "Feeder Three, Fargo. How copy?"

He heard Daman, "Got you five by. Sit is static. Headcount is now two thirty-six on two fronts. Widest front oriented on the west side, one sixty there, the remainder to the north, they're using projectors shouting slogans, but nothing overt at this time. Don't see any more protesters trickling out."

Fargo switched to the shuttle's map screen and replied, "Looks like we're, give or take, twelve segs out, coming in ballistic."

"Rog. Your spot is clear."

"Where is the other suit?"

"Umesh is geared up, in the cargo door, waiting to see where he's needed."

"Rog, I'm suited up, Senior Grayson is not. He says he can't do medic from a suit."

"Concur… Oh shit!"

Fargo watched as people started dropping, like wheat being mowed down in a field, "What? Who fired on them," he yelled.

Daman said, "It wasn't us. It wasn't us! And there are people down north of the site too!"

Fargo watch as people stampeded away from the site, barely hearing Boykin saying, "Grounding in one seg. Prep." When he didn't respond, she yelled, "Prep, dammit! Thirty seconds! Get your ass to the ramp! You are released. Move your ass, Captain!"

Fargo looked down with the camera and saw Grayson give him a thumbs up, then he stepped slowly forward to the ramp, and positioned himself in the center of it. Grayson, his medic gear bag over his shoulder, moved up to the ramp controls. He focused back on the feed, noting that the Ghorkas were boiling out of the Hab and surveillance vans, grabbing whatever medical gear was handy. He keyed up, "Nobody out of the site. Everybody stand by. Umesh, on me as soon as I unass from the shuttle."

He heard Umesh roger up, and saw the blip move on his HUD even as Boykin landed the shuttle pointing nose toward the western side of the site. Grayson hit the ramp switch and charged off the shuttle as the ramp dropped. He heard somebody say something about incoming fire from the overwatch position, and saw the vid zoom in on the window in the building to the west, with what appeared to be a rifle protruding from the window and recoiling. "Gahdammit Grayson, get your ass under cover."

He stepped off the ramp, cleared the side of the shuttle and told Cindy, "Gustav, thermobaric up." He felt the momentary vibration as the Gustav rifle deployed, ammo was loaded and the rifle's carat appeared on his HUD.

"Gustav up, Captain," echoed through his mind, even as he took in the situation.

The world seemed to slow down as his neural lace kicked fully into combat/command mode, and he said calmly, "Back blast clear. Target. I will take the window. Standby to jump, Umesh. I'll jump and fire down into the building, I want you to jump just short of the building, to the left of the window. You'll be on my left."

He heard the double click, jumped and centered the carat on the window, "Firing. One round, one round only." He made the firing motion with his finger and the round rocketed out of the gun, impacted the back wall of the room, and blew out the window. He saw at least two bodies come flying out, and called, "Impact." He used the flight time to catalog any other possible weapons. Seeing none, he said, "Drop sonics and repulsors, medical support up. WO, stand by to receive injured. Activate GalPat protocol for wounded, notify ORBCON we'll need maximum medical support. Chief, get Colonel Zhu to dispatch…"

He heard Horse break in, "Feeder Two taking fire. And protesters are down. Before you ask, we did not fire either."

Barun chimed in, "Feeder One, no action. Wait, protesters are dispersing. Now running in a panic. We have not fired either."

Grayson was already running out of the site, heading toward the pile of bodies on the west side, as Fargo and Umesh landed in front of the building.

Fargo focused his camera on what was left of the window and saw a rifle barrel pointing at him, but realized there was no one behind it. Panning down, he saw one male body, obviously dead, lying between him and Umesh. A second body lay near his feet, and he heard a moan. Carefully flipping the body over, he recognized Eric Smallwell, badly burned, and missing a hand. Scooping him up, he said, "Umesh, remain here on guard until the security forces get here. I'm taking this one to Grayson, maybe he can save him."

He jumped back over the spread out bodies, landed and walked forward to where Grayson was, "Senior, need you to treat this one."

Grayson looked up, annoyed, "Why? I've got my hands full here."

"This one needs to answer some questions and go to trial for murder. He killed Shanni and Lev."

Grayson popped up, "I can do that. Put him over here." Fargo lowered Smallwell and stepped back, surveying the scene as Grayson bent over him, "Yeah, I'll *gladly* save your ass so I can watch you hang, you sumbitch."

Daman waved, "Got a shooter over here. Looks like a needle gun. It's been modified to fire full auto. And this seems to be the center of the damage to the protesters."

"Mark it, but don't move it. I'm jumping to the northern side." Fargo jumped and landed near the bodies on the north side, just as Cheetri broadcast, "Found another pistol over here. Right in the middle of carnage. Looks like ten dead over here."

Daman counted, "Forty-eight dead over here, path of needles appears to be twenty yards wide, most damage plus or minus five yards from the shooter, then extending to the left."

Grayson said, "At least twenty wounded here. Probably half won't make it."

Fargo said, "Daman, get somebody questioning the survivors and recording answers."

"Already on it."

"Feeder Two, status?"

"Ten down, fifteen in *custody*. Needler over here too. Marked, vid captured, questioning survivors. Looks like eight dead, two may not survive."

"WO, you ready to lift?"

Boykin came back, "As soon as I need to. Where to?"

"Let's load the wounded here, then jump to Feeder Two, pick their wounded up and buster to the Palace. Have the medics meet you there. Grayson, you'll go with them."

"Rog. Need some help moving the wounded."

"All hands turn to. Move the wounded to the shuttle."

Umesh called, "Security is on scene. They are wanting to know what happened."

"On my way. You go on the shuttle in armor."

"Roger. Jumping."

Fargo jumped to where the security forces were standing around, landed and keyed his external speakers, "Who is in charge here?"

A slovenly security force sergeant turned around, "I am. Get outta that rig. You're under arrest for…"

Fargo took a step closer to the man, *Just what I need, a fucking bully. Gotta end this now.*

"I don't think so. Are you going to be an idiot, or are you going to listen?"

The sergeant blustered, "Arrest every one of these idiots for murder. Stupid off-worlders, come in here and fuck everything up."

Fargo saw the four other security personnel look at each other, but none of them moved. "Smart move, gentlemen. It's not in your best interest to be as stupid as your sergeant right now. My men are a bit touchy at the moment. GalPat has been notified and is on the way. And, if you'd bothered to check, all of my men are armed with bead rifles, not needlers."

The sergeant pointed up at the window, "That wasn't done with a needler!"

"No it wasn't. I did that with the Gustav on my shoulder, since the dead man right there was trying to kill my troops with a bead rifle that you can see hanging out of the window. I took action to save my troops."

"But you're not allowed to use armor!"

"On the contrary, our ROE specifically allows us to defend ourselves. Also, you will find illegal needle guns, modified to fire fully automatic in the middle of both groups of dead. We never fired at the protesters."

"They didn't kill themselves," the sergeant yelled.

"Effectively they did. Our defensive measures caused their rounds to bounce back into the crowd," *And I hope to Deity I can prove that from the surveillance vid. Otherwise, we're screwed.*

Two sonic booms interrupted their confrontation, as two GalPat shuttles did crash arrivals, one inside the site, and one south of the site in one of the safe zones.

Fargo, looming over the sergeant, reached for his mind, and pushed, "I'd suggest you secure this site and that building until you are relieved by GalPat." With that, he turned and jumped toward the shuttle inside the site.

Chaos

The GalPat captain in charge of the platoons had thrown out a perimeter of troopers in full armor extending into the edge of the village, even as Fargo and his troops retreated to the site. A lieutenant was with each platoon, and they'd gone to TACCOM settings on their armor, preventing Fargo and the others from hearing what orders were being given.

Fargo and Umesh climbed out of their armor, closing it up, but leaving the suits crouched in plain sight, as they waited to see what would happen next. They were assailed by the stench of ruptured bodies, blood, and death. Fargo pinched his nose, swallowed and turned as Daman came out of the surveillance van, closely followed by McDougal, "What do you think, Captain?"

"I think we've got chaos personified here and at Feeder Two. Have you locked the recordings from the systems?"

"Yes, all locked down and transmitted to the Chief as soon as she called for them. She's collating all the data at the Palace. I didn't see your data, though."

"I was linked to the shuttle, not to you. I'm pretty sure the warrant has forwarded it. *At least I hope to hell she has.* "Any of our people hurt?"

"Negative. And all weapons are safed and back in the weapons locker, just in case." Daman nodded toward the GalPat armor on the perimeter, and the shuttles with weapons ports open.

"Good! Now all we can do is wait." He glanced at McDougal, "Well, looks like your little system worked. Probably a little too well."

McDougal gulped and turned an interesting shade of pale, "Yes, sir. I never tested…never thought…rocks…"

Fargo projected calm to him, "Not blaming you, Mac. You probably, no, you *did* save our folks' lives. We'll deal with the impact on the protesters at my level or higher, okay?"

"Thank you, Captain. I—"

Grayson limped over, covered in blood, "Well, *that* is a clusterfuck I don't want to repeat."

"What are you doing here? I thought you were on the shuttle?"

Grayson shrugged. "I did what I could, but we had more injured than would fit on the shuttle. I triaged them, loaded the worst ones, and sent… somebody with them."

Daman replied, "That was Jeewan. His secondary is medic."

"Twelve turned over to the local medics. Most of them will make it, some will need some reconstructive work. Your shitbird was alive when he went on the shuttle."

Fargo stepped into the surveillance van, followed by the others, "What have you got for a count?"

Daman slumped into a chair, "Looks like fifty-eight dead, fifteen, no, twenty-seven injured. Hari marked all the positions as we swept the site. Fifteen transported. Two weapons IDed in the crowd, both full auto needle pistols. The one to the west was empty, the one to the north had a half mag left. That one was in a female's hand."

Fargo winced, turning to Hari he said, "Contact Feeder Two, and see what their status is, please."

Hari keyed up, "Feeder Three, Feeder Two. Ekavir wants a count. Dead and injured."

Moments later, Horse responded, "Ten dead, five children. Nine injured, three children. Archer City medical has the injured. We waved the shuttle off since medical already had the wounded. We had a perimeter set, no one is anywhere near us right now. Security forces took over the perimeter, but I think most of them are in shock. One of them IDed the guy with the needle gun as Hayden Archer."

Hayden Archer, why does that name ring a bell...wait, isn't that one of the names Nicole and Jace kicked out as being... "Interesting. Tell him thanks, and to forward that to Nic...Chief Sergeant, if he hasn't already."

Grayson sagged in a chair, and Fargo noticed his hands trembling, "You okay, Senior?"

"Adrenalin dump. I'll get over it."

Daman said, "I'll get an emergency bar." He opened the door and Fargo followed him out, "How are you doing, Daman?"

"Okay. This isn't nearly as bad as the Sonneburg riots."

Fargo flinched, "You were in that mess? Didn't they have something over a thousand dead?"

Daman shrugged. "We had to go clean it up. We didn't get there until three days after it happened. This is clean compared to that."

"Damn. Not to change the subject, but food is probably a good idea. All I've had is… breakfast. Hope the warrant got rid of that box lunch I left on the shuttle."

"Or Umesh grabbed it. He eats more than anybody I've ever seen. I don't know how Aliza keeps him fed."

Fargo shook his head. "Not going there. One thing I learned is never get between folks and their food. Hopefully there is coffee in this one," he said as he punched the autochef on.

"There is, but you may not like the food selections. We…uh…modified them."

"Oh deity…Not peppers. Or Curry."

Daman sighed, "Sorry. Want me to order for you?"

"Please."

                              ***

A div later, they heard another shuttle coming in for a landing, and Fargo got up with a groan. He shook Daman, "Looks like more arrivals. Make sure we've got everybody's statements on those data cubes. I know whoever investigates is going to want them. And hopefully, these are the investigators." *I cannot believe we've been sitting here for almost three divs without a single person talking to us. Not even anyone from security force has shown up, nor has anyone been allowed inside the GalPat perimeter to start recovery of the bodies.*

As they stepped out of the Hab, they saw the shuttle shifting back and forth on the descent, and Daman said, "What the hell?"

"Dodging beams. WO could bring it straight in since the shuttle is hardened, but why cause more problems than we already have. One of the reasons we picked the site as a landing spot. No beams in that direction."

"Huh, didn't realize that. I'm not a flyer, so I've never dealt with them."

Fargo grinned ruefully, "Well, we did once, remember?"

"Oh, yeah. That...was ugly."

The shuttle finally grounded to the south of the site, and the back ramp grounded slowly. Colonel Zhu, Master Chief Horschel, Chief Justicer Freeman, PLANSEC director Meecham, and prosecutor Park walked quickly down the ramp, followed by Nicole, carrying a data comp and vid recorder.

"Looks like we got the whole crowd. This is going to take a while."

Daman growled, "Or they just want to see the blood and guts."

"I don't think so. Freeman and the female, Park, are with planetary justice shop. Meecham," pointing to the heavyset man in uniform, "Is head of PLANSEC. I don't know who the Master Chief is."

Daman chuckled. "Horschel. I wondered whatever happened to him. He was Third Herd back in the day. Good troop, this must be his retirement tour."

"Haven't seen him around the Palace. Or at least not that I remember."

"He's not a spit and polish guy. He's always been a field troop. He's probably spending as much time as he can as far away from the Palace as he can."

Fargo projected, *"Nicole, anything from your review of the feeds? Any ideas? We're in deep shit here."*

"I ran the analysis of the vids in slow motion. It looks as if the two shooters here, and the one at Feeder Two were attempting to shoot the sonics and disable them. It appears the rounds…bounced, for lack of a better word, right back at them and took them out, along with the others behind them and to either side. I've already turned over my analysis to GalPat, and I'm sure the colonel has it, or at least has been briefed. I also confirmed there were no rounds fired by our troops.

"Thank you! I love you!"

Nicole shook her head minutely, *"Not now. Pay attention. Facts, not conjecture. Just facts."*

"Yes, dear." He saw Nicole shake her head again, and huff out a breath, while covering a smile as Colonel Zhu walked up, closely followed by the others. Fargo and Daman snapped to attention, saluted, with Fargo saying, "Colonel. How would you like to proceed?"

Zhu returned the salute, "What in the hell happened here, Fargo?"

Fargo nodded to the others, "Sir, what we have here is a failed attempt to overrun the site. I believe the leaders attempted to breach the perimeter by shooting the sonics and disabling them. However that didn't happen. Our people fired no rounds. The only round expended here was one round by me, against a sniper in an overwatch location in the village. Two people were in the location when I fired against it. Planet Security has that site secured. We did medical assists as soon as the sniper position was nullified, and evacuated the wounded to the Palace. As soon as your people got here, we pulled back into the site and have remained inside, with no further interaction with either the locals or the bodies. Two modified needle pistols have been identified and are marked with locator flags." He pointed to the flag in the west, then the flag in the north. "We have not touched them, other than to verify they were safe. All that is on video."

Colonel Zhu turned to Freeman, "Mr. Chief Justicer, how would you like to proceed?"

Freeman looked over to Mrs. Park. "Your recommendation?"

Park looked around, then turned to Fargo, "Did you detain any of the protesters?"

"No, ma'am. We were more concerned with the medical triage. There are only ten personnel at this site, and when I responded with Senior Sergeant Grayson, the medic, that only brought the count to twelve. By the time we had cleared the sniper, most of the protesters had dispersed."

Freeman and Park stepped to the side, and Fargo reached out, brushing Park's thoughts and picked up, *"I've reviewed the videos. I need to go find the PLANSEC supervisor and see if they have anyone. If they don't…then we need to take a hard look at them. These troops were set up, from what I've seen. And after the whole Perez thing, I'm wondering who is really running or trying to run this planet. This is another generation of Firsties causing trouble. With Smallwell in custody, and apparently Archer dead at Archer City..."*

Freeman nodded. *"I will stay here and keep them occupied. Send a couple of junior PLANSEC folks with scanners, and let's see how many of these bodies we can identify."*

Freeman turned to the colonel, "Mrs. Park will make contact with the PLANSEC supervisor here, and detach personnel with scanners to see how many of the bodies we can identify in situ." Pointing to Nicole, he continued, "I'd like to use the chief sergeant to record what we see and whom we identify. I have been impressed with her data analysis thus far."

The colonel nodded. "Fine. I will accompany you, Master Chief, I'd like you to collect the data from the surveillance module, any maintenance data available, and data from the armor."

Fargo noticed that Master Chief Horschel had a bag over his shoulder, as the master chief responded, "Yes, sir. I'll get right on it." He stepped forward and nodded to Fargo and Daman, "Lead on, gentlemen."

Once they stepped into the surveillance module, the master chief's attitude changed completely. "Warrant, haven't seen you in a while. Heard you'd retired." He glanced around the module, then at Fargo, "What's a captain doing in charge of Ghorka? Or are you a figurehead?"

Fargo started to answer when Daman snapped, "He's not a figurehead. He's adopted into the clan. See the *kukri*? Ekavir leads by example."

Horschel held up his hands, "Whoa! I didn't mean…"

Fargo snapped, "Yes, you did, Master Chief. Don't fucking play games with us. Yes, we're militia, yes, we're from off world, and yes, I'm the officer in charge. Now do your fucking job and do it without the lip. We didn't kill anybody, well, I did, but that was a sniper. Daman, take care of this." With that, Fargo stomped out of the module, obviously pissed.

Horschel looked at Daman, "What set him off?"

"You did. Marcus, you can be a truly stupid shit at times. Divide and conquer to try to get troops ratting one another out isn't going to work here. And he's not a poseur. He's a combat Marine, Terran forces, one of six survivors of a clusterfuck where *he* brought the five enlisted suits to the evac point himself. Honestly, he's crazier than a dune lizard. I've seen him kill things that were trying to kill him up close and personal, and never flinch. He's also medically retired from GalScouts. He's seen the nearelephant. Now sit your ass down and collect the data. Standard protocols are in effect."

Horschel sat down and typed in a set of commands in the virtual keyboard, then looked up, surprised, "A full up multispectral surveillance unit? How the hell?"

Daman replied, "It's a loaner from GalPat. Those five data cubes are the interviews and vid caps from all the suits while we were doing med triage. I don't have all the armor vids, only the ones from the two suits here. You'll have to ask the captain for his."

"Gotcha." He pulled the data from the system, filling three data cubes, and randomly checked the data. Looking at the data from the attack, he whistled, "What the fuck?"

Daman looked up, "What?"

"What kicked those rounds back at the shooters?"

Daman smiled. "Oh, that's our little repulsor system."

"Repulsor system?"

"You'll have to talk to the Captain about that."

Horschel quickly checked the other cubes and swept them into his bag, "Okay, open up the weapons locker and let me inventory it. Where's the armor?"

Daman unlocked the weapons locker and stood back as Horschel went through the pistols and rifles racked there, "Huh, little bean shooters? Where's the real stuff?"

Daman sighed, "This was a security detachment, not a wartime detachment. And those little bean shooters will kill you as dead as anything else. Glass beads, five thousand FPS. Good to four hundred yards."

"Well, you ain't got any needle guns, so that's good. Lock it up, now the armor?"

"Out back. I'll show you." Daman led him out between the Hab and maintenance modules to where Fargo's armor knelt.

Horschel walked up to it, then stopped. Backing off, he walked around the armor, looking at it from all angles. "Um, this armor… It's not GalPat standard. It's…" Stepping up he leaned into the armor and punched the main power on, found the slot for the data cube and plugged it in. He said, "Authorized override, four, alpha, six, six, three, oscar."

The AI said, "Override not authorized. Contact appropriate authority for approval."

Horschel looked down at Daman, "Now what the fuck? Who's appropriate authority?"

Daman smiled. "Well, I can guess it's the captain. And no, this is not GalPat standard. It's an advanced unit we're testing."

The master chief wilted, "Okay, I give. Go find the captain, please." As Daman walked off, he mumbled under his breath, "How the hell did they get this stuff? And I still gotta find out what this repulsor module is…"

Fargo came around the corner, a bulb of coffee in his hand, "Yes, Master Chief?"

"Uh, sir, I need access to download your data from this morning. My override…"

"Didn't work, did it? Master is on?"

"Yes, sir."

"Cindy, override, both units, my approval. Download from zero seven to fourteen, today only."

"But I need…"

Glad I had to come out here, otherwise I wouldn't have thought about McDougal's little toys. I need to have Jace get those plans to DePerez, and probably a patent for McDougal. At least this way, he's protected, as long as I can get him to keep his mouth shut on anything other than the basics. "No, Master Chief, you only need today's data. And as soon as you collect that, I need to take you over to the maintenance module to see a repulsor module. You will not be allowed to vid that, nor will you be allowed to provide any parameters in your report. That unit is also a prototype unit for GalPat, just like the armor and is restricted access under GalPat regulations."

Horschel pulled the data cube out when the AI said the data was transferred, and he flipped the master switch off. Climbing down, he moved to the second set of armor and repeated the process. Finishing that, he swung down and said, "Whenever you're ready, Captain."

Fargo led the way to the maintenance module, stepping inside, "Senior Mac, the master chief needs to look at a repulsor module for his report."

Mac nodded. "Yes, sir. Let me grab one." He rummaged in a locker, the pulled out one of the modules, "Here you are, sir. Master Chief, if you have any questions?"

Horschel said, "Nope, no questions, Senior. That's it?"

Fargo stepped in smoothly, "They connect much like the sonics do, with a little better spacing between the modules. They require a closed loop, just like the sonics, and ground to negative pole."

Horschel backed up, "Okay, I need to see where they are emplaced." He turned and stepped out of the module, with Daman following.

Fargo turned to McDougal, "Put it back, Mac, and stay low profile. People don't need to know about your design, nor do I want anybody to get specifics of it. This is GalPat restricted, understood?"

"Yes, sir. Understood." Fargo stepped out of the maintenance module, and McDougal flopped down on his stool, wiping a sleeve across his suddenly sweating brow.

Fargo and Daman stood watching as Master Chief Magar escorted Horschel around the perimeter. The colonel, Chief Justicer, Meecham, and Nicole had finished the northern group of bodies, and were now stepping carefully among bodies on the west side, following the two Planet Security men with scanners. "I wonder what they're finding."

Fargo glanced at him, "Not a clue. But I'm betting there will be a bunch of *unregistered* indentures or out of work people. That's usually the kind drawn to free stuff. And I'd bet *somebody* was giving them free stuff to participate."

Daman nodded. "That's what Sonneburg turned out to be. Lots of proles out of the worker's areas. Really poor."

"And they fall for that shit every time, on every world."

***

The sun had set and Eros was rising in the west before the final bodies had been scanned and counted, with Chief Justicer Freeman was looking the worse for wear. Mrs. Park had finally returned, scowling, and she and the chief justicer had returned to the shuttle by themselves. *That doesn't bode well, I wonder what she found, or maybe didn't find?* Fargo thought, as Colonel Zhu approached, Nicole and the master chief in tow.

"Fargo, your people are provisionally cleared. There are a number of *issues* that the prosecutor and chief justicer have to work on, and I've been notified your contract will not be extended."

Fargo stiffened, "Not extended? For what reason?"

Zhu shrugged, then his temper flared, "I'm not really sure. All I got was a terse message from Director Vaughn, via Meecham. And he's hot about the repulsor. He wants to know what the hell it is, and why he wasn't notified. Also, master chief tells me your armor is non-standard. Is there anything *else* you want to tell me about? Like how *somebody* slipped a warrant for Smallwell through the GalPat system without my knowledge *or* how *somebody*, not anybody that works for me, suddenly became experts on surveillance and planetary databases?"

"Colonel, I can honestly say I do not have those answers, other than the armor and repulsor systems are test articles for GalPat, and thus restricted."

"Then why the fuck is a militia, a deity damned *militia* doing testing on a backwater planet for GalPat," he almost screamed.

Fargo smiled. "Colonel, think about it. I have one hundred retired Ghorka. All warrants, E-eights and E-nines. *All of them* are combat veterans, with an average service length of forty years. That is *four thousand years* of experience. And remember what Warrant Boykin told you?"

The colonel looked almost apoplectic, "Get back in your fucking perimeter and stay there. We're releasing the bodies to their families. Their *grieving* families, thanks to you and your men."

Colonel Zhu turned and stomped off toward the shuttle, not bothering to wait for Fargo to salute. Fargo cocked his head. "Well, we know where we stand now."

Daman chuckled. "Yep, going home in fourteen and a wakeup!"

Winding Down

Boykin had finally come back at twenty-three to pick up Fargo and Grayson, who walked on board gratefully. Fargo climbed into the cockpit and slumped in the seat, and looked over at the Warrant, "Thanks for the pickup. I was beginning to wonder if I was going to have to spend the rest of the contract out here."

Boykin grinned tiredly, "If they could figure out a way, probably. There was one hell of an argument on the way back between the colonel and the PLANSEC guy. The old guy finally had to step in to calm them down. Something about plots and missed or missing indentured and third gen Firsties. I didn't catch all of it, since the mic is back by the ramp, but damn, they were going at it!"

Fargo smiled. "Good. I might have been less than forthcoming about our systems, and I used what you told him, whatever that code was, about not being able to talk about things like advanced armor or the repulsor modules."

Boykin lifted off and set a course for Capital, leaned back and said, "That's a good question. How *are* you going to handle that?"

"I'm lumping it in with the armor as test or prototype units. Gonna try to get McDougal a patent for it. The more I think about it, those damn things saved people's lives, at least on our side, today. I *think* I have a way to get them into the GalPat system."

Boykin smiled. "You know you turn that over to GalPat, it will disappear into the black hole, never to be seen again."

"True, but if GalScouts also has a set of plans…"

"Oh… sneaky, *very* sneaky, Captain."

"If we'd had something like this, I can think of at least ten or twelve scouts that would still be alive. Sonics doesn't stop everything. Never have, never will, especially on some of the Exo planets we were scouting."

Boykin busied herself with the comms with ORBCON and when she turned to ask Fargo a question, he was sound asleep. She smiled and turned back to flying the shuttle, humming softly to herself.

A div and a half later, she landed the shuttle softly at the spaceport, refueled and lifted again without ever waking Fargo up. Coming into the Palace on anti-grav, Fargo finally woke up, and she said, "We're home, for this version of home."

Fargo stretched, and chuckled. "Home is where the gear trunk is, right?"

"Pretty much. And we're down."

"Thanks again for coming to pick us up."

"No problem, Captain. We live to serve."

Fargo laughed, got up and eased down from the cockpit as Boykin finished the shutdown procedures. Kicking Grayson's foot, he marveled once again at his ability to sleep in the contorted position he was in, and said, "You're off until tomorrow at eighteen. I'm assuming you're going to do your restocking tomorrow?"

Grayson yawned, "Nah, I'll do it tonight. Sure as shit if I don't, something will blow up on us."

"Okay, and thanks again for your help today."

"Just doin' my job, Captain. Just doin' my job."

"Well, you did a *good* job. You saved lives today."

Grayson shrugged and headed for the medical pallet stored on the forward bulkhead, as Fargo walked slowly down the ramp.

Nicole met him at the bottom of the ramp, and it was all he could do not to reach out a hug her. "Why are you still up?"

"Somebody had to monitor the radios, and I was the only somebody here. I also dumped all our data up to the ship, just so we have a pristine copy, just in case."

He reached out to her, *"I'm sorry you got stuck with waiting for us."*

"I didn't mind, I got some work done, and I've been running data correlations for the last couple of divs."

Boykin walked down the ramp and he said, "Both of you hit the rack. I'm going to flip the comms to alert mode, and we'll worry about the follow up tomorrow."

They nodded and started for the billet, and Fargo projected, *"I love you, Nicole."*

"Love you too, now stop that!"

"Yes, dear."

He heard a most unladylike snort and saw Nicole shake her head, as she said something to Boykin.

***

Daman caught Master Chief Magar as he exited the Hab, "Paras, you seen McDougal?"

"Nope," he thought for a sec, "He came off watch at all balls. He should be in the rack."

"He's not. He seemed real nervous when I went off at twenty last night. I never saw him come in the Hab. All balls?"

"Midnight for you ground grippers. Shit, where could he have…"

"The maintenance unit." They turned and both headed around the Hab to the maintenance unit. Daman popped the door and sighed, "There he is." McDougal was face down on the work bench, snoring softly, surrounded by pieces of hardware, trailing cables to his data comp and the maintenance comp. "Mac! Wake up, Mac."

McDougal jerked up, staring wildly around, "Wha… Did something… What time izzit?" He finally focused on Daman and the master chief and slumped. "How much trouble am I in," he asked softly.

The master chief glanced at Daman and stepped forward, "None. We were worried that you weren't in the Hab sleeping."

McDougal swept his hand vaguely toward the hardware, "Trying to figure out why I killed all those…"

Daman interrupted, "You didn't kill anybody. You saved *our* lives."

"But innocent people…"

"They weren't innocents, they wanted to overrun us, and you can damn well bet they would have killed us, given the chance!"

Mac mumbled, "Not like war, I didn't mean…"

Master Chief Magar motioned toward the door, and Daman took the hint, leaving the two of them in the maintenance unit. "Mac, war, police actions, and security details like this aren't a lot different when you come right down to it. People are still trying to kill you, either for the land, whatever you're protecting, or the detailee. Except they aren't in armor and they tend to hide in the general population. Think about it. These turds had illegal fully automatic needle guns. That's not something law abiding people do."

"But there were women and children out there…"

"Who were active participants? One of the needlers was used by a female. Remember, the female of the species is always the more deadly."

Mac shook his head. "I didn't mean to hurt people, I only wanted to stop the… projectiles."

"And you did a damn good job of it."

"But it wasn't supposed to kick them back, not like that!"

Magar laid his hand on Mac's shoulder. "Son, I'm not complaining. You built something that worked. Granted it didn't get fully tested, but it *worked* at the right time!"

Mac punched up the maintenance comp, stabbing his finger viciously at part of the circuit on the screen. "This… This is what I fucked up. I didn't dial down the max rejection loop. If I'd scaled that with the rest of it…"

"Deity be damned! Senior Sergeant, you did your fucking job and a lot more. It is *not* your fault they died. Get that through your thick Euro ethnic skull. I'm putting you in for a damn medal for what you did. Shut this shit down and go get food, then take your ass to the rack. You go back on watch at eighteen. Do you hear me?"

"Yes, sir, Master Chief. But I'm afraid…"

"The captain will cover for you. He's not one to leave his troops hanging out. Now either go, or I'll go get an injector and put your ass under."

Mac reached up and shut down the maintenance comp and picked up his data comp. "Going Master Chief, I'm going." He groaned as he got up and walked slowly to the door.

***

Three days later, Fargo knocked on the colonel's door. Zhu glared up at him, "What?"

Since he wasn't invited in, Fargo said, "The troops are wondering what is going on with Smallwell, the local feeds aren't saying anything about him being charged with the murder of our two troops."

Zhu killed the holo in front of him in disgust, "That should be the least of your worries. Meecham is wanting to charge you and the two troops at the sites with murder for killing those *innocent* civilians. And that whole thing with your jumping in armor and firing that cannon into that apartment. The owner is complaining that the whole upstairs of that building is going to have to be renovated…"

Fargo reached out and felt the colonel's anger, worry, and distaste for the entire situation. Probing a little deeper, he felt the thoughts of whether or not to tell Fargo what else was going on. "Colonel, you've seen the vids, what would you have had me do? I had unarmored troops in the open, being sniped at." He pushed a little on Zhu, to see if he would talk to him.

"Come in and close the door," the colonel said. Fargo did so, and assumed the position of parade rest in front of the colonel's desk. Zhu looked up at him, frustration in his eyes. "First it was you killing Perez, and now this cluster. PLANSEC is supposedly *trying* to round up some of the *peaceful* protesters from both sites, but apparently not with much success on anything other than the proles. No Firsties have been picked up, and they haven't even notified ORBCON to check the station for escapees, nor has GalPat been formally notified. Matter of fact, the director directed me to keep it low key and she doesn't want any GalPat involvement. It's to the point that they have officially listed Halvorson senior and Archer senior as missing and presumed dead in a liteflyer crash somewhere between the two properties."

Fargo glanced down, "What? They know from DNA…"

The colonel held up a hand, "I know. Apparently both Freeman and Park are having problems with some of the dead identified at both sites, too."

"Firsties?"

"That, and apparently some of the second wavers were involved, at least one of which is related to Freeman himself. But the company has apparently directed that all this be kept quiet, which is why nothing has been on the local feeds. There have been a lot of FTL comms in and out of the Palace by the director's office in the last three days."

Fargo whistled, "That can't be cheap."

Zhu shoved back from the desk and got up, pacing back and forth. "No, and it's all coded in private code. Have your troops seen any more protesters, or anything else?"

"Nothing. Not a soul, no movement showing up at all on surveillance, and nothing on the comms frequencies we were monitoring. And direct liaison with the TBT reps has indicated that they are seeing nothing interrupting the beams, and nobody causing any problems anywhere. That's quite a change from the last two months, which apparently has them worried."

Zhu snorted. "They should be thankful for that."

"I don't think that it's as much that, as they are waiting for the other shoe to fall. I've never seen an optimistic techie in my life."

Zhu planted both hands on his desk and looked at Fargo, "Who are you?"

Fargo reached for his mind and felt the honesty in the question, but he said, "What do you mean, Colonel?"

"You're not the normal militia captain. You don't cower when you come in here, you've got loyalty from a GalPat warrant and medic, you didn't hesitate in either of the situations to do what you needed to, and last, but damn sure not least, you've apparently got the loyalty of an entire company of very senior Ghorka, all of whom are combat vets."

"I'm… just an old retired GalScout. I did a tour in the Terran Marines before I came over to the Scouts."

"You were never GalPat," Zhu asked incredulously.

"No."

"Combat?"

"I was in the Cluster Skirmish. That was at the end of my career."

Zhu looked down, then back up, "The lost Marine company, you're *that* Fargo," he asked softly.

Fargo could only nod.

Zhu said quietly, "You personally carried the five survivors in their armor to the LZ, which was not supposed to be possible. You tried to kill the Intel weenie that gave you bad data. Courts martialed, then overturned. No wonder they'll follow you into hell."

"I don't…"

Zhu stood, walked around the desk, bowed and offered his hand. "I apologize for the way I've treated you, Captain. I cannot make any excuses for my behavior."

Fargo reached out and took it, sensing Zhu's mind, *Damn, he's actually scared of me and what I'm liable to do. And he truly believes they'll follow me in anything I do.* "I don't believe you owe me anything, but I will accept the apology. We'll be out of your hair in another ten days. That is the best I can offer."

Zhu nodded. "I will press the director to put Smallwell on trial before you leave. I will impress her that it would be in her, and Endine's best interest to do so. I will *hint* that if they don't, GalPat may be forced to step in."

"Thank you, that's all we can ask. I'd like to be able to have our folks know the killer is getting his just desserts. If you'll excuse me, I need to get back for comms checks."

"Dismissed."

Fargo stopped by the mess and grabbed a bulb of coffee, then walked slowly back down the hall, trying to determine how best to tell the sites the current lack of status on Smallwell. Stepping back in the office, he was surprised to see Nicole sitting at the console typing away. "What are you doing here?"

Nicole held up one finger, and went back to typing. Finishing up, she turned with a flourish and a smile, "Covering for you, as usual."

Fargo cocked his head. "Say what?"

"You had an encrypted from Captain Jace. It was tracking data on the Firsties. They've all gone to ground at their ancestral homes. Well, except for the Abruzzi clan, they are business as usual."

"Did you... did that end up in..."

"No, it's not in GalPat's database. I don't share *everything* we get." She got up and gestured to the chair, "All yours. I'm going to pee, get coffee, and go back to the Intel section."

She gave him a quick kiss in passing, and walked out the door smiling.

Boykin and Grayson came in a seg later, just as Fargo was saying, "Okay, all sites listen up. Here's the latest on Smallwell. There isn't an update, per se, but Colonel Zhu, the head of the GalPat Det is going to the director of Endine with a strong hint that if they don't do something, GalPat is going to step in and take over the prosecution."

Boykin shook her head, and Grayson said, "Fuckers. GalPat *should* step in, should already have stepped in."

Horse came over the radio, "The good colonel understands we're not happy doesn't he?"

"I impressed that on him this morning. He doesn't want us to go rogue, especially after what happened the other day."

Jiri said quietly, "He does understand, I think. The captain got him off the credit chip. Ten days gentlemen, ten days. Remember that."

Packing Out

Hyderabad sat at the last module at the space station, and Captain Jace sat on the bridge scanning the cameras incessantly. Liz glanced over, "Captain, I've got these. You don't have to sit here and watch them."

Jace shrugged. "So you're telling me to go away?"

Liz smiled. "Politely, but yes. You've got more important things to do. Keldar, Wallace, Khalil, and Klang are all waiting for the stores to be delivered, and Evie's off talking to ORBCON about our pickup and departure routing. The Ching is in his hole as usual, and you're as antsy as a nearporcupine. We're not due for another comm with Captain Fargo until eighteen, and yes, you're getting on my nerves.

Smiling ruefully, he got up, "I can take the hint. I'll go bother them. If anything comes in…

"You'll be the second person to know, Captain."

Jace grinned and walked off the bridge without another word. A div later he stood at the hatch as Wallace walked back aboard, "We're good, Cap'n. Topped off the H2O, stores are loaded, fueling is complete. I'll have you a load sheet shortly, along with a revised weight and balance."

Jace nodded. "Thank you, Wallace. As soon as Evie gets back, I plan on undocking and resuming our orbital parking slot."

Wallace nodded, wondering, *Normally, every captain I've served with pores over weight and balance like a... What was that fish, Piranha? Yeah, Piranha over a piece of meat. This one, he glances at it and files it. Either he's awfully good, or... No, he's that good. I've never seen such smart ship handling in a pig like this one. In all my years, I don't think I've ever seen such a bastard configuration. It's armored like an assault shuttle, but it's not... But, it's got the hardened main deck, the clamps, and... there are a lot of spaces blanked off. And there's a lot of military hardware on here for a supposedly civilian ship.*

Wallace and Liz sat in their cabin after dinner and Wallace turned to her, "What do you think about this ship?"

Jace, sitting on the bridge, perked up, *I wondered when Wallace would get around to this. Time to bring him and Liz in and sign the NDAs.*

Liz looked up from her data comp, "It's got some interesting equipment. Some of it is more advanced than what I used."

"And the crew?"

Liz cocked her head, "They're an interesting mixture. And they seem to get along all the time." She lay her data comp down, "What are you getting at?"

"Doesn't it strike you as odd that there are so few of them? And we don't usually see them? But maintenance still gets done, and all the PM paperwork is always filled out? And the equipment. Lots of GALSPEC, and it's newer and in better shape than anything I remember on active duty."

Liz said impatiently, "So?"

Wallace looked around, then said quietly, "I think this is one of those spook ships."

Liz burst out laughing, "Those are a figment of some newsie's imagination. Ships like that don't exist. Yes, this one is a little odd, but who knows all the designs out there. Didn't you say the data plate said this one was out of Old Earth India? How could it be a spook? I'm just thankful it doesn't stink of the Vindaloo."

Jace laughed, *If you only knew, my dear. I think it's time to be a little more up front with both of you, and get those NDAs signed before the troops come back aboard.*

***

Fargo, Boykin, and Nicole went over the recovery plan again, and Nicole sighed, "Why can't we just pick up the Habs *with* the troops in them? That would save time and multiple trips to each site."

Fargo and Boykin's eyes met over the holo, and Boykin said, "Well, there is a combat pick up where that is done, but it also assumes the troops are in armor. There are some pretty significant G forces involved when I tractor the modules up to the belly of the shuttle. I'd prefer to not have to scrape bloody paste off the bulkheads, and there is the issue of transferring in space. Kinda hard to do without a spacesuit or armor."

Nicole shook her head. "Oh I know. It's just… They're going to be vulnerable one way or the other."

Fargo leaned forward, "There isn't a better way, not right now. We're leaving the sonics, but we are picking up the repulsors. That will be the last thing loaded, and this plan minimizes the troop's vulnerability. All they have to do is climb on the roof, then step into the shuttle. We'll pick up two teams at a time, Feeders One and Two, then Three and Four. Hyderabad is going to be in a LEO…"

Boykin interrupted, "Do we have the timing for the passes yet?"

Fargo shifted the holo, calling up a larger view, and added the low earth orbit pattern, "Ninety seg orbits. Should put him on top of the sites in numerical order. First and second passes are centered over Feeders Two and Four."

Boykin quickly did the math, "I can work with that. If I buster, haul ass for you ground grippers, after each pickup, I can make those on four passes. That'll be nine divs to get all the players and modules back aboard. Ten and a half divs, it's long day, but that's doable."

"How are you planning to handle the modules?" Fargo asked.

"Same way I did when I picked them up from Hunter. Drop 'em close enough for the Captain to tractor them into position."

Nicole added, "Enough, already. We've been over and over this. Nothing's changed. We can plan until Deity takes us all, but until we actually lift, it's all moot."

Grayson woke up with a snort, "Are we done?"

Boykin smiled as Fargo threw up his hands, "Okay, okay. We're done. Senior, you've got the comms watch until seventeen."

Grayson nodded. "Got it, boss. You want to get outta the chair?"

Fargo shook his head, got up, and motioned. "Your chair, oh watch keeper."

Grayson bowed, "Thank you Captain, my captain," he said with a grin as he flopped down in the chair.

Nicole coughed to cover a laugh, "I need to hit the head, and I'm hungry."

Boykin smiled. "I'm with you. Let's go." They walked out chuckling between themselves.

Fargo headed for the mess, intending to grab a quick meal, but the colonel intercepted him. "Got a minute, Captain?"

"Yes, sir." Fargo followed the colonel back to his office, and stood at ease in front of the desk.

"Sit, this may take a bit," Zhu said. Once Fargo sat down, the colonel continued, "I spoke to Meecham, he now understands you and your troops are, shall we say, untouchable until you leave." He brought up a holo that took a minute for Fargo to understand, as Zhu continued, "You've managed with *two* shots to apparently stop two different plots against the director and the company." Pointing to the holo, he said, "This is a list of the Firsties' family trees." Seven of them lit up at the second generation level. "These seven, including Perez and Archer, were apparently dealing with the Traders and/or Dragoons. They were plotting to take over the entire planet and return it to Firsties' control by displacing the company through breach of contract. There was some kind of deal involving mining that was being either discussed or done. None of them kept many notes, but there were quite a few documents and communications recovered from Perez's estate. That particular plot had been ongoing at least three years, based on what Meecham and his PLANSEC folks have pieced together. It *appears* that no family with a patriarch still living was involved, and they are looking for the other five."

Fargo shook his head. "Why? What the hell did they expect to gain? Didn't they effectively control the planet anyway?"

The colonel cocked his head. "Power? Control? I don't know. I don't think they realized how *little* control they would have actually had, had they been successful. The Traders are constantly probing the Rimworlds for any weakness they can find in the administration of the worlds, since most of them are no older than a century, so the populations are relatively small, not too advanced, and most of them have no real forces than can protect them."

"That hasn't changed. We had one incursion on Hunter that…got taken out."

Zhu nodded. "Got a brief on that. It was local forces and a company of GalPat," he stared at Fargo, "Were you by chance the local forces?"

"We just scouted the location. The GalPat company did all the work, and lost their company commander, chasing a Goon into a cave. Stupid…"

"Scouted, uh huh." Fargo shrugged and the colonel lit a group of names on the third level of the family tree. "Now this is where it gets interesting. Similar families involved, but a totally separate plot. PLANSEC found an encrypted data chip in the remains of the comms device you blew out of that apartment in Kwamaine. They couldn't decrypt it, and passed it over to us for help. Our Intel section broke it last night, and it was a treasure trove of information. Smallwell and Archer were apparently the ringleaders, with these twenty one others as active participants. It looks like five or six were the second level of the organization, and the other thirteen or fourteen were the grunts. Apparently there was one female in that top group, and she was killed at Feeder Two. She was apparently the other shooter."

Fargo looked up at the ceiling, then back at the holo, "Who were *they* working with?"

Zhu grimaced. "You'll love this. Only themselves. They wanted to take down the feeders, dump the planet back to the primitive stage, kill off their elders, and establish their own oligarchy."

"How, if they took the feeders down…"

"All of the Firsties home sites have nuke power. Ninety years ago they didn't have TBT up and functional off Earth. Their plan was to take the world back to a feudal society with each family that bought in as *owners* of those that they selected to be allowed to survive."

"Deity! How stupid…"

"Yes, it is… was… Meecham says they are in the process of rounding up the remaining participants, and some of them are… singing like the nearparrot in the cage." Zhu closed the holo and looked at Fargo, "None of this can go any further than this room for now. This is why Smallwell hasn't been tried yet. Chief Justicer Freeman was brought in on the evidence this morning, and the question place before him is *which* of the charges should be brought. Murder or treason. Either carries the death penalty. It will be up to the Chief Justicer and the director as to which way it goes. Their goal is to, shall we say, get the populace's attention with these trials. I foresee a number of public executions, either here in the Palace, or in each of their hometowns."

"Colonel, on behalf of our folks, I wish you'd push them to bring Smallwell to trial for murder. I don't want to have to deal with fifty pissed off Ghorka who feel their tribe has been dishonored."

Zhu shivered, "I see your point. I know I don't want them to go on a rampage, and I know they are capable of that. There are rumors about some… *cleaning up*… that was done on Mars Base thirty years ago. And that was supposedly only four or five Ghorka." Zhu stood, "Thank you for coming with me, and please, hold this close."

Fargo got up, "I will, sir. But I have to tell them sooner or later."

"After you depart Endine, I don't see why not. But I'd ask they not spread it far and wide."

Fargo nodded. "With your permission?" Zhu inclined his head, and Fargo left the office.

***

The day before the recovery started, it was finally announced that Smallwell had been indicted for the murder of the two Ghorka. Fargo quickly got on the comms and put the word out to all sites, and ensured they were going to be ready for the recovery procedures.

Fargo grumped, "Damn zero dark thirty shit, why is it always zero fucking dark thirty," as he made one more pass through the billet and keyed his trunk to follow him out to the shuttle.

Boykin had already preflighted the shuttle, and Grayson was slumped in one of the chairs, sound asleep when he stomped on board. Boykin leaned down out of the cockpit, caroling, "Good morning, Captain! Are you ready to depart this dirtball?"

Fargo shook his head. "How the hell are you so damn cheerful, WO?" Nicole came aboard, trailed by her trunk, and he said, "Morning, Nicole."

She smiled. "Morning. I'm ready to go home! Are we there yet?"

Fargo rolled his eyes, "Oh no, don't start that shit." He reached out, "*I love you, but please…*"

"*I can't wait to get you in the rack tonight. Not being able to be with you is driving me up the wall.*"

Fargo blushed, "*I... uh…*"

They were interrupted by Colonel Zhu, in full uniform. "Captain, could all of you please step out here?"

"All of us?"

"Yes, including the senior sergeant and the warrant, please."

Nicole looked at the colonel curiously as Fargo yelled up to the cockpit, "WO, muster outside please." He kicked Grayson's foot, "Up and at 'em Senior."

Boykin dropped out of the cockpit as Grayson got up, grumbling. They followed the colonel down the ramp and were surprised to see the Palace GalPat Det standing at attention in full dress uniforms and Doctor

Vaughn, the director also standing there at a lectern. The colonel started marching toward her, and they automatically fell into step behind him as he marched to stand in front of the lectern, "Director, the awardees are present."

Doctor Vaughn nodded. "Thank you, Colonel. Ladies and gentlemen, I apologize for the early div, but this needs to be done before you leave. Warrant Boykin and Senior Sergeant Grayson, front and center please."

The warrant and senior marched to stand directly in front of her, "I am pleased to present you both the Endine lifesaving medal for your responses during the unfortunate incidents at your sites involving the treasonous behavior of some of our citizens. Through your efforts, over twenty lives were saved that would have otherwise been lost." She stepped around the lectern, taking saucer sized medals and dropping them over their heads. She shook both their hands, and stepped back, saying softly, "Return to your places please."

"Chief Sergeant Levesque, front and center please." Nicole marched to stand in front of her, and she smiled. "I have the pleasure of presenting you with the GalPat Intelligence medal for your service in breaking up the two plots to take over the planet. Colonel?"

Colonel Zhu smiled as he stepped forward and pinned the Intelligence Medal on Nicole's grays. "Congratulations, this will be entered in your official record Chief. And my personal thanks for your work."

Nicole whispered, "Thank you, sir. But I…"

"You did the work, you get the credit. Dismissed."

Vaughn smiled at her, "Captain Fargo, front and center please." Fargo marched up and saluted her as she read, "For your heroic actions on two occasions that broke up not one but two plots against our planet, I am proud to present you with the Founder's Medal. Normally this would be accompanied by a considerable tract of land, but since you are not a citizen, that has been changed to a monetary award of five hundred thousand credits." She hung the medal around his neck and handed him a credit chip, then two more. Stepping back to the lectern, she continued, "Additionally, we are awarding two one hundred thousand credit death benefits to your two Ghorka who died at the hands of our people. And finally, we will be naming the holiday of the anniversary of the attack on your sites for your two men, so that their names will never be forgotten, nor will your service to Endine. I would have preferred that this be done in front of all your troops, but needs must. Please pass on my and the planet's thanks for what you've done, and Deity bless."

Fargo stood stunned for a moment, then said, "Thank you Madame Director. I will pass this along. And thank you for the benefits, I'd truly rather have the men back, as would their families, but these credits will be taken back to them."

Doctor Vaughn nodded, turned away from the lectern and walked slowly toward the executive wing of the Palace as the Colonel called the assembled GalPat troops to attention then dismissed them. He walked over to Fargo and the others, "I'll send you the vid we took. Thank you for what you did."

Boykin growled, "We need to be in the air in ten, I've got work to do."

Zhu smiled. "And the warrant takes charge. Deity bless, and thank you." He shook hands, starting with Boykin, who promptly headed for the ramp, grumbling to herself. Finally only Fargo was left, and he shook his hand, saying, "I would be proud to serve with you, Captain. And I apologize for the way I treated you. You taught me something that I will carry for the rest of my life about leadership. Thank you." He turned and marched away as Fargo looked after him.

Recovery

Ten divs after liftoff from Endine, Boykin maneuvered the last two modules ahead of the *Hyderabad*, and stood off as Captain Jace recovered them and tractored them into position. Fargo sat in the mess, watching the external camera as he neatly tractored them into the stack on the bottom of the ship, and jerked as the camera flipped to the shuttle bay, doors open and Wallace standing there.

He heard Wallace said, "Nose first?"

Boykin answered, "Rog, nose, and then spin."

They saw Wallace look up and confirm the lights were flashing red and yellow, "Confirm zero G, no atmo."

"Roger zero/no. Have the ball, closure forty fps." They watched as the shuttle closed the side of the *Hyderabad*.

Wallace held up one stick, now lit green. "Bring it."

Wallace said, "Drop ten."

"Thirty fps."

"Three hundred, centered."

Wallace said, "Drop ten."

"Twenty fps."

"Keep it coming. Two hundred, centered."

"Roger."

"One hundred, centered, drop ten."

"Ten fps."

Wallace started waving the wands, moving slowly backward as the shuttle nosed into the hangar. Moments later, he crossed them over his head, "Spin it."

"Going right."

"Stop. Down one fps. Three, two, one. And you're down. Standby for locks."

"Standing by."

Wallace shuffled back to the interior bulkhead, pulled a switch down, look back at the shuttle and said, "You are locked."

"Roger locked, starting shutdown." The bay doors started closing, and Fargo stood, stretched and headed for the autochef.

He'd just programmed a coffee when Nicole walked in smiling. "Do one for me, please?"

He was interrupted by the IC coming on with a pop, and Evie saying, "All hands muster in the crew lounge in fifteen segs, I say again, all hands muster in the crew lounge in fifteen for ship briefing."

Captain Jace came in, glanced at Fargo and asked, "You want to show the vid of the ceremony after I do the safety brief?"

"I'd like to. I've talked to everyone, but I haven't told anyone about either that or some other information." Fargo reached into his shipsuit, "While I'm thinking about it," he handed a data chip to Jace, "I want to get McDougal a patent for this repulsor he developed if we can. He saved our asses down there."

Jace took it with a smile, "So that's how all those idiots ended up dead."

Fargo grimaced. "Yes, and McDougal is still apparently having some problems with it, saying he killed innocent people."

"Not from what I saw. Let me send this out and see what can be done. It looks like it's got a lot of potential applications."

***

Fargo stopped the vid and handed the three credit chips to Jiri, "I'm also donating my credits to the Enclave. Now I want to brief you on a couple of other things you may or may not be aware of." He brought up the first holo that Nicole had helped him build, *Thank Deity for neural laces giving me almost a photographic memory.* He called up the memory of his conversation with Colonel Zhu, "This is a list of the Firsties' family trees." He finished explaining the interactions between the generations with the different plots, then put a fourth up, "Now this is where it gets interesting. Similar families involved, but a totally separate plot that we became peripherally involved in by taking the security assignment. PLANSEC found an encrypted data chip in the remains of the comms device that came out of that apartment in Kwamaine. They couldn't decrypt it, and passed it over to GalPat, their Intel section broke it with the chief sergeant's help, and it was a treasure trove of information. Smallwell and Archer were apparently the ringleaders, with these twenty one others as active participants. It looks like five or six were the second level of the organization of that group of twenty one, and ironically when the chief sergeant was undercover, she actually served them at the restaurant. The one female in that second level group was the shooter who was on the north side at Feeder Three. She was found with the needler under her."

Fargo paused and looked around, "Now this is the interesting part, they were *only* out for themselves! They wanted to take down the feeders, dump the planet back to the primitive stage, kill off their elders, and establish their own oligarchy."

There was a rumble of sounds, "'That's stupid', 'idiots'," and other derisive comments, and Fargo waved, "Understood, but all of the Firstie home sites have nuke power. Ninety years ago they didn't have TBT up and functional off-Earth. Their plan was to take the world back to a feudal society with each family that bought in as *owners* of those that they selected to be allowed to survive. PLANSEC were in the process of rounding up the remaining participants, and some of them are supposedly singing like the nearparrot in the cage."

Fargo shut off the holo, "The reason you are just now finding this out is that Colonel Zhu wanted this close hold, because Chief Justicer Freeman was trying to figure out *which* of the charges should be brought. Murder or treason. Either carries the death penalty. It was to the Chief Justicer and the director as to which way it goes. Their goal is to, shall we say, get the populace's attention with these trials. Apparently there will be a number of public executions, either at the Palace, or in each of the participant's hometowns as a lesson to the others."

There was a roar of agreement from the Ghorka, and Fargo smiled as he stepped out of the lounge, leaving them to celebrate amongst themselves.

***

At 0300 ship time, Wallace, now briefed into the fact that Hyderabad was a remote intel gatherer, stood impatiently in front of a bay hatch that had *appeared* in front of him. It slid open and he whistled as he beheld the little stealth shuttle parked there. Checking his soft suit, he stepped across the threshold, "I'm in the bay. Suit checks good."

Jace answered, "Closing hatch. Go ahead and activate the outer door, the probe is five hundred yards out and closing at ten feet per second."

Wallace turned, making sure the inner door was closed, hit the control for zero G, pressure dump, and outer door. He felt the suit stiffen as the atmosphere bled off, and his weight go away. Looking up, he saw the flashing red and yellow beacons, and clomped around the nose of the shuttle as the outer door slid noiselessly open. "Outer is open. No visual on the probe."

"Try now," came over his headset, as an IR pinprick of light hit his visor.

"Got the IR. How do you want to do this?"

"It will drive itself into the bay and park over the sled. All I need is for you to ensure it's aligned with the cradle and push it down."

"Got it." It was eerie to watch the probe as it maneuvered itself blindly into the bay, turned and parked itself over the cradle. "Centered in the cradle, right," Wallace asked.

"Centered is correct."

Wallace pushed it about a foot forward, then gently pushed down on the nose, which settled into the cradle. Walking to the aft end, he pushed it down, and it clunked into the cradle. "It's in."

"Okay, you can secure back to quarters now," Captain Jace said, as the sled quietly disappeared through a hatch in the aft bulkhead.

Wallace shook his head in amazement, clomped back around to the hatch and reversed the sequence, closing the outer door, repressurizing, and finally opening the inner hatch. Once he stepped through, the inner hatch closed and a panel slid to cover it. *This… this is just fucking amazing. Bays that appear out of nowhere, a stealth shuttle, spook fucking probes. And nobody knows about it.* He peeled out of his soft suit, stowed it in the maintenance locker, and headed back to his cabin, smiling.

The next morning Fargo and Nicole sat in the crew's mess, quietly eating breakfast, smiling at each other. Fargo reached out, *"Thank you for last night."*

Nicole smiled from ear to ear, *"Oh no, thank you! That was… satisfying, to put it mildly."*

Fargo laughed. *"Satisfying? Is that what you call it? I'm just glad the cabins are pretty soundproof."*

She reddened slightly, saying, "I don't care. Everybody here knows about us, and it has been three months." Liz stuck her head in, and Nicole asked, "You need me?"

"If you're not too busy. There's something you need to see."

Curious, Nicole got up, dropped her tray in the recycle and said, "I'll see you later," winking at Fargo.

Nicole followed Liz up to the bridge, "What's up?"

Liz plopped in the seat she'd adopted as her station and brought up one of the large screens, "What do you think of that?"

Nicole looked at the vid, "A moon? With some kind of... surface expression... No wait, that's a..."

"Mining operation maybe?"

Nicole cocked her head, "But that surface doesn't look right."

Liz stepped through the vid, and the picture expanded greatly, "Definitely mining. But that doesn't look like any equipment I've ever seen. And that plume... Volcanic, no... Gas or maybe liquid? There's a... rim around the caldera?"

"How about ice? This is Eros, Endine's moon. And it's an ice moon. I think that's a Goon or Trader ice mining operation. There was an alert a couple of months ago about ice blocks with *unusual* composition showing up in some locations."

Nicole sat down, "I obviously didn't see that. Where did this data come from?"

Jace stepped onto the bridge, "From a stealthed drone we dropped the last time we were here. It was sent in on a ballistic trajectory to check out the other things in the system. We picked it up last night, and it captured this."

"Have you reported it?"

Jace laughed. "Not yet, the analysis is not complete. There are some *strange* things in the data." He leaned over, "May I?"

Liz nodded and moved over, as Jace forwarded the data to a particular location, "What do you think of that?"

Nicole bumped the frames forward and backward, "It... It looks like a ship is coming out of that geyser!" She zoomed in until the frame blurred, "That *is* a ship! How?"

Jace stood back smiling, "Remember Enceladus?"

Fargo stepped into the hatch, "Permission, Captain?"

Jace waved magnanimously, "Enter, sir. What do you know about Enceladus?"

Fargo looked around in confusion, then up at the vid, "Uh, moon of Saturn? That Enceladus?"

Jace nodded. "That one."

"Isn't that where we got a lot of our ice for the exploration and colony ships?"

Jace sighed, "You'll never make a spacer. Enceladus was an ancient discovery orbiting Saturn, in the eighteenth century, and was first closely observed in two thousand five, by an early probe called Cassini. It was determined that there was ice and plumes of water coming from its South Pole. In twenty-one thirty, the USSF made the first landings and determined that in fact there was an eight to ten mile thick ice sheet covering the entire moon and under that was a ten to fifteen mile deep liquid ocean below that. They drilled out one of the vents, and sent probes down, finding a thin layer of atmosphere between the ocean and the ice. While it wasn't quite habitable atmosphere, they were able to place some specialized Habs down there that floated on the water. They also, starting in twenty-one fifty, started mining the surface ice using 'Stroid procedures and lasers to cut ice blocks to size. They developed a specialized *tractor* to pull the ice blocks up, put them in Saturn's orbit and marked them with beacons so the colony ships could get ice to use as water and micrometeorite shields."

Nicole asked, "Did the miners… live below the ice?"

"Yes, apparently it was quite the plumber's job. There was considerable gravity compared to the 'Stroids, about point five G, and no danger of being thrown off a 'Stroid during the mining. It was mostly automated, and they did three year tours, then had a year off."

Nicole looked at the images again, "I wonder… could this be the same technology?"

Jace nodded. "It's on the off side of the moon, not visible from Endine, and that piece looks like a pressor. It could shove the ice blocks into space away from the planet, and nobody would be the wiser."

Fargo, confused, asked, "What… are we going to do anything about it?"

The other three shook their heads in unison, and Jace answered, "No, we'll do an analysis, send it in, and let the nearelephants make that decision."

Jace glanced at the ships clock on the center console. "And we have thirty segs to the first transition. I'd suggest everyone go back to their cabins and secure for transition."

Evie turned, a smile on her face, "I'll do my best to make it a smooth transition, sir."

Surprise

Fargo groaned as they spit out the far side of the hyper gate, *Deity, I truly hate transitions. I can't understand how people put up with this time after time. It's like being torn apart and put back together every time… I wonder where we are, this time.*

The IC came on with a pop, "Translation successful. We have a six div transit to the next gate. Passengers are free to move around for the next five divs. Clean up crew to compartment C-23-4 starboard, again."

Fargo winced in sympathy, apparently Devi had even more problems with hyper translations that he did. He puked *every* time, and apparently missed the sick sack every time too. Fargo got up, stretched, popped his shoulder, and rotated it slowly. *Not forty-one anymore. I know the surgery was successful, but dammit, it still hurts when the weather changes, or I do shit like this.* He dilated the hatch and headed for the mess, glancing at his wrist comp to see if it was lunch yet.

Nicole pushed him in the back, and he jumped. "Hurry up. I need coffee." He stopped and turned, pulling her into his arms. He kissed her, and she pushed him away. "Coffee, not kisses. Cofffeeee," she caroled.

Fargo laughed. "Okay, okay, coffee."

Evie purred, "I saw that PDA, Captain," as she stalked down the passageway. "The captain would like to see you at your convenience."

"Okay, let me get some coffee in me first."

Evie nodded. "I will pass that along."

After getting their coffee bulbs, Fargo and Nicole sat at one of the tables, "So, how's the AAR coming?" Fargo asked.

"Almost completed. We've documented the actions, both at Feeder Three and Feeder Four, including videos, interviews, and diaries from the duty folks. We're still working on the ambush of Lev and Shanni. The videos from GalPat's surveillance cameras aren't the best, and it was a block from the nearest one. At least they took out most of the attackers before that one asshole shot them in the back."

Fargo's face darkened, "And Jiri is still mad that I wouldn't let them go hunting. I know their culture is pretty strict on retribution, but I had to bow to GalPat on that one. At least GalPat caught him, and they're finally putting him on trial."

"Shouldn't have been a trial. He should have been shot. He admitted, hell, even *bragged* about it, when they arrested him!"

"I agree..." Suddenly the IC popped on, the lights flashed red then back to white. A discordant thrumming started up and Fargo tensed, remembering the last time he'd felt that. A two toned siren sounded, "General Quarters. Prepare for maneuvering. All passengers return to your cabins. Captain Fargo to the bridge, please." It repeated twice more, but Fargo was already running for the bridge as Nicole sprinted for her cabin, the two coffee bulbs left on the table in their haste.

As Fargo slid through the hatch, Captain Jace turned to him, "Seat please, Captain. We have a situation."

Fargo slipped into the captain's chair as the hatch closed and he felt his ears pop as the positive pressure system came on, "What kind of situation?"

"There is a beacon from a shuttle, pinging in free space and drifting toward the jump point. There is also a target attempting to hide behind the fourth planet. Analysis shows it to be the Ex-*Ganymede*, which was sent to the breakers in twenty-eight sixteen. There is also a distant track, heading for the local sun that appears to be a dead ship."

"What is here? Wherever here is. Didn't we go through this before with a phantom ship?"

"Nothing here, and yes, we did. It's simply an intersection between two jump points. There was a habitable planet here many years ago, but was destroyed during a battle between GalPat and the Dragoons in the first war, by a planet buster. We are on a ballistic approach to the shuttle and see if there is anyone alive."

"Ballistic approach?"

"Simply, we are coasting for about another thirty segs. We have not powered up since we dropped into the system."

"What do you intend to do with the shuttle?"

"Depends on what we find. If there is anyone alive, rescue them. If not, salvage if possible. If not, vector to the sun for destruction."

"Vector to the sun?"

"The shuttle is a hazard to navigation. It's not noted on any star charts, and it could merge with a ship at the hyper point, which would not be good. Therefore, we toss it into the sun. That way it's out of the way."

"So why the GQ? And why Fleet tones?"

Jace grinned, "Why not. It's something everyone on here is familiar with. As far as why GQ, we don't know what the destroyer is going to do, if anything. But if people are strapped in, I can maneuver up to the human limits without risking killing someone for being out of position."

"Human limits?"

"We can pull thirty Gs, but humans can only stand twelve to fifteen. The IGPs can offset all G forces up to fifteen, but beyond that, it's a one for one. In other words, at twenty Gs, you would feel five Gs. Link with the ship, please."

Fargo pulled his hands out of his lap and placed them on the armrests, and felt the tingle and ping as the ship interfaced with his neural lace. Data started flowing faster than he could functionally review it, and he had to remember the technique Jace had taught him to allow his mind to catch up. He also realized he was *seeing* all the inputs from the various sensors, including tracks, merge points, and the ranges to the shuttle, the destroyer, its estimated pop-up position, and a countdown clock until that pop up point was reached. All of the planets in the system, their tracks and the jump points were also displaying.

Fargo glanced at the screens and realized that they had *flipped* and were now showing the combat screens, as he thought of them. "Are you going to hail the shuttle?"

"Once we put it on the starboard side. With a tight beam, that points away from where the destroyer is. No need to let them have any warning."

Fargo wondered where they could put the shuttle, if they brought it aboard, and he called up the ship's schematic while they waited to close. There was another entire shuttle bay that he hadn't known existed, aft of the forward bay. Nosing around the schematic, he saw another set of bays on the port side, with the aft one a much smaller bay. Just as he started to ask, the ship's radio came on, "Unknown shuttle. Unknown shuttle. Ship *Hyderabad* hailing on Galactic distress. Is there…"

A female voice answered, "Oh my God. Yes, yes!" She screamed, "We're alive! We need rescue."

"How many souls and origin?"

"Four. Three human, one Dragoon. And one Dragoon casualty."

Jace looked at Fargo, who shrugged. Jace nodded. "Per Galactic law, we are required to save them, regardless of origin. Will this be a problem?"

Fargo shook his head. as the relevant portion of the law popped up on the screen, "No. Touchy, but we'll do it."

"Shuttle, are you able to transfer?"

The female voice, much more calm replied, "Negative. Only one suit. We are the only survivors of Star Lines ship that was blown up by unknown parties when we transitioned."

A male voice broke in, "*Hyderabad*, Spacer two Lherson, I have twenty segs of fuel left. I flew scooters in GalPat, but not shuttles. Also, I blew emergency disconnects to get us out of the ship."

Captain Jace arched an eyebrow, and Fargo saw the starboard aft bay door cycle open. "Standby, we will tractor you into the bay. Please strap into couches at this time. We are one thousand yards aft and closing."

"Now," the female voice asked.

"Yes, now. We will pick you up as quickly as possible."

Fargo glanced at the destroyer track and timer, noting it was at 30 seconds and counting. "What about…"

Jace's grin was feral, "We're hot. Both lasers are deployed, counter battery missiles are tracking, and we have good ranging to the target exposure point. If they fire, they will die. We may, or may not."

Fargo shook his head as he watched the screens. *So fucking glad I went troop. At least I wouldn't have to wait to die, and see it coming. Spacers are bat crazy…*

A disembodied voice that he thought of as voice one said, "Missiles away. Destroyer is max accel."

Fargo suddenly felt like the weight of the world was pressing on his chest as the ship went from coasting to maximum acceleration and the rumbling growl he'd heard before increased in pitch.

A scream was heard over the radio before it was choked off.

Voice three said, "Counter battery away. Only two missiles inbound. Firing dorsal lasers in three, two, one." The groaning sound increase in pitch, rising to nearly a scream, as the mechanical voice continued, "9, 8, 7, 6, 5, 4, 3, 2, 1. Cease fire." There was a *'ting'* and the loud noises stopped almost immediately, as the destroyer was blown to pieces when the containment failed on the power plant in an actinic blast.

Fargo turned to Jace and grunted, "Why. Accel. Like. This?" He gasped out.

"Just in case there is something else out there, like a stealthed missile. At this short a range, the missiles can't turn, so anything would be a proximity explosion, not directly on us."

"Oh…" Fargo slumped unconscious. Five segs later, the acceleration came off, and Fargo looked around wildly. "What… What happened?"

"Nothing. We're proceeding to the jump point. You might want to go check on the people in the shuttle. I fear they are still unconscious."

Fargo wobbled to his feet, mumbling, "I'm not much better."

"I will send Klang and Khalil to assist. If you could provide guards?"

"Okay. Page Boykin and Jiri and tell them to meet me at the shuttle bay with two Ghorkas for guards."

Walking slowly down to toward the shuttle bay, he knocked on Nicole's hatch, "You moving?"

A mumbled, "Barely," was heard.

"Might need you. We apparently rescued a marooned shuttle in the middle of killing a destroyer."

The hatch dilated and Nicole stared at him, "Say that again?"

"C'mon. There is apparently at least human female on this shuttle, along with a Dragoon. I'm hoping Boykin is up and moving. Just in case, can you come too?"

"What in the hell? And how do you know... Never mind. Not asking."

The IC came on with a ping, "This is the captain. We had a minor issue with what appears to be a rogue destroyer. We are sorry for the acceleration, but it was necessary to clear the area. If anyone needs medical assistance, please speak up and a medic will respond. We have four divs to the next jump."

Three segs later, they stood at the hatch to the shuttle bay with Boykin, Jiri, Devi, Klang, and Grayson. Grayson had his med kit slung over his shoulder as Klang asked, "Desired is the hatch open first, Captain?"

Boykin interrupted, "My preference would be that they crack the hatch, we get an air sample, *then* we go in. Can you plug an IC cable into the port by the hatch for the Captain?"

"Plug the cable, I will. Dedicated circuit, do you wish?"

"Yes, please."

"Comply I will." Klang went through the hatch, pulling a headset and cables from one of the storage bins adjacent to the hatch. Striding to the shuttle, he plugged the cable in, plugged a second cable into the first one, then plugged it into a jack next to the hatch. Stepping back through, he plugged another cable into a jack, handing it to Fargo. "Live, it is. Dedicated it is."

Fargo put the headset on, and keyed the mic. Hearing a pop, he said, "Shuttle, this is *Hyderabad*. Can you hear me?"

He heard a groan, but no answer. "Shuttle, this is *Hyderabad*. Can you hear me?"

A cough followed by a weak voice answered, "Hyd… Shuttle. Lherson. I hear you."

Glancing a Klang, he said, "The bay is pressurized. If you're equalized, can you go ahead and pop the hatch? We want to get an air sample before we come in."

Another cough was heard, then, "K, give me a seg… Been in zero for… for a lot of days. Bridget and Cedar are unconscious, and Ton is really bad off."

A little more than a seg later, they saw the aft hatch swing open, a disheveled bearded figure leaning against the door frame. Fargo turned to Khalil, "Air quality?"

Grayson looked at his data comp, "Appears to be good. Possibly some fecal matter, and… Vomit?" He cocked his head. "Yes. Vomit. I would recommend breathing masks." He opened a compartment and pulled out seven breathing masks, "Please gear up, and we will secure the hatch as soon as we go through. Will you have the bridge run the scrubbers on high for this bay, please?" Klang nodded.

Everyone took the masks, put them on, and checked the seals. When that was done, Klang opened the hatch and they filed quickly through, with Fargo in the lead. Lherson was now sitting in the hatch, and looked at them curiously as they approached.

"Fecal matter and vomit. We're scrubbing the air," Fargo said. "Ethan Fargo. Supercargo. Klang is crew, Grayson is a medic, Nicole and Boykin are here for the women. Jiri and Devi to guard the Dragoon."

Lherson coughed again, "Ton doesn't need guarding, he needs a med comp. We've basically been out of water for two days. Apparently his hydration requirements are much higher than ours. He's young too, which might have something to do with it. His mother is… well Matriarch, died after we escaped, and is in the offside airlock. She's in a soft suit. We kept that depressurized the entire time."

Nicole asked, "Where are the females?"

"Bridget is in the cockpit, Cedar is in the forward compartment." Nicole and Boykin were up and in the shuttle before he could finish the sentence, Grayson following closely behind. He said, "Ton… Ton, if he's still alive, is in the aft compartment. He… he gave his parole."

Fargo said, "We'll get you some water. Klang, can you get the Dragoon?"

Klang nodded slowly, "Get him, I will. Place him where?"

"Med comp."

Klang stepped lightly into the shuttle, and Fargo turned to Jiri, "Can y'all go with him?"

Jiri nodded. "No problem. The med comp is automatic, right?"

"Yes. See if you can find a shipsuit that might fit him while you're at it. Ask one of the crew."

Klang stepped out, the young Dragoon lolling loosely in his arms, "Good shape, he is not. Grayson says rush."

"Med comp."

Jiri and Devi headed for the hatch and had it open before Klang got there, as Nicole yelled, "Fargo, need a little help here!"

Lherson was mumbling, "We made it, can't believe we fucking made it." Tears rolled down his face, and Fargo patted him awkwardly on the shoulder, "I'll be back, and get you some water, and a fresher, along with a clean shipsuit."

Hopping into the shuttle, he made his way forward in the dim lighting, and saw Nicole and Grayson bent over a young girl. "Can you carry the other one, she's in the cockpit with Boykin? She's, hell, both of them are still unconscious."

Fargo picked up the older female after he and Boykin got her out of the copilot's seat. As they came back, Grayson picked up the young girl. "I have this one. She needs hydration… she may need more."

Fargo said, "I had Klang put the Goon in the med comp. Do we need to pull him out?"

Grayson shook his head. "Not right now. He's the worst of them." I need these two to medical and I'll get IVs and nanites going."

***

Three divs later, Fargo, Captain Jace, Jiri, Boykin and Astrogator Bridget Solly sat in the crew's mess. Solly had just finished the story of their escape, since

Lherson was still sedated in the med bay while the nanites and rehydration did their work, alongside Cedar. Solly twirled the bulb of liquid, "I still cannot believe we've survived. We were to the point that we were talking about dumping atmo, and just ending it all. I don't think Ton would have lasted another two days, and Cedar was failing rapidly too. Dean was just amazing. He did all that with at least one or two broken ribs. And managed to set Cedar's arm, and get Ton to not try to kill us."

Captain Jace leaned back, "Amazing story. In many ways, simply amazing. I can't help but wonder if that was an accidental attack, or on purpose, to kill Ton'Skel. We won't know until somebody examines what the matriarch has in her craw. We might do an x-ray, but somebody is going to have to…"

Solly saw nods around the table, "Her craw?"

Jace replied, "If Ton'Skel really is heir to Ton'Mose, she would be carrying something that proves both her and his patrimony."

"Is he important? I mean…"

That generated laughter around the table, and she blushed, as Jace continued, "Ton'Mose is… literally *the* head Dragoon. He is their equivalent of the president." Turning to Fargo, he said, "The only thing we can do is go to Star Center, now. Effectively, we've just become a Diplo mission. But we're going to have to go in quiet, in case there are others that might want to finish the job. Don't know what, or who the destroyer was working for."

"Oh, I had no… I mean, maybe the Captain knew who he was, but the crew didn't."

Grayson came in, dialed up a bulb from the autochef and leaned against the next table, "Captain, I am happy to report the Dragoon will live. I estimate another eight divs of treatment and we can pull him out and put the young girl in. I have them both sedated right now, and she is in a new plascast for her broken arm, with an IV of hydration running. Ms. Levesque is sitting with her now. Whomever set it, they did a good job."

Bridget colored, "We both did it."

Grayson smiled. "Well, you did good! She will only need about four divs of treatment."

The IC popped on, "Hyper in fifteen segs. All crew report to stations, all pax report to your cabins."

Captain Jace stood, "Well, back to work. Another nine days to Star Center. I'll put a note on the transit file for your folks Captain, to ensure they get paid for the extra days. It's not like they have any choice. And I'm not going to declare us as a diplo. We will only use that if we have to."

Star Center

When Ton'Skel came out of the med box, both Captain Jace and Fargo were there, along with Lherson. When the med box was opened, Jace leaned in and placed the portable GalTrans around Ton's neck. He immediately looked at Lherson and asked, "My Matriarch?"

Lherson nodded. "She is aboard and safe. She has been transferred to a special compartment onboard with two of their troops who died."

Ton started trying to sit up, and Fargo extended his hand. Ton looked up at him, then put his hand out. Fargo gripped it and said, "When you are ready."

Ton pulled himself to a sitting position and asked, "Where are we?"

Jace answered, "We are on the way to Star Center. Our understanding is that was your destination before you were attacked."

Ton nodded. "I… I was to get a medical… pro… procedure? There. I am prisoner?"

Jace looked at Fargo who said, "No. If your parole is still good, you are not a prisoner."

"You make that decision?"

Fargo nodded. "I can, for the troops on board. The rest is up to Captain Jace and you."

Ton stood shakily, then looked squarely at Fargo, "I, Ton'Skel, heir to Ton'Mose, do give my parole."

"Parole is accepted. You are allowed anywhere on the ship except the bridge and engineering," he replied with a side glance at Jace. "My troops will not harm you."

Jace said, "You can eat in the crew's mess, if that is more comfortable for you. That way you are not among the troops."

Ton nodded in understanding. "Food?"

Fargo said, "AI, please page Senior Grayson to the crew's mess. It's not an emergency."

The IC clicked on, "Senior Medic Grayson, Senior Medic Grayson, please go to the crew's mess. Non-emergency."

Fifteen segs later, Grayson was working with the autochef and Ton'Skel to come up with food that he could eat, as Grayson fed him bulbs of enriched water to keep him hydrated. Fargo had gone down to the troop mess and was sitting with Jiri, Horse, Nicole, Daman, and Barun. "Here's the plan. We're going to deliver Ton'Skel to Star Center. He's given his parole, so I don't want anybody reacting to his presence. He's allowed the run of the ship, excluding the bridge and engineering. If he asks any questions, the troops are allowed to answer them, and if, big if, he wants to eat down here, he's allowed to do so. Remember, he's young, so he's got to be curious. And if anybody gets info from him about anything related to his family or home life, let Chief Levesque know. And one more thing, the young girl Cedar considers him a friend, so nothing to see there, and no overt reactions."

There were nods around the table, but Horse had to say something, "You do realize that GalPat is going to have slashlizards when they find out who we're transferring, and they are going to want to take him."

Fargo grinned, "Which is why we're not going to tell them. This is now a diplo mission, which puts it out of GalPat's hands."

Horse shook his head and laughed. "Ekavir you have more balls than sense. They will hang you from the highest yardarm at the academy if they ever find out."

Fargo laughed. "Which means they won't find out, right?"

Jiri chimed in, "Not from us. What about the woman and spacer? Or the kid?"

"Star Lines has NDAs, anybody that violates them will never work in space again. I think Cedar can be impressed that it would not be in her best interest to tell the story."

***

Three days later, Ton wandered into the cargo bay as the troopers were working out. They were just finishing the kukri workout, and starting the hand to hand portion. Ton looked around and found Jiri leaning against a piece of equipment, coffee bulb in hand, and he walked over, "Jiri?"

"Yes?"

"I hear talk of honor and respect, but I do not understand."

"What do you mean, Ton?"

"I hear people talk about Fargo, but with different name among troops. And respect."

"Do your people not rule that way?"

Ton shook his head. and the GalTrans gave some sound that Jiri figured was laughter, "Oh no. Govern? Is right word? With power. Must be better than others. Honor is to powerful. Those who fight/kill." He waved his arm at the troops, "They fight/kill?"

Jiri smiled. "No, they *practice* to fight/kill. Only fight/kill enemy. Not among ourselves." He took a sip of his bulb, then continued, "Fargo, or Ekavir in our culture, is admired for his bravery and willingness to do everything we do. He does not set himself above us. He leads by example."

"Then what honor?"

Jiri shrugged. "It is like another word for respect. Meaning much respected. We are honored he is our captain."

"He does not rule by fear? He does not punish? Did he fight you for lead?"

Jiri laughed. "No, he does not want to be the leader. We forced him to do it."

Ton cocked his head in amazement, "Not leader, leader? How?"

"Because he does not like to kill. But he is very good at it. And does not want troops to die."

"But tr… fighters are meant to die for glory of leader."

"Not in our culture, Ton. Not in our culture. Now you might want to leave, we are going to increase the gravity levels to two gravities to practice."

"Twice gravity, why?"

"We never know what kind of environment we may have to fight in. So we practice in different environments. Hot, cold, thin air, high gravity."

Ton nodded. "Smart. I leave now."

Jiri made sure to catch up with Nicole as soon as the practice session was over and reported the conversation to her. She laughed. "Nice job Warrant, you've probably just confused the hell out of that young Dragoon. What you've just told him goes against everything he's probably been taught."

Lherson and Solly sat in the crew's mess each lost in their own thoughts, even as they shared a table. Cedar, now out of the cast, sat at the far end of the table, playing with a puzzle that Klang had made out of bits of metal for her. Lherson finally said, "Sol... Briget, what are we going to do?"

"I'm not sure, Dean. We'll have to report in. I'm pretty sure there is either an agent or an actual Star Lines site at Star Center. The captain was good enough to salvage the shuttle, so we've got that, but there is so much neither of us knows about what happened..."

Lherson shook his head. "Nothing we can do about that. All we can report is what we did. At least we survived, which is..." Glancing at Cedar, he continued softly, "the best we could do." He toyed with the coffee bulb, "Do you think we'll be met?"

"Well, the captain told me he's not telling anyone what happened to us, in case they try to... finish the job. Said he would report it after they got Ton off the ship somehow."

"Isn't that illegal? I mean in GalPat, our skippers immediately reported incidents to higher as soon as they could."

She shrugged. "Commercial isn't necessarily that way. Lots of stuff, both good and bad, stays in the company. They don't want competitors to gain any advantage."

"Even for safety things?"

"Well, maybe not safety."

"I would have thought they'd report the destroyer they killed."

"Why? They killed it. And this ship is a little strange…"

Lherson laughed. "I think this is an old military transport. It's got all the markings. Lots of what I'd guess are reconfigurable holds, space that could be turned into billeting, and there are some suspicious bulges on the hull that make me wonder. And the extra bays."

Klang tromped into the mess, another thing with dangly bits in his hand, "Miss little, puzzle you like," He asked as he crouched next to Cedar.

She smiled at him, "It is hard, Klang. Can you show me? I can't get past here," she said, shoving the puzzle at him.

Klang took it gently, and rotated it in his massive hand, then said, "This piece, you see?" He picked one up and slid it into the center, "Like this it goes. Piece next." A few seconds later, he'd demonstrated and explained it and Cedar clapped.

She reached out, "Let me try now!" He put it back to where she had been, and she repeated his moves, tongue sticking out the side of her mouth as she concentrated. Once she completed it, she crowed, "I did it! I did it!" She set it on the table and turned to him, "You have another," she said excitedly.

Klang picked up the pieces and dangled them in front of her, "Once you I show. Harder."

He carefully did one piece at a time, as Cedar concentrated intensely, then said plaintively, "One more time, *please*?"

Lherson and Solly both grinned at her tone as Klang promptly undid and redid the puzzle. Solly said softly, "Got every man in the crew wrapped around her little finger."

He nodded. "And she's got a *lot* of daddies now. A bunch of daddies I wouldn't want mad at me. You do *not* want any Ghorka pissed at you, that's a terminal illness."

***

Captain Jace slid the *Hyderabad* into her docking bay without a bump and said, "Release the passengers." As the call was going out over the IC, he turned to Fargo, "Can you set an armed guard? I just squirted a routine encrypted report to the local GalPat office, and I'm putting Solly on line with the Star Lines office now. I've also requested the ambassador from the Dragoon embassy meet the ship immediately with equipment to receive a Dragoon casualty."

Fargo nodded and keyed his wrist comp, "Jiri, can we post a four man watch? Side arms only two in, two out on the main hatch?"

Jiri answered, "Not a problem. They will be at the hatch in fifteen."

Jace nodded. "It will take that long to connect the umbilicals and position the module and pressurize it."

"That's good Jiri, thank you." He looked at Jace, "So you're betting the 'Goon will get here before the Star Lines or GalPat people?"

Jace grinned, "I might have given the Dragoon the diplo code..."

"So how long do you figure we have?"

"A half div before the Star Lines folks, and a full div before GalPat gets here. Ton'Skel and his mother should be long gone."

Ton'Skel sat disconsolately in the bay adjacent to the main hatch, his hand resting on the casket containing his matriarch on the raised platform. He looked again at the small space underneath the casket, and shivered as he thought about having to crawl in there again, but he also understood that there might be another attempt on his life here, and the humans were doing everything they could to protect him. Lherson and Solly, both in new Star Lines uniforms stood off to the side, with Solly holding Cedar's hand. Captain Jace and Fargo had agreed they needed to be present, and available to answer questions if the ambassador had any.

Five segs after the main hatch was opened, the Dragoon ambassador and three others with a grav sled were seen approaching the hatch. Captain Jace told Khalil to immediately admit the ambassador only. After a little bit of back and forth, the ambassador walked stiffly through the hatch and bowed to Captain Jace, his GalTrans growling, "What body do you have?"

"And your name is?"

The Dragoon visibly restrained himself, "I am Ser'Mose."

"Are you related to Ton'Mose?"

"He is my brother," the GalTrans snarled, as the ambassador took a step forward.

Jace said, "I am Captain Jace. We picked up a shuttle from the Star Lines mission…"

"Get on with it!"

Jace nodded. "Come with me, please." He turned and walked to the bay hatch, "There is something you should see."

The ambassador was on his heels as Jace dilated the hatch, and he took three steps into the bay before Ton'Skel's presence registered. The ambassador's steps faltered and he reached out saying plaintively, "Ton? Ton!"

Ton's head came up, and he rushed toward the ambassador, knocking the chair over as he ran into the ambassador's arms. There were quiet words, not meant for anyone else, then the ambassador asked, "Who is in the casket?"

Ton answered, "My Matriarch. She… She saved my life, along with these three." He said, pointing to Lherson, Solly, and Cedar. "We are the only survivors. My Matriarch lived for… a while, but we ran out of medication."

The two of them walked slowly to the casket, and the ambassador put his hand reverently on it. Jace said, "It's not sealed. You can open it."

Ton stepped to the side, and Cedar ran to him, hugging him with tears in her eyes, as the ambassador slowly opened the casket, looked in, and bowed his head silently. Then he gently closed the casket and turned, surprised to see Cedar holding Ton's hand. She said, "You can't be mad at him. He did everything he could to save his mama. Mine… my momma and daddy died…"

The ambassador looked around in anger, "Who, how?"

Jace answered, "We believe they were attacked by a rogue destroyer, which we killed. Neither Solly or Lherson know for sure what happened, but they got Ton'Skel and his mother out, along with Cedar. They drifted for over thirty days before we dropped into that sector and were attacked." He handed the ambassador a package with six data cubes, "Here are the details from the shuttle and from our ship. I apologize for the quality of our ship data, we are a simple merchant with only basic defensive armament and sensors."

"Have you reported this to GalPat?"

"That report is going through channels. We thought it best to notify you *first* in case this was an attempt on the heir. He is the heir, correct?"

The ambassador stiffened and finally said, "Yes. Ton is the heir. There have been *issues* at home."

Jace said, "We have a way to get him off without anyone knowing, if you want. There is room below the casket for him under the drape. Are your men trustworthy?"

"Yes, they are family."

"Then I suggest you bring the sled aboard and we do this. I expect Star Lines and GalPat to be here shortly. I will tell them they may contact you for further information concerning your casualty."

He nodded decisively, "I will get them."

Five segs later, the ambassador bowed to Lherson, Solly, Cedar, and Captain Jace. "We thank you for what you did. You will be named in our hall of honor for your fighting deeds." The Dragoons marched solemnly back up the module and disappeared into the station.

A little over ten segs later, a harried man in a Star Lines uniform rushed down the module, closely followed by a GalPat major, with both of them requesting immediate access. Captain Jace invited them both to the crew's mess, and pointed each of them at the stack of data cubes, then began the laborious task of answering as many of their questions as they could.

Four divs later, the Star Lines rep left, accompanied by Lherson, Solly, and Cedar, with a promise to recover the shuttle within one day. The GalPat major looked around at Captain Jace, Fargo, Nicole, and Jiri, shook his head and said, "Why do I get the feeling I'm not getting the whole story here? Again, why didn't you broadcast an emergency and run to the nearest planet?"

Jace smiled tiredly, "Simple Major. The mission was to here, not an intermediate location. We were afraid to stop anywhere else, for fear of being attacked. The same reason we didn't broadcast an emergency."

Turning to Fargo he asked, "So you nor your people had *anything* to do with this?"

Fargo said, "No, for the umpteenth time. We were merely passengers. We assisted with recovery of the

Goon, but that was it. And we provided security when we docked here. That's it."

"So this Goon *ambassador* has the body? And you gave it up without our approval?"

Jace stood, "We did what is the accepted practice in the galaxy. We notified the next of kin, if you will, and provided a dignified transfer, as I've shown you on the video on cube seven. To do anything else would have contravened accepted practice. In any case, what would a dead body have told you that we didn't already note?"

The major grumbled, "Don't go anywhere. Plan on a three day hold until this goes up the chain. GalPat will provide compensation for dockage fees." He gathered up the data cubes, put them in his satchel, and stomped out, trailed by Jace.

At the hatch, Jace said, "Am I to assume we are not restricted to ship?"

"No."

"Thank you Major, have a pleasant day."

Homecoming

Evie piloted the *Hyderabad* as smoothly as ever into what Fargo now thought of as *her* parking spot at the Enclave. All of the members of the Enclave were standing at the edge of the village as the forward ramp came down, and the Ghorka, led by Jiri and Horse, marched off in column. Fargo stood on the ramp, saluting them as they passed, Nicole at his side, along with Captain Jace, Wallace, and Liz. Once they were at the village, Barun, Horse, Daman, Jiri and three others, along with the priest, returned to the ship. Fargo looked at Jiri, who nodded at the caskets and asked formally, "Please assist us, sir."

Fargo nodded silently and stepped to the rear of the left casket. He knew it was Shanni's and he also knew he didn't want to face Rami, his wife. Lev hadn't been married, but he would be mourned by the entire village. The priest said a short prayer, and Jiri took charge. They picked up the caskets and marched off the ship with them side by side. They carried them all the way to the village, with Rami stepping out of the crowd and laying her hand on Shanni's casket, as if she had known which one he was in. He saw a single tear roll down her face, then she faced forward and marched the rest of the way to the chapel with them.

They were placed on two biers side by side at the front of the chapel, and the priest said another prayer as they stood with bowed heads. Once that was completed, they left the chapel, leaving Rami to her private grief. Lal stepped up to his side, "There will be three days of mourning, then we will send them into the next life. We would appreciate it if you would participate in the funeral."

Fargo raised his eyes to the sky and blew out a breath, "Are you sure you want me to? All I seem to be able to do is get your people killed, Lal."

Lal laid a hand gently on his arm, "You are not to blame. This we know. You are their commander, and it would be in their honor to have you participate in their send off."

"I hate this Lal. I purely hate losing people."

"We know. That is why we follow you. You do not throw men away in fruitless causes."

Fargo sighed, "Then I will be here. Thank you. I also have memorial credits from the director of Endine for the families."

"We will talk of that later. Please invite Warrant Boykin, Senior Grayson, Senior McDougal, and Chief Levesque also."

"I will."

Lal patted him on the shoulder again as he made the long walk back to the *Hyderabad*, lost in thought.

As he walked back aboard, he heard Captain Jace say, "Ramp is coming up, prepare to depart. Captain Fargo, if you will meet Chief Levesque and the others at the shuttle, Evie will drop you at your respective homes."

Hyderabad was cleared for low orbit as Evie eased the shuttle out of the bay, "Captain, we will drop you and Nicole first, since Rushing River is closer, if that is acceptable."

Fargo looked at the others and saw Wallace and Liz nodding, "Okay."

"Also, Warrant Boykin has completed the placement of the modules on planet, and she, Seniors Grayson, and McDougal are now back in their billets."

"Thank you, Evie."

A div later, Evie parked the shuttle in front of the administration building and Fargo and Nicole walked down the aft ramp, trunks bobbing in their wakes. Fargo told Nicole about the funeral plans, and she nodded sadly as Holly came running across the ramp, closely followed by Ian and Inga, while Luann marched determinedly after them.

Fargo reached out to Nicole, "*I love you. Looks like Holly is glad to see you back.*"

"*I love you too, now get out of my mind. Call me in a couple of days.*"

"*Yes, dear.*"

"*Men!*"

Fargo chuckled as he withdrew and crouched, catching Ian and Inga, "Oof! You trying to knock me over Ian?"

"No, Unka. I wanted to be first to say… Wel… welcome home?"

"Yes, welcome home. Hi Inga."

Inga hugged him shyly, "Uncle Ethan, I am happy to see you."

He hugged her back, "You have been practicing your words, I'm proud of you!"

She beamed up at him, showing a missing tooth and said, "I try. Momma says I need more words."

"Women always do, Inga, remember that." He stood as Luann got to him, "Sis?" He felt her conflicting emotions, fear, relief, and anger as he hugged her.

"Ethan Fargo, you need to stop doing this. It's not like you need the credits. I swear… Men!" She stepped back, wiping a tear away, "I went up and cleaned your cabin. Did you know there are animals prowling around it? I saw all kinds of tracks, some even coming right up on your porch! You need to take one of those sonic alarms up there and use it!"

He heard a beep, and the ramp starting to retract, "Time for us to move. Come on kids, let's get off the ramp so Evie can take off." Taking them by the hands, he nodded to Luann, "Let's go." He saw that Nicole and Holly were already at the edge of the ramp, and Nicole had her arm around Holly, with Holly resting her head on Nicole's shoulder. He also noticed that it was cooler than Endine had been, and it was a beautiful day. He could even smell the nearpines, and inhaled in relief. *I'm home. Now I just have to deal with Luann. And I know she's going to feed me. I need to see OneSvel. I need to get copies of everything that went on to him, so he can...wait, if Jace has already sent it...oh hell, I'll give it to him anyway.*

Luann interrupted his thoughts, "I've got dinner in the oven. We need to get back before it burns. And Misha can take you up to your cabin tomorrow."

"Okay, that sounds good." They walked up to the runabout, and he shook hands with Mikhail, "All your stuff was working when we left."

"So I heard. And I heard it got *interesting* again."

Fargo shrugged. "A little bit."

Luann hissed, "Not in front of the kids."

Fargo and Mikhail looked at each other, and both nodded as Ian asked, "What did you bring me, Unka?"

Luann rolled her eyes, "Ian!"

Fargo laughed. "Sorry Ian, this was a working trip. I didn't have any time to sightsee or do any shopping."

Ian frowned then kicked discontentedly at a rock, "Oh, okay."

Luann chided him, "Ian, you can't expect Uncle Fargo to bring you something *every* time he goes somewhere. Get in the runabout, please."

Ian and Inga climbed in the back seats, but he asked, "Why not? Papa does!"

Luann patiently said, "It's because your uncle's job isn't like your daddy's job."

Luann had pulled out all the stops, making Fargo's favorite meal, and dessert, and the whole time he sensed her fears. Once the kids had been sent upstairs, he finally said, "Luann, what's bothering you?"

She shook her head as she put the dishes in the recycler, "Nothing."

He reached out and turned her to face him, "Lu, don't give me that." He was tempted to reach for her mind, but pulled back.

"I… I was afraid *you* were dead. I… It's not fair. You're all I have left of family, and you go gallivanting off trying to get yourself killed, either by animals or people, and I have to find out what you're doing from somebody else!" Tears rolled down her face, "I can't lose you Ethan! I just… can't."

He did reach out now, pushing calm, and reassurance as he replied, "Luann, I don't take stupid chances, I go after the animals because they are worth a lot of money, and I know how to kill them. That saves lives. The militia, that's a responsibility to this world I call home. I don't go fight the battles, that's what others do. Now I just sit behind the lines and provide communications and some limited direction."

She hugged him, "I'm sorry. I don't mean to…"

He picked her up, eliciting a squeal, "I know. And I'll do better, I promise."

She pushed him away, "Go, I know you and Mikhail *need* to talk without me around, and I have dishes to do. Go!"

***

The next morning, as soon as they finished breakfast, he borrowed the runabout and drove down to the clinic. As he had hoped, OneSvel was there early, and let him in. Handing him the pouch of data cubes, he said, "Here's the complete report, including what's been sent to GalPat. There is ice mining on Eros, their moon. We think it's Traders. There's also some scans in there on an empty star system with two gates and a busted planet. There might be hydrocarbon mining going on there, but we were too busy fighting off a destroyer to stop and look around, so the visuals are not really good. Jace thinks they might be mining hydrocarbons off the remnants of the C3 planet that was there."

OneSvel exuded a pseudopod and took the pouch, his GalTrans twittering, "I will pass this information today. It has been quiet here, other than having to fix a couple of GalPat troops who got a little bit too enthusiastic in a bout with the locals. It seems that five to one odds does not bode well for the troops."

Fargo laughed. "Ego overloaded their asses?"

"Apparently, and the application of blunt instruments reminded them of that. Only a few bones were broken. How are you?"

Fargo shrugged. "I'm here, nothing's changed."

"Sit please." OneSvel extended a pseudopod. "May I?"

"Sure," Fargo said resignedly.

"What is the matter? You do not seem happy."

"Many things. I lost two men on this trip. We have to bury them in two days. If it were not for Captain Jace, we would have died in space when the destroyer attacked us. And we saved a Dragoon, and took him to Star Center without notifying anyone."

OneSvel almost physically recoiled at that, *"What?"* Fargo opened his mind and felt OneSvel probing his memories for what seemed like a div. Then he withdrew, *"You did what is right by law and convention. That is not on you or anyone on that ship; that is Galactic law. That he is the heir makes it… complicated."*

Fargo chuckled. *"You think so? All I want now is to go to my cabin and get away from people."*

"All people?"

Fargo looked at OneSvel, "All but one, okay?"

OneSvel withdrew the pseudopod. "That was not, how you say, appropriate? But, I make humor."

"Joke, OneSvel, it's called a joke. And Taurasians don't have a sense of humor."

"Oh, but Doc Grant has been working with me on… jokes. And how to tell them."

Fargo shook his head sadly, "Oh, Deity. This is not going to end well."

"If you are going to Enclave to bury troops, may I accompany? I would like to check on the young girl we saved and see how she is doing."

"Let me check with Lal."

***

Fargo sighed as he taxied the liteflyer up to his cabin, seeing Canis, Cattus, and Urso sitting on the porch. They knew not to approach it when it was moving, but he sensed their joy and as soon as he shut down and opened the canopy, they charged down the steps toward him. He barely managed to get out of the liteflyer before Canis and Cattus knocked him down, growling, woofing, and licking him. Urso was a little slower, and she moaned as she looked for a place to lick him, finally settled for licking his hair.

He finally got out from under them, and came up spitting drool and wiping his face, "Really girls? Really? *This* is how you welcome me back?" But he was laughing as he said it, and projected his gladness to see them as he petted each one. He unloaded his trunk, put it on the porch and collapsed the liteflyer before pushing it into the storage shed.

Stepping into the cabin, he sighed, *Luann… Dammit, you cleaned and moved things. Now I'll have hell finding...* Laughing as Canis and Cattus ran around smelling things and looking for their food bowls, he walked into the kitchen and checked the autochef. She'd restocked it, and he opened the refrigerator to find that she'd also stocked it with meat for the animals. He was sure she didn't know what he was doing with all that meat, and laughed again, *She's probably thinking I cook steaks every night, and don't ever eat vegetables.*

He took out portions for all three animals, dropping Canis and Cattus portions in their bowls, then carrying Urso's bowl outside where she could eat. *I wonder how they would react to flying in the liteflyer. I wonder if... Maybe I'll try that later. Eventually Luann will find out, and when she does...Gah!*

He dialed up a 1200 calorie meal, and brewed one of his cups of coffee as he checked the e-tainment system for messages. Thankfully, there weren't many, and he decided to eat in peace before he looked through them.

After dinner, he plopped down on the couch, called up the e-tainment and decided to watch an antique movie, rather than looking at the messages. Three divs later, he woke up with a crick in his neck, and Canis pawing at him and whining. "Okay, okay. Lemme get up and I'll let you out!"

He got up slowly, groaned and stumped to the door rolling his head, grumbling, "Getting old. Still don't see how Grayson sleeps like he does," as he opened the door and Canis and Cattus shot by him, heading for the grass. Urso was sprawled peacefully on the porch, and didn't move, other than to twitch an ear as they pelted off the porch.

***

After a solid nine divs of sleep, he stumbled into the fresher, set it to rejuve, and let the fresher bring him to life. Two bulbs of coffee and a breakfast later, he felt human enough to actually check messages. As soon as he brought the e-tainment system up, it pinged, "INCOMING MESSAGE. IMPORTANCE HIGH. Fargo sighed, "Now what? Display message."

F- PALETTE, R MAJ
T- FARGO, E MIL CPT/LEVESQUE, N MIL SC
S- REPORT TO WHITE BEACH
R- GALPAT OPORD 28240536

GALPAT COL KEADS REQUIRES REPORT ON MILITIA MISSION TO ENDINE. CPT FARGO/SC LEVESQUE TO REPORT IN PERSON TO COL KEADS AS SOON AS PRACTICABLE. ADVISE ETA ASAP.

S/PALETTE

He growled in disgust, "You've got to be shitting me. I know the damn report was sent from Star Center, what the hell else…" Hitting the remote, he said, "Vid call." The screen came up and he continued, "Levesque, Nicole."

He heard a click and a beep, and Nicole answered with no video, "What? Do you know what time it is?"

"Um, morning? Have you checked your messages yet?"

"No, I was blissfully sleeping before you rudely interrupted me, why?"

"Palette sent us a flamer to report *immediately* to White Beach to Colonel Keads."

"Do you think he's that desperate to see us?"

"Not really, I think this is Palette, the colonel probably said something like, ask them to come see me next time they're in town. This is Palette being the officious little shit that he is."

He heard a jaw cracking yawn, and Nicole finally answered, "We're going to the funeral, right? And that's in three days?"

"Yes. We could go on to White Beach from there, and spend the night."

"That has... *possibilities*."

"Good possibilities?"

Nicole laughed, and Fargo had a momentary picture of her nude coming out of the fresher, "Oh, yes, good possibilities. Eight divs with you, without anyone to bother us."

"Okay, I'll message back, and you can concur. Love you."

"Oh, Holly mentioned last night that she's been seeing tracks in the vineyard."

"Tracks?"

"She thinks wolf and cat tracks, big tracks."

"That's... odd."

"She said they apparently started right after we left."

Fargo leaned back and looked at Canis and Cattus, "I wonder…"

Impatiently she snapped, "Wonder what?"

He leaned forward, "I'll come down tomorrow. Can we eat dinner at the winery?"

"Sure, why?"

"I might know, but I want to… confirm something. Don't say anything to Holly other than we'll have dinner with her."

"Alright. I'm going back to sleep. Goodbye."

He went on to the next message in the cue and sighed.

F- RAGSDALE, T. PURCHASING AGENT
T- FARGO, E HUNTER, RUSHING RIVER
S- FURS?

MR FARGO, RAGSDALE HERE. WONDERING IF YOU HAVE ANY FURS. LAST BATCH VERY WELL RECEIVED. AS DISCUSSED WILL ACCEPT AT YOUR LOCATION. SAME PRICE POINT IF SAME QUALITY.

SEMPER FI/RAGSDALE

He quickly drafted a response, and vowed to get back in the Green, knowing there was money to be made, Luann's worries or not. He also drafted a reply to Palette, saying they would be available after the funeral, and asking for Boykin and Grayson to be allowed to attend. He proposed Boykin pick them up and bring them back from White Beach the following day.

The next message brought a smile.

F- HYDERABAD, CAPTAIN JACE
T- FARGO, E
S- MCDOUGAL INVENTION

CANNOT DO PATENT, BUT DE PEREZ GALACTIC OFFERS ONE (1) MILLION CREDITS TO PURCHASE RIGHTS, PLUS ROYALTIES OF ONE (1) PERCENT. WILL YOU ACT AS LOCAL AGENT? ARRANGE MEETING WITH SENIOR SERGEANT MCDOUGAL WITHIN SEVEN (7) DAYS?

R/JACE

He quickly drafted a reply and sent it, smiling as he did so. *This might work out better for Mac. I don't know how much longer he has on this hitch, but I don't see him staying in after this. He was really torn up by what happened. I hope he's talking to the captains or the major.*

Challenges

Fargo glanced back to see Canis sitting up, avidly staring out the side of the liteflyer, her nose pressed against the window, and Cattus curled contentedly on the seat. He smiled, remembering stories from his dad about riding in the ground car with his dog Rex sticking his head out the window and slobbering down the side of the ground car. He felt the liteflyer shift and heard both animals growling. *Now what the hell got into…* He banked sharply to the left, beginning to circle and the animals shifted sides quickly, steepening the bank, "Whoa! You two take it easy back there! He reached out and sensed their hate/prey/fear drives, and wondered what set it off.

As he came around, he saw a shadow moving across a small clearing, and reached out with his empathic senses. *Shit, Silverbacks! Where did they come from?* He spiraled lower, straining to sense whether this was a pair or a single. He reached up and dropped a mark on his nav screen and looked closer at the area, *Damn, it's a pair; they shouldn't be this close to Rushing River.*

Dropping down in altitude, he sidestepped the TBT beam to Rushing River and tried to locate the pair visually, but without success. Both Canis and Cattus continued to growl, noses pressed to the window, and he decided to try something. He reached out to them, on their 'frequency' so to speak, *"Warn others, danger do not fight.* He 'felt' them doing something, but he wasn't sure what it was, as he picked back up above the beams and headed back to the cabin.

Urso was pacing the landing strip when he touched down, and she came loping up to the liteflyer as he shut it off in front of the cabin. He opened the canopy, and she reared up on the side of it, causing him to wince, as she stuck her head in, making sure Canis and Cattus were okay. He chuckled. "Girl, just because you don't like to ride in here doesn't mean they don't. Now get down. He gave her a little mental push, and stepped out as Canis, then Cattus jumped clear of the back seats, and padded over to Urso. He once again 'felt' them communicating, and it frustrated him to be so close but not be able to fully understand them. As MobyDineah had told him, it had taken them years to get the rapport they had with animals, and he couldn't expect to have that happen overnight.

Looking at the sun, he decided there wasn't time to go hunt the Silverbacks today, as the closest place to land he'd found was at least a mile away. He wanted to do another airborne scout tomorrow, maybe two, one on his way to Rushing River, and a second coming home. And he needed to let somebody know where he would be, remembering the incident at the feeder site. After putting the liteflyer away, he quickly called up the mail component of the TBT, posting a notification to the GalPat reps, Sergeant Omar, Nicole, and Luann to spread around Rushing River.

Luann and Nicole both answered immediately, and both asked if he was coming to town tomorrow.

Shaking his head and laughing, he replied he would be there for lunch, telling Luann he would be bringing Nicole with him. Running through the rest of the messages, he groaned when he got to the messages from Horse and Jiri, and glanced at the data comp, *That time of the damn month. Why oh why did I let myself get volunteered for the militia, much less put in charge?* Three divs later, he'd finished signing off on the monthly reports, forwarded them to Colonel Eads, and let the animals out.

He pulled the bead rifle out, tore it down, cleaned it, reassembling it and checking the charge on the power pack. It was at 80%, so he pulled the spare out, put it on, verified it at 100%, and put the original power pack on the charger. That done, he allowed himself a real cup of brewed coffee.

Once the brewing was finished, he poured a cup, then went onto the front porch and settled into the chair as the sun descended in the east. He looked to the west, watching the dual moons rising, and thought about the information both he and Jace had passed up the chain about the ice mining on Eros, Endine's moon. *I wonder who they're going to send to take care of that little problem.*

He finished his coffee as George and Celeste rose in sequence, and Canis, Cattus, and Urso came around the corner of the cabin. Canis and Cattus made for the door, while Urso padded over to him. Fargo scratched around her ears, and Urso moaned contentedly, until he picked up his cup and stood. "Enough." He pushed a thought of contentment at her, and she sighed, sprawling in her accustomed place on the porch. *I'm glad she hates being closed in, having her in the cabin wouldn't be good. Not good at all. Of course Canis and Cattus aren't much better, but at least they don't weigh 300 plus pounds. Guess I should be thankful for that.*

He opened the door and Canis and Cattus stampeded by him, heading for their respective feed bowls. "I'm coming, I'm coming, you two. Just calm down." Putting his cup in the fresher, he opened the refrigerator and pulled out four nearrabbits he'd gotten yesterday up by the waterfall, "Dinner is served. Sit." He reinforced the words with a mental push, and both sat, staring avidly at the food in his hands. Dropping two in each pan, he said, "Okay. Eat," as he stepped out of the way.

He sat in the living room and turned the e-tainment unit on, then decided to send a message to Mikhail that he would be hunting the Silverbacks tomorrow, and when and where he would be. *Better safe than sorry. And Mikhail won't tell Luann, which is good. I want to get there early, so...* He ended up eating a quick bite and headed for bed. Three was going to come early.

***

Fargo moved as quietly as he could, hoping to get to the small meadow he'd observed yesterday before the Silverbacks became active. He could distantly sense them, and they seemed to be close together, so they must have a den in the area. *Another hundred yards, that's all I need. The sun is rising and I need to make sure I'm positioned so I'm not going to have to look into it.* He extended his empath senses, and felt the wolves and mountain lions in the distance, and a couple of bears at his liteflyer, *Helluva backup. Not that anybody would believe it. And if they come in… it'll probably be too late.*

He found a spot he liked, checked the footing, and tramped down some of the grass, making sure there wasn't anything to trip him up if he had to move fast. Now it was a waiting game, depending on the Silverbacks to come out of their den, wherever it was. He sensed it wasn't far, and he scanned the ridge ahead of him, figuring it was somewhere up there. The other Silverbacks he'd taken had all denned up as high as possible. His empath sense picked up separation of the Silverbacks, and he caught movement out of the corner of his eye. Bringing the rifle up, the ridge jumped into focus and he saw a Silverback disappearing behind some boulders. *Well, at least one of them is up and moving.*

He felt the wind shift, and sighed, *Well, the game's on now. I'm betting they'll come after me as soon as they get the scent.* He heard a coughing roar, and saw movement about the same place he'd seen the other Silverback, *That's got to be their den. Not that it'll do me any good right now. Maybe later.*

He turned to keep their mental presence in front of him, and smiled as they came down off the ridge together. *Come on, stay together, please give me a shot!* He was disappointed when they split, and both of them stayed downwind of him, which lessened his worry. He finally saw one, pacing just inside the tree line, and he turned toward it, honoring the immediate threat.

He felt the other Silverback moving away from its mate, while not quite getting directly behind him, but it had done the same thing he'd seen before. He glanced over and didn't see the second one, and turned back to the one that was visible, and saw it turn its back on him. *Oh please, please. Do that again!* He brought the rifle up, making sure the safety was off, and watched as the holo sight popped on as soon as it touched his cheek. The Silverback gave another coughing roar, and turned to pace the other way, and Fargo put two beads into its hindquarters, dropping it in its tracks.

The second Silverback, now broadcasting hatred charged out of the woods as he pivoted, and he started shooting. Left, right, left, right, then three centered as the Silverback launched itself at him. He went to dodge, and his foot slipped, dropping him to his knees. He threw up the rifle in front of him, and it landed between the Silverback's jaws as it bowled him over.

Time seemed to slow as, he managed to get one hand free, pulling his vibro knife. He stabbed up into the belly of the Silverback and ripped down, when he finally realized that it wasn't moving. He squirmed out from underneath it, grunting and pushing, and doing his best to stay clear of the claws. *Gotta get out, not sure if the other one is dead, Deity this sumbitch is heavy!*

With a final panicked heave, he got clear, vibro knife in his hand and he pulled frantically at the rifle. He managed to pry it out of the Silverback's mouth, and saw that the holoscope was destroyed. *Dammit! That is… inconvenient.* He cycled the action, stepped back and fired a round into the ground. The rifle cycled, and he limped over to the first Silverback, pumping two more beads into it from behind. That one never moved, and he grunted in relief.

He turned off the vibro knife, sheathed it, and started limping back to where he'd left the lightflyer, *At least I survived that. And those two pelts are going to be worth something. They look heavier than the other ones. I'll bring the flyer back up, skin them out, and...* He sensed other presences, and felt the wolves, mountain lions and bears moving in. *Maybe get it done before they tear the hell out of the pelts.* He picked up the pace and made it back to the lightflyer, climbed painfully in, and quickly flew it back to the meadow. There were animals around both carcasses, but thankfully hadn't torn into them yet. He landed and stepped out of the liteflyer, then walked slowly toward the first carcass. The animals opened a path for him, and sniffed at him as he walked by, radiating as much peace as he could.

The female wolf he thought of as the matriarch walked up stiff legged, and licked his hand before she squatted and peed on the carcass, followed by a mountain lion, and then the female bear he recognized from the waterfall. He thought she might also be Urso's mother, but he wasn't sure. After she'd finished, they all sat off to the side, looking intently at him.

Figuring that was his cue, he started skinning out the male Silverback, and cutting chunks of meat. He made three separate stacks, about ten feet apart as he skinned it, and was about 2/3 of the way through, when he felt a gentle push *"Captain? Are you alright?"*

Confused, he stood, looking around. *"MobyDineah? Where are you?"*

"We are south of you. We can feel you are surrounded by animals and slightly wounded?"

Fargo laughed, looking around he saw about fifty animals, *"I'm fine. I took out a couple of Silverbacks, and one of them landed on me. Twisted my knee a little bit. There are a few animals waiting patiently for me to feed them."*

"Can we help?"

Fargo looked around and found the female wolf, he shut off the vibro knife and limped over to her, then reached out, remembering MobyDineah and doing his best to send a picture of them from his memory. He sent what he hoped was the right direction, thinking of downwind, but was stumped on how to send a distance. The matriarch cocked her head, barked once, and trotted off in the right direction, *"Um, if a big female wolf comes up to you in the next few segs, I think she'll bring you back here. If not, stay away until I get these damn things skinned out."*

He felt Dineah's 'softer' mind touch, and her humor, *"Sounds like you've been working with the animals."*

"I think this one is Canis' mother. I think… I'm roughly in the center of the meadow, about twenty yards west of the liteflyer." He went back to skinning and cutting meat, making bigger piles and marveling at the intermixed animals sitting patiently, except for one lion cub, who dared to dart forward and try to grab a

chunk of meat. It got smacked down, picked up by the nape of the neck, and carried back to the pack.

A couple of segs later, MobyDineah sent, *"Yes, the wolf found us, sniffed us, and is now looking at us."*

"Okay, start walking this way, and let's see what happens." Maybe five segs later, just as he finished up the first carcass, he saw them walking slowly behind the matriarch, looking around in wonder.

"We *have never seen anything like this. We cannot believe these animals have not attacked you or the carcasses. Amazing. And they truly do intermix. What can we do?"*

Fargo hoisted the hide up on his shoulder, carrying it slowly to the liteflyer, *"First thing is to get this one loaded, then I'm going to skin the other one do the same piles on the meat. Let me walk to you, and lead you to the other carcass, it's in the edge of the woods."*

They stopped where they were, and Fargo limped over to them, shook hands and said, "You are braver than I would be. If I'd sensed this many animals, I'd have been gone in the opposite direction in a hurry."

Dineah trilled a laugh, "We were *watched* from the time we cleared the settlement and got in the woods. But they never tried to charge us or anything else. We heard the shots, and stopped. That's when we reached out, not realizing it was you."

Fargo smiled. "So you were just out for another little stroll?" He started leading them through the animals, then changed directions, "Might as well introduce you to the other matriarchs. I think I told you the hierarchy is backward, with females in charge?"

Moby nodded. "You did." They stopped in front of the mountain lion, and they both held out their hands. She sniffed both of them, then licked their hands, "She just sent something. Maybe a scent and taste for us?"

Fargo shook his head. "I didn't catch anything." He led them to the bear, and she did the same thing. This time he concentrated, and felt something, "I felt something that time, but nothing... specific."

Dineah replied, "I think scents. Didn't you say they all smelled you?"

He nodded as he led off toward the tree line. "Every one of them did. I was scared spitless."

Moby grinned as Dineah trilled another laugh. Some of the animals followed them, led by the matriarchs while the others separated by species and began eating the mounds of meat Fargo had carved. Fargo laughed. "I think there is one cub that's in *serious* trouble, it tried to grab some meat earlier, and now it's being herded over here with us. That's gotta be frustrating."

Dineah said, "I think it's called a learning experience." Moby and Fargo laughed as she said, "Can we help with the skinning?"

"If you want to. If you do, this will go quicker and the sooner we're away from them, the better, before they get frustrated. I know if I was hungry and there was fresh meat, I wouldn't want to be sitting around waiting."

They got to the carcass and Moby said, "Only two rounds? I thought you said it takes a lot more."

They flipped the carcass over, and Fargo quickly slit the skin down the belly of the female, then split the gut, showing them the hearts and lungs, "A couple of shots from the rear can get to the hearts and lungs without having to break the pelvic bones. She turned far enough away to give me a decent shot and I took it before they got their attack set up."

Moby and Dineah quickly took over the skinning, leaving Fargo amazed at not only their quickness, but how precisely they took the hide off. He was cutting and carrying meat as quickly as he could, and there was soon another three piles of meat spaced out just outside the woods.

Once they'd finished, Moby deftly folded the hide, picking it up like it weighed nothing, and they headed back to the liteflyer. He sent what he thought of as gift to the matriarchs as they cleared the meat piles, and the animals fell to with a vengeance, with the little cub leading the way. All three of them smiled at that, and once they were back at the liteflyer, Moby easily hoisted it into the cargo area.

"Are you going back to your cabin?"

Fargo looked down at himself, "Yes. It wouldn't be a good idea for me to show up at the spaceport looking like this, and my sister would probably kill me on general principles." He looked around, "Um, I can reconfigure the liteflyer, and you can ride with me, if you want."

He started to reach for a hide, and Moby picked them both up. "Go ahead. I'm assuming there are seats that reconfigure?"

Fargo reached into the cockpit, pressed the appropriate switches, and two additional seats popped out of their storage positions. Moby set the two hides on one seat, and climbed in. Strapping the hides in before he started on his straps. Fargo shrugged. "Dineah you want to climb in?"

She climbed in the right seat, and Fargo followed, then closed the canopy. He ran through the checklist, then lifted off slowly, oriented himself with the TBT power lines, and climbed out toward the cabin. A half div later, he taxied slowly up to the cabin, and they were met by Canis, Cattus, and Urso.

Fargo cussed, "Dammit, I forgot to bring them any meat. I'll feed them first, before we unload the hides. Otherwise, they're liable to eat them to pay me back."

They laughed and Moby said, "Especially after they smell the blood on you."

All three animals crowded the liteflyer as soon as they stopped, with Urso rising and sticking her nose into the back, sniffing the hides, then growling, which set Canis and Cattus off. Fargo got out, sending 'friends' to them as he headed for the cabin door. He came back moments later lugging three haunches of neardeer he'd gotten yesterday. He called the animals, then sent 'eat' and they fell to eating with enthusiasm.

Moby and Dineah piled out, and Moby grabbed the hides as Fargo reconfigured the liteflyer and pushed it into the garage. "Drop those on the bench and come on in. I need to clean up, but I can offer a cup of real coffee."

Dineah smiled. "Oh, please."

Moby grumbled good naturedly, "That's all you want, woman. Coffee."

She stuck her tongue out at him, "*This* is real coffee, not like the crap in the mess or autochef. We will greet the animals while you clean up."

Fargo took the hint, and headed into the cabin as they walked toward the front porch. Ten segs later, he stepped out on the porch to find Urso and Moby mock wrestling, and Dineah with Canis on one side, Cattus on the other and both with heads in her lap being petted. Fargo mocked, "This… is what I get. Abandoned by the three of you for the first people that show up."

Cattus looked around at him, then put her head back in Dineah's lap with a sigh and a purr. Moby and Dineah laughed. "We communicate with them, just a little better than you do." Moby pushed Urso down and he felt him send a sit command. Urso promptly sat, and put up a paw, as if wanting to shake hands. Moby took it, then ruffled her scruff as he turned to Fargo. "The real reason we hoped to catch you home was to talk to you about Senior McDougal."

Fargo, rather than answering, waved them through the door, then said, "In what way? Sit while I make some coffee."

Moby continued, "He is… depressed. Something happened on the detachment that has caused a change in his outlook."

"Why do you want to know?" Fargo asked bluntly. He started the coffee brewing and took out the cups and got a glass of water for Moby, handing it to him.

Dineah projected, "*Part of our job, if you will, is assisting the captains and major with maintaining order among the troops. That entails… probing… um, psyches if you will. He has not spoken to anyone, and is actively avoiding the medic."*

Fargo dumped his memory of the action to them, along with his talk with McDougal, and what he had done for him. *Damn, I didn't realize I'd retained all that. I wonder if my neural net is active all the time.*

Moby projected, *"Yes, sir. Yours is active, and it's high function. Yours seems to be more… fully developed than even the major's is."*

"That's interesting. I haven't used it in probably thirty years. It is a Marine command neural net. Installed when I graduated from TBS. I remember it was painful, and it took a while to figure out what it was doing, or helping me do. It was supposedly deactivated when I was… Court martialed."

"Maybe you haven't consciously used it, but I think it's been active for a long time. That level of recall and detail is… almost like being there." Fargo dropped out of the link, "Thankfully it doesn't include smell-o-vision." He poured two cups of coffee, handed one to Dineah, and sat down, sipping his with a smile.

Dineah inhaled deeply, her smile spreading and she took a sip, "Oh, *so* good!"

Moby just shook his head sadly, "I don't see…"

"Hush you. You are… what is ancient word, Phoenician… No, Philistine. You cannot appreciate good things."

Fargo snorted his coffee, and Moby laughed. "I joined with you, didn't I?"

"Well, maybe *some* good things."

Fargo watched the byplay as he cued dinner in the autochef, "Will you stay the night?"

They looked at each other and nodded. "*If it is alright with you, we would be grateful. We can help you with the hides if you wish.*"

"*Please.*" The divs passed quickly, and finally they were both scraped and prepped. "Well, I think we're done," he said.

Moby replied, "We can take your rifle back with us. Our armorer is good, and bored. He would be happy to work on a rifle that nice, and he can probably fix the holoscope too."

"I have to fly down to Rushing River tomorrow. I'll gladly trade a ride for a repair."

Moby looked at Dineah and he felt them communicate, then Moby said, "Deal!"

Duty Calls

Fargo parked the liteflyer in the space assigned to him and walked around the front of the administration building. He found Sergeant Omar sitting in his runabout, and asked, "Ho, Sergeant. Favor you can do?"

"Need you have, Lieutenant of the retired," Omar's GalTrans spit out.

"Ride to GalPat compound is needed."

Omar straightened, "Ride, I can give." He motioned and Fargo climbed into the runabout. Ten segs later, he dropped Fargo off at the gate to the compound, "Ride to return, you need?"

Fargo shrugged. "Know, I do not."

Omar nodded and held up his radio, "Call can be made."

"Thanks are owed."

The androgynous corporal on the gate shook his/her head, saying in a soprano voice, "I hate trying to parse what they say. Can I help you?"

"I'm Captain Fargo, with the militia, I'd like to talk to either of the captains, the major, or Command Sergeant Major Aphrodite if they're available."

"Standby one, sir."

He decided the corporal was a she, as she spoke into the air, and a moment later nodded. "The major would be happy to receive you. Do you know the way?"

"Yes, I do, thank you." Five segs later, he sat in Major Culverhouse's office, along with Captain Culverhouse, Captain Garibaldi, and the CSM. He juggled the bulb of coffee as he thought through what he wanted to say. "I wanted to give you some feedback on the ops, and see if you were satisfied with the condition of the modules."

CSM Aphrodite replied, "Well satisfied. They actually looked better than when we loaned them to you. Although the maintenance module was short some electronic spares."

Fargo nodded. "That's one of the things I wanted to talk about. But first, I'd like to say we could not have been more appreciative of the Fleet people that accompanied us. Warrant Boykin was outstanding, as was Senior Sergeant Grayson, and Senior Sergeant McDougal. They have all been put in for awards, and Senior Sergeant McDougal *invented* something while on the Det that saved our lives."

Major Culverhouse looked sharply at Captain Garibaldi, "Did you know about this, Bob?"

He held up his hands, "All I know is *something* went on. McDougal came back changed. He's never been real social, and he's even more withdrawn, but his work ethic is still there, and he's ahead on all the maintenance."

The CSM asked gently, "Did he have to kill someone?"

Fargo shifted, "A sniper tried to kill him about a month into the Det. What he invented killed about ninety civilians who were trying to overrun our sites. He took it pretty personal, and our master chief and warrant had a few heart to heart chats with him. I don't know how much longer he has on this hitch, but I don't think he's going to re-up."

Major Culverhouse asked, "What the hell did he invent that killed that many people? And why don't we know about it? He didn't submit anything to us, did he?" The two captains and the CSM all shook their heads.

Fargo interrupted, "Because we told him not to. Due to the nature of the development, it is truly a game-changer in site defense. It was actually classified by Intel, and the design was pushed up via other channels."

The CSM looked angry and started to get up. Fargo snapped, "Star level classified, CSM. Sit down." Major Culverhouse looked at him speculatively as he continued, "I will tell you it ties into the sonics, and repulses *projectiles* at reciprocal velocities away from the barrier."

All three of them started talking at once, "That's not possible." "How did…" "Can't be done."

He interrupted again, "It is, he did, and De Perez Galactic is willing to offer him a significant amount for his innovation, with royalties."

Captain Culverhouse laughed. "Oh that is just… perfect. I'm guessing he gets no *official* recognition, right?"

Fargo shrugged. "Above my paygrade. I was asked to see if he would be willing to meet with a De Perez representative within the next seven days."

"Why you?"

"I guess because I'm here, my name was on the initial report, and that's one less person that has to be read in? I really don't know."

Major Culverhouse shook her head in amazement, "McDougal is a frikken lightening rod! She glanced at her desktop, "He's got… ten months left on his enlistment. We're supposed to be picked up in two or three months, and that would give him time to transit back and out process. I can only wonder what the brass thinks about this, considering…"

Captain Garibaldi smiled. "You tell me when, I'll have him there, wherever there is."

Fargo looked at each of them, "Any problems with that?"

It was obvious the CSM did, but she elected not to say anything as Fargo got up, "Thank you for your time. As soon as I get a date and time, I'll message you. They wanted to meet at the administration building here."

The duty driver gave Fargo a ride to Rushing River, and after a long lunch with Luann, and a review of the work schedule with Mikhail for more upgrades to the TBT system, he finally got away and walked slowly toward the winery. Glancing at his wrist comp, he picked up the pace, *Damn, where did the day go? It's already seventeen! I told her I'd be there early.* He got to the winery a few minutes later, slightly winded, and found Nicole standing grumpily in the office. He asked tentatively, "What's wrong?"

"Holly's been bottling wines. I really don't want to go through the same bullshit I did last year with hauling it to Star Center, but…"

"Why not have them come here?"

Nicole looked askance at him, "Yeah, right. That was probably a one-time sale, and who the hell is going to come to our little backwater Rimworld to buy wine?"

Holly interrupted them, and Fargo was surprised to see McDougal with her. "Mom, Fargo, this is…"

They both said, "Senior Sergeant McDougal."

Holly, confused, looked between them and Mac, blushing, "Uh… I don't know…"

McDougal said, "Captain, Chief, I didn't expect…"

Fargo smiled. "What are you doing here, Mac?"

"I asked if I could get a tour. I've never seen a winery, but I'm interested in how wines are made." Fargo had a random thought, *I wonder if Grayson's stories about illegal booze and the Scots/Irish maintenance mafia are more than just stories.*

Holly asked, "How do you know my mother and Fargo?"

"I was detached to them for the mission on Endine."

Nicole smiled at him, "Would you like to stay for dinner?"

Fargo smiled when Mac looked first at Holly, who nodded, and then said, "If it's not too much trouble, I would like to."

Nicole and Holly served neardeer tenderloins with a hunter sauce, greens, beans, and potatoes and one of their bottles of red wine for dinner. Mac didn't say much, but cleaned his plate quickly. He finally pushed back from the table, "That has to be one of the best meals I've ever had." He looked at his wrist comp, "I'm sorry, but I need to get back to the compound. I didn't sign out for an overnight, and muster will be in a div. Thank you very much!"

Holly walked out with him, and Nicole and Fargo had bulbs of coffee as they sat contentedly at the table. Fargo looked at her, "She could do worse."

Nicole looked at him, "What do you mean?"

"He's going to be offered a million credits and royalties for his repulsor. And he's only got ten months left on this hitch."

She laughed. "You don't know Holly, do you? She's not... interested in him."

It was Fargo's turn to laugh, "Maybe not now, but he's interested." He got up and started picking up dishes. "As soon as she comes back, I want to take a walk in the vineyard."

Nicole picked up the other dishes, "Are you thinking about that wolf and mountain lion? Would it be safe?"

"As safe as anything. If you two don't want to go…"

Holly came back in, "Go where?"

Nicole answered for him, "Walking in the vineyard. In the dark."

Holly looked between them, "Is it... necessary?"

Fargo shrugged. "Maybe not, but it might confirm some things."

Nicole threw up her hands, "Men." She reached for her jacket, handed Holly hers, and grabbed two hand lights. "Lead on, Mister Mysterious."

Fargo led them to the back fence of the vineyard and said, "Turn off the lights." When they did, he reached out with both his empath sense and his mind on the 'frequency' of the animals, projecting welcome.

A seg later, he heard a soft woof, and a purr that was more felt than heard. He knelt, putting out his hands, and felt a wolf under one hand, and a mountain lion under the other one. He got a sense of protection, and watching over cubs. He said softly, "Nicole, Holly, come kneel by me. Don't be afraid if you get nosed or licked, okay?"

He heard Nicole sigh, and Holly's quick intake of breath, but they both knelt next to him. Nicole laughed musically when both animals licked her hands, and Holly sighed, "So warm. And that purring. You can *feel* it!"

Nicole said softly, "They were patrolling weren't they?"

Fargo sent thoughts of thanks and welcome to both animals, and he got what he thought was probably as close to an acknowledgement they were capable of. "I think so. Nicole, I got a sense they were protecting your *cub*, Holly"

Holly asked, "Cub? Me?"

Nicole laughed. "Oh, this is just… unbelievable."

Fargo stood, helping both of them up, "Maybe, but it's not something we can ever tell anyone."

"Why," Holly asked.

"Because every Xeno in the galaxy would be here experimenting on them. They are… sentient in their own way. There is another species…"

Nicole chimed in, "The bears, right?"

Fargo nodded. "The bears also communicate with each other and across species. I know those three species interact with purpose."

Holly shivered, "That's scary."

***

Boykin had picked up Fargo, McDougal, and OneSvel at Rushing River, and flown them to the Enclave earlier in the day. OneSvel, with Grayson helping, had done a medcall for the village, and Grayson was surprised to find so few problems among either the children or the elders.

OneSvel chittered, "Mountain air. Very few particulates, too cold for most viruses and bacteria. And they keep their village and themselves very clean."

Grayson nodded. "That makes sense. Come to think of it, I've never had the chance to work in an environment like this. I'm usually patching up drunks, and stupid troops. And battle wounds."

OneSvel chittered a laugh, "Welcome to remote duty. There is not much of that here. Tomorrow, can you point me to the hospital in White Beach? I have medications to pick up for Doc Grant."

"Sure, that will get me out of the compound for a while. Glad to do it."

After they finished the medical call, a buffet lunch was provided by the village as the people started changing into what Fargo thought of as their funeral clothes. A div later, Fargo stood on the bank of the lake, staring morosely at another funeral pyre, this one built for Shanni and Lev. *I truly hate this. They… should not have died. I should never have let the troops go into those towns. That was stupid on my part.* Nicole stood next to him, lightly rubbing his back, out of sight of the others. Boykin, Grayson, and McDougal lined up beside her.

"This is *not* your fault Ethan, just like the last time. I can feel your anger, and you're wrong. You can't lock them down like children. They're all grown men and women, and they knew the odds. They could just as easily have died in camp. Deity has her own way of taking those she wants, and we have no control over that."

Fargo tasted her emotions and knew she *believed* exactly what she was saying, but that didn't ease the pain, "No, if I hadn't allowed them liberty, it wouldn't have…"

The priest and Lal marched down the bank to the pyre. Lal lit the first torch out of the fire pit, and handed it to Fargo, then handed the next torches to Horse, Daman and Jiri as the priest chanted the dirge for the dead in the background. The four of them went to the four corners of the pyre, as when Lal nodded, they simultaneously touched their torches to the pyre, and then Fargo followed the others in adding the torches to the pyre as its flames grew.

He went back to stand by Nicole, thankful that the winds were blowing away from them, as the fire leapt higher and higher, until the bodies were consumed. The priest continued his prayers as the fire burned lower, and Nicole translated for the others that the families have eleven days of mourning, then a celebration of life after that time.

When the funeral ceremony was completed, the Ghorka formed a line, each shaking their hands, or in OneSvel's case, a pseudopod, with the exception of the little girl whose life he'd saved. She hugged one of his tree trunk legs, and thanked him in halting Galactic. Rima hugged each of them, and whispered to Fargo that she did not hold him responsible. Shanni had been Shanni, there was nothing he could do. He hugged her, "I'm sorry Rima. I'm sorry," was all he could say.

***

Three divs later, Boykin brought the shuttle in to White Beach, landing at the compound, and saying, "Thank you for flying Ass and Trash Airlines. We do not assume any responsibility for lost luggage, misplaced body parts, or anything else. Don't let the ramp hit you in the ass on the way out."

Fargo laughed as he picked up his bag from the netting, "Always a pleasure WO. You're in an awfully good mood."

She smiled as she climbed down from the cockpit, "I had the *pleasure* of returning the Wizard to Lieutenant Edwards this morning, and he's well and truly pissed."

"Oh, the blooding, so to speak?"

She nodded laughing, "Yes, *and* the fact that I'm now an ace. And a woman. And a warrant."

He laughed with her, "So a threefer, fourfer?"

Grayson said, "Ah shit. Here comes Palette."

Since they were all in uniforms, they saluted him as he stomped up the ramp, "Late as usual. What did you do, Warrant? Take the scenic route? You were told to be back here ASAP."

Fargo bristled, "Major, we came direct from the funeral."

Palette snapped around on him, "And you! The colonel directed you report *immediately*, and you don't bother to show up for three days? You should be court martialed and relieved of rank for that."

Fargo started to answer when Palette spotted OneSvel, "Who authorized *this thing* on a GalPat shuttle?"

Boykin said sweetly, "Colonel Keads did. We are doing a medical assist for Rushing River, in addition to a medical assist for the Ghorka Enclave. OneSvel is a Galactic certified medtech, and he is approved for travel on GalPat transport. If you have any further questions…"

Palette glared at her, then turned to Fargo, "You and her," pointing to Nicole, "Are to report to the Colonel at eight. Or should I tell him you'll be there when you show up?" he said, his lip curling.

Palette took a step back when he saw Fargo smile. "We will present ourselves at eight as directed. May we depart now?"

Palette turned and stomped off without answering and Grayson said, "Well, guess that answers that. You're still on his shitlist there, Captain."

Nicole laughed. "I think we all are."

OneSvel's GalTrans twittered, "I can *fix* his problem. Permanently."

Nicole batted her eyes at them, "Would you please? I think we would *all* be better off."

***

At seven-thirty, Fargo and Nicole were standing in the hallway as Colonel Keads came in, "You have coffee yet? I haven't. Let's go to the mess." He led them to a senior table in the corner, then came back with three bulbs of coffee, "So, sounds like things got a bit interesting out there. I've read the reports, is there anything else I need to know?"

Nicole asked, "Sir, were you aware of the Major's insistence that we report immediately?"

Keads winced. "No, and that's not what I told him. I… am not going to get into that." He finished his bulb, "Let's go to my office, bring your coffee with you."

They followed him into his office, and he sat at the conference table, gesturing for them to sit. "Now, the issue I need your input on is this apparent ice mining on Eros, is it?"

"Yes, sir," Nicole answered. "It meets all the indicators for a Trader operation, well inside the DMZ, and a prohibited action on the part of the Dragoons and Traders. The equipment and ship seen exiting a vent are not of GalPat design, as best we can determine."

Keads leaned back in his chair, "That makes for an interesting situation. We need to respond, but there is only a destroyer that is anywhere close. We have a company of troops here, but I can't transport a full company on a destroyer. Do you think we could use that ship you used for the Endine mission?"

Fargo nodded. "I believe that could be arranged, sir."

"The next question is, would you be willing to accompany them? You haven't actually had boots on the ground, but you've seen what is there, and you've seen hard combat in unfriendly environments."

Nicole looked sharply at Fargo as he sighed, "Sir, can I have time to think about that? If I go, what would I go as?"

Keads looked closely at him, "I could activate you as a Lieutenant Colonel, or send you as the local liaison. Your choice. We're looking at sending them in two weeks, as soon as the destroyer gets here. I'll need your answer by next week. And a contact point for the ship you used."

"Can I have that week, sir?"

Keads nodded. "Certainly. I know this is over and above, but you've exhibited all the qualities I'd expect of a senior officer. And you have the respect of everyone here."

Fargo nodded. "Thank you."

Keads stood, "Dismissed, if you have nothing else."

They got up, "No, sir. Thank you."

They heard a knock on the door, followed by Major Palette saying, "Colonel, I haven't seen those two militia…"

"They were waiting when I got here, Palette. We've completed what we needed to do. Have you completed the assignment I gave you?"

Palette gulped, and Fargo and Nicole took the time to exit, closing the door quickly behind themselves.

They heard the colonel's voice raised, and smiled as they walked down the hallway.

Decisions, Decisions

Boykin dropped them at Rushing River. OneSvel thanked her and quickly left the shuttle, his GalTrans twittering, "I must get these medications to the clinic and into the refrigeration. Will I see you tomorrow, Fargo?"

Fargo nodded. "I'll come by in the morning."

He and Nicole walked off more slowly and Nicole put a hand on his arm when they got to the edge of the ramp, "Are you going to go?"

"I don't know. I know the colonel wants me to, but I'd be a fifth cog."

"What was this about activating you as a light colonel?"

He grabbed her hand, "Come on, let's go to your place. I'll tell you there." Twenty segs later, they were in her quarters behind the bar at the Copper Pot. She'd set one of the honey and nut desserts on the table and they both had bulbs of coffee. He said, "I'm going to let you into my mind, you can see everything. It will be easier than trying to explain. He lay is hand over hers and reached for her mind, "*I've dropped all my barriers. Here's the story.*"

Nicole convulsively grabbed his hand as she *saw* his memories, all of them. She sensed his pain from the loss of his wife and son, the loss of his troops in combat, his fears, and the depth of his feelings for her.

Tears rolled down her face as she saw his recollection of the vid from General Cronin, and she jerked away, jumped up from the table and ran to the bedroom.

Fargo sighed, finished his bulb of coffee, and sat quietly, *Well, that didn't quite go as well as I'd hoped. I guess telepathy with no barriers isn't the right thing to do, but what else could I have done? I'd be here all night trying to explain...*

Nicole came back and wrapped her arms around him, "I'm so sorry. You... have to go. Oh Deity, I'd never realized what a command neural net entailed. How do you live with that... level of detail in your mind?"

Fargo reached for her arms. "I seem to be able to *compartmentalize* the memories. And it's like having an on call AI, with tactics and other things loaded. I know in combat it... makes time slow down? I don't know another way to describe it. The other... stuff, it will never go away. I'm sorry, but I didn't..."

Suddenly she was in his lap, her arms around him and kissing him hungrily. They came up for air, and she replied, "All I know is I *do* love you, and I don't want to let you go, but I know I have to."

She got up, trailing her hand across his chest, and pulling lightly on his arm. He got up and followed her, momentarily looking back at the dessert left of the table, then smiling as he followed her into the bedroom. Divs later, they lay tangled in a nest of sheets, exhausted by their lovemaking, with her asleep on his shoulder.

Fargo looked at the ceiling, letting his mind run free. *I think we've just made a life commitment to each other. And she's right. I do have to go, for myself if no other reason. If I can save lives, I owe it to them. Captain Jace is supposed to land at twelve, and I need to meet with him about this op. And McDougal's meeting, need to be there for that. Got to go see OneSvel too.* He faded off to sleep, thoughts still churning.

He got to the clinic so early it was still locked up, and he leaned against the wall next to the door. He felt OnSvel's touch and projected, *"I'm outside. Take your time."*

"We will be there in a moment." Shortly the front door was unlocked and he stepped quickly inside, "Getting a little chilly out there. Winter is coming."

OneSvel's GalTrans twittered, "We still do not understand this seasonal component you humans seem to enjoy."

Fargo laughed. "We don't like the same weather all the time. Seasonal changes invigorate us, and being both warm and cold reminds us we are alive."

"But what about the people on the stations, and on the ships?"

"Well, not *everyone* likes to be reminded of seasons, or they don't particularly like being hot or cold. Just like there are people that don't like to smell the outdoors, or have significant allergies, or get bitten by bugs."

If OneSvel could have, they would have shaken their head, instead they continued, "What is your plan?"

"I am planning on accompanying the GalPat company. Half the company will go on the destroyer, the other half will follow in *Hyderabad*. This is an older destroyer, so they are limited in passenger capacity."

"May we accompany you?"

Fargo stiffened, "You? Why?"

OneSvel's pseudopods rippled in what Fargo thought was embarrassment, "This is a place no Taurasian has ever been. And there is always the possibility…"

"You realize this is an ice moon. There is no atmosphere. You will not be able to get out of armor. Speaking of, do you have your armor stored somewhere?"

"My GalScout armor is at the spaceport. Also, there is only one medic with the company. If there are problems, we may be of assistance. The destroyer is a Liberty Class, the *Lincoln*. She only has three medboxes, and a four bed sickbay."

Fargo knew OneSvel was right, but he wasn't sure how GalPat would take it, nor whether Captain Jace would allow it, "Let me check with the powers that be. I'll talk to both the ship captain and the GalPat major today."

OneSvel extruded a pseudopod, touching his temple lightly. "*GalScouts want both you and us to go. Apparently there is a chance of collecting data from the site that might lead to discovering other incursions deep within the DMZ.*"

"*Understood, I will push it, but we may not get to the surface.*"

"*If we get close, we can collect data. That is better than what we have now, which is nothing.*" Retracting the pseudopod as Doc Grant came in, he continued, "This injection will help that knee heal. You are not forty-one anymore, and don't need to be out hunting in the wild without backup."

Fargo winced as the injector shot the nanites into his knee, as he said, "Morning, Doc. How come OneSvel's injectors hurt, and yours don't?"

Doc laughed. "According to *most* of my patients, it's the other way around. And listen to them."

Fargo got up and tested the knee, "Okay, I'll take it easy." Fargo nodded to both of them and walked slowly out of the clinic, debating whether to go by the store on the way to the spaceport or after. *After, that way I'll have a better idea of what's going to happen, and I can get Luann to feed me lunch.*

***

The *Hyderabad*'s shuttle landed promptly at twelve, and Captain Jace and a blue tinged Kepleran from 62F carrying a document pouch walked off together. Fargo met them at the door, and nodded to the Kepleran, "Have we met before?"

"I am Klamat. You were the bodyguard last year when I bought the wine from Mrs. Levesque. Where is this senior sergeant?"

Fargo glanced at Jace, "I'm assuming they are in the conference room. And I wasn't a bodyguard." *Frikkin Keplerans are all alike, assholes of the first order. Almost could be a brother to Keldar, but I'm not about... Oh, damn, that is just plain sneaky, if he's what I think he is.* He preceded them up the steps, and dilated the entry, "After you, gentlemen."

Jace winked at him as he went by, almost as if he knew what Fargo was thinking. He shook his head, *Damn, how many of those simulacrums do you have hidden away Jace? And what's your real role in De Perez Galactic?* He led them down to the conference room, and saw Major Culverhouse and McDougal standing looking at the holo map of Hunter. "Major, Mac, this is Captain Jace of Hyderabad, and Mr. Klamat, a representative of De Perez Galactic. Major Culverhouse is Senior Sergeant McDougal's commanding officer."

They shook hands, and when Fargo shook hands with Klamat at last, sent a quick probe. There was no empathic or sense of any thoughts, confirming Klamat was a simulacrum. They took seats at the end of the table, and Klamat pulled a package of documents from the pouch, sliding them across the table to McDougal, "Please verify this is your design, and you are solely responsible for this design. It was not done by anyone else, nor did anyone else contribute to it."

Fargo just sat back and watched, marveling at Jace's ability to control the two simulacrums independently. *I don't know why I should be surprised. He's controlling an entire ship full of them. But he's doing this outside the ship. Is there a limit when he doesn't have… Huh, interesting question for later.*

Mac nervously picked up the documents, reading through them carefully, even though the Kepleran did everything but pound on the table and tell him to hurry up. Major Culverhouse sat quietly, watching everyone else and doing her best to keep her curiosity in check. Finally Mac put the last document down, cleared his throat and said, "Yes, that is my design. I never intended for it to…"

Klamat rudely interrupted, shoving another pile of documents to Mac. "De Perez Galactic, as authorized in the JDA with GalPat dated twenty-eight thirty-five Septober twenty-eighth, extends the following offer to one Ian Sean McDougal, Earth Four, for rights to device two three eight one three alpha. Said rights are irrevocable once signed. Royalty agreement starts on page six, and is set at standard rate of two point two percent of sale value, reviewable in ten year increments. Ancillary agreement offer is for software modifications to items one six nine six quebec, zero three six three zulu, and one nine two four echo. The ancillary agreement is also irrevocable with no royalty attachment."

Stunned, Mac took the documents, "JDA? Device? And what did I do to the sonics, cabling and control functions?"

Klamat replied brusquely, "Joint Development Agreement. You know what you did with the midpoint entry exit modifications."

"Oh that. It needed to be done. Security breakdown if you have single point entry/exit." He started reading through the documents slowly, then looked up white faced, "One million credits?"

Klamat shifted impatiently, "That is the offer. Accept or refuse. No negotiation."

Fargo and Culverhouse exchanged confused looks, and Jace held up his hand, miming he would explain later. Mac kept reading, page after page, his hands shaking by the time he finished. He finally looked up, staring blindly around as if in a daze, he came back to the Kepleran, "This is no shit for real?"

"Is real. Accept or refuse. No negotiation."

"Where and how do I sign?"

"Pages five, eleven, thirteen, and seventeen. Sign and date," turning to Major Culverhouse looking her up and down, "You are serving GalPat, so you will suffice as witness. You sign with name, rank, serial number."

She bristled at his tone, and Fargo shook his head minutely at her, as she stepped around to McDougal's side. Once he finished signing, she signed as the witness, and Klamat took the documents back. He stamped them with a holostamp, then somehow split the pages, and holostamped them again, handing the second set to Mac. "Where do you want the credits deposited?"

Mac held the documents for a moment, shook his head, then said, "Uh, I guess my GalPat pay account."

Culverhouse interrupted, "What about the tax hit? Is the senior sergeant going to be responsible for that? And how many units are you talking about delivering at what cost?"

Klamat almost snarled at her, but visibly calmed himself, "The one million credits will be after tax. De Perez will take care of that. For the royalties, part of the provisions on page eleven and thirteen specify that taxes will be withheld from royalty payments."

Fargo jumped in, "So when will he expect royalty payments? And how often?"

"Twice yearly. At six month intervals on delivered systems." He took the documents, returned them to the pouch, and got up, "We are done. I am ready to return to the space station, I have other work to do."

Jace stood, "I will escort you back to the shuttle, but I have a short meeting with these folks, it should take less than a div."

Mac looked down at the documents, "I'm... Fuck... Sorry, Major. What am I going to do? A million fu... credits! And two hundred credits a unit. Shit... What do I do with the paperwork? I..."

Culverhouse said gently, "Senior, we can log the paperwork in for you, that makes it a part of your record, and we can keep the copies in the company safe for you. As far as what you do, that is up to you, but I wouldn't go overboard spending those credits."

Mac shoved the documents to her, "Please, ma'am. If I may, I'll walk back. I... need to think."

She picked them up, "Dismissed, Mac." After he walked out, she turned on him, "How the hell did you..."

Fargo held up his hands in defense, "I didn't do anything. I just passed the design up the chain. And he stands to make a lot more off the royalties than he does the original agreement."

"You think so?"

"GalPat has how many dets? I know GalScouts have over a thousand teams. One unit per team is two hundred k credits. And if you add in the diplos, and who knows who else in dot gov."

"Damn, he's... going to be truly rich. And the point two percent for the software, I think... I don't even know how many sonics units there are out there."

"Thousands, tens of thousands? Who knows?"

Jace interrupted their musings, "So, I understand I have a contract to carry part of your company and accompany a destroyer somewhere?"

They spent the next div hashing out the details, and Fargo was surprised when both Jace and the major were amenable to OneSvel coming along as a backup medic. *And I hope to hell he doesn't have to blow his cover and do any major surgery. I wonder if... He was always talking to DenAfr when we came back. Could he be a sifter too? I wonder if they all are?*

He took the runabout back to the clinic and told OneSvel that the major had invited him to accompany the company on their tasking, and explained to Doc Grant that the *invite* was more in the vein of an order, especially since OneSvel was a former GalScout. Doc shrugged and took it fairly well, looking at them and saying, "As long as I see you back here in thirty-five or forty days. Langdon's system isn't that far away."

Fargo looked at him sharply, "I never said anything about where we…"

Doc laughed. "Not hard to figure out. Where have you been for the last three months? You come back for a week, do secret squirrel shit, and boom, you're gone again."

Sighing, Fargo asked, "Please don't extrapolate any further. And keep it to yourself."

Doc bristled, "I did my time. I know the rules. I don't know what kind of game you two are playing, but I'm not a dumbass. You've got some kind of lone ranger mission out here, and this one," jerking a thumb at OneSvel, "is your Tonto."

Fargo looked at him, puzzled, and OneSvel's GalTrans twittered, "Tonto?"

Doc laughed again, "Go figure it out. Now get out of here, I've got patients to see."

***

Fargo sent the animals back to their respective packs, and buttoned up the cabin as the BIT check ran on the liteflyer. Once it was finished, he double checked that his trunk was secured in the cargo area, and climbed in. *I gotta tell Luann, she's going to throw a fit, but I can't lie to her. I just hope Mikhail hasn't already let it slip, since I had to use his shuttle to go get my armor. I'll spend the night on the ship, since she grounded this morning, that way I'm away from both Luann and Nicole.*

Mikhail picked him up at the parking area, "Your armor is already aboard. You want to drop your trunk now or later?"

"Now, if you don't mind. I need to go by and see Nicole too."

Mikhail chuckled. "She's at the store. Luann asked her to help cook dinner, and to stay for dinner."

"Damn. *That* is not what I planned," he shrugged. "I guess it's going to get interesting."

After they dropped his trunk off with Klang, who assured him it would be placed in his cabin, and that his and OneSvel's armor was onboard, along with the two platoons of company armor, they watched a combat shuttle blast off, and Mikhail said, "That's the third trip today. I thought combat shuttles could take a platoon at a time."

"Normally they do, but I'm guessing they're also taking extra supplies, and probably some admin stuff up too." He glanced at his wrist comp, "Guess it's time to go beard the lions in their den."

A div later, as they sat down to dinner, he still hadn't figured out how or when to tell Luann, when she looked directly at him, "You're leaving again, aren't you?"

He glanced at Nicole, then faced Luann squarely, "Yes, but I'm support only. And we should only be gone a little over a month."

She nodded. "Okay." And started serving the kid's plates.

Oh shit. She's pissed. Now what do I do? I... He felt a gentle pressure on her knee, and saw Nicole shake her head quickly, mouthing, "Not now!"

The dinner was excellent, and Luann was actually cheerful, even showing patience with Ian when he didn't want to eat his greens. Fargo complimented her, and she smiled tentatively. "Thank you, but Nicole helped, in more ways than one. You and Mikhail get out of here while we clear the dishes, then we'll have coffee and dessert. I made a nearapple pie for you." She looked at the kids, "Ian, Inga, kiss your uncle good night and upstairs with you."

He crouched and Ian tried to bear hug him, whispering, "I love you, Unka. Bring me something back, okay?"

He kissed him back, and whispered, "I'll try, but no promises."

Inga hugged and kissed him quickly, "Love you," then darted for the stairs.

He and Mikhail walked out onto the back deck, standing under the infrared heater to stay warm, "I don't understand. I thought sure she would blow up at me."

Mikhail cocked his head. "Unless Nicole said something, but I'm not about to ask."

"No, me neither."

Nicole dilated the hatch, "Dessert."

They trooped back in, and Luann served coffee in real mugs, along with the pie. "I suppose you're going to stay on that ship tonight?"

He nodded. "It's an early go in the morning, and I know how much you like to let the kids sleep when you can."

"And it's because you don't want to deal with a crying wreck in the morning, right?"

He winced. "Lu, it's not that. It's…"

Luann laid a hand on Nicole's arm, "No, I understand now. She explained it to me. I was… being selfish. If I try to control you, all I'll do is drive you away. So finish your dessert and go."

He got up, walked around the table and hugged her, kissing the top of her head, "Thank you, Lu. I don't ever want to hurt you, but I've got… responsibilities."

She sobbed once, then grabbed his arm, "I know, I don't like it, but I know now. I love you, Ethan. And I have to love you enough to let you go."

Fargo looked at Mikhail, and nodded toward the door. He nodded, and got up. "I'll run him out there and be back in a few."

Nicole got up and came to him, as he reached out for her mind, "*I love you. Thank you for whatever you did. I'll see you in a month or so.*"

"*I just told her the truth. It takes special people to put up with military personnel. I love you too. I'll see you in a bit.*" She kissed him fiercely, then pushed him away and turned back to the table.

At the ramp, Fargo shook Mikhail's hand, "Thanks for the ride. I hope Luann won't take this out on you. And if Nicole needs anything…"

"Don't worry on either count. I'll handle it."

Fargo walked out to the *Hyderabad*, looked back, but Mikhail was already gone. Coming aboard, he was stopped by a young GalPat trooper, "Sir, who are you?"

Fargo produced his data chip, "Spare cargo. I'm your liaison with Endine."

"Yes, sir. You're on the manifest. You know where your cabin is?"

"I do, Corporal."

The corporal saluted, and Fargo weaved around the armor and up to the crew's mess, looked in and didn't see anyone, so he went to his cabin. Unpacking, he got settled in, and was drifting off to sleep when the hatch dilated and Nicole came in.

"What the hell are you doing here?"

Nicole dropped the robe she was wearing, "Going with you. Now scoot over."

***

Sixteen days later, Fargo, Nicole, Captain Garibaldi, Sergeant Major Aphrodite, the two platoon lieutenants, and Captain Jace sat in the crew's mess, looking at the vid screens showing the battle watch center in the *Lincoln*, on tight beam laser. Major Culverhouse completed the final briefing. "So, one more time. The attack shuttles will launch from here, drop on the extraction unit on the surface, and return to Hyderabad, load out, and drop the third platoon on the vent. Fourth platoon will be reserve and security. We are," she glanced over her shoulder, "Twelve divs out. Everyone should be in EMCON until we're engaged. Captain Fargo, Chief Sergeant Levesque, I'd like for you two to maintain this link for the duration."

Fargo glanced at Captain Jace, who nodded. "We will, Major. Any specific tasking?"

"I'd like the chief sergeant's take on any changes she sees from the previous data collection. That data is now about two months old, and we all know intel ages out quickly. Anything you note, pass it in the clear to the watch officer. We don't have time to do in depth analysis."

Nicole nodded. "Will do, Major. Direct report to the battle watch. Will your unit be linking their sensors via this beam?"

"Standby one." The major stepped out of the camera view, coming back moments later, obviously frustrated. "The CO says he can't share classified data with a civilian ship."

Nicole pinched her nose, "Okay, we'll do what we can with what we have. Are you sending any intel personnel down?"

"Not on the original drop. When we do the sweepers, we'll send one or two down."

Captain Jace interrupted, "Major, we will be up on your frequencies, as a reminder for your shuttle pilots, our callsign is *Limit*. Our beacon will be channel twenty-nine when activated, which will also give you our range and bearing from *Lincoln*."

Culverhouse looked off to the side, "Shuttle ops you got that?" She nodded and turned back to the camera, "They roger up for it. I'm squirting specific platoon assignments now, same as what we worked up, CSM, Captain, do your final briefs and put everybody down for at least five divs. I want everybody ready to mount up in ten divs. We're done unless there are any further questions?"

They looked at each other, and Fargo saw nothing but head shakes, "We're good on this end, Major."

The captain, CSM, and platoon lieutenants data comps all pinged nearly simultaneously, as she said, "Okay, we're out here. We will stand up the battle watch in eight divs." With that, the screen went to the Lincoln's logo, and a data stream across the bottom of the vid.

Fargo looked at Garibaldi, "What can we do to help you?"

"Nothing right now. We'll go brief the platoons again, put them down, and gear up to be ready to go at ten."

"Alright. I'm going to go check with OneSvel and see if they have the sick bay ready to go." He got up, and Nicole came with him as Garibaldi and the lieutenants headed back to the lounge the platoons were using.

Jace turned toward the bridge, "If you need me, just yell."

Nicole laughed. "Yell at you, or the AI?"

"Either, or."

They found OneSvel pseudopods deep in the medbox and Fargo asked worriedly, "Is there a problem?"

"Not really, just preventive maintenance."

Fargo interrupted, "We need to go down for a few divs. The captain wants everyone in armor at ten."

"We will be ready. I have this sick bay and the secondary sick bay prepped."

"Secondary sick bay?"

"There is a ten bed sick bay at compartment three-zero-five three hotel."

"Oh, okay. I'm going to rest. I'd suggest you do the same."

"We will."

Fargo and Nicole left the sick bay, with Fargo mumbling, "What *else* is hidden on here?"

Nicole shook her head. "This ship is... odd... isn't it?"

"More than you know," he sighed.

Fight's on

Fargo, Nicole, and OneSvel's armor were against the bulkhead, forcing them to weave among the rows of armor, with Fargo following appreciatively behind Nicole. She caught him looking and said, "*Really*? You're watching my butt now, of all times?"

He shrugged. "Men are visual, and your *visuals* are nice."

She stuck her tongue out at him, then stopped in front of her armor. She grabbed him and quickly kissed him, then climbed in before he could do anything. Laughing, he climbed in as OneSvel began the laborious process of folding themselves into their specially constructed armor. *DenAfr hated their armor with a passion. They always said they felt cut off when they were in it.*

Fargo powered up, and felt the frisson of the armor closing around him as the AI snapped into sync with his neural lace, "Good morning, Captain. I sense we are aboard a ship in transit."

"We are Cindy. Combat BIT please. Two point oh divs to depressure and operations."

"BIT commenced. Would you like to run any sims?"

"Once we are up, that would be a good idea. When you complete the comms portion, connect with the ship net and display data on the right HUD please."

"Will do, Captain. Two segs to comms complete."

After the comms checks, Fargo checked in with Garibaldi, Jace, Nicole and OneSvel. Tonguing over to a private channel, he asked Jace and Nicole, "Who is watching the vids?"

Nicole came back, "I have them on my HUDs now. We're a little far out, but it looks like the plant is in a slightly different position relative to the vent than the last time."

Jace chimed in, "It is, it's closer. They must move it when they reach the extension on the cutters. I'm not sure what the *Lincoln* is doing. It is not on a tactical approach, it is cruising in without any attempts to minimize signature. I am going to drop back and down, putting the plant down on an event horizon, allowing us to maneuver as required to minimize our signature."

The hair stood up on the back of Fargo's neck when Jace said that, and his command node started pinging tactics at him. *Stop that*, he thought, *I'm not in charge.* "Cindy, display TACSIT on left HUD. Display combat armor down to sergeant level center HUD, maintain display on right HUD."

"Completed, sims, Captain?"

"Reduce available manpower to two platoons. Start from scattered in landing spots on surface."

"Level of alert?"

He sighed, "High."

Cindy's dulcet voice said, "Starting in three, two, one…"

The HUDs changed violently, now showing from ground level, so to speak, the plant five miles away, with one platoon engaged by heavily armed defenders, and the platoon he was with standing around staring at the vent, weapons up. He started sweating as he 'listened' to the incoming attacks, and watched combat armor go from green to yellow to red with startling quickness. He let it play out, and ten segs later, they were all dead.

"Reset. Move third platoon off axis from the plant entry. Add fourth platoon squads one and two to assault. Squad three is reserve, squad four is vent guard. Begin."

Three more iterations, three more losses, and he slumped against the straps. *Well, shit. If this truly goes sideways, this could get ugly.*

His questioning was interrupted by Jace, "It appears the *Lincoln* is going for Geosync. That will put them less than one hundred miles above the surface, and she has just launched both shuttles."

Startled, Fargo looked at the countdown clock, "Copy all. Nicole?"

"No changes, other than plant is definitely moved. It appears their cutter range is around… Shit! Hot spots! I see three, no four, um… Break, break, *Lincoln* be aware possible self-defense modules activating planetary north of plant."

They felt the ship dip suddenly enough that they lifted in the straps as *Hyderabad* maneuvered violently. Captain Jace came on, "*Lincoln*, Vampires, vampires, vampires. Estimate two four launched. I say again two four launched."

Fargo was thrown violently to the side, then pressed back into the harness as more violent maneuvers happened, he heard the ship groaning and wondered how many Gs they were taking. Captain Garibaldi asked quietly, "What's going on, Captain?"

Jace answered smoothly, "Evasive maneuvers. Twenty-four vampires launched and I was not going to take any chances of them locking on us. We are now below the event horizon for the plant and maneuvering to come over the local horizon orthogonal to our original track. Increasing speed, will maneuver as required. We will have comms back in one four segs. *Lincoln* has not come up on broadcast."

"So we're out of touch with higher?"

"Completely."

Fargo heard a sigh, then Garibaldi asked, "Captain, what would you do in these circumstances?" When he didn't answer, Garibaldi asked, "Captain Fargo? Are you up?"

Fargo shook his head, not that anyone could see it, as his command neural lace kicked in and time seemed to slow. Thinking back to the sims, he answered, "I'd assume no help, and what you see is what you have. I would scatter deploy around the plant away from the entry or hangar, with everyone except one squad and I would put them on the vent. I'd go in hot, shoot first and ask questions of the survivors."

"But that exceeds our ROE, we're supposed to give…"

"ROE be damned, you've already been fired on, this is now a combat situation, and *combat* ROE is kill the enemy."

He heard a click, and CSM Aphrodite said, "I agree with Captain Fargo, sir. We need to go in hot and fast. We don't know if anyone else made it down, and we've… possibly lost half the company. Captain Fargo, are you planning to disembark?"

He looked at the top of his helmet, sighed, and keyed up, "I can. I will go with the squad to the vent, if that is acceptable."

Garibaldi answered, "Please. And can you ping your plan to me? What do you think of our chances of success?"

"Fifty-fifty," he answered brutally. "Against trained, well equipped troops, nil. So I hope they are slackers that got dumped out here on a punishment tour."

Aphrodite's laugh rang across the circuit and she said, "Deity, I love honest officers!"

Eleven segs later, they crossed the *Lincoln's* horizon, and Nicole said, "*Lincoln* is turning away, I'm seeing one shuttle returning to it, and I've got a distress beacon from the other shuttle. No comms with *Lincoln* at this time."

He heard Jace on broadband, "*Lincoln, Lincoln,* this is Q-ship. We are up and up, proceeding to objective."

A panicked voice came over the radio, "This is *Lincoln*, abort, abort, abort. One shuttle is lost and we have damage. Abort, abort, and stand by to assist us."

He heard a snarl on the circuit, and wasn't sure who it was, maybe it was even him. Nicole said, "They're fucking running! They're max accel back toward the gate and leaving the other shuttle! What the?"

Jace interrupted, "Plan?"

Fargo answered automatically, "Continue. We will attack the site. One squad at the vent, everyone else attacks the plant. Can you take out the missile sites?"

"Yes. Prepare for depressure and max decel. We will open the aft ramp in one seg and remotely unlock each row of armor as the ones in front clear the deck. Entry and hangar will be on the left as you exit. I will arc around to the right of the plant."

"Captain Garibaldi, CSM?"

They answered in chorus, "Do it!"

"Depressuring now, ramp coming down now," the G forces slammed on, "Decel."

Nicole gasped out, "No guards appear to be outside. Vent is clear. No activity at missile launchers but they are still hot."

"First rank unlocked. Go, go, go!"

"Second rank unlocked, third rank…"

Fargo shut that out as the remaining troops ran off the back ramp, until it was down to the last squad. "Turning to vent, how close do you want to be?"

"Put us one hundred yards off it." He realized he was still on the command channel and went to the all call channel, "Standby for the vent. Go stealth as soon as you go out."

"Unlocked, go, go go!"

Fargo charged off the ramp after the rest of the squad, realized they were only a hundred yards up, and was amazed at Jace's flying. "Cindy, stealth, deploy laser and Gustav, HE round up. Gravity estimate?"

He felt the weapons deploy, and she replied, "Stealth, laser, Gustav HE up. Grav measures point three G." Fargo hit the ice and grunted, looking at his

HUD, he said, "Sergeant Rescoe, spread the squad on a tac front to cover the vent and keep an eye on the plant if we need to respond. Light G, use anti-grav as necessary."

"Tac front, aye, sir."

He heard Jace, "Going after the disabled shuttle, we'll be back as soon as we can. I think they've shot their load on the vampires."

"Roger," he watched the *Hyderabad* arc up and away from the moon, as the other platoon and squads maneuvering on the plant with part of his attention, amazed that no shots had been fired, when he heard, "Holy shit!"

He looked up to see 'something' emerging from the vent, "Hold fire. Hold fire! It was a weird looking shuttle, and when it got free of the vent it moved slowly toward the closest missile launcher, which was about a mile away. A wild idea came to him, "Rescoe, give me two troops."

Two of the dots pinged, "Cornelius, Virginia, go with the captain."

The three of them started bounding after the shuttle as Fargo quickly tasked them, "Let's see if we can take it. It may only have cargo. Tac spread on the aft ramp. As soon as it drops I will jump the ramp. Cornelius, you're my backup, Virginia, you're reserve and security." He blinked their tasks to them as he spoke, and they clicked mics in understanding.

Less than a seg later, the shuttle settled on the ice adjacent to the first missile battery and the aft ramp rumbled down. Fargo started to jump, but a reload pack sliding out on a grav sled stopped him cold.

"Hold position. I can't breach." It slid out of the hatch followed by a being in a soft suit, then an obvious guard in a hard suit, "Take the hard suit!"

He pinged Garibaldi, "Status?"

Nicole broke in, "Just broke their encryption, a shuttle full of guards come up from somewhere."

"Moving into position. No external oppos…"

A scream breached the net, and Fargo saw a suit go red, then Garibaldi saying quietly,
"Okay, take 'em."

Fargo said, "Standby the vent. Another shuttle coming up, take it out. Ware the crossfire."

With no atmosphere, there wasn't anything to hear, but he saw the guard going down under Cornelius shot, and the person in the soft suit trying to hide behind the missiles. He vaulted the missile pack, charging into the rear of the shuttle and fired on another hard suit that was swinging a laser toward him, "One down inside." He hit the cockpit door with a shoulder of the suit, and saw a startled face in a soft suit quickly hold their hands up, gabbling at him.

"Don't shoot the soft suits. Nicole, got a freq for comms?"

She pinged it to him, and he added to his monitoring, hearing "Oh, please don't shoot, we are slaves, please. Please. No shoot!"

Shit! Last Deity damned thing we need is slaves. That fucks… dammit. Tonguing the all call he broadcast, "Don't shoot soft suits, they have slaves in soft suits." He held up his hand, then scrambled out of the shuttle, "Virginia, get in here. Bring the other soft suit with you and guard them." He started bounding back toward the vent as he saw the nose of a shuttle coming out of the vent. "Take it! Take it, dammit!"

He targeted the Gustav on the cockpit of the shuttle and calmly fired the HE round, knowing he was probably killing a slave. *Deity, I hate killing innocents. May Deity have mercy...* The cockpit of the shuttle disintegrated, along with the rest of the shuttle as the squad fired into the hull as it went by, shedding pieces and guards in hard suits. "Make sure you kill the hard suits!"

He heard "Breaching charge!" and felt a thump through the ice as he landed. Swiveling his suit vids, he saw air exploding from the plant, and saw a blizzard of laser fire converging on various parts of the plant. "Nicole, any more guard chatter," he asked on the command channel.

"Negative. And we have recovered the shuttle. Two dead, pilot severe. OneSvel working on him now. We're coming back down. *Lincoln* is still outbound."

Another suit blinked orange, then red, and he winced. *Dammit.* He heard the CSM, "Shugart, left, Thomas right, looking for the control room. *Do not* shoot anyone but hard suits."

"Hard suits, Aye."

"And go!" Moments later, he heard, "And we have entry," another suit turned orange, and she added, "Shugart you are one *stupid* troop. Didn't I *tell* you to shoot hard suits?"

A gasp was followed by, "Yes, CSM. I... no excuse."

An exasperated CSM replied, "And you're going to hurt for it, right?"

"Yes, CSM, I am."

"Medic… Shit… we don't have a medic. Thomas drag her sorry ass out."

"Dragging, ma'am."

Fargo watched as the squad finished off the few hard suits that survived the shuttle explosion and turned back to the shuttle sitting forlornly on the icy plain. He jumped to it, and walked aboard, then up to the cockpit. Reaching out, he touched the pilot's mind, seeing him jerk convulsively, *"I will not hurt you if you obey me. Do you understand?"*

Frantic nodding accompanied, *"I… how are you… What do you want?"*

"What is below the surface, and how many guards are there?"

"There are three…modules. About ten miles down. One for guards, I think between twenty and thirty. There is one module for the plant workers and beings like me that are capable of…outside work. The third module is power, food service, and…rooms where they do things to us. That is where the Dragoon lives too." He pulled additional details, and shook his head, more slaves below? Not good.

"A Goon is here?"

"Rumor is it is a prisoner. It is said it cannot see or speak."

"Leave the aft hatch open and fly back to the vent. Stop a hundred yards short."

"The ghosts will kill me!"

"Do it, or I will kill you now!"

Fargo came up on the command channel, "Three modules below. One for guards, one food and power, one Hab. They are *floating* on water. There is at least some atmosphere. It's about two miles thick, and about ten miles down. I'm going to take this shuttle and the squad and go take care of it."

The shuttle settled softly and he called, "Mount up! Virginia, stay here with the soft suit."

A disappointed, "Yes, sir," was followed by Virginia poking the soft suit and following it off the shuttle.

He reached out for the pilot's mind, "*Close the ramp and take us down. Where do you normally dock?*"

The shuttle's aft ramp rumbled closed, and the pilot lifted off, "*I have to go vertical to line up. It will be dark and rough. I dock at the service module in the center. There are passages to the other two modules from there.*"

He keyed up, "Going to go vertical then down, hold on, the pilot says it's rough and dark going down. Will dock at the center module." He was trying to figure out who to send where when he noticed an extra suit on the shuttle, he blinked the link, and said quietly on the command channel. "Where did you come from, CSM?"

"I want to kill them all. They purposely breached the control room, killing everyone there. Six, *six of them*, were female."

"You want to lead on the guard's module then?"

"Yessss," the CSM hissed, sending shivers up Fargo's back.

"You've got it." Switching back to the troop channel he continued, "CSM will pick who goes with her to the guard's module. I want two," he blinked on two icons, "To clear the… slaves' module for any guards. Do not shoot any slaves. The rest of us will clear the center module, and be aware, there is apparently a Dragoon prisoner. *Do not* shoot that prisoner!"

A rectangular shape loomed out of the mist and darkness, then slid by as the shuttle turned toward a misty light source. *"Open the ramp,"* he directed the pilot, who looked quickly around at him.

"But we're not inside! I have to close the hangar door…"

"Open the ramp, now! We will be out and moving as the hangar closes."

The landing lights showed three hatches at the back of the hangar and he broadcast, "CSM, left hatch is yours. Slave module, right hatch, the rest of us up the middle." The ramp rumbled down and he said, "Let's go. Do not breach hatch until there is air in the hangar."

He heard double clicks, and as the shuttle settled on its legs, he projected, *"Stay here, if you leave the cockpit, you will die."*

The troopers charged off the shuttle, closely followed by Fargo and he suddenly realized there was going to be a delay before the hatches could be opened, and there were probably vids on the hangar walls. "Dammit, I screwed up, cameras on the bulkheads are going to let them know we're here. And we've got to wait for pressure equalization, so nobody charges through a hatch. Open and clear first, understood?"

A flurry of clicks answered him, as he mentally beat himself up, *What else can you fuck up and get people killed? You should have let CSM lead, you're not even close to qualified.* He realized he was 'hearing' whistling through his external mics, and said, "Prep the hatches and stand clear."

He lay down on the deck in line with the center hatch, "I'll take anybody that tries to shoot through the hatch." Suddenly the hatch popped open, and there wasn't anyone there. He 'heard' the sizzle of laser fire, slewed his vid left, and saw laser fire coming through the left hatch, with CSM throwing a grenade through the hatch. Slewing back right, he noted the two they'd detailed were through the right hatch and gone. "Go, go, go," he said, as he charged from his kneeling position straight through the center hatch. He slid to a stop in the mess area, orienting to the left, in case there were guards, but all he saw were melting or destroyed hard suits.

Tagging two dots he said, "Right hall," Selecting one remaining dot he blinked the info, "Reetina, you're on me. Left hall." He stalked carefully down it, using the arm with the laser to clear each room. The last room door he opened bloomed with laser fire, slagging his external pack on the right arm before he returned fire, holing the hard suit. Once the guard went down, he cleared the rest of the room, and then the next room, where he found a dead Dragoon, the center of the chest missing, and one other being who had also been burned down. "Goon is down and dead."

He stood over the Dragoon and sighed, then used the vid to record the body and its condition. It was obvious the eyes had been burned out, and he very carefully pried the mouth open, the tongue was also burned off. Shaking his head, he turned and started back down the hall when he felt a 'thump' and one dot went red and a second red, then back to yellow on his left. He heard air whistling and Cindy's quiet, "Pressure loss, three segs to zero pressure."

A panicked voice came on, "CSM is down. She… they blew up… something."

"Get their armor back, retreat to the center module! Reetina, look for a hatch or soft seal!"

He moved back to the mess area and was greeted by the rest of the squad with one suit of armor. When he pinged the other one, it was still in the left module, "Where is the CSM?"

"It's sinking, we couldn't…"

He bowled over the troops as he dove through the passage, "Seal the hatch behind me." The module was definitely sinking and tilting away from him. He plunged into the liquid, tearing through walls until he ran into the other suit of armor. Grabbing it with his manipulator, he started dragging it back toward the passageway, *Deity, let me save this troop. We don't ever leave a troop behind, Deity*… He finally made it to the passageway, lifted the CSM's suit and pushed it ahead of him. Once he'd scrabbled five or six yards into the passageway, he turned and used the laser rifle to cut the passageway free of the sinking module. When it sprang back, it bounced both of them off the ceiling and floor multiple times. He rolled the suit on its back, and breathed a sigh of relief as the telltale still glowed yellow. Reaching out, he found the CSM's mind, *"Don't you die on me. Dammit CSM, don't you dare die on me!"*

Escape

Fargo tongued over to the command channel, "Garibaldi, status?" He heard nothing, then said, "Nicole? Jace?" He got no answers, and looked at the comms portion of the HUD. There was no signal showing on the command channel and he tongued back to local, "Reetina, status?"

"Uh, everyone is back, Seekamp says thirty-eight host... slaves, mixed beings in the far module. What do you want us to do, sir?"

"Is the center module holding pressure?"

"Yes, sir."

"Move the slaves to the shuttle. Get as many in as you can, with a guard. Two guards if there is room. Leave enough room for CSM's armor."

"How are you going to..."

Fargo dropped his head, *Fuck. I didn't think that through. Can't go through the hatch, unless they depress the whole module. Unless... No, that wouldn't work. Can I fly the armor around to the hangar? I did that once...*

"Have you started loading the shuttle?"

"Yes, sir."

"What I want done is for the shuttle pilot to depress the hangar and wait. I will fly the armor with CSM's armor around to the hangar. Then the pilot will close the hangar and pressurize, load the CSM, and depress again. Then off you go. You should find *Hyderabad* on the surface waiting. They are up on the command channel, work with them to get the shuttle in a bay, empty it, then come back and get us."

"Um, sir, is that possible?"

"We'll find out. How is the load out coming?"

"Moving the last two now, sir."

"Let me know when the pilot starts venting the hangar. And tell whomever is going up as the guard on the slaves to let the ship know they've been in point three G for Deity knows how long."

Five segs later, while he continuously watched the CSM's telltale, he finally heard, "Depress starting now, sir."

"Rog," then to Cindy, "Store all weapons, prep for antigrav with another suit of armor in tow."

Cindy answered, "That will potentially damage your armor to the point of failure."

"Cindy, I'm a Marine. We don't leave anyone behind. Recommendation for carry?"

Moments later Cindy replied, "Recommend arms extended, use manipulator to hold armor horizontal on arms. Estimate eight zero percent chance of one or both arms failing."

"Copy." He dragged CSM's armor back to the end of the passage, feeling it sink dangerously, "Antigrav now." He maneuvered out of the passageway, rotated, and sank down until the extended arms were level with the floor of the passageway, then used the manipulator arm to pull the armor to him. He quickly started sinking, and said, "Cindy, increase antigrav. Prep lateral movement."

He felt the armor creaking, and said a quick prayer, then leaned right. The suit bobbled then moved slowly along the side of the module, as the hydraulics started flashing yellow and Cindy said, "Twenty percent failure, right arm. Thirty-five percent failure, right arm."

"Silence alarm." He'd never heard the armor groaning like it was, and was beginning to wonder if he was going to make it, *Fuck it. I'm not leaving without the CSM, if I die, so be it.* He saw a dim glow getting slowly brighter as the hangar door hinged open, and he leaned forward, then quickly left. Planting his feet on the hangar deck, he said, "I'm in, close the hangar and repressurize as quickly as possible!"

He heard the door start rumbling down, seeing six suits of armor facing him, he continued, "I've got her, she's still alive. Is there room?"

Reetina answered, "Sir, there is room for the CSM and one more. You should..."

"No! Send someone else. I will be the last one out."

Cindy said, "Imminent failure, right arm. Ninety-five..." The arm gave way with a screech, and the CSM's armor slid slowly to the deck as he lost control.

Reetina replied, "Seekamp, you're up. Help me get the CSM on the shuttle as soon as the ramp opens, then you steady her." Two suits stepped forward, and Fargo stepped back, then moved toward the hatch. He sagged in the harness, wondering if he could even keep going, and Cindy said, "Human factors, you are crashing, Captain. Administer stim?"

He mumbled, "Stim." He felt a prick in his thigh, a burning sensation, and he drew a deep breath, knowing what was coming. It suddenly felt like the top of his head was coming off, his eyes teared up, and he groaned as the stim hit his system, but he was fully alert and ready to fight the world.

The ramp came down, and he got the first look at the slaves crammed in the hold, seeing a Taurasian, a couple of Arcturians, three blue Keplerans from 62F, and four from 62E, their fur matted and patchy, a couple with almost white muzzles. Without thinking he tried to Salam toward them, but his right arm failed. Reetina and Seekamp moved the CSM's armor into the shuttle, and the last view he had was of Seekamp crouched and stabilizing her as the ramp closed. He heard the diminishing whistle as the air was evacuated, then the shuttle moved carefully out into the darkness and disappeared.

***

Two divs later, he limped off the shuttle and through the hatch onto the main deck. He looked at the open slots and backed his armor into a set of clamps, "Captain, I'm in the clamps, lock me in please."

"You're locked, Captain. Welcome back. I need to see you at your earliest opportunity on the bridge, if you will."

"Let me get out of this, and hit the head, then I'll be there." He started the shutdown, "Cindy, report maintenance issues to the network, and thank you for bringing me back."

"Shutting down. Maintenance report completed." He knelt the armor and climbed slowly out. Once he was on the deck, he stretched and rubbed his thigh where the shot had been given. *I hate those fucking stims. That's gonna be stiff for a week.*

Nicole flew into his arms, almost knocking him over in the light G as she babbled, "You had me… us, so worried. We lost contact." She kissed him then stepped back, "And you *stink!* And we've got a problem."

Fargo recovered his balance, "Light G because of the slaves? And what problem, Captain Jace wants me on the bridge, ASAP." He started loping forward and up the decks.

She paced him, "Yes, the G is for them. A total of six lost. OneSvel couldn't save the shuttle pilot, he… was fried. The sick bay is full of the worst of the slaves, and they are operating on Aphrodite. She's badly chewed up in her legs, OneSvel's probably going to cut them off below the knee to keep her alive. And Captain Garibaldi brought back all his dead. We've got Captain Culverhouse and all his platoon in the spare bunks, and we don't have enough rations or air, or water to get back."

He skidded to a stop, "Get back where?"

"To Hunter."

He let out a breath, "That's not a…oh shit."

"Endine is the only place we can make, and they…"

"Are a three decimal planet for humans only? Well, *that* is going to go out the window now."

He went through the bridge hatch, Nicole on his heels, "What do we need to do, Captain?"

Jace turned, "Well, first, what are we going to do with this plant?"

Fargo scrubbed his face and slumped in *his* chair, as he thought of it. "What do you mean?" Turning to Nicole he asked softly, "I know I should do it myself, but could you please get me a bulb of coffee and an energy bar? I know I shouldn't ask."

Nicole looked at him, then smiled. "Since you know better, and admitted it, I'd be happy to."

His next thought was, *I'm going to pay for that. Sooner or later, I'm going to pay. What does he want, dammit. We've taken the plant, but don't have a force to occupy it, and where the hell is the destroy...* "Belay my last. We don't have a force or ship support to occupy the plant. We've evacuated or killed everyone. We leave it and notify GalPat. Speaking of GalPat, where is the *Lincoln*?"

Jace's laugh had a dangerous edge, "She was last seen heading for the hyper gate. Apparently they had a pressor down here too, and threw a rather large chunk of ice at her. She took some apparently minor damage, but ran like a scared… nearrabbit. She never tried to recover the shuttle, and apparently barely slowed down enough for the other shuttle to catch up. I have filed a report through *channels* on her and her CO's behavior."

Fargo winced. *That's not going to be pretty. Leaving troops behind in combat is…* His thoughts were interrupted by Jace, "And we have issues with the sheer number of bodies we now have onboard. We don't have bunk space, food, or water enough to get back to Hunter. And we could use some fuel too.

However, Endine is the only actual planet on the shortest course to Hunter. I have queried their station, and they do not have medical quarantine spaces for thirty plus former slaves. They said they will take the GalPat troops assuming they are human."

He snorted. "Really? They have stated they will violate GalPat law and convention?"

Jace nodded. "And I have it on tape. They will not even allow us to dock, saying they will only allow their shuttle to come to us. This was even after I identified us as the Fleet Auxiliary Transport GSS *Sampson*."

Fargo's head snapped up, "GSS Sampson? We're…"

"Properly beaconed, with the correct external markings."

"How… No, don't answer that. I don't want to know. So what rank are you?"

Jace puffed out his chest, "Oh, only a lowly lieutenant commander. That's the appropriate rank. And beards are legal in the GSS, and yes, I even have the appropriate uniform."

"And if anybody checks, of course we *exist* right?" Jace grinned and nodded as Fargo shook his head in wonder. "Can you get an open channel to Colonel Zhu at the Palace?"

Jace smiled. "Of course. Would you like that now?"

Fargo's smile was feral, "Why not. And send him copies of all the vids and data of *Lincoln*, plus our *battle* to take the ice mining plant. Can you page the GalPat captains to the bridge before we connect with the good colonel? And I guess we better brief them on our identity."

A div later, they had comms with Endine and the GalPat Detachment. Colonel Zhu glared at the vid, "They did *what*? That's illegal by every convention and rule of law."

Jace, now dressed in his uniform, continued, "And *Lincoln* left us high and dry. We had no choice but to continue the approach, rather than get shot down. Captains Garibaldi and Fargo succeeded in capturing the ice mining operation, while we recovered the damaged assault shuttle. However the additional personnel and recovered slaves are straining our resources. We need at the minimum to offload the thirty-eight slaves, all of whom need medical care, but they are not all human."

Zhu rolled his shoulders and cocked his head. "Well, Fargo, you've done it again," he said with a sigh. "You do realize how much of a shitstorm this going to cause here?"

"Colonel, I'm simply the liaison for this mission. I'm not conversant on every GalPat law and treaty, but this is a humanitarian issue. And if I remember correctly, that overrides any particular world's peccadillos."

Zhu barked a laugh, "Three digit human requirement is a peccadillo? That's…rich."

"Well, this whole thing probably ties into the plot to turn Endine over to the Goons, so as far as I'm concerned, they have created this nightmare for themselves."

"Captain Garibaldi or Culverhouse, are either of you willing to offload your troops to provide security?"

They looked at each other and said in chorus, "No, sir. Our tasking was to take the ice mining operation, and return to base. We have dead to return, injured that need rejuve and need to find our other platoon. Also, all of our troopers are Herms."

Zhu put his head in his hands, then glared at the vid, "Screw it. Bring your ship here. I'll meet you with enough hospital personnel and gurneys to move everyone to an isolation ward at the Palace, *and* I'll make the director understand they have to help them under GalPat law, at least until I can get them moved to a refugee facility."

Jace leaned in, "Sir, our ETA is seven divs. When you say here, do you mean the main spaceport at Center?"

"I do." He reached up to punch the connection off, and they heard, "Deity damn you Fargo," as the vid faded to a black screen.

Fargo turned to Culverhouse, "Where are MobyDineah? Were they with you?"

"No, they were on the other shuttle with... Jackie. I don't know..."

Jace said softly, "They were recovered by the *Lincoln*, and appeared undamaged."

Culverhouse slumped, and a tear rolled down his face before he angrily swiped it away, "Thank you. I didn't know. We lost all comms, and I really didn't want to ask."

Garibaldi put a hand on his arm, "C'mon Mack, let's go check on the troops."

**

Jace gently touched down on the corner of the space port as directed, and the IC came on, "On deck, Center Spaceport. Crew and pax are released. Captain Culverhouse, please post guards at aft ramp. Litter bearers report to Captain Garibaldi at the mess."

Fargo headed for sick bay, and found OneSvel with NasTess the rescued Taurasian working over the medbox containing CSM Aphrodite. "How is she?"

OneSvel twittered, "She will live. We managed to stop the major bleeding and suture the internal injuries prior to getting her into the medbox. Having her data has allowed us to start the regen process immediately."

"Why is...NasTess here?"

"We are both healers. NasTess was outbound to their residency when captured. They were the doctor and caretaker of the Dragoon on the moon. They have information you need to know, and they want to return with us."

"How do I?"

NasTess extended a pseudopod, and Fargo nodded. They touched his temple lightly with it and he felt what he decided was a female mind. *"Thanks be to you for saving our lives. We are... Doctor, not yet surgeon like OneSvel, but cared for slaves as well as we could. Ton'Kalt was the Dragoon held there. They had blinded him and cut out his tongue before he ever got there. That was about eight or seven of your months ago. They did not know we can... talk like this, very few outside our home world know. We were able to convince Ton'Kalt to eat and maintain his health after he found out he could communicate with us. He was a hostage to...something like a...how you call, a coup? His, we do not know lineage, but younger family member was/is head of Dragoons. Another...family? Was attempting to overthrow them and go back to full scale war, saying the family was not getting the respect and opportunities? That Ton'Kalt's family did. There were a total of six five slaves when we got there, two four were killed/lost before you saved us."*

"How many slaves were there when we landed?"

"Five one. There are three eight left. One three are gone, including all that were sent to plant for shift."

"How many guards?"

"Three three. They were all human. Not good men. Abused females, killed...a number with perversions. Beat us when we could not save."

"I am sorry. Do you not want to recover here?"

"No! We wish...ask...to go with our mate. We have...things to do."

"Do you—"

"Yes, we know what/who OneSvel is."

OneSvel exuded a pseudopod and touched Fargo's other temple. *"We would like this to happen for...many reasons."*

Fargo raised his head, dislodging both pseudopods, "Both of you are a bit overwhelming. Sorry. I will talk to Captain Jace and recommend that NasTass stay with us. What was done to decontaminate the slaves?"

OneSvel twittered, "They were given nanites, they are all clear."

The IC came on with a pop. "Captain Fargo, OneSvel please report to the aft ramp. Captain Fargo, OneSvel aft ramp."

Fargo grimaced, then spoke to the ceiling, "On our way."

At the ramp, he saluted Colonel Zhu, who returned it stone faced. "Captain, the Director would like to meet with your medic over the *people* you are transferring."

"OneSvel is the medic," Fargo pointed to him, "And he has data cubes for each *person*. We will only be transferring thirty-seven."

Director Vaughn stepped forward. "Captain, nice to see you. OneSvel, did you say?"

"Yes, ma'am. OneSvel, meet Director, Doctor Vaughn. She is the…President of Endine, for lack of a better term, and also a medical doctor."

OneSvel sort of bent a knee, and extended three data chips in a pseudopod. The two of them quickly lost Fargo with their medical conversation, and he walked over to where the colonel was standing. "I honestly didn't plan for this to happen, Colonel."

Zhu's mouth turned up for a moment, and he replied, "Captain, first rule of combat, no plan survives first contact with the enemy."

Fargo smiled. "Oh that's true. But this one—"

"I've reviewed the files you sent. And used them to beat the director and PLANSEC into submission on this. There will be a ship here in two weeks that can take the slaves to a refugee center, but there are a lot of questions that will need to be answered. I've requested a full GalPat investigation, in addition to a detachment to take control of the ice mining plant." He looked at Fargo curiously, "Did you really go after the CSM with no help? And manage to save her?"

"I don't leave people behind, Colonel. It was a close thing, but she's alive right now. We'll transfer her to a regen center as soon as we can."

Zhu shook his head, "You never do anything by halves do you? Let me go *supervise* these transfers so you can get on your way back to Hunter."

Fargo came to attention. "By your leave, sir."

Zhu returned the salute. "Dismissed, Captain. Pardon me for saying this, but I hope I never see you again." With that, he turned and stalked toward the line of grav gurneys that were lining up on the ramp.

Epilogue

Fargo smiled as Nicole snuggled closer to him, "Doan wanna get up!"

"Not even for brewed coffee?"

"Thas' bribery." Nicole squeaked as Canis' cold nose hit her in the back, "Go way, Canis!"

Cattus jumped on the bed, conveniently landing between them, and Fargo laughed. "I think you've been outvoted." Throwing the covers back, he got up and padded through the cabin to the front door, letting the animals out. Detouring by the kitchen, he started the coffee brewing, then made his way back to the bedroom.

"You want first shot at the fresher?"

Nicole sat up crossly. "Next time, we stay at *my* place. I had other plans for this morning, but I'll settle for coffee in bed." Her smile belied the comment, and Fargo bent, kissed her thoroughly, and headed for the fresher.

Ten segs later, they sat at the small table in the kitchen, silently savoring their coffees and Nicole asked pensively, "Why did the GalPat Det cremate the troops that died? I don't remember that being done before."

Fargo took a sip of coffee. "I think they do that when it's too long a delay to send the body home, wherever that might be. We had the cans, and that's what we sent back to their home world and families."

Nicole shuddered. "Barbaric custom, but…it does make sense. The military has always been a little more…I hate to say it, but comfortable with death."

Fargo leaned back in his chair. "Well, considering it's our job, so to speak, you do become… I don't want to say hardened, but more…understanding? Inured? Comfortable? We know we can die at any time, and tend to live that way. At least I know we did in the Corps. And you never thought it would be you that got killed, always the other guy."

Nicole lay a hand on top of his. "Well, get rid of that idea, mister! That's off the plate with me!" She finished her coffee, looked out the window at the snow covering the ground and sighed, "It's so pretty, and so deadly. I don't see how Canis and Cattus manage, and Urso is, what, hibernating I think you said?"

"They have fur coats, which helps. Urso is up near the waterfall, tucked in a small cave up there, she's been hibernating for about three weeks now. And don't forget, snow is actually insulating. They can burrow down and stay warm."

She laughed. "Speaking of staying warm, the Culverhouse's were in the other night, apparently the CO of the *Lincoln* is being cashiered. Cowardice in the face of the enemy didn't go over well, and apparently Jace's vids and Major Culverhouse's testimony did him in. Seems he was a Polapp, and only saw combat once as a gunnery lieutenant. They had to smuggle him out of the court and then the brig, apparently there were some GalPat troops that were, ah, *less than happy* with him."

Fargo winced. "What's a Polapp? Wonder if he'll get off the planet in one piece?"

"Oh, political appointee, somebody owed his family a favor, apparently. Who knows? Speaking of who knows, apparently your guy Mac has, shall we say, been hanging around the winery."

Fargo cocked his head. "Really? And Holly is putting up with this?"

"She isn't chasing him off. Matter of fact, they are plotting something, I'm just not sure what."

"That could be *interesting*, considering Mac's past exploits."

Nicole shrugged. "It's her life. And if she's *occupied* then she's not looking over my shoulder." She got up and set her cup in the fresher, "I'm going to clean up, and we can head back to Rushing River."

"Okay, I'll drag the liteflyer out. You mind if I take Canis and Cattus with us? I'm trying to get them used to flying."

"Why?"

"Well, they seem to sense Silverbacks before I can. And there seem to be a pair somewhere near another one of Remington's logging operations, based on the message he left me."

"You're not going to take them into town are you," Nicole asked sharply.

"Oh no. Just down and back."

***

Fargo landed the lightflyer and taxied around the corner of the administration building, then stopped it in the sunlight, reaching out on the animal's frequency, he sent, *"Quiet, down. Cover."* Cattus merely looked up and yawned, but Canis whined a little then lay down in the other seat. He reached back and pulled the cargo cover forward, leaving a little gap for them, and opened the canopy.

Helping Nicole out, he said, "Mikhail is going to pick us up for drill on Friday. Are you going?"

"Planning on it. I want to talk to Kamala about some seasonings. Lal and some of the others are wanting me to serve some of their favorites at the Copper Pot, and if I do, I want them to be right. Hugh is willing to cook them if, big if, I give him exact directions and amounts. For some reason he's scared to death of the Ghorkas."

Holly came around the corner in their runabout, with Mac riding in the jump seat. Nicole smiled at Fargo, "See?"

"Mom! Guess what? We've figured out how to make booze!"

Fargo thought, *Maybe there is something to that Scottish mafia thing after all. Second time Mac's been tied to that. First Grayson, and now this…*
"Interesting. Well, they're here, and I need to get back. See you Friday?"

Nicole hugged him, "Of course."

Holly said, "I was hoping you could stay for dinner. I've figured out…"

MobyDineah, CSM Aphrodite, and Sergeant Omar came around the corner, and Fargo sighed, *This is not what I needed. I hope Canis and… oh shit!* The cargo cover started moving, and both animals popped up looking eagerly at MobyDineah.

Sergeant Omar's GalTrans chirped, "Animals of danger. Take care of, I will," as he drew his service pistol.

Fargo stepped between Omar and the animals as they snarled, and Moby reached over and clamped a hand on Omar's arm, "No Sergeant. Not dangerous. Friends of us and the Captain. You will not shoot."

Fargo reached out, projecting, *"Sergeant, they are trained. They are not wild. You will not shoot. You will forget you ever saw them. You will leave now."*

Omar stiffened, then chirped, "Captain of the retired is here. I must go back to my duties." He turned and walked stiffly away, leaving the rest of them staring at Fargo as Canis scratched at the canopy.

Fargo sighed, pushing the canopy back as Canis and Cattus bounded out of the liteflyer. Moby and Dineah went down on their knees, and were being licked by both animals as Holly and Nicole shook their heads. He saw that Mac had moved between Holly and the animals and smiled to himself.

CSM Aphrodite looked at him, then said, "You *did* talk to me when you pulled me out, didn't you?"

Everybody looked at him in confusion, and he sighed, "I told you not to die on me. And yes, I have psi talent. You are the only people that know that. I would ask that you not tell anyone else about that, or the animals. The wolf is Canis, the mountain lion is Cattus."

He projected to the animals, "*Friends.*" "Walk to them quietly, hold your hand out palm down for them to smell."

Aphrodite looked down at MobyDineah, "You knew about this?" She put out her hand tentatively, and Canis then Cattus sniffed her then sat back down."

He felt the two of them 'talking' and Dineah said, "Yes, CSM. You know what we are, and what we can do. Fargo can also do that."

Mac sidled over, and he said, "Mac, they're not going to eat you." Nicole snickered, and Holly smacked her arm as she stepped up beside Mac, extending her hand. Canis smelled her then licked her hand, tail wagging as Cattus sniffed Mac's hand. Cattus yawned, then shouldered Canis out of the way, licked Holly's hand and walked over and head butted Nicole in the thigh, rocking her back.

Nicole swatted her, "Stop that Cattus. Yes, she's my daughter. You know that."

Fargo's looked at the sinking sun, "I need to go. Please don't say anything about this, please."

Aphrodite nodded tightly then said, "I will not. But we need to have a *conversation*."

Fargo nodded. "Friday morning? Will that be soon enough?"

Aphrodite nodded again, then stalked off. Fargo picked the animals up and put them back in the cargo area. He nodded to MobyDineah, who were smiling, kissed Nicole, and climbed into the cockpit as Holly and Mac walked back to their runabout, Nicole following behind.

***

Friday morning, Fargo landed at Rushing River just after first light. Climbing out of the liteflyer, he pulled his jacket closer, *Damn it's getting colder. And this snow…I hope Jiri doesn't decide to do any outside drills today.* He was startled to see the CSM drive up in a runabout, considering he'd never see her without a driver. She opened the door, "Get in."

He climbed in and before he got the door shut, she'd already stomped the accelerator, "Where are we going?"

"To your damn clinic." She stared forward and he sat back quietly, *Well, this is off to a good start. Why are we…oh shit, OneSvel. He saved her. That's…dammit, how can we explain this and keep it quiet?* He settled into a funk, frantically trying to figure out how to not reveal what they were doing. Segs later, she slid the runabout to a stop in front of the clinic, "Out!"

He climbed out and at least beat her to the door, dilating it as she stomped through. Doc Grant came out of the back, "Can I help you?"

CSM Aphrodite came to attention and ground out, "I would like to see *medic* OneSvel if they are available, please."

Doc glanced at Fargo, "Ah, give me a seg, they are in the back. Please have a seat." He disappeared into the back of the clinic, and Fargo sat, while she continued to pace.

She finally stopped in front of him, "Why did you save me?"

"What?"

"Why did you save me? Your kind hates me."

Fargo jumped up, "What the fuck are you talking about? Hate you? Where the fuck did you get that…"

She sliced a hand down, "You are a Marine. Marines hate Herms. You should have let me die, yet you saved me! Why?"

Fargo got nose to nose with her, "Because you're a fucking troop. I had the privilege of commanding you, but I also have the responsibility for you! I don't like my troops to die. You weren't dead, and I've got enough dead troops on my conscience already. Maybe GalPat has a different *mentality* than the Corps, but we take care of our own. As far as what you are, I don't give a fuck. I don't care if you're a pitcher, or catcher, or whatever. You do a good job, and *that* is what counts. Now get out of my fucking face, troop! Do you understand?"

Doc Grant interrupted, "Ah, do you want us to come back later?"

Fargo snorted. "No, I've had my say. Sorry for the fuc… language."

OneSvel twittered, "Can I help you CSM?"

She turned to him, and they saw tears running down her face, "What are you? You're not a medic! No medic could have done what you did according to Seekamp. You had your 'pods inside me before they even got me out of the armor. She said she's never seen anybody move that fast, much less work around somebody being extracted, who was technically dead. She said I'd gone red on the way up. And regen my legs? That's only done at a major hospital, not in a fuc…med box on a damn weird ship. You…I can have you drafted into the Patrol for your *expertise* for the good of the service, and I'm sorely tempted."

Doc Grant burst out laughing and CSM yelled, "What are *you* laughing at?"

He finally got his giggles under control and said, "Oh CSM, oh you poor thing. You can't draft him."

"Why not?"

Fargo was wondering what to say when Doc replied with a smile, "You can't draft somebody that's already in service. Meet Colonel-General OneSvel, Galactic Medical Corps. Oh yeah, he kinda out ranks you too, so you might want to salute him, rather than screaming at him."

Fargo fell back into his chair, *Colonel-General? OneSvel? He's a contract…he never…what the…*

OneSvel twittered, "I see you found us out Doc. Why did you not say something earlier?"

"You were a little too good. And showing up not long after Fargo, and leaving *stuff* in storage tweaked my interest. There aren't many Taurasian doctors, much less surgeons around. And your saving that girl up at the Enclave really piqued my interest, since I knew I couldn't do that surgery with better than a fifty-fifty chance of success. That narrowed the search even more, and I reached out to a few people. Low and behold, one Taurasian Colonel-General surgeon was TEMADD to the GalScouts, but currently on sabbatical. Two and two added up to five, and voila, here you were. You two are up to something, but I don't give a shit."

CSM said weakly, "Colonel-General?"

OneSvel waved a pseudopod, "Afraid so, CSM. You were a *bit* of a challenge, but no more than putting Fargo back together a couple of times. At least you don't have *his* issues."

The CSM collapsed into a chair, burying her head in her hands, sobbing. Fargo decided it was time to be elsewhere, and headed for the door as Doc Grant sat down next to her. He had to go drill with the militia, and being on time was critical, especially since he was the commander, *Yeah, that's my excuse and I'm sticking to it.*

***

Fargo decided Jiri was a closet sadist as he racked his pistol and rifle after qualifying, then cleaning them outside. *In the freaking snow? Really? And advance/retreat drills in the streets? And practice dispersals? I haven't slept in a tent in…Deity knows how many years.*

Warrant Boykin just *happened* to drop by just as they were finishing up, and offered him and Nicole a ride back to Rushing River, which they gladly took her up on. As it turned out, she was coming down to do a survey on the shuttle she'd named Wizard, and was, with Colonel Keads backing, hoping to get to keep it, and send Stuttering Sally back for retrofit and depot level repair.

They stood talking on the edge of the ramp, and she was filling him and Nicole in on the BS going on at White Beach when Fargo's wrist comp beeped, and he looked at it. INCOMING MESSAGE- JACE REQ U MEET HIM AT CABIN ASAP. "Well, looks like *Hyderabad* is back. Captain Jace wants me to meet him at the cabin, so I need to go. Thanks for the ride, WO."

He hugged Nicole and gave her a quick kiss, "See you in a couple of days?"

Nicole grumbled, "Maybe I'll be warm by then. Militia my ass. Go away. I'm going to go get warm."

***

Fargo landed on the antigrav at dusk, which was a little tricky with the snow. He saw the small stealth shuttle sitting in front of his cabin and wondered, *Now what the hell? Jace is paranoid as hell about that little shuttle, why...* He opened the canopy saw Canis and Cattus flat on the ground, ears back and in attack mode, and other wolves and mountain lions streaming into the field. *What the hell?*

He jumped out and headed toward the shuttle, only to have Canis and Cattus crowd in front of him and try to stop him from getting to it. He heard snarling and spitting and looked around, startled to see that he and the shuttle were surrounded. He projected, *"Calm, no threat. Friends,"* and that quieted things down a bit.

He got to the hatch and Jace cracked it about half way open, "Ah, there seems to be an issue here," waving his arm at the animals surrounding the shuttle.

"I don't know what set them off. I've never seen that kind of behavior before. It's almost like you've got a Silverback on here."

Jace nodded solemnly, "Pretty damn close. Can we make it to the cabin?"

"We?"

"Ton, come on back."

"Ton?" He glanced forward to see Ton'Skel come walking back from the cockpit. "What are you…What is he…?"

Jace repeated, "Can we go to your cabin? I… we need to show you something."

Fargo shrugged. "Well, that explains what the animals are upset about. They must have smelled Ton'Skel, and I know they hate Goons. Okay, come here Ton, you will need to step out with me. I will *introduce* you to them and we'll see what happens. Just so you know, if you go down, I'll go down with you, because you are my guest."

Fargo turned to the hatch, projecting, *"No threat. Friends."* He repeated it over and over as he led Ton'Skel to Canis and Cattus. "Stick out your hand, palm down. Let them sniff you."

Ton'Skel extended a trembling hand, and Fargo noted the claws extending then retracting as Ton visibly calmed himself. Canis whined, then sniffed him with a tentative tail wag. Cattus sniffed, then licked his hand, tail twitching, then sat and yawned. "So far so good. Come on Captain, let's walk *slowly* to the cabin.

They got about halfway there, the animals sniffing as they walked by, until Fargo saw what he recognized as the two matriarchs blocking their way. "Stop and hold your hand out again. These are the matriarchs. They are the alphas, if you have ever heard that term. They are the leaders of their respective packs." The two matriarchs sniffed Ton'Skel, then licked Fargo, and he sensed them sending what he could only think of as greetings. As soon as they did that, all the wolves and mountain lions disappeared into the tree line.

Ton'Skel turned to him as Canis and Cattus padded behind them, "You control those... beasts?"

Fargo laughed ruefully, "Not even close. They tolerate me. These two," he pointed to Canis and Cattus, "And one more, a bear are bonded to me mentally."

Once they got inside, Fargo gave Ton a big mug of water and looked at Jace, "You want to tell me what's going on?

Jace shrugged. "How about a message from Ser'Mose." He handed a data cube to Fargo and pointed to the e-tainment system.

Fargo plugged it in and sat down, watching Ton out of the corner of his eyes. Basically, Ser'Mose was requesting asylum for Ton'Skel for three months, after three attempts on the Dragoon embassy on Star Center. He said that there was no other place where he believed Ton would be safe, and the reason he was asking, was that Fargo had demonstrated he was a man of honor.

Fargo looked at Ton, "Are you willing to do this?"

Ton stood and faced Fargo, "I Ton'Skel, heir of Ton'Mose do give my parole. I... do not wish to impose, but I..."

"Ton, sit down. This is not going to be easy, but we will work this out. Having to keep you hidden will not be easy, nor will it be fun for you."

"My uncle has agreed to pay you, Captain Jace has that payment."

Fargo shook his head. "I don't want your credits. I don't need them. What I need is for you to be willing to do what I tell you. Will you agree to that? It will be lonely here."

Ton nodded. "Lonely and alive is good. I will do as you say."

Fargo leaned back, *Now what the hell do I do? I've got the heir to the entire Dragoon hierarchy sitting here, and we're at war. Damn you to seven hells, Ser'Mose, damn you...*

About the Author-

JL Curtis was born in Louisiana in 1951 and was raised in the Ark-La-Tex area. He began his education with guns at age eight with a SAA and a Grandfather that had carried one for 'work'. He began competitive shooting in the 1970s, an interest he still pursues, time permitting. He is a retired Naval Flight Officer, having spent 22 years serving his country, an NRA instructor, and a retired engineer who escaped the defense industry. He lives in North Texas and is now writing full time.

Other authors you might like are on the facing pages- I highly recommend them all!

You can either use the embedded link (Kindle), type the URL, or search for them on amazon.com by author name or title under books or Kindle

https://amzn.to/2EH22lC
https://amzn.to/2LsF4yT

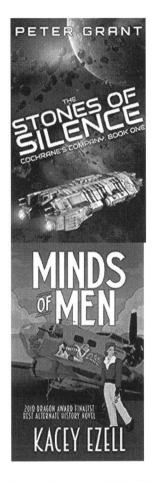

https://amzn.to/2CsnIPV
https://amzn.to/2SiKFe

Made in the USA
Columbia, SC
20 August 2019